Curse of Flame

by

J. Von Tobel

Dedication

For everyone who has a fire that won't go away.
Especially those who burn too brightly to be ignored.

Chapter One

Olivia hated that the trees spoke to her. Washing her hands in the cool stream, Olivia could worry about the predatory night that would return at sunset or think about the errands to run in the frontier town that whispered rumors about her. It didn't matter how she tried to distract herself. The boughs overhead begged for her to answer them and use her magic again.

The glow of the canopy filled the forest around her. Birds chirped in the branches and leaves rustled as squirrels chased each other. A twig snapped to her left and a light brown fawn, white spots scattered on its fur, stepped out from the tree line. Its black eyes danced over the trees above Olivia before it drank from the stream. The deer paid her no mind.

She repressed the impulse to feed it from her hand. It was the sort of thing that Life wanted her to do. It would try anything to bring her talents back. Gifted with Life magic from an early age, those sorts of beautiful things were once within her ability. Olivia knew better now. Nothing was without a cost. Especially the incredible power she chose to forget.

As she chewed over her thoughts, a clatter of snapping branches erupted behind her. The fawn raced up the small slope of the river and into the trees. An ax broke through brush and boots trampled over wildflowers. Olivia rolled her eyes, already sure of what was crashing through the brambles.

"Could you be any louder?"

A mountain of a woman smashed through twigs with a polished hatchet. She was six years younger than Olivia, but somehow a full head taller than her. Josie's muscular arms flexed as she cleaved through nature to reach the stream. Josie beamed at her older sister and ducked beneath a branch.

"What?" Josie asked.

"You've got to be careful this far out from home. Be quiet, don't leave a trail, all that stuff I've tried to teach you."

"Oh, come on. What are the odds of something bad happening during the day?"

If Olivia was concerned about a large, noisome creature thrashing through the woods, it had already arrived. She would never voice these complaints. Olivia pushed it down, like she did with most things. Be controlled. Be accommodating. She acted the part expected of the first daughter. She was days from accepting ownership of the family farm. After letting go of her magic, it would be the prize she had sweated for.

Leave the childish behavior to the sixteen-year-old, Olivia thought.

"Come on. We haven't even reached the ruin fields yet and sunset won't wait for us," she said.

Once the sun set, it wasn't their world anymore. That was the first lesson pressed upon them when they were children. More frightening would be the chiding she would get for keeping her kid sister out past dark.

It was a short walk out of the gulley and to the edge of the tree line. Her black stallion, Grizzly, was hitched next to Josie's horse at the edge of the grove. The forested hills rose around them like a rumpled sheet. The stream wove through it moving east to west. Far to the north, Olivia could see the Cragged Mountain, their hometown of Hasketter somewhere at the foot of it. The horse's hooves clattered as they rode over the ruins of an old road. The worn stones were swallowed up by pale grass and dirt. Few knew where the road went. Even fewer cared to maintain it.

The hills flattened into a rolling, grassy plain punctuated by imposing ruins. When she first saw the colossal stone towers ahead, she thought they were windmills. They formed a tattered line across the land. Spears were stuck into the ground above impromptu graves. Arrow heads were lodged into ancient barricades and war machines. Trenches that once held a garrison were now choked with scarlet and yellow blooms.

Olivia was used to this sort of old death. It was impossible to escape the broken world they lived in. Once you got away from the guarded, well-lit towns, you could not escape the bones.

It was their turn on border rotation. The empty plains around them were a forbidding barrier to raiders, but that did not always stop them. Each of the major families volunteered to keep an eye out for intruders. Usually, this meant one rider popping out to the ruin fields and then going home. To keep her kid sister focused, Olivia came up with another purpose for their visit.

They explored every nook and cranny of these towers. Each one held secrets of the old world, tarnished pieces of art, and scraps of books that barely survived the centuries. Olivia urged Josie into it with tantalizing lies about what they might hold: swords, armor, or any flashy instrument of death that would intrigue her. It was a white lie, but Olivia knew what was best for Josie. Though this was to keep Josie entertained, Olivia could not deny the thrill she felt at discovering these faded relics.

Their next target was an unassuming, squat tower. Its uneven shape and bleached, tattered banners did not promise much. Whatever was inside was likely well preserved thanks to its intact walls. Their last barrier was the rusted front door.

They left their horses and Josie unpacked a large metal pole. A missing brick along the door frame was a perfect wedge. Three steel hinges were all that stood in their way. Josie stuck the pole into the gap next to the door so that it jutted out horizontally from the side of the wall. She grunted as she forced the pole toward the wall. The wood of the door cracked and iron hinges squeaked. Olivia's protective instincts started wailing.

"I should be doing this, not you," Olivia said.

"We tried that already. You weren't strong enough." Josie gasped and pushed harder. "And don't even think about using any magic. We don't need any of that mischief here."

Josie knew damn well Olivia would never dream of it. She still mentioned it as if only her reminders were stopping Olivia from tapping into her gift. The nightmares were what made sure Olivia would never touch it again.

"Please don't bring it up."

Olivia felt the grass shift like hair on her arms. Small beetles crawled through tall shrubs and rodents hunted after them. These things pushed into her mind without consent. Olivia did not like to remember the night she gave magic up. After her mentor dragged her from the safety of the light. After his crazed eyes demanded her as a sacrifice. It hurt too much to think about.

The door began to splinter.

"I'm your big sister, I've got this." Josie adjusted the pipe and pressed in again.

"Being a big person does not make you the big sister. I am older than you. That makes me the big sister here."

A hinge sprang off the door and struck the ground next to Josie. A second one followed and came within a few inches of her. She flinched and gave the pipe another push. The large door fell away from the building and twisted on its final hinge. Olivia lunged forward and pulled on Josie with all her strength. The final hinge snapped with a clang and the door collapsed against the side of the tower.

Josie patted Olivia's arm and nodded. "Good look out."

"Are you alright?" Olivia's heart hammered as the rush caught up with her. She shook her hands against the tingle and a small, nervous laugh escaped from her.

"I'm fine," Josie said, quick to cover any bumps or bruises.

Olivia offered Josie a hand to get up, which was ignored. They peeked inside the tower, both of them hesitant to charge inside. Sunlight filtered through small cracks illuminating the trickles of dirt and sand falling from the next story. Against the far wall, a ladder led up to the second floor. Josie dropped the steel pole onto the ground and rubbed her hands together.

"Maybe this is a bad idea," Olivia said. "It will be on my neck if you get hurt."

"Then why don't you go first? You promised me a look inside this tower and I'm not leaving until we do. I can go if you like. Go calculate crop yields or whatever boring farm stuff you help dad with."

The effort to entertain Josie had officially backfired. Josie would walk into this death trap regardless of what she told her. Everyone in Olivia's life, from farm hands to merchants, jumped at the Seers's family name. Everyone except Josie.

"It's not that boring," Olivia said.

She stepped inside as the wind shrieked past the newly opened door. Cobwebs swaddled a disorganized rack of weapons. Olivia ran her finger along one of the handles of a sword; brittle flakes of rust crumbled onto her hand. She rubbed it off and walked over to a ladder that led upward. Olivia set her foot on the first rung when Josie pulled her back. She stumbled, but Josie kept her upright.

"Let me try it first. I want to see what's up there."

"Nope, me first, we agreed. You don't always get your way," Olivia said.

Josie cocked an eyebrow and pouted. "Are you saying I'm spoiled?"

"No, you're not, that wasn't supposed to be a—you know what? You go ahead. I'm sure it will be fine. I'm just worrying."

Her sister's frown cracked into a grin and she planted one foot on the lowest rung.

"Too easy."

She moved up the ladder and it quietly groaned under the added weight. Olivia toyed with the knuckles of her hand as Josie climbed higher. Her mind played out the horrific image of her sister falling from the top rung.

She would certainly break a bone. How would Olivia get her back to town? She shook her head and tried to chase out the worries.

Josie paused near the top and set a hand on the next floor.

"Come on up. It all worked out and nobody died. Let's take a—by the Flame!"

Josie stumbled on the highest rung and balanced against the wall behind her. A small shout escaped her mouth as her feet tried to balance on the rusty rungs of the ladder. Olivia's heart quickened to a manic pace. Those worries didn't seem so silly and she moved to catch her. Josie held her footing, but stared across the next floor. Her jaw drifted open and the color drained from the face.

"Shit and darkness!" Josie finally settled herself.

"Josie! Are you okay? What is it?"

Josie nervously licked her lips before looking back down to Olivia.

"There's uh, dead things up here. Skeletons."

"What?"

"Like three of them."

Olivia followed up the ladder and Josie helped her up onto the platform. Three skeletal bodies laid around the room. Two of them laid on top of each other, pinned together with a sword in each chest. Their bones were mixed together in a loose pile. One adversary impossible to distinguish from the other. The last of them sat at a table with a dagger firmly wedged into its spine. In its right hand, it held some sort of golden locket.

"What happened here?"

"Same thing as any other place. Magic." Olivia walked over to a window and kept her distance from the nearest of the deceased. Outside, she could see barren fields pockmarked with wrecked catapults and bones. The remains of the old world stretched southward until the fields faded into dry earth and sand.

"Would you look at all this stuff?"

Josie's fingers hovered above the tarnished armor and weapons clutched by the dead. She walked to the skeleton at the table. It wore ragged, draping robes and gold finery around its fingers.

"Did you know this land used to be covered in trees?" Olivia asked. "The forests back home stretched so far south that you and I could ride out here in the shade."

"They needed something to build all these fortifications out of. Can't all be stone." Josie touched the dagger in the skeleton's back. The handle was made of ivory and wrapped with bands of tough fabric. The blade was the color of charcoal and glimmered like a lake under the night sky. She pressed a finger against the back of the knife and winced as the skeleton shifted.

Josie left the dagger where it stuck.

"And when Flame pressed close to the world, to turn back the Shadow, it burned forests, dried up lakes, and scoured crops." Olivia recited the story everyone was told growing up.

"Are you going to get moody over every old war and bad decision?" Josie asked.

"The stories say they had roads all around the world. You could get from Sallew to Shelter Harbor in just three days."

"Then the mages got pissed at each other and burned the whole thing down. I've heard the stories." Josie moved on to the locket clutched in the skeleton's hand.

It was ovular, golden, and had two loops on the back of it. It was like an ornate set of brass knuckles. The skeleton clutched it not far from its breast. Josie grimaced and lifted the skeletal hand. She pulled on the pendant and the dead fingers let go of its treasure.

"Sorry. I guess I can fixate," Olivia said.

Josie slipped the pendant from the skeletal grasp and held it up to the light. Flipping it over, she saw etched lines emanated from the gleaming, red gem seated in the center.

"I know you are not big on the swords and shields, but this might be more your taste." Josie held it out to Olivia. She was not thrilled about her sister messing with this stuff, but Olivia was as fascinated as Josie.

"You should leave it alone. Flame knows if they have diseases or anything on them," Olivia said.

"Weren't you just talking about wanting to see things the way they were? Here, take a look." Josie handed the relic to her sister. It was small, but heavy and cool to the touch.

Olivia wiped the dust from it with a careful touch. The gem glimmered orange in a thin ray of sunlight. Despite the age, it was unblemished by time. Olivia only heard of the masterwork that the old world was capable of. To see such a thing felt like a reward. Like it was waiting for her to find it. The relic fit perfectly in her hand as she slid her fingers into the loops on the back.

"It is beautiful."

"You should keep it. A reminder that not everything got ruined," Josie said.

Olivia wanted to polish it to a worthy gleam. Maybe read about any meanings in the etchings. Unfortunately, that was behavior fitting of Ruin Raiders: people who made their livelihood pillaging the treasures of the past. They were not welcome where she was from, but sometimes they slipped past to resupply or rest.

Sometimes your dad welcomes his skeezy, egotistical, con artist brother home despite the fact that it was going to be *her* farm soon, she thought.

Olivia gritted her teeth at the thought of her uncle John. He had turned the entire town against him in a matter of months. The only good thing about his company were the stories he told when he drank too much. A Ruin Raider by trade, he had seen every corner of the world. She pretended to ignore these stories, but she could not resist listening.

"I appreciate it, but we aren't robbers. We shouldn't really even be this far out," Olivia said.

"We've never taken a single thing. Why don't we deserve a bit? Especially you. You love this crap."

Olivia bounced it in her hand as she weighed more than just the relic.

"Okay, how about this," Josie said, "We aren't going to be able to close that door down there. You leave it behind and it is certainly going to be sold to the highest bidder when someone snatches it. With you, it will be appreciated. Primevals be damned, you might figure out what it was."

Josie overlooked details and shouldered too much to protect her adopted family, but Olivia loved her infectious exuberance.

"You are convincing when you want to be," Olivia said.

"I have my moments. Oh." Josie looked up and pointed a finger above them. "What is that?"

A trap door quietly waited above them. A leather

strap dangled from it. The hinges rusted to an itchy shade of red. It must have been shut for every minute of the last three hundred years. It reminded Olivia of a brick that the roots of a tree had grown around. They had become one immovable thing. It would be best not to touch it.

Josie did not have the same instincts. She leaped into the air and reached for the handle.

"No, wait!"

Her sister was already airborne and grabbed the strap. The trapdoor opened and the tether snapped, dropping Josie to the floor. It clanged on its hinges and dust shook from the roof as the wooden planks snapped and creaked. Now opened after decades of stillness, the structure of the building shook as the roof began to fray.

The howling wind outside grew louder as the floor quivered. The weakened building shifted and a gout of pebbles fell from the ceiling. A thunderous snap echoed through the tower as age finally claimed the ancient building. Olivia pulled her sister up just as a plank crashed down next to them.

"Time to go!"

They ran to the rusted ladder. Despite the size difference, Olivia felt like she could carry Josie on her back if she needed to. Fear was an inconvenient thing she did not have time for. Once her sister was safe, there would be time for fear.

A brick fell from the ceiling and broke straight through the second floor. Olivia flinched as the old stone dropped next to her with a murderous thud. A support beam snapped and splinters shot overhead. The sisters ran out of the front door as the tower caved into itself with an avalanche of snapping timber and crumbling mortar. A dust cloud blasted over the two and pushed them to their knees. The horses whinnied and stamped their hooves.

Whatever history remaining within was buried in an avalanche of dust and stone. The plume rose high into the air and the ruin settled into a lop-sided mound. Olivia and Josie coughed and wiped caked dust out of their eyes.

"You alright?" Olivia asked.

"Stars, that was close. Is it bad that I want to do that again?" Josie said.

"You seem fine enough." Olivia brushed off her fleece shirt and found the pendant still in her hand. In the chaos, she did not remember holding onto it.

"Hey, you saved it." Josie smiled wide and brushed the dirt out of her hair. "See, now it won't be lost forever under that huge wreck of a tower."

She should not have held onto a trinket when their life was at stake. That was behavior unbecoming of the future laid in front of her. Despite that, the relic was there in her dusty fingers. Its unnatural polish glittered in the sunlight. Something inside of her decided it should be kept. She stashed the pendant in her pack and climbed onto her horse.

"We are leaving. Not a word of this to anyone. We'll make it back with plenty of time before nightfall. Just make sure you get all that dust out of your hair before we get home."

Josie and Olivia took the reins of their horses and rode back along the line of towers. Olivia felt that they were being judged as they left the demolished ruin. There was no sign of anyone on the horizon, but Olivia could not shake the feeling of being watched.

Chapter Two

Olivia and Josie's horses beat a path north until they crossed back into the rolling hills south of their home. The groves cast longer shadows as the sun sank toward the horizon. While the sun was in the sky, it was their world. After that, it became a world of locked doors and shuttered windows as shadow beasts grew bolder.

After an hour, they reached the stone bridge of the Seventh Republic. The Cragged Mountain lorded over all those who called the Seventh home. A large train of merchant wagons stalled on the far side of the bridge, held back by excessive customs inspections. This great bridge forded the Sentinel River, a deep chasm that was difficult for anything without wings to cross.

The bridge was so titanic that entire caravans and armies could cross it with ease. A stone watchtower on each end of the bridge witnessed every passerby. It was built when the Congress of Six protected these lands, a bastion of last resort if the Great War turned against them. A dark day that, thankfully, never came.

They turned east and the town of Hasketter spread out before them. In the comforting shade of the valley, this town flourished out from Hasketter farmstead. That ancestral farm grew beyond its borders and now was a rustic palace. Other farms settled around the Hasketters. Small one-story houses, barns that held armies of animals, and rolling fields of corn, watermelon, and gorgeberry all carved out a place here. Tanners, smiths, taverns, lawyers, and theater companies followed.

Olivia barely remembered the founding of the Seventh. She grew into a woman alongside the foundling state.

"Hey, go ahead home. I have some errands to run," Olivia said to Josie.

Josie split off toward home in a shot, happy to shrug off the threat of errands. Olivia trekked down the main road into the heart of town. Crowds of people wrapped up their day of trading and buying. Weapons were a common sight on people's belts: daggers, swords, and even the odd Coilgun. A relic of another time, they were impossible to replace on the Frontier. Everyone wore tough, durable linen and hemp clothing. Colors varied from tan to green to brown. There was not a dress or high collar in sight, such things only appearing at marriages and season festivals.

Shop keeps lit torches outside of their brick storefronts and town guards fiddled with new buzzing light bulbs. Long, tubular glass housed a wire that would become incredibly hot, but also provide light without flame. It was unclear if their clockwork engine, the only one in town, could keep these lights running for long.

Three dogs, varying colors of brown and black, sat in an alley across a butchery and waited for scraps to be thrown out. Several children tried to lure the dogs over with discarded hunks of vegetables and bread. Olivia slowed Grizzly near the front of the shop. Tying up her horse, she watched the children play.

"Come on, pup. Come get some," the shortest of the children pleaded.

One of the dogs, tall ears and long, black fur,

swiveled an ear in their direction and kept its focus on the side door of the butcher.

"They aren't going to listen," Olivia told the children.

The short boy glanced over and took off his hat and bowed as quickly as courtesy would allow. The others matched his gesture after a moment.

"Good day, Ms. Seers."

"You just watch, Ms. Seers. My father said that I could have a dog if I took care of it. Gonna start out right by giving it a good meal," said a tall, lanky kid.

"Dogs don't eat apples. Well, they don't prefer it. They might eat it," Olivia said.

"What do you mean?" the short kid asked.

"Imagine I asked you all to do my work for the day and I promised you a plate of boiled cabbage for it."

The children wrinkled their faces at the mere concept.

"Can you help?" the lanky child asked. "Dad says you have a way with animals, that you used to do magic."

The other children watched for even the slightest confirmation of the rumor. She clenched her fist and smiled through the frustration. The common gossip always seemed to roll back to her past. That or the scandal of a daughter set to inherit such a historic family farm as the Seers fields. No matter how hard she worked, how considerate she was, that black mark would never wash away.

She felt like a witch at times. A hideous mage that strangled people with vines or wielded the night itself as a weapon. They respected her family name, maybe they even liked her. Yet the possibility of a mage among the farming family elite conjured all sorts of prejudice.

I'm not the town witch, she reminded herself, that title belongs to my old teacher.

"I think your dad's been making things up, but I do have a trick for those dogs. You all stay here," Olivia said.

"What's she gonna do?" one of the kids asked.

"Did she say magic trick?" asked the tall kid.

"Just a trick, normal trick. Get the corn cobs out of your ears," the short child said.

Olivia walked through the chipped, wooden door of the butcher shop. The sign hanging against the back wall read "Meltz and Sons Butcher". The evening sun tinted the room in a blood-red glow cut back by several buzzing bulbs. A symbol hung above the door shaped like the sun held in a pair of open palms.

There was still a fair stock of meat. She counted herself lucky to not have scraps to choose from. She was less enthused to see her Uncle John in a tense standoff with the butcher, Mr. Meltz, and his assistant.

John wore a long green coat and black pantaloons, both stained from too little care. Olivia saw the flash of steel in his pocket. She recognized his flask from the smallest detail.

"This boring, watering hole of yours is a bit more bearable with a good buzz," he once said.

He was as old as her dad, but his hair was pure gray where her father still had a few strands of blonde. Despite his age, John reminded her of the young men in town: reckless and presumptive.

"Your coin is no good here. Take it and go," the butcher said.

"If my money is no good, how about these? Eh?"

Johnathan flashed a pair of bracers hidden under the

sleeves of his coat. They were made of leather, reinforced with slats of unbreaking warden tree. They were worth the butcher's entire store and then some. The butcher did not know this, ignorance she knew John delighted in.

"Get your stinky sleeves out of my face. Probably made of dog skin."

"You're a dog," Jonathan said, "I just want some venison for dinner, you've got plenty right there."

"I heard from Ivalo. He said you were giving us tin shulten! Counterfeit, you cheat."

"I'm surprised the old man could tell the difference. I'm impressed."

"You would admit to it. I thought responsibility was beyond you," Meltz countered.

"Yeah, you—you jerk." The assistant leaned into the argument.

John paused to roll his eyes and give his customary shit-eating grin. "The grown-ups are talking, butcher boy. Run along. Don't you have to close up shop while the old man sits on his fat ass and overcharges for mutton?"

The butcher lunged forward and grabbed Johnathan's shirt. The butcher's sweaty face was inches from John's gray mustache. Her uncle fidgeted, the loose grin on his face looked as if he was thinking of his next joke.

"You can be a bad customer or be a jerk, you can't be both. Why your brother bothers with you, I'll never know. You're out of here."

"Mr. Meltz, I am so sorry for my uncle." Olivia stepped forward.

They did not notice her until now. John groaned. He

knew his fun was at an end.

"Liv. My little niece, so good to see you. Mr. Meltz and I were just having a disagreement."

"Ms. Seers. Sorry for speaking so rough to your kin, but this one isn't anything but trouble," Meltz said.

Olivia ignored her uncle.

"No harm, no foul. Johnathan wasn't exactly being helpful either. Uncle, what are you doing here?" Olivia asked.

"Dinner, venison for dinner. We need some meat to eat tonight, preferably nothing salted either. The sun was getting so low. I assumed that you forgot," John said.

"What are you talking about? There's plenty of time before sundown. I'm here, aren't I?"

His eyes narrowed. "And no trouble out by the ruins? No harm befell the favorite daughter without anyone to fawn over her?"

"No one fawns over me," Olivia said.

"The mothers certainly do. They'd love to marry off their backwoods sons to backwoods gentry. It'd keep your ideals in place. You'd like that wouldn't you?" John asked the butcher.

Meltz went to speak, but was cut off by Olivia's raised hand. John would find something to jabber about unless he was given a distraction. Ideally, something that would compromise his own presumptions.

"Well, I'm here to get dinner. Did you pick up your end of things?" she asked.

John's smug grin slackened. His eyes went to the door past her and his brow furrowed.

"I'm not supposed to get anything."

"You weren't listening when my mother asked you to get salt? Oh, John." She winced. "I can't imagine how she is going to react if you spent all day harassing people and forgot to do the one thing she asked for."

Her mother had not asked for salt. Olivia kept the joy of tricking him inside and doubled down on her grimace.

"I see. It's coming back to me now. Mr. Meltz, sorry about all that. You cut a wonderful figure and you have a fine shop. I need to go elsewhere. Liv—"

"It's Olivia."

"—I'll see you back home."

John waltzed out the door and toward whatever disaster he was set to cause next. She did not know if her behavior would ever wipe away the gossip. As she saw it, what else was there to do? Olivia would fight her past with every breath.

"I am so sorry you had to deal with him," she said.

Meltz eased his elbows onto the counter and rubbed the back of his neck.

"No need to apologize. Just tell your pop I was not so harsh on him, eh?"

"He's been here six months and has the entire town united against him, I've never seen anything like it."

"Which city is he from again?" Mr. Meltz walked behind the countertop and prepared a cutting board and knife.

"All of them as far as I can tell. Five pounds of venison, please."

The butcher nodded and began slicing apart a flank of meat.

"He's had a tick up his ass about everyone and everything since he came here. Once I'm in charge, he better shape up or be ready to ship out. My dad's favors only go so far," Olivia said.

It was an earnest hope. He helped with chores around the house and worked in the orchards two days a week. She could use the extra help. His attitude was repulsive, especially toward her.

"He's bored. I've seen the type," Meltz said. "The kinds of people who wear armor on the day-to-day. I don't know why he came to stay with you, but he needs an outlet."

"He is drunk half the time and if he isn't then he is teaching Josie to throw daggers or blowing off errands—"

"Or harassing the townspeople?" Meltz interrupted. His knife sliced with the precision of a fencer.

"He does like to cook," Olivia said.

"Has it helped?"

She shrugged. "A little, I guess."

"Your folks, you, that tall, Faros girl you all adopted. You're good folks. Your uncle on the other hand is a bad cut of meat. Doesn't fit in with the rest of the plate, you know? Most people in town can tolerate an idiot, but he's pushing it. I'm not the only one who is starting to refuse his business." He wrapped the meat in a few sheets of parchment and tied it with twine. "Twelve shulten."

"I thought it was three for a pound?"

"Consider it a discount for getting your uncle out of here before closing time."

"Thanks. Oh, one more thing," she placed another coin on the table, "I'll take a quarter pound of mutton. No need to wrap it."

The butcher handed her the extra cut of meat.

"Good evening, Mr. Meltz," she said.

"Evening, Ms. Seers."

The children still squatted in the alley. Their apple plan failed, but they were determined as ever. Their heads perked up as she walked out.

"Trade you an apple for this." Olivia dangled the mutton in the air. "It might work a bit better for luring a dog over here."

"Done," said the short child, not waiting to confer with his friends. She handed the cut of meat over to the kid and took an apple in return.

"Nice doing business with you," she said.

They did not respond with thanks, too eager to see if their gambit would pay off. The children advanced down the alleyway. Olivia wiped her hand on her pants and walked over to Grizzly. The animal sniffed the apple for a moment and then bit into it. It chewed for a moment and then took the rest of the apple.

She patted the horse's neck and climbed up into the saddle. The mutton finally lured the dogs to the children. After a curious sniff or two, the black dog with long fur snatched the meat from the short boy's hands. It turned tail and ran off behind the building, the despairing children in tow. Olivia smiled and took off eastward toward home.

The Seers Farmstead was on the edge of town. It was a large lot of property set aside under their titles and deeds. They were crop farmers and owned some of the rolling fields that surrounded Hasketter to the north and east.

She rode into the organized rows of cherry and apple trees. Grizzly slowed a few times, aware of the sweet things that hung from the limbs, but Olivia drove him on. He would get plenty later. Beyond the small trees was a majestic farmhouse. It was two stories tall and made of the finest oak that her ancestors were able to lay a hand on. Wide windows looked out over the never-ending rows of trees. A handful of out buildings surrounded the property. Sweaty farm hands returned their tools before heading home. They waved or gave short bows to her as she passed toward the stables. Olivia smiled and nodded back to them.

It was important to appear gracious, she told herself. Whether the market is up or down, despite discontent or good humor, the master of the farm must be reliable. Her father moved slower than a decade ago. Retirement was so close now. She would never be rid of their help though. It was the least she could do after years of their love.

She rode into the low and wide stables. Josie's horse, Swift, happily ate inside. She dismounted Grizzly and led him into his pen. She grabbed her bag, locked the pen door, and made for the farmhouse.

"Do you see how late it is?" Dalton Seers hollered from the door of the farmhouse.

A balding man, he wore a wide hat that saved him from the sun on long days. His small, barely managed beard defined his chin. He held his hands on his hips as he walked out to meet her, but the warmth in his eyes betrayed that he was happy to see her.

"Careful talking to the master of the farm that way. And I am back before sundown, can't you see that bit still above the trees?" Olivia asked.

"Mhmm, I'll remind you that I'm not retired for another eight days and six hours. Not that I'm counting." He cast his eyes down the road that led back into town. "Your uncle still isn't back."

Olivia held her tongue. She was told that anything

she said about him came off as condescending.

"Was he…you know?" Dalton mimed a bottle on his lips.

"Maybe a little. It's hard to tell what sober looks like."

"Still not great," Dalton said. They stood in silence, her father's thoughts heavy enough to weigh down any other words.

"I won't be tolerating him much longer. You know that, right?" she said.

Dalton did not look away from the road and recited the same answer he gave every month for the last six months.

"Just a few more weeks. He's my brother, your uncle. That's worth a few more chances."

"It would be different if he was accommodating in the slightest measure. The only people he's seemed to warm to are you, mom, and Josie."

Her father sighed and slipped the hat off his head.

"I know he hasn't been easy on you, but his line of work was stressful. He's gone through a lot and he's my brother. Think about what you'd do for Josie."

She hated to see her father defend him. Dalton Seers moved sky and soil to keep his brother comfortable.

"Then why does he say he's bored? Why does this raider get a pass because he's our blood?"

"Because—" Dalton bit his lip and shook his head.

She came so close to pulling the truth out of her father so many times and each time he relented. For all the stories John told, he never said why he retired.

"Two weeks. Can you give him two weeks for me?" he asked.

Another failure, but he could only hide it for so long.

"Fine. I'm starving," she said.

Their home consisted of a large, shared room with several others connected to it on the first floor. Dominated by a dinner table that could host fifteen, the kitchen laid to the left of it. To the right was a row of windows and a sparsely filled bookshelf. The loft above filled half of the angled ceiling. A staircase wound upward on the far side of the room.

Candles burnt next to the front door and many were set about the main table. Salty, savory scents of dinner drifted from the kitchen and spread across the house. Eggs, meat, butter. Josie was busy at work on dinner alongside their mother, Elena.

There was no question that Olivia was Elena's daughter from the shared dirty blonde hair to the same thin nose on their face. Her dark brown hair was almost a perfect match to her adopted daughter. Elena was dwarfed by Josie, but commanded her about the kitchen without hesitation.

"Diced not chopped, Josie dear. Liv, have you seen my brother-in-law? I can't believe I'm going to say this, but we could use his help."

"Olivia, please. She press-ganged me into this, help," Josie pleaded.

"You're a natural, Josie. No sign of Johnathan." Dalton walked over to Josie and motioned for her to leave.

"Go ahead, I've got this handled."

"Bless you, father," Josie said.

"Before you wash up, Josie," Dalton said, "I need you to chop a bit more wood."

"What? There's plenty," Josie said as she walked away.

"You did some this morning. Not plenty. Putting off chores doesn't get rid of them."

"Listen to him, Josie," Olivia added.

"Fine, but I'm using my ax," she said.

"Careful with that. I'd hate to see you spending an entire day polishing it again," Elena added, her eyes firmly rolled upward.

Josie hurried up the stairs to their room. Olivia set the venison on the kitchen counter and went toward the stairs. The front door opened and Johnathan walked in, a heavy sweat gleaming on his face.

"Hello family," he said.

Josie gave a rousing greeting that dwarfed any other response.

"There he is! You're late. I'm taking your cut of meat now."

"I will fight you for it, dear niece. I got the salt. Already deposited in the basement for you, Elena," John said.

Elena squinted at him and paused her cooking, letting her befuddlement simmer like the onions in the pan.

"Salt?"

"We needed salt, so I picked some up earlier. You're welcome," he explained with an irritated titter.

"Well, I appreciate the extra stock, but I never asked for any."

"No, no, you asked. Olivia told me—" The words choked in his throat. Olivia smiled wide and took her time waltzing over to the stairs. John waggled his finger at her before turning back to Elena.

"I must have heard you wrong. All the same, it's yours."

"Well, I need your hands in here," Elena said.

John walked into the kitchen and Olivia slipped up the stairs. The upper hallway flickered with candles. The torch outside glowed against a window at the end of the hallway to her right. Josie came out of their room. In her hands was an ax half as tall as she was. A polished wooden handle and a shining, iron ax-head bore a sigil on it: a stylized F for Faros, her last name.

Olivia walked into the first room on her right. The last rays of sun shined over an unlit, simple chandelier hanging from the ceiling. She grabbed a set of matches on her bedside table and climbed a step stool under the chandelier. She struck one to light and brought the small flame to each candle.

The shared room was the last vestige to go before she assumed ownership of the farm. Once complete, her parents would move to the guest house and she would inherit the generational farmhouse that so many Seers worked in.

The room Josie and Olivia shared was large enough to have two beds on either side and plenty of space between the two. A wide window looked over the backyard and the dense shadows that swallowed it. Josie walked to the lumber pile near the back of their property, barely discernible through the evening sun. Olivia double checked the window latch and dropped her bag onto the bed.

On Josie's side, there was a collection of books on sewing she had not read, family trees of the Seventh Republic, and a copy of "War of the Fire Keepers", an adventure novel. Olivia's side had a larger collection of books, and her possessions were kept in neat order. A chest next to her bed held most of her belongings, including a hunting knife she never found time to practice with.

Olivia sat on her bed, ran her fingers through her hair, and undid the one tie that held her locks back. Hard work was a way of life in the Seventh and made for strong and lean people. Olivia's body fell somewhat short of the first tenant. What she lacked in brawn she made up for with speed, her thin waist and strong legs easily able to weave among the orchards. She was not tall enough to be elegant and not short enough to be cute. However, she could reach whatever she needed from the work shed and that was all that mattered to most around here.

Whatever conventional anxieties she had about herself were nothing compared to the worming desire to smother any magical talent left in herself. Her presence did not sprout daisies on summer days like when she was a kid. There were only the whispers left, but she wanted it all gone. Only then would she be able to forget Mage Yorker, her former mentor.

She pushed her bag aside and felt the hard lump within. Olivia forgot about the pendant and slipped it into her hand. The gem in the center of it was the color of a blood orange. She swore she could see a flicker of light inside of the crystal. Turning it over, she decided it was a trick of the light. The embedded lines in the oval pendant lead away from the center, alternating straight and wavy like a simple depiction of the sun. She let her fingers loop through the grips and flexed it around her hand.

Voices rose in the room below. Too loud and nervous to be idle conversation. Their pitch changed to fear as something metal clattered to the floor.

"Get down!" John shouted.

Glass shattered and wood cracked as a deep, feral roar echoed through the house. Olivia ran from her room to the edge of the balcony that overlooked the first floor. In the midst of the room below, amid shattered glass and splintered wood, a black-furred beast howled for blood.

Chapter Three

A beast stood in the middle of their home. Black as the night outside, its fur barely caught the light of the candles. It was five feet tall at the shoulder and stood on four legs. Claws like filet knives scratched their wood floors. Its powerful jaws were laced with serrated teeth. It snarled and glared at Olivia with its four green eyes.

Olivia's mind told her to run, save her parents, anything, but she was rooted to the spot above the creature. So used to how things always were, the presence of this aberration inside their home was near impossible to comprehend. Just as she felt that the dreadful stillness might swallow her whole, it was broken by a brutish yell.

John charged the creature with a kitchen knife. He jumped off the long dinner table and drove his knife down. It swung up at him, claws extended. They shredded cloth and snapped buttons along John's arms, but the warden tree bracers held. John landed and stabbed the knife into the creature's side. Dalton followed behind his brother. He threw a heavy cutting block at the creature's head, cracking its brow and forcing the beast to stagger on its feet. Her father grabbed a poker from the nearby hearth and threw that as well.

"Get the militia!" Dalton shouted to Elena.

Her mother rose from behind the kitchen table and ran out of the house. There was a bell outside of their home that would raise the alarm across town. It was the only real answer against a monster like this.

Olivia left the railing of the loft and went to her room. She grabbed the hunting knife before running back to the stairs and sliding down the banister. Her other hand balled into a fist, barely aware that the golden pendant was still in hand.

The beast pushed John closer to the far wall. Dalton drove his knife into the monster's back leg. It howled in pain before it knocked her father backward, throwing him into the stairs. Olivia fell off and landed next to her father. Her knees stung from the impact, but she was back on her feet in a heartbeat.

"Run!" He pushed her toward the front door.

"I'm not leaving you." Olivia ran toward the monster as John dove under the main table to avoid it.

Water and Flame, where is Josie, Olivia thought. The lumber pile was not that far away and her sister would never hesitate from defending her family. Olivia hoped her sister and that well-used ax were on their way.

The four-eyed creature tore at the main table, John hidden underneath it. It snapped in half and John rose from the far end. Gripping the knife by the tip, he threw it at the creature. His aim was sharp and it dug into one of the four, green eyes. Dark red blood spurted into the air as it shrieked. The monster knocked the knife out of its eye and the metal blade clattered on the hardwood floor.

Olivia drove her hunting knife into the creature's muscled forearm. She twisted as best she could, but it felt like stabbing a tree. The chords of its arm stopped the blade from twisting. She was almost afraid to pull it out. The creature was so much broader up close.

Above the clamor, the alarm bell clanged in the yard. She pulled her knife back out and readied to stab again. It spun on its feet and knocked Olivia onto her back. The monster smashed through the front doors and ran for her mother and the shrill alarm bell.

She gasped for air as she staggered to her feet. A distant scream, her mother's scream, put nails of panic in Olivia's lungs. She wouldn't lose her family. Not like this. Not after everything they worked through.

Olivia dashed out before the two men. Her mother screamed as the monster bit into Elena's arm. Blood ran black with only the faintest light of day left in the sky. Olivia reached the creature and swung a stab toward its ribs. Its three eyes rotated to Olivia and casually swatted at her with a free paw. The strength of the blow knocked her to the ground next to her mother. Olivia reached out to her just as the beast pulled her mother away.

Olivia heard the pounding footsteps of John and Dalton nearby, but the creature moved like a gust over an open plain. Olivia reached out toward the monster. The pendant, still in her left hand, began to glow as cinder flaked from it.

The only thought on her mind was how helpless she felt. A burning desire coursed in her mind and left no room for anything else. A scared, familiar part of her rose through the pitch-black panic and reached out to the magic that existed at the edge of her mind.

Kill it.

Something answered. It was not the rustle of grass or a quiet voice in her ear, but a deep, furious rage that boiled in her chest and flooded her arms and legs. The pendant in her hand grew as bright as a torch. It fed off her fury. As she raged, it grew stronger.

It jumped to her fingertips and exploded outward. It burnt like sunlight and roared like a bonfire. The blast singed the stretch of grass in front of her, flew past her mother, and cut straight through the creature's heart. The fireball lit the yard brighter than any torch and sent John and Dalton ducking for cover.

The monster shrieked as its flesh boiled. Unfocused paws took a few lingering steps before its great mass collapsed. Cindering fur glowed around the cauterized wound and smoke trailed from within its charred corpse. Its wide jaws yawned open, letting a plume of smoke escape before it dropped its head to the earth.

The pendant's glow faded. Olivia's shallow breath barely filled her lungs as she focused on her mother's prone form. She did not move, slumped next to the dead beast. The moment of dread felt like a lifetime until Elena took a deep breath and wailed.

"Mom," Olivia stumbled to her feet and ran to her, followed by John and Dalton.

Elena's right leg was sliced to ribbons and deep holes in her arm bled freely. John ripped off the sleeve of his shirt and tended the wound. A bell rang down the road and the faint glow of torches approached.

"Over here! She's hurt," John shouted.

"It's okay, hon, you're safe." Dalton cradled her in his arms.

Olivia rested a hand on her mother's good leg. She cried tears of fear and joy, relieved that the danger was gone. Josie appeared from behind the house. Her clothes were torn and the once shiny ax was bloodied. She dropped it and fell in alongside the rest of the family.

"Josie, where were you? What happened?" Olivia asked.

"Shadow damned lumbira. I heard screaming in the house and it was waiting in the yard for me. It ran off after that explosion. What was that?" Josie asked.

"Two of them? They never come this far, never mind more than one," John said.

He was too focused on stopping the bleeding to hear what Josie said. Dalton looked at Olivia as the memory caught up with him.

"What was *that,* Olivia?" Dalton asked.

The column of militia made it up the main road. A square-jawed woman wearing green cloth and brown leather settled down next to them as the others fanned out around the property.

"Lumbira, shadow wolf. One's dead, the other's slipped off," John explained, his voice tense and focused.

"Sweet sunlight, they killed one?" a nearby guard asked.

Several of the arriving militia gawked at the carcass of the great wolf and the steaming hole shot clean through it.

"And there's still another. Chase it off before it gets to the livestock," John said.

As the small crowd dispersed, the square-jawed woman cursed under her breath. It must have been as bad as Olivia suspected.

"I can stabilize her for the moment, but she needs healing magic. Hey," she shouted back to a nearby militia guard who stared at the dead monster. "Head back into town and get Mage Yorker. Bring him here as fast as you can."

"Yorker?" asked Olivia.

Her heart seized up as though the other lumbira returned. The name alone was enough to quicken her breath.

"Horses are in the stable, use one of those," Dalton said.

The woman finished wrapping Elena's wounds and looked between the two men. "I need to get her inside. Help me carry her."

The three of them lifted her mother. She gasped in pain, but ground her teeth together to stop from screaming. The two sisters trailed behind as their mother was shepherded back into the shattered house.

Josie grabbed her sister's arm, tears coming freely. "Is this our fault?" she asked.

Be strong, Olivia. This is the kind of stuff you're supposed to be ready for, she thought.

Despite the assurance, it sounded silly in the face of this. Almost losing her mother and facing down a full-fledged shadow beast were the smallest of her fears. What made her want to crawl into a hole was knowing her gift came back. However, this was not the Life magic of her youth. She only knew this power by an infamous name whispered as a warning to mages and common folk alike. It was the scouring True Flame.

Olivia sat next to her mother as they settled her onto a table. The guard rubbed medicinal herbs in the lighter cuts. John and her father pressed bundles of cloth against the gaping wounds in her leg while Josie held her pale hand. Elena passed out several minutes ago, her skin as white as chalk. Only the guard's insistence that she still had a pulse kept the family from falling to pieces.

Yorker's name set Olivia on edge. It was a name that was not welcome in their home. Despite that, she knew his magic was the only thing that might save her mother. She still feared his appearance. Horse hooves clattered up the road and stopped in front of their home. Two people dismounted and quickly entered their home. The first was the guard that collected the mage. She braced herself for the second.

Yorker was the only known magic user for miles around. His white hair was oily at the roots. The full beard of gray hair hid most of his face save for the nervous, sunken eyes that searched around the Seers home. He looked over the wounded woman and the family around it, but his eyes settled on Olivia. Panic flashed in his face and Olivia felt her stomach roil. The beard was new since she last saw him.

Yorker looked away from her as fast as his neck could stand. He hurried to the kitchen table with a withered twig and a handful of nourishing gorgeberry in hand. Dalton looked up from his injured wife with an uneasy scowl. The others in the room regarded Yorker with an ill quiet. Dalton raised an eyebrow to his daughter with an unspoken question. Olivia nodded back and conjured a weak smile.

"Evening all. How do you do, oh my. Dalton, what happened?" Yorker babbled as he entered the circle of people around Elena.

"Pair of lumbira. One of them broke into the house and the other attacked Josie. Damn near got away with Elena," John said.

"Lumbira? Shadow wolves this close to populated lands, strange things. Were they commanded?" Yorker asked.

"How should I know that?" John snapped. "Wasn't like I could ask."

"This isn't going to hurt her, right?" Josie asked. She clutched her mother's hand and seemed ready to yank her away from the mage's touch at the first sign of trouble.

"This is the best thing for her right now. You can rest easy, Josie."

His words did not ease her. Olivia appreciated that no one else in the room felt good about Yorker's presence here. It was not enough to comfort her, but it gave her a bit more strength. The mage popped a few bright, purple gorge berries into his mouth and chewed quickly. He gestured for the others to give Elena some space and gathered her hand in his. He held the withered twig over her.

Yorker took a rattling breath and closed his eyes. Memories of their lessons were thrust into her mind. The recognition of the magical arts made her squirm and she stepped away from the table. Her heart pounded with the suspicion that he would invoke the darker powers onto their home. Tearing her eyes away from the ritual eased her worries.

"Pull my vitality into her. Sustain this body with my blood. Heal Elena, please," Yorker whispered to himself.

The withered twig shifted and veins pulsed against his wrinkled skin. Buds bloomed from the twig and flowered. Elena's wounds began to knit together. Her pale skin gained a hue of red as blood coursed through her veins. Broken bones mended with small snaps and pops. Elena winced and wriggled on her back.

Josie clutched at her mother tighter, uneasily watching the magic at work. She knitted her lips together as she cried. Her large shoulders sagged, a degree of relief finally washing over her.

Olivia turned back to the table. It was working, Life would heal her.

Dalton rested his head next to his wife's and whispered something in her ear. Pendant in hand, Olivia fumbled with every detail she could find. Even as he saved her mother's life, the distant memories brought the hair on her neck standing.

His bright eyes gleaming in the darkness, the whispering thing in the shadows and the pounding at the door. Come outside, child. It is waiting for you.

Yorker drew the twig away from her. The deep gashes and tears closed with only pale scars left on her skin as a memory of this nightmare. Yorker braced himself against the end of the table. Blinking against the weakness, he fumbled into his pocket and drew a few more berries. He spoke as he chewed the sweet fruit.

"Much healing to be done still, but not enough in me to finish the job. She should be fine." Yorker patted her leg tenderly. "The lumbira, what drove them away?"

John and Dalton shared a silent glance.

"There was fire, an explosion," Josie answered.

"Flame?" Yorker asked.

John nodded silently. "Honest. True Flame."

The mage knitted his brows together and looked among the faces around him.

"Well, where is this mage?" The last word caught in his throat. He did not look at Olivia, but she could hear his thoughts bending toward her.

"I think you know where," Dalton said.

Olivia looked back at the pendant in her hand. The damned thing, the shiny bauble that seemed so innocent a short time ago. Yorker saved her mother. Now she wanted him gone.

"Olivia, is this true?" he asked.

She said nothing, afraid that confirmation might be

seen as an invitation to linger. Her father cleared his throat, the noise full of expectation. She looked up and found that John's face had gained edges. The sarcastic, self-assured layers peeled back. All that was left was a brutal earnestness. She nodded and finally looked at Yorker. The eyes, nestled in his white beard, were softer than she remembered.

"Yes, I made fire," she said.

"And what is that you have?" Yorker asked.

John and Dalton stood up from the table, now aware that something was cradled in her hands. Josie shrank in her seat as she gripped her mother's hand.

"What is in your hand?" Dalton asked.

Olivia looked between the waiting eyes, but did not find a convenient excuse. She raised the pendant over her head. The gold metal shone in the candlelight around them.

"By the Triad: Earth, Water, and Flame," Yorker whispered and made a sign with his hand.

"What is that?" her father asked.

"It's a magical Focus. Where did you find that?" Yorker pressed.

The word sent her nerves skittering up and down her neck. No, she would have known better, right? For all her vigilance against magic, she could not have just slipped so easily could she?

"It's not a Focus. I would never think of it, you know that."

She thought over how it had felt when she touched it. It felt like a reward. It was waiting for her. Her skin crawled and heat washed over her. That was not right. Olivia would have let the damn thing be buried if she knew what it really was. The one time she did not feel the tug of the elements and it happened to be a Focus of some dead mage.

Each Focus was different. They could look like anything. It was an item through which mages could speak with the elements. Every mage made their own or dedicated a found item to the elements. Olivia could not remember what she did with hers.

"I was scared. Mom was almost gone. That thing had her, she was going to disappear—"

"Into the shadow," Yorker finished.

The room felt warm. The damned heat lingered since she killed the lumbira. She tried to speak, but she could not describe the feeling that came over her. It felt like raw power. Pure, untouched, indomitable power in the palm of her hand. It felt like she could have ripped the monster limb from limb herself. Dalton crossed the room to stand next to his daughter.

"She put a hole through that damn thing. It saved our family. Does it matter where she got it from?"

"Not particularly, I guess," Yorker said. He tented his fingers together, the twig held between them.

He took a few steps closer toward Olivia. Her nerve failed her as a kind smile gathered on his face.

"Olivia, I'm so sorry that I failed you. Dalton, same to you. I've paid for my transgressions in more ways than you might know." Yorker ran his fingers along the blooming twig, the flowers on it already dying. "We need to confront this. You need to get her to someone who can help her. Flame magic is dangerous."

John shook his head, a laugh and a smile breaking his stony expression. "She hasn't used magic in ages, what are the odds?" he asked.

"What is he talking about?" Olivia asked.

"Bringing a Focus under your control is normally a long, painful process. I don't know where you found it, Olivia, but if you've conjured True Flame then you may already carry the affliction," Yorker continued.

"I haven't been in danger since I learned under you. You are the only thing I'm afraid of in this room," Olivia said through her teeth.

Yorker took a deep breath. "Olivia."

"That's enough." Dalton pointed toward the front door. "Go. I am grateful to you for saving Elena's life. You can consider our bad blood to be thinned. Tonight though, you must leave."

"You don't understand. With her talent, her conjuration of Flame has to be addressed. You sweep this under the rug at the risk to your daughter."

Dalton approached him with a mean look on his face and balled fists. The mage stumbled back from the glare.

"You are scaring my daughter and you know damn well why. Get going."

Yorker gave a final glance toward Olivia before walking out of the room. The guard rose from their mother's side and headed toward the front door.

"She will still need time. No hard work, no travel, keep her on bed rest. I am going to leave some people outside. Expect a change of the guard in four hours. I will be back in the morning to gather an official report."

"Thank you," Dalton said.

Josie and John gave a deep nod of thanks as she passed. Yorker and the guard climbed onto the horse and rode off into the night.

"Enough of that crack pot. He's caused our family enough pain," Dalton said. "Let's go to bed, deal with all this in the morning."

John cleared his throat and ground his shoe against the floor. His voice was a wilting murmur as he spoke. "He might be right, Dalton. I wish he wasn't. Liv manifested Flame magic. Flame burns kindling."

"Don't tell me you're agreeing with him," Olivia said.

"Flame is the enemy of Shadow and can cut through anything it might offer. The catch is that Flame needs kindling. You are kindling. That is the flame affliction he was talking about," John said.

She rolled her eyes and snarled. Olivia wasn't willing to accept any guff after everything that happened tonight. "What do you know? You're a con artist, not a mage."

"It's how this magic works, Liv. I've seen it before. There's a reason there haven't been any fire mages since the war."

"So I'm sick? I'll stay in bed for a few days. We can push off my inheritance of the farm for a few days," Olivia said.

She would not let this slow down her plan. Magic could not, would not, screw up her life again. Olivia needed that. Josie left her sleeping mother's side, but could not tear her gaze away from her sister.

"If Yorker is right, you're dying."

John spoke like he was handing down a death sentence. The silence was as deafening as the flame that killed the shadow wolf. The thoughts of everyone in the room threatened to spill into the open air and shred the quiet night to ribbons. The two sisters and their father spoke in a flurry.

"Stars above John!"

"Dying? She's fine, look at her."

"How long? Can we cure it?" Dalton asked.

"Maybe. How do you feel? Are you warm?" John raised his hand to feel her forehead, but Olivia stepped away from him.

"Yeah. Ever since I killed that thing, I've been burning up."

"That could be just the shock of the fight. That means nothing," her father said.

Josie wrapped her arms around Olivia. She squeezed with desperation, like her sister would slip away with any less of an embrace.

"I shouldn't have grabbed it. I should've just left it like you said, I'm so sorry," Josie whispered in her ear. John and Dalton argued too loudly to hear her.

"I'm a mess alright, but trust me on this. Flame magic is nothing to sneeze at. It starts as a fever. It gets worse, you'll sweat and say it's the heat. But it won't go away. You're thirsty and burning up and all the remedies stop working. You'll cook from the inside out."

"Damn it, John. I'll run you through if you keep talking to my daughter that way," Dalton moved toward his brother, but winced after two steps. He massaged his side against a blooming pain.

"Shit, I'm sorry, Liv. I didn't think," John said.

"You never think," Olivia said. "You love getting a rise out of us and I can't wait to throw you out of town. Why should I listen to a thing you have to say?"

"Because as much as you don't like me, I would never hurt you. Ever. You've got a good head on your shoulders and you're better than the rest of the town put together. You're my niece. I wouldn't betray my brother like that," John said.

Better than the rest of them? He did nothing but

scrutinize her every move since he arrived. When he was not stumbling around in a self-aggrandizing haze, he would tell her what a hayseed she is and how she does not understand the outside world. John must have noticed her silence.

"Don't read into that, alright. I don't like seeing people die."

Josie pulled herself from her sister's shoulder. "How do we cure it? If she is sick, where is the cure?"

John pulled a chair from the upended table. He took a seat, slipped the flask from his jacket, and took a drink.

"East to Sallew, capital of the Congress of Six. I've heard that the Church of the Sun messes with this stuff. They might know."

"That's almost a six-day ride," Dalton scoffed.

"I'm not leaving home. There's too much to do. Mom is hurt. They were supposed to retire soon, this can't happen," Olivia said.

John chuckled and leaned on his knees.

She wanted to find her hunting knife and stick it into his eye. "Do not laugh at me, Johnathan."

"You don't have a choice, Liv. Well, you do, but you aren't going to like what happens if you stay."

"Damn magic. It's not messing things up again, not twice. Not after everything I've done to avoid it. I was almost out of it." A sob escaped her chest and she kicked a chair. "I was almost free of what I used to be."

Josie followed her sister and put her hand on her shoulder. She swallowed a growl, fighting the urge to shove her sister back.

"Stop it, Josie."

"He's right," Elena said, "You have to go."

Their mother propped herself up on one arm. The

rest of the family came back together around her. Olivia sat by her side and the rest of the family stood nearby. Elena looked as if she was on death's door when Yorker arrived. Now she only appeared exhausted.

"I can't leave you like this," Olivia said.

"I'll heal with time. I won't stand for my daughter to die because of something we could have stopped," her mother said.

"But the harvest, your retirement. This is not how things were supposed to go," Olivia said.

"Don't you worry about that. If what John said is true, then you are the only thing that matters right now."

Tears rolled down her face and she shook her head. It made sense, but Olivia did not want to give in. She had tried to dominate this weakness for years. Now she was back to square one. Maybe somewhere worse if she was being honest.

"I knew it was going to kill me. Nothing good can come of it, this damn gift."

"It's always been a part of you. We let you turn away after what happened, but maybe that was a mistake. Things you push down have a way of surfacing eventually. There's always a debt to be paid. You've got to go."

Dalton sat next to his daughter and rested his hand on her shoulder. "You can't go alone, but I can't leave. Your mother is not fit to travel; someone has to keep an eye on her. And, well, I'm not doing so great myself. I think my ankle is messed up too." He winced as the pain in his side bit.

Olivia began to consider a solo journey to a city she had never been to. The thought intimidated her more than she liked. Dalton grinned and turned to face John.

"Luckily, we have someone who knows how to get to Sallew and any other place you might need to go. He'll go with you."

"What?" John capped his flask with a loud clink.

Olivia was not sure what could have made this situation worse, but her father found it. She had no desire to spend a trip in his company, much less one where she was slowly dying.

"No, we can find someone else," Olivia said.

"Listen to your daughter, she's right," John added.

Dalton raised a finger, his whole body tensed and ready to fight this point. "No, she's not. Who else in this town of hayseeds, as you said, has any idea how to get her to the right people in Sallew? Who else could possibly know what she'd be up against."

John wriggled and toyed with his flask. "I want her to be safe. I'm really not qualified for this."

"Bullshit," Dalton said.

"I'm a wanted man. Stars above, I'm supposed to just walk back into town and hope they don't arrest me?"

"Blend in. Hide. Do all those things you said you were good at. You've only been retired for six months, you can't be *that* rusty," Dalton said.

"John, please," Josie said. "I haven't heard much else from you besides stories about all the ass you used to kick."

He sneered and cursed under his breath. John opened his flask again and took a long swig. His eyes contemplating the rafters above them. Olivia knew they were right. He was the ideal pick. If she was truly ill, time was not on their side. She could ride around the Seventh Republic blind, but beyond their borders was a wild place. She would never say it, but she wanted this cocky asshole as a guide.

"I guess I could do it. We can get there in five days if we move quickly and pack light. But we need to get going. We're leaving at first light. Be packed."

Dalton nodded his head. "Thanks."

John rolled his eyes and walked to his room on the first floor. Dalton groaned and ran his fingers over his head. Olivia looked back to her dad.

"Are you sure about this dad?" Olivia asked.

"On my life, Olivia. He'll get you there."

She felt that she should be feeling better, but the tumble of emotions in her chest were worse than an hour before. At the same time, she wanted to crawl into a hole and also run as far as she could.

Chapter Four

The city stood on the crumbling ruins of what it used to be. Tall buildings with dirty shingles towered over the cobblestone streets. Dingy light bulbs desperately buzzed over the heads of street traders that hawked their wares to huddled throngs. These streets stretched from the brass city center and out to where the aged lights faded. The abandoned, broken outskirts stood beyond their shelter.

Near this border was a row of taverns and inns that catered to vagrants. One of these taverns rose above the others. Locals called it the Guild Hall, though the only decisions made there were whether to drink yourself blind or just enough to feel fuzzy. It was not home to any club anymore. Like the city around it, it was a memory of better times. It was the perfect place for deals that even the rest of this jaded city would hesitate to take.

Tomis and Peter did not shy from such deals. They walked through the streets of Shelter Harbor from the glowing city center to this forgotten place. They were just like the many who defied the rain. In a city where desperation was expected, cunning was a requirement. Tomis much preferred the second option. His hands fiddled with the buttons of his jacket. Clients usually wanted artifacts and treasures from the Great War.

Tonight, their parcel was a wrinkled scrap of paper. Peter dripped rainwater onto the tarnished, hardwood floors of the Guild Hall. Tomis followed and tried to shake the water from his jacket. Wide tables were scattered around the room, many pushed closer to a large hearth that burnt scrap wood. Two men spoke in low tones near the fire, pulling drinks from the same almost empty bottle of liquor. A third person slept beneath a coat with an enormous hound at their feet. Its chocolate fur had deep wrinkles that collected drool from its mouth. It sat up as Tomis entered, ears raised.

A wooden bar, carefully polished and cleaned with cheap soap, ran alongside the opposite wall. Ahead of them was a grand staircase that went to the floors above. Tomis took his coat off and ruffled his dark, thin hair. His knees ached and the rain made his right elbow stiff from an old injury. He was nearing his fourth decade of living as a scoundrel. This sort of wear and tear was expected. Though his jaw was marked with a long scar and his hair was flat as wet parchment, he was happy to only have a few gray hairs.

Peter stood at the bar and spoke with the innkeeper. Where Tomis was frail, Peter could haul carts of merchandise by himself. A gut bulged against his shirt, fed by a steady diet of bread and ale. His calloused palms ran across the bar with a slow, appreciative move.

"Anything that overlooks the alley will work," Peter said.

The innkeeper retrieved a set of keys and set them on top of the bar. Her braided top knot was dyed green, the remainder of her long, dark hair running down her back.

"Ten shulten for the night."

"All I've got is talons. Will that do?"

The innkeeper's fingers closed tight around the keys

and she pulled them back.

"Thirteen talons and you've got it."

"Talons are a royal currency, friend, recognized in any port city worth its trade."

"They're harder to spend around here, but I've got people taking shulten all day. Thirteen."

Tomis nudged Peter. "We've got a schedule, just pay her."

Peter grunted and laid the bronze coins on the table. The innkeeper pushed the keys over to them and scooped the talons up.

"Room 12, top floor. Keep the windows shut tonight, the breeze pushes the rain in and I don't want any more water damage."

"We are actually expecting someone. If anyone asks for Peter, direct them to us," Peter said.

The innkeeper gave no response besides a blank stare and returned to cleaning glasses with a rag. Tomis and Peter climbed the stairs to the higher floors. The wood was blackened by a parade of unwashed boots and squeaked loudly under their feet.

"You seem nervous," Peter said.

A quiet hallway, lit with dim candles, led off from the stairs and onto the second floor. The rainy night pressed against the window at the end of the hallway. The dark outside leered through vacant windows and open doorways.

"This feels off. No goods, just information. What'd you say the client's name was?" Tomis asked.

"It's not important. What's specifically different?" Peter eyed Tomis. He finally removed his coat and laid it over his shoulder as they mounted the stairs for the third floor.

"Just a feeling."

"We've had deals go bad before," Peter said, reading Tomis's mind. "I bailed your ass out last time. You still owe me for that, by the by."

"I don't think bringing ten thousand shultens' worth of war relics to an abandoned warehouse for a handoff was a good idea."

"Why'd you do it then?"

"Because you told me it was a good idea," Tomis said.

Peter chuckled. The green carpet of the third floor was stained the same as all the others, but the wind howled against the windows. One of the candles at the end of the hall fluttered, the shadows squirming to smother it. The small wick barely kept its fire and the darkness pulled back.

"I mean it now, what if it really goes bad again? We're right outside the edge of the city, it would be nothing for them to slink off afterward."

"It wouldn't be hard for us to slink off either. I got an alley facing room for a reason. Would you settle, you're making me nervous now," Peter said.

Peter unlocked the door and stepped inside. Tomis followed closely, swinging around to check the corners of the room as they stepped in. The room was a coffin. A single bed was pushed against the far wall and a rain-streaked window stood over it. The short table next to the bed was stained with something. A small door led to a toilet shared with the next room over. Rainwater collected on the floor, dripping from the open window.

Tomis glanced into the alley below before closing it. Peter sat on the bed and rifled through his pack. He pulled out a small bottle and took a drink before offering it to Tomis, who refused with a wave.

"I'd rather we were both sharp going into this," Tomis said.

"You've gotta calm down or they're gonna think something is up."

Tomis's nerves were getting worse since he started planning these handoffs and purchases. He rubbed his aching elbow and thought over what would come next, how much they agreed to sell the information for, too many details. He felt sick.

Their third partner, John Seers, was forced to retire almost six months ago. Tomis was always getting the goods and trinkets, but John made the plan. He knew where to look for them, how to get them past borders, and into the right hands. Whether the artifacts were real or not, whether the clients were satisfied or not, it always worked out.

Tomis was upset at first. Retiring to his brother's farm in the middle of nowhere hardly seemed a fitting end to the wise cracking con man. It was out of his hands. John had nowhere else to go. All the same, Tomis still missed him. Tomis wondered how much longer he could keep this up.

"You have it, right?" Tomis asked.

Peter reached into his pocket and retrieved the note. A set of coordinates were scribbled on it in ink.

"Nice and dry. They'll be happy and we'll get paid."

Tomis still fidgeted with the buttons on his sleeves.

"You don't have to say anything. I can do all the talking, sound good?" Peter asked.

"I wish John was here, he always calmed me down."

"And I don't?"

"You're like me. You know better than to be calm,"

Tomis said.

Lightning flashed against the windows and thunder rolled after it seconds later. Tomis took a deep breath and glanced outside again. He could not see anything in this downpour.

"Look, just go into the bathroom and wait. I can handle it."

"No, no. That's not fair," Tomis said.

"Would you look at yourself? If you pissed yourself at the next bolt of lightning, I wouldn't be surprised." Peter's pudgy, grizzled face softened and he nodded to the bathroom. "Go."

Of course, he was right. Tomis knew that. His hands were shaking and he could not bear the idea of sitting down. Peter lacked almost all the charisma that John had, but he was far from heartless.

"Thanks. I'll be waiting."

He stepped into the cramped room and closed the door. The air was close and humid, the smell was worse. It was the sanctuary that he needed. It did not quell his worries. He could not escape the feeling that something was wrong.

You've done this a hundred times, calm down, Tomis thought.

The meetup was remote. The client was vague. They asked to find a location from the Great War. Not some filigree or tapestry or even a sword. She wanted them to find her an old battlefield. Particularly, the last place some old mage was seen last. They spent two weeks with their noses in books and faded scrolls of parchment, but they found it all the same.

Tomis heard three sharp knocks on the door to their room and his chest tightened. The bed rattled as Peter stood up. His footsteps went to the door and the hinges squeaked as it opened. Tomis cracked open the bathroom door enough to see in.

"Peter?" a woman asked. Her voice was edged with impatience. She spoke with the same tone of a courier at the end of their route.

"Guessing you are Faldir. Come in," Peter said.

The floor groaned as Peter walked back into the room followed by two people. They each wore black cloaks, dark as the night outside of the window.

The first was a woman, her hood removed to reveal a tight bun of dark brown hair. Her face was chiseled into a scowl. Three piercings dotted her jawline, the only interruption to her smooth skin. By the look on her face, Tomis thought she would be as hard as stone if you touched her.

The second person's cloak was heavier. Soaked with water from the rain, they still did not remove it. It was pulled as far over them as they could manage and stretched to its limit. Bulging arms peeked out from under the hems, a tangle of wild, brown hair grew from the forearms. The rumble of their breath reminded Tomis of some great, toothy predator.

"Where is it?" Faldir asked.

Peter ignored her urgency. He could not help but antagonize at times, something Tomis hated.

"Can you believe this rain? Your friend can take his coat off, get comfortable."

Her breath hissed as she exhaled. "We won't be long. Where is the mage's grave?" she asked again.

"No chit chat huh? You aren't in the treasure hunting business often are you?"

They did not answer.

"I've got it, I've got it. Keep your shirt on," Peter said.

"Good. Will your compatriot be joining us?" she asked.

Peter paused. The floor groaned as he shifted his weight. Tomis held his breath, praying to be left unknown.

"Nope, he's lining things up with another buyer."

"Too bad, I would have liked to meet you both."

"I'm sure he would be sorry too. All the same, I've been trading in goods from the war for years. Sorting through old graves and ruined castles long enough and you pick up a few things the history books don't know. But I found it; the last resting place of Adar. Looks like he stopped breathing east of here, in the ruin fields."

"I paid you for coordinates. Not directions."

"Well, I'm not doing this for free."

Tomis could see Peter's grin in his mind. She reached into her pack and handed a modest bag to him. It clattered with coins and Peter shook it.

"That's what I like to see. Here, all yours."

Peter handed the parchment over to Faldir. She opened it quickly and read silently. The walls creaked as the wind rattled the windows. The breath of her hooded friend filled the room, louder than the drumbeat of rain.

"Are we done here?" Peter asked, "It's been a long day and I'd like to sleep."

"We are done here, grave robber," Faldir said.

She nodded to the Hooded Man. With that small notice, he leaped at Peter. The figure's hands were muscled like an animal with claws to match. He threw Peter across the room and onto the bed.

Tomis backed up against the door to the other room.

He could barely see Peter laid out on the bed as the Hooded Man leaped upon him. Tomis opened the door to the attached room and looked back. His friend was a seasoned criminal who had fought for his life before.

I should help him, I should be fighting, he thought. His frantic heart assured him that he would die if he did.

Peter swung his fist into the creature's face, a loud crack followed by an agonized whine. He kicked hard and propelled the creature head long into the wall next to the front door. Peter rose and rammed the creature's throat. It gasped and stumbled. Peter drew a dagger and turned to face Faldir, but found her ready for him.

She held no blade or coilgun. In her raised hand was a small rod of onyx, her magical Focus. She pressed it against Peter's chest, her other hand catching Peter's arm. The shadows in the room pulsed, the candles flickered, and a horrid screech filled the air. A bolt of purple and black erupted from the onyx rod and shot through him. Peter's breath left him before he could scream. The magical death stroke cut clean through and crashed into the brick wall behind him, just a few inches above the Hooded Man.

"My legacy is not yours to pillage," Faldir said.

Peter's body crumpled to the ground, the edges of the wound shriveled and black. Tomis took a backward step into the other room and leaped for the window. No one was inside, not that Tomis would have cared. He flipped the latch on the window and swung it open. The metal hinges screeched and the intruders turned to the bathroom door.

"Get in there!"

The bathroom door crashed open.

Tomis stepped out and settled on a stone ledge on

the side of the building. The woman leaned out of the window and raised the onyx Focus. As the bolt of killing magic flew at Tomis, the stone ledge crumbled under his feet and he fell.

He fell through the rain and flailed for anything to grab onto. His hands almost caught the window ledge on the second floor, but he slipped. He crashed into the canvas roof of a closed street shop below. The wooden poles snapped and the smell of spices and herbs kicked into the air as crates and barrels within were upended. The canvas folded over him and a cloud of red and yellow incense swallowed him. He shouted in pain as he climbed out of the rich smelling wreck. His heartbeat hammered in his ears and every instinct screamed for him to run.

Tomis climbed out of the small tent store as another purple bolt struck the ground behind him. He dove behind a crate full of fruits as another streak of magic crashed into the spot where he had been. An older man passing by the alley shouted and ran away. Calling an alarm would have been pointless. There was no one who would answer it.

Tomis ran into the streets and ducked into the next narrow alley he could find. Down that soaked street, he turned on to a lantern lit main drag. He ran toward the heart of the city. Tomis did not hear anymore screaming shots of death, no more growling monsters in cloaks, and no more Peter to look out for him. Tomis was alone.

Chapter Five

Olivia sat upright in bed, broiling under her woolen sheets. Her sheets were soaked as if she went swimming in the night. The room was dark, but a candle lamp burned on the other side. Josie was dressed and busy packing two bags. One was on her bed and held Josie's clothing, bed roll, and some tools. The second was for Olivia. It laid on a table they shared near the center of the room. Josie took a handful of her clothing and lumped it next to the bag. Olivia saw the shelves of her cupboard were opened and emptied.

"I can handle my own bags," Olivia said.

"Oh good, you're awake. I just got us a head start. I know what you would wear on a trip like this, I've got a sense for it. You can change it, but I think you will be satisfied with my ideas."

Josie was jabbering. Olivia got up and rubbed her eyes. She pushed the shelves of her drawers shut, checking inside each as she did. What clothes remained were pushed aside or unfolded by her hurried sister.

"What time is it?" Olivia asked.

"About an hour till dawn. I was going to let you sleep a little longer before I woke you."

"Has John been up yet?"

"He came by, seemed to have been awake for a while."

Josie glanced at the partially open door. Olivia could

hear someone making noise in the main room below. The concept of John awake at this hour was hard to believe. In addition to being a general pain in the ass, he once slept through a tornado that came perilously close to their farmhouse.

"I don't think I've ever seen him up before sunrise," Olivia said.

Josie's frenzied packing paused.

"I think you're right."

She resumed sorting and Olivia organized her possessions into tight piles: spare socks, undergarments, shirts, hunting knife, travel coat, her mental tally went on. Josie continued to ramble in the background. She was hunting for meaningless things to throw into conversation.

Olivia shook off the topics with vague agreements. She glared at every fold and wrinkle in the clothes she packed. If she had not picked up that relic or if Josie was not so curious, she would be peacefully sleeping the night away. She would not be stuck going all the way to the eastern coast with a guide who openly disliked her.

Or my mother would be dead, she thought.

She stuffed more clothes into her bag with a violent shove. The heat of the day must have been trapped in their room. She couldn't cool off. A strong breeze shook the trees across the nearby yard and through their open window. It should have been cool in their bedroom.

"You're both awake. Shocking."

Olivia jumped as she became aware of John standing in the door. He wore his warden tree bracers and dark green jacket, but it was joined by a leather chest piece. On each side of his hips were new additions. A straight bladed short sword rested on one hip. On the other was a hand crossbow. Her father said only killers would find use for such things. Despite the bags under his eyes, he seemed alert.

"Same to you. I figured we would have to wake you up," Olivia muttered.

"You are looking mighty dangerous," Josie said.

He smiled and crossed over to the table where Olivia packed her things.

"I promised your dad not to take them out ever again, but you never know what you'll meet out there."

"And he is fine with you having them now?" Olivia asked.

"I'm not telling him."

He fiddled with the hand crossbow, but subtly watched Olivia. The edges of his eyes were barely noticeable in the dim candlelight. She must have been as hard to see because he gave up the ruse after a moment.

"How are you feeling?" he asked.

Olivia glanced back at her bed. "A little warm."

"Turn to the light." He reached out and tried to twist her face toward the candle before asking. She smacked his hand and jerked her head backward.

"Don't touch me."

"Could you please face the candlelight? I want to take a look at you."

He crossed his arms and waited, but his tongue probed the inside of his cheek. Olivia turned to face the light after a long moment, but John did not have to say anything as his brow furrowed. Olivia had seen that face in people who were bit by venomous creek vipers. They knew bad times were coming.

"It's not too bad yet," he lied. "Don't give her any ideas about special treatment."

"I don't need any special treatment," she said.

He ignored her and walked back toward the door. "Meet me downstairs, wrap this up. And uh, golden child, pack that Focus too."

"Why?" Olivia asked.

It was a relic of the past, something she would have loved to study under any other circumstance. Now it was trash. She wanted to toss it into the Sentinel River valley. Even if it survived the fall, no one would ever find it once it washed out to sea.

"I don't know too much about magic and certainly don't know anything about snuffing flame affliction. What I do know is that a mage without their Focus is a ship without a rudder," John said.

"Who needs a rudder for a ship they aren't going to use?" Olivia asked.

He rubbed his hands together and a flash of genuine concern crossed his face again.

"Better to have it and not need it. Once we cure you, then do what you want with it."

He left them and went downstairs. Olivia walked over to the chest at the foot of her bed and grabbed the golden relic. She turned it over in the pale moonlight.

"We should just smash it. No good will come of it," Josie said.

"I was thinking about that, but he's got a point. Unfortunately."

Olivia weighed it in her hand then slipped it into her pocket. If her father valued John's judgment enough to send them into the wilderness with him, it was surely trust and not desperation that motivated him. She wondered if it was time to give the con artist a chance.

"I don't want to see that damned thing." Josie tied

her bag closed and slung it over her shoulder. "I wish John did not even bring it up."

"I wish we didn't have to bother with this whole thing, but here we are."

****

The sun broke just over the trees, the heat of the day yet to arrive. The scent of dew lingered in the air, sticking memories of other early morning errands around town. Olivia never guessed that she might face her last one so soon. Olivia stood in front of her parents, Josie and John close behind her.

"Stay rested after you're cured. It's a long ride."

Elena leaned on Dalton's shoulder. Her bruised arms wrapped around her eldest daughter. Olivia had the impulse to make one more play to stay home. She could come up with some disagreement or some condition for a delay. Anything. The faint moisture on her forehead and the persistent heat was beginning to convince her otherwise. John's warning still lingered in her mind.

First, you'll start sweating.

"Watch yourself. Lands between here and the Congressional's are wild. You too, Josie. You are not the strongest thing out there," Dalton said.

John held the reins of their three horses as the family said their goodbyes. Each wore their respective packs. John's horse carried a bag full of supplies and food. Josie stood patiently behind her sister. Olivia let go and gave her parents a smile.

"I'll keep an eye on her," Olivia said.

"We'll be back before mom is healed up, I know it," Josie said as she stepped forward.

"Listen to your sister. She's still the older one," Dalton said.

"Like I ever listened to her."

John handed the reins over to Olivia and walked to his brother. John hugged both Dalton and Elena, his embrace not lasting as long.

"You keep them safe John. This is on you now." Dalton's voice slowed as he spoke, as if to impress each syllable on his brother.

"It's not too late to find someone else."

"We're not playing games," Elena said. "They know the wilderness, but you know what's out there. I'm counting on you to protect them."

John made a show of side-eyeing the sisters before nodding to his brother. His voice fell, clearly trying to keep something between the two of them, but she still heard him say, "On my life."

They climbed their mounts and the horses stamped in anticipation. Olivia scratched Grizzly's black mane before grabbing the reins and moving him to action. The three of them turned their backs to the Seers family home, where she should have been preparing for her time as owner. As they skirted the edge of Hasketter, Olivia looked down the road leading into town. She could make out the sign for the tanner and a bakery. So much for a sendoff. That's the last look she got of her hometown: bread and leather.

John took the lead with the black spotted horse that his brother lent him. Olivia and Josie had no trouble matching his pace. At times, they could have ridden faster than him, but they needed to make the horses last. Riding them to death would do them no good for the return.

The ruin fields loomed to the south, but they stuck to the road. It was not paved, but rather beaten down and cleared off by the hooves of horses, the wheels of wagons, and the steps of tired travelers. They stopped every few hours to relieve themselves, give the horses some water, or eat a small bit of food.

The day dragged on and the sun rose overhead as the three rode past merchant caravans. These grand convoys of wagons and people stuck together against raiders during the day and shadow beasts at night. Some watched the three with a passing curiosity.

They were drawn from the entire continent. Salvaged ship sails on wagons signaled those from the coasts. Gargantuan, polished beetle shells made up the wagon covers of those from the southern nation of Shavuhnsten. Many were a mix of materials, woods, and flags from every corner of the land. Some wagons were the size of houses and just as fortified. Some were handled by the same family for generations. Others focused on their own skinny horses and scrap wood wagons, afraid that they might not reach the next stop on their path.

They left the caravan behind them and Olivia found herself in the shadowed hills and groves north of the ruin fields. She imagined that leaving the farm would have been her decision. Instead, she was riding to the distant city of Sallew to cure a curse. Any hope of burying the past was shattered. It might be her that they end up burying, she thought.

Olivia told herself she could put her talents away after this. She had done it once before, hadn't she? All the same, she could feel the Focus jostling in her pack as she could feel the wind wash over the fields of tall grass. This other sense was like a stranger sitting right next to her. Impossible to ignore, but it would never speak without being asked.

Hours later, the sun lowered toward the horizon. An entire day spent in travel with only a few words shared between them all. The merchant caravans were miles away at this point and no one traveled the roads at night.

"John, shouldn't we stop here and start setting up a camp?" Olivia asked.

"Oh, yeah." His eyes darted to the setting sun and they slowed their horses.

"I thought you said you were a famed traveler?" Josie teased.

"Just a little rusty. There," he pointed to a hilltop not far from where they were. It was barren save for a tree that was bent low against the wind.

"How about at the bottom of it?" Josie asked.

"Bottom?" John raised an eyebrow.

"The wind is too rough up there. We won't keep a fire going for long and we'll be visible for miles." She traced her finger from the breezy hilltop to the shaded slope. "See that spot at the bottom? It's perfect for the three of us. If we camp at the base—"

"Yep, excellent thinking, foot of the hill it is," he said.

Olivia barely suppressed her annoyance. They rode their horses to the foot of the hill, just off the road, and dismounted. They set torches around their camp and Olivia portioned out some bread and cheese from their supplies. John passed a piece of flint from his pack to Josie and she began snapping sparks onto gathered lumber. He looked at Olivia's hands and then back to the wood and sticks.

"Think you could uh, you know, give us a little help? Just a cinder or two. Should be easy."

Her face flushed. A snarling anger rose in her chest and threatened to rip through her throat with a flourish of curses. She focused on her breath and the ache in her back. Riding was not uncommon for her, but it had been months since she rode so far so quickly. Hungry, tired, irritated, she somehow conjured the patience to stay quiet.

"Too soon," Josie said.

John shrugged and repressed a chuckle.

Night fell and the shadows pressed close against the warm glow of the campfire. It flowed like an ebbing tide. In the presence of fouler things, Shadow would become excited and wriggle wisps of itself out from the oppressing mass of night. She heard stories of the night reaching out and snuffing torches all on its own when properly incensed.

Olivia heard the quiet, scampering noises though. The things of the night never really went away, they just waited for a chance to emerge to the surface again. They were small in these lands. They were mostly just swollen, chittering rats or foxes with long, needle teeth for snatching rabbits from their dens and fish from rivers. They kept their distance from fire, but would not pass up the chance to swarm anything that lingered beyond its light for too long.

They lurked around the perimeter of their camp. She followed the bounding shapes of three large rats, yapping with their tiny throats. They skittered toward where Grizzly slept, but the horse was not new to the wild. It stomped its hooves on the ground and neighed, enough to send the small creatures running for the tall weeds.

John raised his flask toward the two sisters.

"Cheers," John said, "to finding a cure for Olivia."

"Cheers."

"Mhmm," Olivia grunted.

John settled into his bed roll and gazed up at the stars. He was clearly settling in for the night, but they had not discussed the basics of running a camp in the wild. Josie glanced at Olivia and then back to John. Her sister likely had the same thought as her.

"Amazing things," John said. "A friend of mine said that the stars themselves were one of the primeval elements. Just like Fire and Water and such. All they are waiting for is someone who can talk to them. He got hit in the head a lot though."

"Watches?" Josie asked.

"What?"

"Don't you want to set up watches before you go to bed? Or do you want your nieces making sure you get your beauty sleep?" she continued.

"Of course. My brother did teach you well, didn't he?"

"This is kind of our lives. We have to be good at it," Olivia said.

"Right, you've been out in the sticks this whole time. Shade, when you were little there wasn't even a regional militia. The Seventh wasn't even a country."

"And what did you do when you were out in the wide world?" Josie asked. She smiled as her interest bled through her annoyance.

"I made my way. Did some things I would not advise doing." He smirked and took another sip from his flask. "Some things I wish I could do over again. But I'm retired now. That's all in the past. Spent most of my time in cities, ports, and palaces."

"Hold on." Olivia straightened up and swallowed a

piece of bread. "You were sent by our father to guide us. That is what my mother said. Guide. And you are saying you never spent a night in the wilderness alone?"

"It's not the wilderness guiding you will need from me. I was someone who, uh…oh how do I say it." He sat up. Olivia could swear that he hid a grin. Maybe he enjoyed telling stories as much as she enjoyed hearing them.

"People sold things that were valuable and I made sure they went to the right buyers. There's a lot of money in being a middleman. Business took me all over: Shelter Harbor, the Kingdom of Margecei, the Northern Communities. You two have been in this little bubble of suspicion and deep woods. Sallew is a big city with lots of things you two have never seen before. When we get there, you'll be glad to have me around. Besides, if we get into trouble, I can be handy."

"Is that what the assassin's weapon is for?" Olivia asked.

"Maybe, but I'm tired now. You'll have to ask your dear uncle more questions tomorrow night."

He collapsed back into his bed. Josie groaned and prepared to ask about the night watch again. She tolerated his jokes more than Olivia could. Admittedly, Olivia never joked very much with John. He was a scumbag, front and back. That was a convenient box to sort him into, at least.

"Watches," Josie repeated.

"Shit. Yes, yes," John sat up and pushed a finger into his chest, "I'll take the first watch. I'll wake you up for the second watch." He turned his finger toward Josie.

"And I'll take third?" Olivia asked.

"No, you need your rest."

"I'm not an invalid. I can help."

John shook his head. "I'm supposed to keep you safe and alive. If we are going to reach Sallew in time before you go all crispy—I mean, before it's too late, you will need your rest."

"I'm supposed to lay here and do nothing?"

"This affliction you've got, it's like any plague in the land. It doesn't kill all at once, it wears you down like water over a stone. Your health is the only thing that will slow it down and we need you as strong as you can be. You are not doing nothing. You are saving yourself."

Olivia shook her head. "I don't like it."

"I don't care. Lay down, go to sleep."

Olivia settled under the fur-lined wrap and pulled her bag under her head. Josie watched her, a nervous light in her eyes.

"Night, Liv," Josie said.

"Goodnight," Olivia answered.

With the silence of her thoughts, she could feel the persistent heat on her brow. She almost wished they pitched camp on the windy hilltop. The scathing breeze, ice cold by now, sounded soothing. A few minutes later Olivia was dreaming. Her head was full of green eyes, gold pendants, mothers screaming for help, and a familiar monster just beyond the fire light.

Chapter Six

A rickety, covered wagon bounced along the sun-scorched, dirt road heading east. Under the canvas cover, Tomis carefully traced a dull knife along ripe, red apples. The bumps in the road made him reconsider every slice, painfully aware of how close his fingers were to the edge. The wagon was in a train of twenty or so merchants. Each had its own product to pitch or service to offer. Cutlery, pots and pans, clothing, leather, fortunes told. Tomis found himself in the sweets-making business.

He stuffed the apple slices into a boiling pot of water next to him. Once boiled, he was instructed to dump them into jars along with a mixture of brown sugar, syrup, cinnamon, and a secret ingredient. After extensive tasting, taken out of his employer's sight, he was certain it was ground almonds.

His employer, an old woman named Wandala, hired him as a laborer for the trip from Shelter Harbor to Sallew. She hummed a small tune in the seat of the wagon that Tomis could not place. Her gray hair ran to her shoulders with frazzled ends. Wrinkled fingers clutched at the reins, occasionally swapping hands and flexing with a wince.

He slipped in with merchants every few years. There were always a few caravans taking "the Elbow": a route from Shelter Harbor, east to Hasketter, further east to

Sallew, then south to Gazal in faraway Shavuhnsten. They restocked, sold their wares, rested for a day, and then did it all over again. These long trips were useful when he needed to get away from jilted customers or irritated debt holders.

"Don't eat all of those," Wandala said, not looking away from the road ahead, "It wasn't in our agreement to eat the product."

"I wasn't, ma'am," Tomis said after he swallowed a wedge of fruit, "Making a good dent into the stock though. You should have plenty when we reach the markets in Easterton. Might even have enough to sell some in Sallew."

Wandala squinted at Tomis. Creases ran from her eyes to a long scar on her lip.

"A little chatty for a traveling laborer."

Tomis did not admit that he was running from someone. He certainly did not say that he was a Ruin Raider and she thankfully failed to notice how quickly he urged them to get out of Shelter Harbor. There was still no sign of Faldir or the Hooded Man.

He could not shake the feeling that Peter was dead because of him. It was Peter's contact, Peter's deal, Peter's location, but maybe Tomis could have helped. He was useless in a fight, but maybe if he distracted them, Peter would have found some advantage.

No, I'll fall to pieces if I go down that road, he thought.

He was not acquainted with the inner workings of mages and their various sects, but the thugs were unmistakably worshipers of Shadow. That heaping hulk of a man might have been twisted by the gift of creation. Anyone who spent too long in the deep shadows would find themselves changed by degrees. If you submerged yourself in the darkness willingly, it would mold you like clay.

Faldir had carried the crackling weapon of the old world: Void magic. It was the gift of Shadow that started the Great War. That power would cut through steel and anyone with the gift could command it with even a slight devotion to Shadow. Tomis truly hoped they lost his trail.

"Day laborers are a somber, silent type then?" he asked.

"Last person I hired to help me, I swear, they only knew the words: 'Yes Ma'am', 'No Ma'am' and 'Pay me, Ma'am'. The one before that, she just nodded or shook her head."

"You don't have to hire people like me. I'm sure it would save you some money."

"I'd love to skip the expense. But my fingers are too tired to be cranking jar lids and that pot's burnt me too many times. I'm also somewhat certain you aren't a day laborer, at least you weren't until recently." She turned back to watch the road.

"Just trying to get a cheap ride to Sallew and make some coin in the process, ma'am." He returned his attention to not cutting himself.

"Can you ride a horse?" she asked.

"Aye. I could get us to Sallew by the end of tomorrow if it was just the one horse." He rolled his eyes and bit his lip. It was critical that she forgot him as soon as their journey ended.

"A stable groom then?" Wandala guessed. "You made it a habit of riding your master's horses in the down time, now you're striking out on your own."

"No and I'm a little old to be striking out on my own for the first time."

"Anyone under forty years looks the same to me. You're all children," she said, "Okay, not a groom?"

"No."

Wandala looked up at the sky and hummed to herself again.

"But you ride horses well. A messenger then? You don't look meaty enough to have been a cavalryman or a soldier."

"Thank you for reminding me of my less-than-heroic stature."

She was getting closer to the truth. He tapped the knife against the skin of an apple and thought over all the lies he told in the past.

"You know what, you got it right. I used to carry mail from town to town. Worked for the, uh," Tomis rubbed his forehead, "Oh Flame, something with a G. I can't remember. It's been a few years, but I never liked the gig too much."

"I had a sense you were turning over a new leaf. I've known some people who've done that before," Wandala said.

The conversation died. Tomis breathed easier and busied himself with the jarred treats. The sound of turning wheels, the huffing of horses, and the distant conversations of other merchants drifted through the air. It was busy. It was the sound of company. Tomis found himself smiling as he listened.

"Did you hear about the accident in Hasketter? Happened to hear a touch of it when I was buying those apples," Wandala said.

"Hasketter? The Seventh?"

His stomach pulled tight, his guts threatening to coil. He knew Hasketter. It was where John retired to.

"Yeah, you know that place where you lifted all those heavy barrels?"

"I remember that, thank you. What happened?"

Tomis looked back to the apple in his hand and took another slice out of it. He focused on every word and syllable Wandala said.

"A shadow wolf, maybe two, hit a farm in town. Way out of their territory right?"

"When?"

"Two days ago."

"Strange." He waited for details.

"Smashed up a big, fancy farmhouse, hurt the farmer's wife. You know, those rich farmers who have shulten to blow. Serves them right. They'd do well to have a little taste of what the rest of us have to deal with."

"Anyone die?"

Please say no. Not both of them in the same week, he thought.

"That's where it gets weird, messenger boy."

"Not a boy," Tomis reminded her.

"No one died. One of them got mauled. Seers farm, I think. The one with all the apples and the cherries. We bought enough goods from them. They'll be able to afford the repairs."

"Seers you say?" It was as bad as he thought it might be. He closed his eyes and swallowed. The sickness in his guts threatened to well up.

"You know 'em?" Wandala asked.

"I know the name."

"I haven't gotten to the weird part yet."

He looked up at his boss in the seat of the wagon.

Weird could be a lot of things. Weird could be a family member found out as a criminal. Weird could be a disappearing man, gone on the lam.

Wandala turned around with an arched eyebrow and a mischievous smile. "The beasts got scared off by Flame magic."

He almost laughed. "You're picking daisies."

"Honest, Flame magic, as true as the sun above."

"What mage would play with that? The only crazies who would try are in Sallew or Katoia," Tomis said.

"No one knows. The one mage in Hasketter is some codger. A Life mage who is over the hill like me."

"And?"

"That's the end of it. Some things don't have an ending yet. Oh, I lied, I heard one more thing. The Seers family, some of the family and an uncle left the farm. They were heading east like us," she said.

"Uncle on the mother's side?"

You damn fool, he thought.

"What does that matter?" Wandala asked.

Tomis licked his lips. He thought of details, reasons. Why? Why?

"The mother got hurt, you said. Curious if the uncle that left was just going back home or trying to get her medicine."

"Well, how should I know that?"

"You shouldn't. Just wanted to ask," he said.

Wandala shook her head.

"Strange one," she chided, "We're at the border."

"Already?"

"I've got the cargo papers. You just need to give me your name and let them take a look at you."

Tomis looked ahead as the caravan came to a halt.

Horses snorted and merchants stretched their legs. All eyes were directed toward the soldiers that descended on the first traveler.

A group of six moved from wagon to wagon. They wore red cloth and gold armor. Metal seals bore the image of grain and the sun emblazoned on a shield: the mark of Congressional Militia. Their wide-brimmed, metal hats were adorned with a sprout of wheat. They were professionals. It was the last thing Tomis wanted to see. Three of them carried short-barreled coilguns, two had swords, and the last one wielded a quill, ink, and parchment. The last of these frightened Tomis the most.

"Let me pack this all away. I will be up in a minute," he said.

The soldiers moved through the first five wagons faster than he hoped they would. As they finished one, they waved it through and onto the open road ahead. He reached into his pack and retrieved a flint, tinder, a small flask of torch oil, and drew a small knife. He slipped out of the back flap of the covered wagon and a set of snorting horses greeted him. They trotted nervously as he shushed them. Their driver had stepped out onto the road, too occupied with the vista to notice Tomis.

A lucky break.

He skulked between the pair of horses, stroking their manes as they stamped. He ducked below the tongue and crept under the wagon bed. Tomis craned his neck low and looked back. The soldiers just reached the wagon ahead of Wandala. He scraped at the wood of the wagon's back end with a knife. Beneath was flammable wood grain underneath. He dug into it with the tip to make a small tangle of splinters. He put his knife away and dribbled a touch of oil over this exposed kindling.

He knocked sparks onto it and a fire followed.

"Come on, come on."

The soldiers were about to reach Wandala. The fire was spreading, but might be too slow to save his skin. He was out of time and would have to hope it worked. He stepped out and walked out to the side of the caravan opposite where the guards were. Tomis pitched his arms high and waved at an imaginary friend. It made a few idle merchants look away from him and Tomis slunk to the back end of Wandala's wagon.

He heard the guards on the other side. The wagon ahead had been waved through and was making a fast-track east. Almost free. He just needed Wandala to buy him some time with her rambling.

"Papers and name please," the scribe said.

"Here you go. That's for both of us."

Wandala handed over the cargo receipts. The scribe looked them over with no urgency.

"Baked goods?" he asked.

"Sweets. I can spare some hard sugar candy for each of you if you like."

"That's awfully kind of you, but we're working. Wouldn't be appropriate. Says here you have a laborer in your employ?" the scribe said.

"I do. Hard worker, but don't tell him I said that."

"Where is he?"

"In the back."

The soldiers moved toward the back of the wagon. He closed his eyes and held his breath.

"Fire! Fire! My damn cart! Damned shade and Death, help!" A voice shouted from behind. Tomis smiled and immediately moved up to the seat.

The wagon behind them went up in smoke as the fire

caught the cover. The soldiers rushed over and unlatched the horses from the growing blaze. The kicking, neighing horses did not make it easy or quick. The owner, a squat man with a trim beard, flung his hat onto the ground and howled.

"My spices, you gotta help me! Get in there, please!"

He tugged at the soldiers and pleaded as Tomis crept up into the seat of their wagon and grabbed the reins from where Wandala left them. She gawked out of the open flap.

Screwing people over did not bother him anymore. His conscience was covered with a thick callus. Something inside of him wriggled uneasily as the man's livelihood went up in flames, but he pressed that discomfort down.

"What's happening?" Tomis asked.

"Fire! The wagon just caught fire." She continued staring at the scene unfolding.

"How horrid."

He whipped the reins and the horses grumbled as they pulled forward. Tomis glanced back once as they gained distance, the wagon behind them now resembled a bonfire and blocked the rest of the caravan.

"Shouldn't we help?" she asked.

Tomis shrugged. "What are we gonna do? Put it out? Wasn't like we caused it."

Wandala finally tore her eyes from the smoking wreck and settled onto a seat. Her eyes lingered on the floor.

"I guess you're right."

The wagon of sweets rolled well past the border and into the Congress of Six. Tomis knew they would be in

Easterton within a day and a half. Sallew a few hours beyond there. Once he hit those docks, he was a free man.

Chapter Seven

Olivia splashed the river water over her head. It still held some of the cold from its headwaters on the slopes of the Cragged Mountain. She gasped with relief and scooped another handful. This single river stretched far to the east, almost mimicking their journey. It wandered too much to be a reliable guide though. Instead, now a day out from reaching Sallew, she and the river finally came together again near to the northern shores.

Mid-day sunlight trickled through the canopy where it could. These were not like the young saplings from home, so content in the sun. These low-lying boughs dwelled in shadow even during the day. Their roots were thick and their leaves were the darkest shade of green. Here, out of the worried sight from the others, Olivia could indulge her illness without concern.

Three days had passed since they left home. The horses were beginning to tire. They took more frequent breaks from the hard canter, letting them rest with a trot before resuming. When the sunset neared, they found the best place to camp they could, lit a fire, and stewed.

The fire inside of Olivia only grew. Try as she might to conjure excuses, she could not deny it. It was not a literal flame inside of her heart, but more like a heat that flowed through her veins. She felt like she was sitting next to a blazing hearth at all times, even when she threw off her traveling coat and opened her arms to the breeze.

John was right. She was sick.

Her patience with this heat wore thin. John certainly was not helping her endurance either. Though his behavior was slightly more bearable, he remained a weight around their ankle.

John had no idea how to make rations last or which to eat first. He could not tell a poisonous berry from a wild snack. Whatever he did in his life before now, he clearly was guarded by others. He barely remembered to stay awake for the first watch last night.

She splashed more water in her face, the cool water running from her scalp to her neck. The heat finally began to relent here in the shade and she took a moment to breathe. She tried to push out the persistent irritation that built in her since she left home.

I'm not an invalid. I don't need help. I can take care of myself, she thought.

Illness was not a familiar experience to her. Of course, she had colds as a child. She did better as the one giving aid, rather than receiving it. Even as it became clear that this was not a passing bug, she was determined to not burden the others as long as she could.

"Liv, where are you?" Josie shouted from around the bend of the river.

"I'm over here. Give me a minute."

She plunged the mouth of her waterskin into the river. Once that was filled, she did the same for a second one that John brought for her. He insisted that she would need more water than the both of them. She had no intention of letting him know he was right.

Josie ducked below a branch that Olivia merely walked under. Her eyebrows knitted as she looked over her sister.

"Did you fall in or something?"

It would have been easier to go for a swim. At least, that would have been easier to explain away. She could not bear to tell Josie about her condition. Her sister worried after her enough, explanations would only worsen things.

"Almost. I splashed myself by accident."

Josie snorted, but her uneasy stare still lingered for too long. If Olivia looked as awful as she felt, then her sister might start making assumptions.

"Just don't take a bath. We need to hit the road soon. John's getting antsy," Josie said.

"Are we doing a load of laundry back there? Or just swapping gossip about boys?" John called from around the corner. Olivia capped the second waterskin and slung her bag back onto her shoulders.

"Only another day and a half of this. Then we're done with him," Olivia said.

"I don't know, it's been kind of fun."

"Fun?"

"Well," Josie kicked at the dirt as Olivia walked back to where John was waiting, "Sure, he's a pain in the ass, but in a joking kind of way."

"You only feel that way because he likes you. He only tolerates me," Olivia said.

"You two just butt heads. Both of you made a bad impression on each other and it stuck."

Olivia thought her sister was too hopeful and far too willing to believe things would work out. It was admirable that someone who lost her parents at such a young age could be so optimistic.

"If he was such a big shot, relic-dealing, con man, where'd all the money go?" Olivia asked.

"I'm still waiting and that sun is not rising any higher," John shouted.

Josie shrugged and walked around the bend and toward their horses. Olivia followed and covered her eyes as she walked back out into the harsh, afternoon sun. John sat on top of his spotted horse with a cocked arm against his hip.

"They emerge at last. Was there a hot spring back there?"

"Do you ever stop?" Olivia asked.

"By all means, take your time. We're only racing the clock here."

"I'm keenly aware of that." Olivia tried to rub away a small headache building behind the bridge of her nose. When she looked back, she found John was trying to relieve a similar frustration.

"It's been a long ride. We're almost done. I'm crabby," he explained.

"What's your excuse every other day of the week?" Josie asked and stuck out her tongue as she climbed onto her horse.

"It's being stuck in the armpit of civilization that explains the other days. Not so much as a decent bottle of wine to while away the increasingly long days."

He broke from his reverie of insults as Olivia came closer. He had the same look as Josie. Maybe it was how her eyes were persistently red or how every step felt heavier than the last.

"How're you feeling, Liv?"

"What do you care?"

"Look, I got carried away. Your dad asked for me to watch after you and—"

"I'm fine," she snapped. Olivia grinned with as

much venom as she could conjure before climbing onto Grizzly. "Like you said, let's get this over with."

John chewed on his lip and muttered a few indistinguishable words under his breath. Her father did the same thing when he felt guilty.

They resumed the hurried pace toward Sallew. The frequency of travelers grew as they came closer to the port city. Olivia only visited this remote region a few times with her family, but never the renowned capitol city. It was a town that John was never keen to talk about. Whether that was because his stories of it were boring or he did not care to share them was unclear.

Olivia dabbed at her forehead as discreetly as she could. She took swigs of water regularly at first, but increased in pace as the rest of the day wore on. Without the shade and water of the forested gulley, the flame affliction burned brighter. For a brief moment, the world tilted and she felt herself slip to the side of the saddle.

Panic closed her fingers around the reins and she leaned forward in her seat. She took a deep breath and tried to shake away the bleary feeling at the back of her head. Neither of her compatriots noticed the slip, something she was grateful for. Josie would only fret. Olivia was not sure what John would do at this point.

The day came to a close and the sun lingered low in the sky. As the shadows grew deeper, they heard a few strings from a lute somewhere ahead of them. Several horses were tied to a fallen tree, torches lit around them. Nearby, a tall bonfire flickered against the dark and a group of six or seven people talked, ate, and played music. Their camp was settled in the circular remains of a tower. The remains of the walls were no higher than two feet at most. If the bastion was ever something of note, it now was little more than a fence worthy of livestock.

"Well, that's handy. Won't have to make our own camp tonight," John said.

"I thought we were supposed to be leery of people on the road?" Josie asked.

"And you should be, but if they wanted to rob us, we wouldn't see them coming. Let me do the talking and don't use your last name."

Olivia scoffed. "Why?"

"Trust me, come on."

John took the lead and the sisters followed. Olivia left her doubts unsaid. The dangers of the road were baked into their heads. Though Shadow made people cooperate, there were still those who found it easier to steal than to work together.

Closer to the camp, the words of the song became clearer. A man wearing a wide-brimmed hat plucked at his lute to a slow, mournful song. The woman next to him wore a patchwork dress of many colors and a low cut, puffy shirt that clung to the hems of her shoulders. Her voice was incredible, reaching high notes and carrying them long in the rhythm of the tune.

The bonfire danced higher and lit a number of barrels that were taken off their mule. Olivia could see a logo emblazoned on the side of it in blue ink: an "A" with waves behind it. John pulled his horse to a stop.

"Woah, woah. Actually, we should keep going." He did not look away from the logo.

"But, we don't have to make our own camp," Josie said.

"I know. I know what I said, but these," his mouth opened and closed with a dozen different excuses. He was not scared, he was embarrassed. "I've never met any of these people. It would be rude."

"It is only natural to help someone so close to sunset, provided you keep them at arm's length and a wary eye to them. It's nothing to be embarrassed about," Josie said.

"He isn't nervous about that, Josie. You know those people," Olivia said.

John's nostrils flared and his jaw pulled tight. "It's complicated. You wouldn't get it."

"Did you rip them off? Piss off the wrong group of people? Is that why you're hiding out with my family?"

"I don't have to tell you a thing. Let's go. We can find another camp."

"But the sun's almost set. We'll be pitching camp in the dark if we have to go all the way past them," Josie said. "And I'm getting really tired of that cheese that dad packed us. Maybe we can trade for something else? Can't be that bad, right?"

It was far too late to go looking for a camping spot now. They would have to ride well past this group to avoid them. It was not impossible, but she did not look forward to kicking nipping rodents away from her as they tried to make a fire. By the look of John's resigned frown, he knew that as well.

"I am so damn tired of that cheese," he muttered. "Fine, fine. Rules are the same. Don't use your last name and don't call me John. Got it?"

He pointed his finger directly at Olivia, the one who would take the risk to upset him. Olivia had enough sense to not put John, and by extension themselves, at more risk than they had to.

"Deal," she said.

They trotted to the campfire and John called out to them just before the edge of the firelight. The music stopped and the group turned. They wore soft, loose-weaved shirts and work pants in shades of brown, tan, and white. Only the woman and her lute-playing partner looked distinct from them. The woman's brown hair was wrapped into a pair of braids and dangled down to her waist.

Her partner raised his head and set the lute aside. His ruddy skin was broken only by the speckles of a graying beard. He squinted and wiped his button nose before standing.

"Who's out there?" He spoke with a low, deep voice that dwelt on the O's longer than usual. Olivia heard the same accent on someone from the southern land of Shavuhnsten.

"Some travelers looking for a place to sleep. I'm Gus. These are my nieces, Liv and Josie."

"Do you have your own food? We're happy to share a fire, but we're a little lean on vittles," the hatted man said.

Josie groaned at the prospect of another night with the same food.

"We just need a fire. I promise we won't be a bother," John said.

The group muttered amongst itself briefly and the singing woman gave the final head nod. The man in the hat waved for them to come closer.

"Come on then. Wouldn't want the shade rats to start nipping at your heels."

John lowered his head. "Do not call me John. Our last name is Leeds. Yeah?"

"Would hate for you to pay back some people that

you owe," Olivia said.

"It's not like that." John climbed off his horse and hiked his hood over his head.

"Josie Leeds, easy. What are you so nervous about?" she asked before dismounting from her horse.

Olivia climbed off Grizzly as well, and they walked their horses to where the others were tied up for the night. A bucket of water and another of oats sat nearby and their horses quickly ate their fill.

The bonfire crackled with splintered, dry boughs of a tree. Other logs and sticks were placed under it, but now the piece of lumber burned on its own. A handful of other torches were set around three or four tents out of sight of the main road. The circle of travelers adjusted to allow the new arrivals around the fire.

Olivia sat on a felled tree that was rolled over to use as a bench. Josie and John fell in next to her. Most of the group, what looked like two men and three women, resumed their conversations. Some still chewed on the last bits of their dinner, the bones of a small animal cleaned of meat lingered on the ground at their feet or a plate set off to the side. Closer to their supplies, Olivia could read the name "Abaghi Courier Service".

Josie pulled some food from her pack and divided it between the two of them. A few of the others toasted them quietly and drank from half-full cups of mead and water. They talked about things they saw at the edges of the world, good bargains they made in the markets of Sallew, and important sounding things in foreign lands. Olivia did not join into these conversations, wary that details might tread too closely to John's rules.

After a few minutes, the man in the hat and the singing woman seemed a bit keener on them. The man set aside his lute and wove his fingers together.

"You seem tired. Have you all traveled far?" he asked.

John said nothing but looked to Olivia for an answer. His eyebrows twitched with a reminder of their rules.

"Not terribly far. Just from the Seventh," Olivia said.

John clicked his tongue. He did not like that answer.

"The Seventh?" The man sat back. "Lots of farms there."

"We're farmers," Josie said.

John coughed and skidded his heel toward Josie.

She seemed to pick up on the message. "Well, at least we sometimes are farmers. Traveling hands, we've been all over. Sometimes we fish, sometimes we farm, sometimes, we don't. Farmer was not accurate."

"Sweet sunlight," John grumbled.

"Enterprising lot you all are. I didn't get your family name."

Josie answered reflexively and caught her mistake halfway through. "It's See—Leeds."

"Sealeads?"

"Stop talking," John whispered to Josie.

Olivia's own nerves grew as Josie fumbled with the answers. There was something about the man's intensity that set her on edge.

"I don't think we got your name though," Olivia said.

"I never did, did I?"

The man in the hat smiled and squinted over the campfire. He was not looking at Olivia though. John was his focus.

"It would be polite to give us your name. We're all friends here, right?" Olivia said.

"Some people already know it." He gestured to the crate with the symbol on it. "Abaghi's my last name. My wife, Cota, shares that name. In the Congressional tradition. I do a lot of trading, here and there."

"What kind of trading?" Olivia asked.

"Relics. War Treasures. Fine goods. That sort of thing. I've worked with a lot of Ruin Raiders over the years."

John wriggled in his seat.

"Most of them are forgettable. It's a mixed bag of scum and worthwhile partners. There was one that sticks with me above all of them. A real handsome face and a smooth talker, arrogant as all Shadow."

Josie leaned forward. "What was his name?"

"Well, he's right here," the man in the hat said. "Been a while, John."

John cursed under his breath and pulled his hood off. "Good to see you again, Bruce. I didn't realize I was that memorable."

The others around the circle gawped and spoke to each other in low tones.

"I thought he was dead."

"He'd be better off dead."

Bruce laughed and slapped his knee. The rest of the group laughed with him. The other conversations had petered out and everyone was listening. Bruce straightened up in his seat and smiled. His teeth gleamed like a cat that cornered a mouse.

"Of course. How could I forget the one Ruin Raider that burned so many bridges he went into hiding."

Chapter Eight

John wrinkled his nose, lips pulled into a tight frown. He did not challenge Bruce's claim or answer Josie's look. His eyes went to Olivia, a manic light in them hoping to smother this conversation. With Josie being his favorite niece, Olivia assumed it would have been the other way around.

"I was good at what I did," John said.

"Oh, one of the best. Where do you think I got this lute from?" Bruce spun the instrument around in his fingers. "At least you're still alive. After that last deal of yours, I wondered if you were breathing."

"What deal?" Josie asked with a little too much excitement. Olivia wanted to hear as well. It was a chance to make John feel small for a change, but she also could not resist a good story.

"They don't need to hear about that." John waved his hands.

"No? I figure they deserve to know they are traveling with a murderer." Bruce looked into Olivia's eyes, the light of the campfire dancing on his own.

Her curiosity shriveled. Anger pounded in her throat and flushed her face. The idea of a cutthroat living amongst her family made her want to throttle him. The Focus pulsed in the bag at her feet. It stoked the fire in her chest, fear and anger dousing it with fuel.

Olivia reached for the knife at her belt when John

set his hand on her shoulder. She considered shoving him off her, but something kept her from a larger reaction. In her experience, John was a jerk and a lout. He was not violent.

He pointed a finger across the fire. "It wasn't murder, don't you go filling their heads with those rumors."

"Does your brother know these rumors?" Olivia asked.

"They're just stories. One deal went really bad and I had to call it quits."

"Why don't you enlighten them?" Bruce purred. "Clear all this confusion up."

Olivia did not understand Bruce's goal. Admittedly, she knew nothing of Ruin Raiders and their business. Why would Bruce want to humiliate him with no clear financial gain at hand?

"Why're you doing this, Bruce? I always played it straight for you. The lute works, right?" John said.

"I'm as curious as anyone. I just know the stories. Would you prefer I tell them my version?"

"No," John almost shouted.

The circle fell silent with expectation. John straightened up and gave his nieces a last look. All the mirth and swagger she knew in him was gone. All he had left was that genuine, mournful look.

"I dealt with genuine relics when I could. But the product was not always there. Sometimes your lead turns out to be nothing. Sometimes someone else beat you to the goods and you came away empty handed."

"But the market doesn't rest," Bruce said.

"I always needed something to sell, so sometimes I bent the truth. You leave a one-hundred year old sword in the rain for a few weeks, bury it for a month, come up with a story about it. It's not hard."

"So you cheated people?" Olivia asked.

"Only anyone who I could cheat. There were collectors, historians, people who knew what to look for. If I tried to pull that on the wrong person, it would only bite me. No, that crap was for the wannabes."

"Idiots, rubes, people who want something that looks like a relic, but don't care about the quality," Bruce added.

"One such idiot wanted a set of bronze plates and silverware I faked. I didn't know why, I didn't ask. I also did not really know who I was dealing with. They were a well-to-do husband and wife. Fast to laugh, faster to gossip. I took their money and gave them the fakes."

"Who were they?" Olivia asked.

John rolled his eyes.

"Some big business type with connections with the city of Sallew. All that matters is that they used the plates in a soiree. I've been told, they made a big stink about having authentic relics. One of their guests was the type who knew what to look for."

Bruce grinned. If this story ended with John exiling himself to Hasketter, maybe it also ended with this man taking over business that used to be John's. Bruce seemed to be enjoying himself as the story wound on.

"It turns out the easy laughing, well-to-do types had a mean streak. They thought of themselves as far more important than they were, but they had the money to act the part. The little embarrassment at the soiree cost them investors or something. Maybe it just hurt their egos. Point is, they did not just let the authorities know. They hired some muscle to deal with me. I don't know if they hired them to kill me, but it sure as sunset felt like it."

John stared at the ground, unable to meet anyone's eyes.

"I defended myself. Didn't really intend to kill him, but it didn't matter. I just reacted. The people who hired them put it together and made sure everyone in town knew John Seers was a murderer."

"And you came to stay with us because you had nowhere to go?" Olivia asked.

"Your father didn't have to take me in. We both came up from nothing. Born into dirt and hunger. He took the high road and I went elsewhere. Even after everything I've done, your father saved my life. That's a kindness I can't swerve from. Everything we did and earned. Everything I made of myself and it was washed away by some spoiled brat. Some wealthy, land owning—" He cut himself off and clicked his tongue.

These were the same words he had used against her. He was wounded, not sour. Bitter, not bored. Olivia reminded him of the privileged few who burnt his life to the ground. She thought about saying something to him, anything that might soothe him in the slightest bit. However, she had no idea what to say to someone who had lost everything.

"They only named me. My partners were free and clear, but no one wants to work with a middleman who might kill them and take their money. That was what some people told me."

"They put a bounty on his head, biggest at the time. It's gone down a little bit," Bruce added.

John's eyes swiveled up to Bruce.

"Bounty?" he asked.

"Oh yeah." Bruce pushed his coat back and rested a

hand on the pommel of his sword.

The hair on Olivia's neck stood up. Bruce seemed to be leaning much further forward than before. The singing woman drew a dagger from her boot and played with it between her fingers. Olivia noticed the shadows at the edge of the fire wriggling. Tendrils of darkness broke from the dark of night and reached toward them. The night pressed against their backs.

"Enough to, oh, I don't know," John slowly reached for the hand crossbow on his hip, "murder a man in front of his nieces?"

"Wouldn't dream of it, friend. Bounty says they want you alive," Bruce said. His smile was as large as the moon overhead.

Josie moved in front of her uncle like a castle wall. Olivia drew her hunting knife. She could feel the Focus in her bag as if it were shouting at her. It pleaded for her to lose her patience. It wanted to feel that horrible thrill of violence.

"Try to touch him," Josie grunted.

Bruce laughed like a loving relative.

"You're big, girly. You'll be trouble. But you're outnumbered, and a long way from home. Don't worry, we just want him. We'll find a use for you two."

The rest of the circle drew their weapons, the plan now plain to everyone. Olivia's stomach turned as she sized up the man nearest her. She remembered stabbing the beast at home. The effort had been frightening against an inhuman beast. Olivia questioned if she could murder if it came to that.

That moment of agonizing fear was broken by a shrieking roar. A black shape lunged from the shadows. It drove its black talons into the singing woman. Her scream cut short as its jaws closed around her neck. Its green eyes swept across the rest of the camp and an enormous paw swiped at Bruce. The hooked talons ripped his arm from his body.

The beast still wore the slashes Josie inflicted on it nights before. It had tracked Olivia. She was not sure what put the thought in her head, but she was horribly sure of it. The lumbira drove the camp into a mad frenzy. The would-be bandits now fled from the campfire and toward their horses with hysterical screams. John, Josie, and Olivia retreated from the beast. Just a few steps away from the horses, the lumbira finished mauling Bruce and turned to Olivia. It growled and took a step toward them.

Ask for it. Let the Flame loose.

It felt like her own idea, but came from someplace else. Her head pounded and her hands shook. She felt the fire rising inside of her.

"I'll end you this time!"

Josie's shout startled the beast. John fired his crossbow and the bolt struck the beast in its shoulder. It reared back in pain before charging at the pair. Josie took a great sweep with her ax and the shadow wolf stumbled backward.

"Olivia, don't use it. Don't even look at it," John said. He drew his short sword and sliced a talon from the creature as it swung it too closely.

Giving in again would be her death. The heat inside of her only built higher with this new threat. She clamped her hands over her ears and ran for the nearby forest. She felt that she was on a ledge and the Flame told her to jump. There would only be more fire at the bottom of that leap of faith.

Behind her, the creature leaped back from John and

Josie, blood streaming from fresh wounds on its fur. Its attention shifted to her again and darted out of the moonlight in pursuit.

Her family shouted something to her as she ran. The sound of screaming and roaring faded and the high grass gave way to bushes and tree roots. She dropped her hands and raised her head. Amidst the thrum of fire in her heart and blood in her ears, she could feel the leaves move in the wind and the owls crouched on top of branches.

Olivia ran further into the forest. She broke through thorny bushes that stung her hands. Her pounding steps snapped sticks and kicked pebbles. Shards of moonlight carved through the dense canopy overhead. After a dozen steps, she was practically blind. She barely had time to duck underneath low branches and rip her feet away from snagging bushes. A low growl echoed off the trees, much closer than she wanted it to be.

She entered a small clearing. The moon shone past the branches of a half-crumbled, dead tree, the bark scored with the claws of squirrels and raccoons. The lumbira was close, maybe only a few feet. Olivia moved to the other side of the tree and aimed her foot at the thinnest part of the withered trunk. A midnight colored snout poked from the shadows and sniffed at the ground. She took a deep breath and kicked. The tree groaned and a long crack shot up its side.

The shadow wolf heard her breath, but its eyes trailed upward to the falling trunk and its mouth pulled closed. Wood beetles fluttered away and dust kicked into the air as the dry wood snapped to pieces and pinned the creature to the ground. The wolf roared and thrashed under the dead branches. Olivia stumbled backward as a mighty paw broke through the corpse of the tree.

There was nowhere to run. Heat built in her chest as she gasped for breath. Her head so warm that she could pass out. She leaned against a willow tree and pulled herself against the trunk. The lumbira snarled as it thrust the trunk off itself. Olivia gripped the Focus in her hand. Flame would kill the beast, but then she would certainly die within hours. She did not even know how to conjure the fire again if she wanted to. She was cornered, exhausted, and soon it would find her.

She thought of another monster in the woods. Yorker lost himself in the pursuit of knowledge, but he was not always like that. She remembered him as he once was.

Life wants to help you because it is in you. It is in me, it's in the trees. It's in those birds too. Ask them to sing. Go ahead, just ask. Life will hear you.

Olivia placed her hand on the ground. She thought back to those lessons years ago. The lumbira took deep sniffs as it tracked her down. She put this danger out of her mind. Flame's voice drowned out the grass under her fingers, the bugs crawling in the branches above her head. She was deaf. She was blind. All she could do was ask.

"Hide me, please."

The fire pleaded. It was her only way out. It wanted to save Olivia, even as it consumed her.

"Hide me," she said, unsure how close the lumbira was now.

Just as it felt that the cinders would burst from her ears, a hand of roots and mushrooms reached from the ground and entwined with hers. It squeezed back. The branches above her thickened, leaves budding from them. The boughs grew heavy and they stooped down to the ground. Bushes and thorns burst from the ground and formed a wall. Twisting roots and vines met the lower branches of the small tree. They wrapped together and knitted shut. The Flame still screamed in her ears, but now another voice whispered.

You are safe.

The lumbira took a deep whiff and walked past the shelter of nature. Olivia almost laughed as she heard it pass. The monster gave an annoyed growl and took off at full speed.

Olivia had little idea of what to say. This was magic. Undoubtedly, unmistakably magic that she conjured as she had before. The voice in her ear was the same one that spoke to her as a child, the one that whispered to her in the wind. She let go of the ground and the dome broke. Vines and grass pulled back into their roots and the boughs lightened as leaves fell from where they budded moments ago. The thrill of survival banished any doubt for the moment and she left her shelter, still following the distant sounds of the lumbira leaving. Olivia rose on shaky legs. She turned the Focus over in her hand and nodded to the tree.

"Thanks."

She quietly went back the way she came. The voice was just as warm as when she asked the birds to sing. Before she fell too deeply into her thoughts, twigs snapped ahead of her as Josie cleaved through a bush.

"Olivia! Oh Flame, you're alive." Josie ran to her, John right behind.

"Are you both alright?" Olivia asked.

"You handled yourself well for a silver-spooned brat," John said. "It seemed to lose interest in us really quick, like it was looking for you."

John did not follow the thought further, but she felt the same. Things were seeming very coincidental to Olivia. Lumbira attacks were a dreadful thing, but rare. What were the odds of being tracked by one over four days?

"Why did you run? We could have protected you," Josie asked.

"No, Olivia did the right thing. She was losing control," John said.

"That sounds terribly close to praise," Olivia said.

He shrugged. "Don't get excited."

"Well, how did you escape?" Josie asked. Her sister barely heard what John said.

Olivia slipped the Focus into her pocket. Her first impulse was to tell them about how nature saved her. How she used the same powers that she once practiced. Magic. The words tasted like hypocrisy. Outside of danger, she winced at the idea of it. She worried that Josie might see it in an even worse light.

It's not worth telling her. I won't ever need it again, she thought.

"It must have lost me. I got into the woods and just didn't see it for a while. I finally came out and found you."

"We messed it up. Maybe we hurt its nose or something?" Josie asked.

John's eyes flickered to Olivia's pocket. A wry grin slipped onto his face, but he kept the antagonism back.

"Probably that. The thing was ready to meet Death. It won't bother us for a while. Regardless, we should go. If it's still around, I don't want to tempt it."

The trio walked toward the tree line. Josie slashed at

branches that were nowhere near their path. Olivia grimaced and thought of the plants that just saved her.

"Hey, no more noise, huh? I think we can make it out of here with the path you cleared already," Olivia said.

Josie nodded. "Sorry, I just got a little carried away. With their ringleader dead, maybe we can still use that camp."

"No, we will need to ride tonight. Even if the lumbira leaves us alone, one of those flunkies might be around. They could cause us some trouble."

Someone had untied all the horses in the mad rush, but they were still close. They milled around the camp, rooting through bags for food. Their horses were among them, but happily came when called. They would have to ride through the night with barely a stomach full of food and not a wink of rest. She was glad that the cool, night winds now swept over them. Olivia swallowed her fatigue, even as her feet began to slip from the saddle. She would fight this as long as she could. Even to a stalwart soul like her, she was not sure how much longer she could hold on.

Chapter Nine

Easterton sat alongside the Running River. It was the bulwark of the Congressional farmlands against the wild, open plains to the west. Tomis rode past one of the tall watchtowers along the river's edge. These wooden towers were a hollow imitation of their stony, ancient peers in the Ruin Fields. They were half the height and only reinforced with steel where required.

Guards in red and gold armor waited idly next to gatling coilgun turrets, capable of putting a rod of steel through plate armor. Torches lined the bridge and wide braziers were lit beyond them. A small group of soldiers chatted and walked from one to the next, lighting each torch as the sun just slipped below the horizon.

Once the caravan set foot over the river, the guarded hesitancy of the frontier evaporated. The guards who looked out at the plains beyond laughed and leaned on their weapons. Tomis repressed a chuckle at their lack of concern. Too many were forgetting the danger beyond their borders. Losing Peter to shadow cultists pressed the danger of the world back into Tomis's head.

Cob farmhouses appeared here and there along the road, each one with a small plot of crops or livestock. Ahead of them, the quiet town of Easterton glowed with a dim electric light mixed with flickering lanterns.

People left their houses with empty baskets in hand, children in tow. The occasional electric bulb was hooked to gaudy, black wires that went from roof to roof and disappeared in the mix of buildings. Runners were hung between street posts. Dried gourds were strung alongside and small candles glowed within. The caravan circled a two-tiered fountain at the center of the village. Children leaped from the upper level and into the lower one with a dramatic splash. Some families walked back from the far edge of town with baskets loaded with fruits, cheeses, and hard to find goods. The caravan left the square and trailed eastward.

The buzzing of delicate, orange light bulbs faded and the yellow glow of torches grew as a city of tents and wagons spread out before him. The sun had set, but the festivities were just beginning.

"Get the product sorted if you can, Tomis. I'll find us a spot to set up," Wandala said.

He left the seat of the wagon and stepped into the back. The cart shifted direction and Wandala shouted at someone to move out of the way as she brought the cart to a halt at the far end of the market. Tomis pulled wooden poles and a shovel from the back of the wagon. A honeycomb vendor next to them waved to Tomis with a welt-covered hand. Tomis gave him a friendly nod and anchored the poles to the ground.

Wandala stepped gingerly from the wagon's seat as Tomis walked back to the cart and grabbed a large piece of canvas. A part of it trailed after him on the ground. Wandala slowly walked from the front of the wagon to the back, grabbing a hand crate of candied apples.

"I'm going to have to find a hired hand who can actually keep up." Wandala chuckled as Tomis finished tossing the canvas over the last pole: three canvas walls and an open front.

"Was that a joke?"

She only snickered and turned back to unloading the wagon. He shook out the canvas walls and clipped open the flap door at the back of the tent. Tomis hurried back to the wagon and slid a long piece of lumber from it. It would have to work as a table for the night. Wandala set the crate of goods down and circled back to get another.

"You don't need to rush. We've plenty of time left for the night market," she said.

"Time is money. That's the gig."

"And your gig was to get to Sallew right?"

He regretted being too friendly. Wandala had let her curiosity be since the previous day. Even after a good lie, she still pressed him for details about his life.

"I needed a ride and uh, didn't have my own. Thank goodness for Wandala the Sweets Master."

"That's not a bad name," Wandala said after a moment of consideration.

Tomis went back and forth in front of her. Every time he stepped back into the tent, there were more people eyeing the sweet candies on display. A line was forming, some already counting out a stack of coins to hand over.

"I meant to ask. What's in Sallew?" Wandala said.

"Big buildings. Lots of fish."

"For you. What is in Sallew for you?"

Tomis grimaced. She was picking at him again, trying to puzzle him out. The lie about his profession either did not convince her or she wanted more. Both options were problematic. He grabbed a barrel and rolled it out of the wagon.

"A ride out of town, off the continent. Thought I would go traveling for a bit."

"Making something of yourself," Wandala guessed.

"Again, a little old to be striking out on my own for the first time."

"I didn't say that. How long were you in the messenger business?"

Tomis deposited the barrel inside of the tent and turned to get another.

"You have customers waiting. You could be helping them," he said.

"Eh, they can wait. If they already have coins in hand, I've got them. Answer the question."

"Why are you so curious?" he said.

"Because I can be. I've got you here and I'm paying for your time."

He was not used to being given the third degree by someone who did not carry a seal of authority. At least there were no heavy costs to resisting her.

"It really isn't important."

Tomis took another box from the wagon and Wandala dropped the line of questions. She went into the tent and shouted for the customers to gather around. Children crowded the table as soon as she sat down. Parents pointed at blueberry sugar-knots, candy apples, or whatever else their kids wanted. Wandala gladly took their coins and handed them gleaming, sweet treats in return.

"My assistant over here can help," Wandala gestured to Tomis, "Come on, help these people out."

Tomis walked behind the table and leaned into the melee. The crowd grew and shrank to the din of coins and clinking jars. He did not consider the risk until someone offered to shake his hand. So many chances to be recognized. John was the one with the bounty on his head, but there was a time when John's compatriots were wanted for questioning as well. Of course, that was six months ago and he never got into trouble anywhere outside of Sallew.

At least, he had not run into trouble until earlier that week.

He tried not to think about Peter in the days since he fled Shelter Harbor. His glassy eyes, limp body sprawled on the floor with a hole shot in his heart. Tomis ran at the first opportunity and now his friend was gone. With both of his partners dead or missing, he wondered what sort of life he could hope to salvage from this mess.

"So, about Sallew," Wandala said, the ravenous crowds finally thinning. "You're good with the horses. You can set up quickly and you can actually handle people without scaring them. Ever think about entering the merchant business?"

It was not what he expected to hear. He briefly considered if he had been wondering about his future out loud.

"Maybe. I haven't thought that far ahead."

Wandala leaned against the table. Her eyes searched for something in him. No, not searching. She was pulling on a rope. She smiled after a moment and turned away.

"You know I ran too. I was out on the north edge of the Oleev desert. My family, my clan, we ran into some Katoian settlers who were looking to put down stakes. You see, we were plains people. Katoians kept wandering north for new lands and new opportunities. These ones got closer to our lands than any of the others. My family took it personally, no love of Katoians among us."

She wrapped up sugar-covered strawberries in some

parchment and waved it at a thin woman who lingered a dozen steps away.

"Two shulten and they're all yours," Wandala said.

The woman stepped forward, tossed two coins onto the table with a silent nod, and left with her treats.

"You didn't let the settlers stay?" Tomis asked.

"I was younger and I wanted to do what my family thought was best. We forced them off the land, took their livestock, then burnt their crops and homestead."

Tomis's mouth drifted open. He had not suspected a drop of cruelty could dwell in her. He reminded himself that she was young and guided to this action. It was not so different from how he came to be this way.

"I'm not proud of it. They looked no different from me. I was told they were different from us and that was enough. We didn't kill them. We just gave them no other option than to leave. We should've though. Those settlers went back to where they were from and spread stories about a clan of vicious desert dwellers who were hostile to the Katoian Empire. We weren't ready when the Fire Keepers showed up."

He almost dropped the jar in his hands. Rumors about Fire Keepers made their rounds among his kind of criminal. The strictest customs agent would be welcome compared to those armored juggernauts.

"They sent Fire Keepers after your family?"

She fiddled with a few coins, her jaw drawing tight at the memory.

"Shade, we wouldn't have been ready for them even if they told us they were coming. They only sent five Fire Keepers to handle our clan. We were about sixty strong, all told. They cut right through us. We couldn't do anything to them."

Two girls with hair like golden wheat approached them, eyes as wide as the moon above. One was around twelve years old, the other maybe ten at most. Their parents watched a distance behind them.

"What's the tastiest thing you've got?" the younger child asked.

Wandala leaned onto the table, hands clutched together.

"Well, I am partial to the dried apricots myself, but that sounds yucky to you. Doesn't it?"

The little girl politely nodded after a moment of hesitation.

"I like apples," the older girl said, "Anything with that?"

The younger girl nodded once more in agreement.

"Apples. My friend here did a great job with these: apple, brown sugar, omod syrup. Sounds good?"

The brightness in the older girl's face faded as she turned over the few coins in her hand.

"We only have three. Is there anything cheaper?" she asked.

Wandala glanced at the parents past the girls and slid the jar over to them.

"Three sounds like an even deal to me."

They handed over the coins quickly and took the jar of apple sweets. With a short thanks, they stormed back to their parents with thunderous steps. Wandala waved to them as they left. The smile wilted off her face as her eyes unfocused.

"Only nine of us escaped. My father and I were among them. He led us north to Margecei, the old kingdom. We hoped that they'd give us a new homestead in the king's land."

She rubbed her hands and winced. Tomis heard enough about Margecei to know where this story would go. It was across the sea and shared none of the democratic principles of the Congress of Six. It was a land besieged by monsters that had grown just as cruel to its people.

"It was not like anything my father told me about. I don't think my father expected it either. The people were poor, it never stopped raining, and all the work was in service to the Hunting Households. We didn't even get that far. They called us desert scum. Word reached the kingdom about our clan. They didn't want to upset the Katoians, so they arrested us and intended to send us south for judgment. I was the only one that slipped away."

Tomis's eyes followed the girls and their family as they went from stall to stall. The youngest was already trying to open the jar of sweets. The mother took it from her and an unheard promise passed between them. The last children he was around were the thin, hungry urchins that stuck to the outskirts of Shelter Harbor. The last time he haggled was for a piece of art over three hundred years old and was worth more than the lives of that family.

"I don't know what kind of trouble you're running from, but you're welcome to stick with me as my assistant. The pay is not great. You have to respect laws and take the taxes on the chin. It's quiet though. All the fruit you can eat too," Wandala said.

She let the question hang in the air between them. The night air seemed warm. A slick of sweat started to build on his back. Tomis looked down at the table of goods and sorted through them, his fingers shaking. This was not part of his plan. It was risky to stick around now.

"We're getting low on a few things. I'll grab some more," he said.

"Be quick. They'll be closing in the next hour and there's always a rush right before they start putting out the torches."

Tomis left the tent. He unhitched the clip and let the flap close. Down the line of other vendors and wagons, they were all left with their doors wide open and crates hastily unpacked. Their wagon was as messy as the others.

Their wagon.

He did not like that the words sprang unbidden. He was getting tied down. Maybe he was getting sentimental after losing John and Peter. Would that be so bad? Tomis remembered the stomach aches, the nausea, the headaches. That final deal was so bad he could not even be in the room. Was he born for this life or had it just been easy to fall into? With that old life crumbling away, he was not certain that he wanted it back.

He tossed a few empty crates as a quiet growl rippled through the air behind him. Heavy footsteps shook the ground and Tomis was pushed against the side of the wagon. Several blades pressed against his neck and hot, stinking breath fumed on his back. They were not knives. They were claws.

"I have to give you high marks for evasion and speed. You are a coward, but you have what it takes to run away and live another day. If you scammed anyone else, you might have gotten away."

Tomis recognized that voice. The deep tones of a Pescan accent and the remorseless inflection. It was the same voice that killed Peter in Shelter Harbor.

"Nothing to say, thief?" Faldir said.

The Hooded Man flipped Tomis around so that he could see them both. He hid beneath his cloak even under the moonlight. This close to the creature, Tomis saw a pair of insect pincers inside of his hood. They clattered with anticipation and the lower jaw was cramped with sharp teeth, each one irregularly placed like it grew in on a whim.

Faldir stood behind him. She wore the same black cloak and dark blue tunic as before. Her sun kissed skin was dotted with tattoos above her jaw piercings. Her eyes were a deep brown and did not hold a sliver of light in their depths. She held the small, onyx rod in her right hand.

"Why did you take it?" she asked.

"I don't know who you are, but please take whatever you need. I'm just a trader on the road to Sallew," Tomis lied.

The Hooded Man made a choking, sputtering sound that was either a laugh or a growl.

"Oh, you're too smart to play the idiot." She smiled and walked closer to him. "You snuck out of Shelter Harbor, laid low across the entire continent, evaded detection by Congressional border guards, and found a place in a local market on the road to the largest port city on the eastern coast. Take pride in your work, Tomis."

He wriggled as she said his name. The Hooded Man's claws pressed into his skin and drew small beads of blood.

"Now where is the Focus?"

"What?"

"Adar's Focus. Golden. Large enough to fit in your palm with a red gem in the center. The Focus of one of the elite fire mages of the Great War. The Focus that your coordinates were pointing to. The Focus was not there when we arrived," Faldir said with a rising tone of impatience. Her lips pulled back as if she were the one who might tear out his throat and not her hooded ally.

"I didn't know it was a Focus. It was Peter's job, Peter's contact, Peter's info. We didn't even go out to where it was. We pieced it together with research. You'd be shocked how much you can find out when you're not threatening people with magic."

Faldir pointed the black rod at him.

"Do not confuse me for some charlatan who has learned the magic of destruction and wields it like a club. You are slowing me down."

The Hooded Man growled and looked back at Faldir. His claws tightened around Tomis's neck and he yelped in pain.

"I don't have it. I promise I don't."

"Kill him. We'll search his corpse and the wagon," Faldir said.

Sweat dripped down the side of his head. He briefly imagined his fate: dead in a gutter without a name. This creature would act within a moment, he had to come up with something fast. There was one thing he still had. It was the last thing that might buy him time.

"Wait, wait! I know who took it."

The Hooded Man's claws loosened.

"I like cooperation. Speak," Faldir said.

Tomis opened his mouth, but his conscience choked his tongue. It was John, his oldest friend. The man's life was already a shell of what he once had. He would be shattering any hope John might have for a happy ending. A part of Tomis was nauseous at the thought. His eyes flicked to the creature in front of him and the claws wrapped around his throat. He would die tonight. That thought silenced any complaints from his conscience.

"There was a farm in the Seventh. Someone manifested Flame magic and killed a lumbira. Mages aren't exactly common up there. You said this Focus is a big deal? What if someone got to it before you? Could it create a mage from nowhere?"

"How does that help us? We go on a wild goose chase all over the damned frontier on a rumor?" she asked.

"It's not a goose chase because I know the farm where this happened. I also know that a group of people left the farm the very next day and headed east."

"Do you have a name?"

Tomis blinked and saw Peter, bloodless and spread on the ground without a drop of life in him.

"Hey Tom, what's taking so long?" Wandala called from the tent.

Tomis's breath left him. The Hooded Man let go of his throat and rushed toward the back of the tent. Wandala's hunched shadow stood against the canvas wall. She was coming to them. The Hooded Man stepped to the side of the flap door, out of sight.

"Who is that?" Faldir asked.

"Just a merchant, she paid my way in exchange for labor. She doesn't know anything," Tomis said.

"Make her go away."

"Hey," he called back, "I've almost got it. I'll be there in a minute."

"It's been a minute. We are out of stock and the rush will be here soon."

Wandala reached for the tent flap.

"Please, just let her go. She doesn't deserve this."

"Shut up," Faldir said. She took a step back from Tomis and lowered her Focus.

Wandala pushed through the flap door of the tent. She smiled as she saw Tomis and then her eyes went to Faldir.

"Oh, who's this?"

Faldir stood quietly and Tomis conjured a grin.

"Can't have a break, huh boss? You go back up front and I'll be there soon. Okay?" Tomis said.

Please just leave, he thought.

Wandala and Faldir eyed each other like wolves from separate packs. The old woman looked at Tomis and then back at Faldir. A looming shadow rose behind her. The Hooded Man's talons flexed like an eagle ready to leap upon a field mouse.

"I know he is in trouble. What kind? Debts? I can make good on it. There's no reason to shake him down like this," Wandala said.

She took a step forward and the creature's claws closed around her throat. Faldir pressed her Focus into Tomis and shushed him. Wandala was able to squeak as she turned to see the chittering maw of the Hooded Man. His jaws closed around her neck and brought her to the ground. The slavering mandibles went to work, ripping and dicing.

"What family?" Faldir asked, her empty gaze not wavering as her companion feasted.

Tomis could not tear his eyes from the carnage. His guts coiled in his belly and wretched. He knew this was his fault. His paralysis was punishment, he had to observe what he wrought. He felt as though the elements themselves commanded him to watch Wandala die.

Faldir grabbed his chin and pulled his eyes from the

Hooded Man.

"Pay attention. Where was the mage? What farm? Who ran east the day after?"

"John. Jonathan Seers. He has the Focus," Tomis said.

As the words left his lips, he imagined John beneath Faldir's boot, a black and crackling hole in his chest.

Chapter Ten

Olivia could still taste the sick in her throat. Slumped against Josie's back, the sun's light was blinding. Its heat was like a broiling oven. She wanted to wail and groan, but that would be admitting her weakness. Her mouth was dry despite her efforts to drown it in water.

She made it to the end of the night after the camp ambush. With only the moon to contend with, she thought that they could make it all the way to Sallew. Once the sun rose, she heaved up her dinner along the side of the road. They moved her to Josie's horse and put a cloak over her to dim the light. Grizzly followed after them, tethered to the back of Josie's horse.

"We made it Liv. Take a look."

They were at the top of a grand hill that looked down on the sprawling city. Sallew spread across the land and built up until it collided with the coastline. The white walls and slate roofs were pushed together so tightly, she thought they were thrown on top of one another by some giant beast. Olivia had never seen so many homes in one place. Each one was a different style or material. Sandstone stood across the street from limestone. Arching, grotesque-clad roofs stood next to squat, flat hovels. Lines of laundry dangled between these towers like spider webs, the colored clothing and blankets made it look as though the flags of one hundred nations flew over the city.

Wide docks extended from the coastline like fingers reaching toward the horizon. The city refused to be contained by the shore. Congressional war ships docked two piers over from unmarked cargo ships. Fishing vessels spilled their scaly hauls next to disembarking passengers. The ocean stretched to the ends of her sight. Dark blue waters beyond the shallow shores rose and fell with mighty, white-capped waves.

"Incredible," she whispered.

John pointed to another hilltop on the opposite side of town. A lonely, ill-maintained street broke away from the dense cluster of buildings and climbed the far hill. At the end of it was a domed building with a tall, reflective pillar at the top.

"That's our destination."

"The Church of the Sun? That's my cure?" Olivia tried to wet her parched lips.

John tilted his head and considered his answer.

"Maybe. They're your best chance to avoid, well, you know."

Josie looked over the city and crossed her arms. She studied the urban sprawl with knitted eyebrows and a frown. She never took new things well, in Olivia's experience.

"Let's get going," John said.

They rode through town at a brisk pace, John glanced nervously at Olivia when he found an opportunity to. He was otherwise busy hiding inside of his hood. No one paid the three of them any mind, despite the sheer flood of people that traversed the streets. She lifted her hood and soaked in every sight and sound. She almost forgot the dreadful reason for their visit.

The streets pulsed with people. Markets brimmed with exotic foods, tools that she did not recognize, and clothing that was dyed with a rainbow of colors. These stall vendors bellowed their deals despite the people inches from them. There were no quiet hellos or idle conversation like back home. Olivia could not imagine catering to the needs of so many. In return, the shoppers were direct and brief. Olivia caught snippets of conversation among the tumult. A short man with a wildly frizzy head of hair hawked brilliant blue rugs.

"I ran from a patrol of beetle riders coming south, because they knew I should have paid twice what I did."

No pity was paid in the market. In this confluence of riches, only the best was acceptable. They passed this jumble of trade and went down shadowed, interior streets. The buildings rose taller, braced with lumber at their corners and pressed right against their neighbors. A grocer's shop was downstairs from a family home that aired its laundry on ropes. Children yipped and shouted as they dodged between the endless flow of strangers.

Parchment was posted to walls and boards, but she did not bother to read them until one was shoved into her hands. A woman stood on an overturned bucket and shouted like a merchant. She possessed no goods though, just this stack of papers. She faced down the tides of people without a quiver of trepidation. Her wide hat had a piece of paper stuck into the brim. Red hair was pulled back into a braid and she wore a too-large smile.

Olivia flattened the flier out in her shaky hands and looked it over. It was a caricature of a man kicking a robed figure in the seat of their pants. The words "Stackos for County Representative" were printed in bold type. Underneath it was a handful of lines about his time in the Congressional Militia, his time abroad, his charity, and other claims that seemed too convenient to be true to Olivia.

"Doesn't everyone get a say here?" Olivia asked.

"It's not like at home." John lifted his head just enough to speak to her. "Too many people, it would be chaos trying to get everyone's opinions. They vote on representatives here."

"Just the one?"

"Oh no. Three per county, six counties—"

"Sounds like chaos," Josie said.

"You don't know the half of it." John shook his head.

John seemed to know this city like an old friend who he owed money to. He glanced at street signs with a knowing nod and silent confirmation as they went. They cleared the other side of town and climbed the steep road toward the shining dome of light on the hilltop. The buildings grew sparse. Small farming plots sprouted from cramped, front yards. The road turned sharply and escaped the forest of brick and mortar.

Signs were stuck along the road leading to the Church of the Sun. Each one was covered in vulgar language and warnings, telling them to turn around or to beware what was ahead. The homes were cheaper and the farming plots sparse. Cracked shingles and warped front doors were more obvious.

"Are we sure about this?" Josie asked. "Mages are hair-brained as it is, but a mage that thinks the elements care about us? Crazier than a bag of shade rats."

John did not answer.

The church was built around the central dome of the

building. An upper ring of glass toward the top of it let the sun pour inside. The front doors were cast open and a man in a white robe watered flowers that grew next to the building. A few small buildings were visible behind the church as well as a clothesline replete with even more white robes hung to dry.

They rode near the main doors. John hopped off his horse and held out his hands as Olivia climbed down. As she spun in the saddle, her world tilted again. Her breath caught in her throat and the colors of the world blurred together. She fell from the mount, her knee buckling as she attempted to hop down. Heat bloomed against her skin. John eased her to the ground and helped her back up with an unsure hand.

The robed, young man hurried over, but kept his distance at first. His auburn hair ran to the bottom of his neck and his brown, sun-kissed skin was dotted with freckles. A gleaming pendant dangled from his neck, the silver icon showing a pair of hands holding the sun. He towered over John, but stood a few inches shorter than Josie.

"Is it plague?" he asked.

"It isn't plague, she has flame affliction. Where's the High Cleric, I don't need an initiate," John said.

The young man snorted and bent down next to Olivia.

"I speak with the High Cleric's authority. You're a mage?"

"No," Josie said.

"Yes," said John.

The white-robed man shook his head and spoke to Olivia.

"Which is it?"

She felt so tired that she could fall asleep right there in the dirt. The cleric picked up her hand and smoothed his fingers along the veins in her wrist. His touch was steady, unshaken by her weakened demeanor. He had the manner of a medicine worker and his brown eyes were calm as the ocean. It was clear to her that he was no stranger to magic.

Olivia considered telling him about her encounter with Life magic in the forest yesterday, but relented again. She was too tired to make sense of why Life listened to her and certainly too tired to deal with the needling concern of Josie if she learned about it.

"It's complicated. I was being trained with Life magic as a child."

The cleric placed his left hand over her forehead and brandished a medallion in his right hand. It was made of tan stone with a yellow jewel seated in the center. The edges were broken as if it were ripped from a statue. The jewel gathered light and small embers wicked from it.

"The Flame is great and rising. What's your name?" he asked.

"Olivia."

"I am Alkis." He took a deep, steadying breath and rubbed her hand. "You're burning too fast. I need you to pull some of my vitality."

"What?" she asked.

"You've used Life magic. Listen to me and I can help you for now."

She could hardly believe this stranger wanted her to use her own magic. The usual hesitancy rose in her. She swore to herself that the incident in the forest would have been the last time. Josie watched Alkis like he was a feral dog, her hands pressed against her lips. John reached into

Olivia's pack and handed the Focus to the cleric.

"This is hers. It bonded with her instantly. I've never seen anything like it."

"She bonded without any ritual?" Alkis asked.

"I didn't mean for her to use it. Why would I ever want that?" Josie said unprompted.

Alkis gave her a confused glance and handed the Focus to Olivia. She wrapped her fingers around it and he guided her Focus to lay against her chest.

"What did you mean vitality?" Olivia asked.

"I'll explain later. Now, I want to help you, but you need to help me first. Close your eyes."

"Don't let her drift off. Please," Josie begged, a quiver in her throat.

Alkis ignored her and kept his eyes trained on Olivia. She closed her eyes, but remained painfully aware of the world around her. The Flame jumped in her chest, eager to see magic at work. She ignored it and reached out to the comforting voice from the forest.

"Olivia, I need you to say the following: Bring this man's life into me."

"I'm not going to hurt you, am I?"

Even though it felt that her head might burst into flames, she was terrified of what Alkis was asking. Magic turned Yorker into a slavering mad man. It nearly made him sacrifice her to that thing, the swirling cloud of darkness.

I won't let it happen to me. I won't let it happen to me. She repeated the thought in her head.

"You won't hurt me. Say the words," he said.

"Bring…. this man's life into… me."

The grass nearby bent toward her. The wind gusted in the wrong direction. The ground trembled under her, but only she could feel it. It was the shake of roots wriggling to answer her call. The voice from the forest rose in her mind, distant and soft.

It's you.

"Good. Again," Alkis said.

"Bring this man's life into me," Olivia whispered.

Another pulse and this time she could feel Alkis's flesh, his skin, his mouth. She could see blood rush through his veins. He gasped in discomfort, but did not let go of her.

"I'm fine. Do it again."

"Bring this man's life into me," she repeated.

Are you sure?

"Yes, he told me to," she said.

Are you sure?

She was not, but she felt his vitality drip into her veins. It was only a leaky faucet. Just enough water to wet your palms and clear off a smear of dirt. As small as it was, it eased her body in ways she had not felt since they left home behind.

"Bring this man's life into me," she said.

Alkis winced as a green light sparked between their hands. The leaky spigot of Life squeaked open and a flush of it coursed through Olivia. She cooled and the red shade in her cheeks faded. Alkis turned ghastly pale, his skin losing the sun-flushed quality. He never wavered, holding her hands as if on a deathbed.

His Focus glowed once again and he pulled his right hand from her. The spigot sealed shut and Olivia's eyes fluttered open. She drank in the smell of flowers and the salty air of the ocean. Her muscles eased and the relief nearly put a tear in her eye. For the first time in days, she felt like herself again. There was still something though,

just a flickering flame in the depths of her heart.
That was not a cure.

Chapter Eleven

It felt like she leeched something from the cleric. She felt the draw of his blood to her fingers. Some energy passed between them, but she gave nothing back to him in return. Olivia flexed her fingers. She felt alive, healthy. Across from her, the cleric was pale and unsteady where he crouched. Alkis grinned and rubbed the joints of his hands. The blood returned to his skin and he shivered as his body warmed.

"What just happened?" Olivia asked.

"What did it feel like?"

"It felt like I was drinking you, I was killing you."

He snorted.

"Not inaccurate. I just gave you a week or two of my life. Should keep you around long enough for the High Cleric to think up something."

Two weeks of his life?

"I never asked for that. You shouldn't have, you don't even know me."

Before he could explain himself, Josie pushed between the two and shoved Alkis onto his back. She hugged Olivia and gasped for air like her life was saved.

"You're safe, you're cured! Shade-damned magic. Vile, wonderful stuff. Let's be done with this."

John helped Alkis back up. The cleric stumbled on his feet, but snapped back to a straight-backed posture. They shared a nod before Alkis spoke to Josie.

"I merely gave some of my life force to sustain hers. She was on the edge of death. I'm surprised it worked," Alkis said.

"But she is safe for now?" John asked.

"Life magic isn't my specialty, but it should keep her around a while longer."

"Thank you all the same," Olivia said, "I owe you my life."

Alkis was a complete stranger, but there was a serene happiness on his face. He was a mage for certain, but nothing about him reminded her of Mage Yorker. He was fit, sure of hand, and ready to save a stranger's life without a second thought.

"Don't be vowing on things you can't give away. We don't have any stables on property. You'll need to take your horses into town. There is one a quarter mile from here though. Tell them you are friends of Elza, that will get you a good price," Alkis said.

"A mage's word getting us a deal?" John asked.

"We have more friends in town than you'd think. Not many are willing to say it publicly though."

Olivia stood and shook out her joints. She even conjured the energy to hop in place.

"I feel so much better."

"What is important now is that you conserve your energy and avoid agitation. You were hours from death. The Flame rises in the hearts of the brave. In the heart of an afflicted as yourself, it finds kindling," Alkis said.

"Are you a poet or something?" Olivia asked.

"I'm a cleric, holy texts and all. I was also a soldier for some time. Made the regiments of scripture a bit easier. You should both come inside. Elza will want to speak with you," Alkis said.

John took the reins of the horses and began the trek down the hill. "I'll be back soon."

"Do you want us to help?" Olivia asked. "I mean, you're not exactly welcome in town."

He waved her off and grinned. "If I meet any tough customers, I'll send them your way."

Olivia gave her uncle a small nod of thanks and watched him head back down the road toward town. She remembered what he said about protecting them: on my life. At the time, she assumed he was lying. The cleric's hand on her shoulder interrupted her thoughts.

The room beyond the front doors was quiet. It was a small welcome hall fit with delicate, stone statues. Sun iconography was etched into every door and stone tile under their feet. The windows were wide with simple panes. Two passages, to their right and left, ran alongside the main chamber and toward the back of the church.

A handful of people loitered in the front lobby. Their outfits did not fit a particular profession or way of life to the point of looking tacky. Olivia imagined they chose these outfits to be as unremarkable as possible. They greeted them with welcoming grins and a small bow.

"Flame keep you," one said.

Ahead of them was the central worship hall. Rows of worship mats surrounded a central dais, a few small slates left on top of it. The upper level of the room was a network of mirrors attached to wooden poles and columns that were evenly spread around the room. A crank sat on each of the columns which could adjust the position of the mirrors. Sunlight poured in through the ring of glass at the top of the church. The beams bounced between the mirrors and together lit the room as though there was no roof at all.

At the foot of the dais was an older woman in the same white robes, but hers had a yellow collar that ran down the hem. Her long, white hair was bound with a red ribbon. She cracked one eye open and finished a whispered prayer.

"Welcome, but you missed the noon service. Come later for our sunset sermon." Her voice was stern and unbending.

"Elza, these are not parishioners. Well, in a way at least," Alkis said.

Josie gripped Olivia's arm like a vice. "If they say one thing about required donations, we're out of here," she muttered.

"Would you relax?" Olivia nudged her sister in the ribs.

"They've just arrived. She is afflicted with Flame, but also a gifted Life mage. She's been stabilized, for now. But the fire rises." He gestured to Olivia.

"She took Life from you?" A flash of concern crossed Elza's face.

"It was necessary. She would not have lasted the night without it."

This news turned the elder mage from the dais to face them. Her wrinkles ran deep and scars covered her hands. They were old burn marks, pale streaks across her light brown skin. She crossed her arms and arched an eyebrow.

"Flame affliction?"

"And still living. I told her that you would know best if a cure were possible."

Elza strode toward them. She was shorter than all of them, but her presence smothered the free air in the room.

"Your name?" she asked.

"Olivia. This is my sister Josie. Our uncle, Jonathan, is taking our horses to a stable."

"But we aren't staying for long. Just fix her and we'll be on our way," Josie said.

Elza's glare could have cut Josie off at her knees if she were any closer. Nonetheless, Josie loomed over the old woman and gave her best glare back. The High Cleric chuckled and looked back at Olivia.

"And you are a Life mage?"

"I was. I haven't practiced in years."

"One never stops being a mage. We aren't so lucky as to leave the Gift behind when we find it inconvenient. You are obviously talented. To be out of practice and to summon the powers of Life while in the throes of advanced flame affliction, remarkable."

Elza spoke to her the way that her father spoke about prize-winning horses.

"I have no intention of joining your...church." Olivia wanted to say cult. "Magic has been nothing but trouble for me. The only reason I'm here is because this relic conjured the Flame inside of me. I didn't ask for this; I won't die for this."

Elza's mouth opened in awe as Olivia showed her the Focus. The High Cleric's eyes went to Alkis with a knowing look.

"It bonded instantly, how she tells it. I thought it was impossible," he said.

"Only improbable. I've heard rumors." Elza played with her hair.

Olivia had the horrible feeling that she was being inspected or measured. Without John nearby, in the presence of two mages, she considered running back out the front door. She had no idea what Flame mages could do. After a moment, Elza looked away from the Focus.

"I would never ask you to recognize Flame's obvious divinity if the spirit was not within you. If Flame's power is not enough to convince you, then nothing will. All the same, we are loath to let others die," she said.

"I thought mages like you just burnt people for disagreeing with you?" Josie said.

"We are not Fire Keepers," Elza said with a harsh edge. "We are practitioners of the True Flame and live in the principles which Flame gave itself to humanity: aid the weak and heal the ill. It is our mission in life to help those in need of it."

"So can you cure me?" Olivia asked.

Hesitancy broke Elza's iron composure.

"I've worked for years to master True Flame and still it eludes me. To handle Flame is to risk affliction. But with your life already in jeopardy—"

"She is not your test subject." Josie reached for a small knife at her hip, but Olivia pulled her arm to the side.

"What did you have in mind?" she asked.

"Are you seriously considering this? You'll be their plaything," Josie said.

Olivia felt almost normal now, but she could still feel the tickle in her chest. She remembered the ill, worthless feeling that this curse brought her down to. She did not ask for this, but it was going to kill her anyway. She would be damned if she let magic define how her life ended. Olivia was not surprised that this was being asked of her. Since the start, she suspected there was only one way to fight it.

"Olivia," Elza said, "you have made it clear there is no love lost between you and magic. But the only way we might discover a cure is for you to master that power. Fighting this fire with more Life will end up killing someone."

"To beat the curse, you need me to use magic again?"

"I need you to remember that you are a mage. The gift never left. You just stopped caring."

Josie snorted. "She doesn't need this. We'll find another way."

Olivia wished it could be that simple. But she knew better. If it infuriated her sister, she would have to live with it. Without magic, her mother would be dead. Without it, she would die.

"When do we start?" Olivia asked.

"What?" Josie let go of her sister's arm and stepped away.

"You will have to stay on church grounds. We have a visitor's lodge in the back that you are welcome to. Alkis, could you see that it is stocked?"

He nodded and headed to a door at the back of the great room. Olivia reached to grab her sister's arm again, but Josie pulled away. Her face shriveled with disgust.

"It's the only way and you know it," Olivia said.

"After magic started all this, you just want to trust them?"

"Do I have a choice?"

Josie threw her hands over her head and walked out of the prayer hall. Olivia took a step after her and then slowed down. Olivia wished Josie would understand, but she knew better.

"She'll be back. She never handles bad news well,"

Olivia said.

"Well, she will have to. I'm forbidding you from leaving the church for the next few days," Elza said.

Olivia jerked her head back toward the High Cleric. "That seems a little extreme."

"You are still sick, Olivia. Flame affliction is not some passing pox. It is a curse. A magical damnation that only has one end: your death. I'm not trying to scare you. I am letting you know what you are up against. The first Fire Keepers wielded True Flame without hesitation or caution and were all consumed within weeks of the Great War's end."

Olivia chuckled. "You run a church devoted to Flame and you can't even use the stuff?"

Elza held her thoughts for a moment. It was impossible to tell if she was annoyed or amused.

"Only the limited sort that modern Fire Keepers use. I am not initiated in their ways. I learned through practice. I would wish Flame to be unrestrained and allowed to burn free as it once did."

Elza gestured to the mirrors above.

"The sun is a reminder of Flame's love. When it saw the world falling to Shadow, it intervened and granted us a touch of its power. Flame burns kindling though, and it burns more than twigs. Crops died, rivers, and lakes dried up and those who used its gift were burnt to ash.

"And you are looking for a way to use Flame magic without all that happening. You need me," Olivia said.

Elza folded her arms across her chest. "I will try to keep you alive as long as I can. It is not the manifesting of Flame that is difficult, it is the controlling of it. I can feel it burning in you now. I can help you master it."

"What good would that do?"

"The elements cannot be commanded. If you learn control and restraint, we can stop it from surging. Instead of fourteen days before you are on death's door again, we may be able to extend it further. Perhaps indefinitely."

Elza reached toward Olivia. "Come to the yard with me. We will begin your training immediately."

They led her out of the church and into a small clearing behind it. The guest house stood a dozen steps away. The cherry wood of the building's pointed roof stooped over a small garden of wildflowers. On the other side of the clearing, there was a rope that ran from the back of the temple to a laundry pole.

Josie leaned against the door frame of the lodge. She watched with nervous eyes as Olivia, Elza, and Alkis walked into the center of the yard.

Clouds blew in from the west and brought some much needed shade. Olivia was glad to escape the sun, even for just a while.

"Keep the Focus low," Elza said, "It is the instrument through which you channel the elements. They will pick up on cues from its position. Wield it like a weapon and the elements will give you a weapon."

Olivia held it in front of her.

"Good. Now close your eyes. Today we are going to help you find the Flame. It is somewhere inside of you and you must be able to find it in order to address it."

"Can't I just speak to it? I can feel it in me," Olivia asked.

Elza paced around her.

"Feeling is not seeing. You have a physical connection to it, but without a mental bridge you can only be so effective. You will be shouting across a raging river, details lost in the noise. Speaking of noise, no more questions for now."

Olivia nodded.

"Clear your mind. Remove any nagging thoughts."

She took a deep breath. The smell of ocean salt came on the wind. Elza's feet shuffled through the grass behind her. The details of the world faded from her ears and she felt as though she could see a dim ember ahead of her. She bent her thoughts toward it. As she did, a scream echoed from deep in the darkness. Olivia flinched as green eyes and a smashed, bloody door manifested in her thoughts.

"Ignore it. The closer you draw to the fire, the more agitated you will become. It will do anything to agitate you."

"What was that?" she asked.

"A memory, a nightmare. Push through it."

The ember flickered just ahead of her. She moved toward it, but the screaming came back again. She could see her mother disappearing into the darkness. Monstrous shadows rose beyond the broken door. Olivia ignored the memory and marched toward the embers. She was so close.

Her fingers closed around it and sparks filled the darkness with a blinding flash. Flames leaped from her fingers and swam past her face. A pillar of fire burst to life in front of her. A glowering face emerged from it with bloody, wet lips and snarling fangs. As it lunged forward, she heard a child scream. She was just a child when she made that sound. Olivia opened her eyes and fell to her knees. She drew her hand back, the Focus almost too warm to touch.

"I got it." She grinned from ear to ear and stood. "I

found the Flame."

The barest suggestion of approval pulled at Elza's face.

"You have talent. I'll give you that," Alkis said.

A panicked shout came from across the yard and her sister charged toward them. Josie sprinted from the door of the guest house when Olivia fell. She slowed just enough to not knock her sister over. Olivia stumbled as Josie grabbed her shoulders, careening to a stop.

"Are you okay? What did they do to you?"

"I'm fine. Making progress for a change. Thanks to them."

Josie glanced at the mages. She gripped Olivia's shoulder as if she might yank her under her arm at a moment's notice. Her glare faded and fingers slackened, but she did not let go.

"I'm sure they barely helped," she muttered.

"This is a good sign, Josie." Elza said, "We should move quickly. Time is not on our side."

Josie ignored them.

"Don't forget these people use the same magic that did this."

"You're being rude, they're just trying to help. Like you are," Olivia said.

Josie's fingers slipped from Olivia's shoulders and she straightened up. Olivia kept Josie's gaze. Her little sister would seize on any leeway in her condition. Any sign that Olivia was uncertain about this would make her dig in against this situation. When Olivia did not cave to her sister, Josie turned to Elza.

"I can't help her, can I?"

"Moral support is always welcome. You might not trust us, but unfortunately you're out of options," Elza said.

Josie pursed her lips. Whatever insult or accusation she wanted to hurl at them, Olivia assumed she tucked it away for later. Her sister groaned and rubbed her forehead.

"I'm starving, Olivia hasn't eaten either. When do we eat?"

You aren't my keeper, Olivia thought. Whether it was the calmer Flame within her or some stronger sisterly urge, Olivia did not speak out.

"Alkis will prepare dinner for you all," Elza answered.

"I am?" he asked.

"Yes, you are the better cook of the two of us. Hardly want to be feeding our guests my flavorless soups. I have research to do if we are going to continue Olivia's training tomorrow," Elza said without a hint of a smile. She walked back toward the temple and Alkis gestured to the guest house.

"Go rest. Feel free to draw baths from the well. I will call when dinner is ready."

Josie ushered Olivia toward the guest house without a parting word to the cleric. Olivia at least managed a small wave to him before being pulled away. He returned it and watched a second longer before leaving. Josie was busy talking about the sleep Olivia needed and the stress she shouldn't be carrying. Even though Josie picked up the Focus in the first place, Olivia did not blame her. Josie had no idea this would happen. With renewed vitality within her, it was easier to push the angry thoughts away.

Olivia ran her fingers along the etched lines of the Focus. Things were still the same. Magic ruined Yorker.

It broke the world. Olivia would never stop hating it. She hoped that these thoughts would drown out the exhilaration of learning once again.

Chapter Twelve

The sun was high in the sky as Tomis entered Sallew. Noon shift guards began to loiter in public commons and at busy street corners. The things of the night could not stand the sun, that was what they were told. On such a glorious day, why would they suspect any different? As long as they carried fire in hand and did not allow fear into their hearts, no terror of the dark could challenge them.

Tomis and his captors walked by without a glance from these sentinels.

They took a long road that looped around the edge of the city and then entered on a scarcely occupied side street. Tomis walked next to Faldir, the Hooded Man behind them. The creature's cloak and hood were drawn high, but he effected a more upright walk. Faldir made it clear to Tomis that if he helped them find John Seers, he would go free. If he ran, screamed, or called for help in any way, the Hooded Man would kill him before anyone could save him. It was all the same to Tomis. Unclear if he might be detained in the hunt for John, laying low was in his best interest.

They put some distance between themselves and the edge of the city before stumbling into the maze-like streets. The warehouses on either side of them loomed overhead and blocked out the day's light. Laborers and task masters hurried to finish out their work. Frustrated shouts echoed down the long road and the narrow alleys that sprung off it.

Tomis's eyes followed the few workers who were out on the street. A group of four, all wearing oily suspenders and stained shirts, held small pendants as they stepped into a sun-drenched alleyway. They knelt down to face the horizon and bowed their heads. Faldir snarled and the Hooded Man let out a hideous, growling gurgle.

"Conquerors and murderers selling themselves as friends and saints," she said.

"They seem pretty innocuous to me."

"They are an extension of the old order. They scoured Shadow and my people from the world. There are no truer enemies left than those who worship Flame and desire its unbound use."

The group moved beyond the alley. Her eyes swept from warehouse to warehouse, searching for something.

"It's all history at this point. No one was actually there, why get so bent out of shape over this stuff?" Tomis asked.

"It's easy to say that as one of the victors," Faldir said, "you were not raised in my family. We were allowed what they deemed acceptable for a defeated nation. Everyone faced famine after the war. We were starved and they called it justice."

"Yeah, yeah famines, scarcity. I know the story."

Faldir gave him a look, her fist pulling tight.

"What I mean is that the rough times are over."

"Not everywhere," she said, "There is still a debt of revenge to be repaid. Revenge for an unjust war. Revenge for driving us from the world. A debt that my companion and I will visit on the cowards who turned their backs on us."

"Twice cursed traitors," the Hooded Man growled.

Tomis jumped away from the creature. Its guttural voice sounded like a chain being pulled from a deep mire, choked with bones and weeds. "Stars above, it talks."

Faldir nodded to the Hooded Man and walked down a side alley. The creature poked Tomis with a claw and pushed him in Faldir's direction. The alley led into a market plaza, one of the many that littered the town. They slowed in front of an old store front. Foggy, glass windows were obscured further by a layer of dust. The wood siding was splintered with age and wind. A sign in the window said "Closed" and another chain and padlock were wrapped around the handle of the front door. Faldir shook it to no avail before stepping aside. The beastly man wrapped his taloned hands around the chain and twisted.

"Flame started this war, not us," she said.

"I'll remind you *that* war is over. Has been for about three centuries."

"Is it now?" Faldir grinned for the first time since he was among them.

It was a nasty, mean thing. He felt like it was only brought on by the promise of violence to come. The Hooded Man grunted and wrenched the pad lock open. If anyone in the plaza heard them, they did not care. Tomis was not sure if they looked away out of ignorance or if they desperately wanted to avoid being dragged into their business. The creature slunk into the unlit room and purred as he stepped out of the sun. Faldir shoved Tomis's shoulder as they both entered the shuttered store.

Dust motes floated through the air to settle on the rotting floor underfoot. A few tables and chairs ran through the center of the room. Cobwebs stretched across the serene relic of a room. A handful of tools were left on the counter. An open doorway was at the back of the room, the door and its hinges entirely missing.

Faldir slid one of the chairs under the handle of the front door. She tested it as the Hooded Man stepped through the door at the back and disappeared into the stifling darkness beyond. The lumbering creature moved into the room, sniffing at the floorboards and glancing into the shadows. Faldir yanked on Tomis's arm and gestured back out to the street.

"My brother will ensure it's safe. You and I have work to do."

"We've already traveled so far. Don't you want to let your hair down? Maybe rest for a minute? "

She shoved him against the wall and pointed out the door. "Now."

Tomis rubbed his shoulder and left the storefront and the beast inside. Faldir closed the door and gestured to the blinding flash of the sun on the sea up ahead. He didn't question the direction. When Tomis was tired he tended to resist further movement, like a boulder in a gulley. He suspected that Faldir vented her irritation on others when she ached. She said nothing as they passed by taverns, slips, and piers.

Their quiet was only broken when she asked where the harbor master was in Sallew. Not far now, they reached it a minute later. Faldir pointed at the pier nearest to the cramped, briny building that sat on the edge of the breakwater. He obeyed without further instruction. She balled her fist as she marched down the pier and opened the door.

The foaming surf crashed against the seawall. Salty, cold spray arced up before splattering onto Tomis's shoulders. He kicked at the roiling sea. The offending wave drew back before his boot touched it. A seagull called as it flew overhead with a noise that sounded suspiciously like laughter.

He looked back at the Harbor Master's office. To his relief, the dockmaster was still alive. Faldir's frustration rose above the crash and hiss of the surf. Despite their short time together, he could tell they were on a clock.

Tomis could slip into the crowd or hide behind a stack of cargo. The boards of the pier creaked quietly under his feet, nowhere near loud enough for Faldir to hear if he walked away. Small crowds of merchants unloaded hauls of crates and nets of slimy fish. He could evade them for some time among the thrum of people, but they first found him without a lead at all. Tomis weighed the danger of attempting it again, especially when he did not have an easy way out of town. He would have to run south or all the way back west to get to the next major port.

The two of them were hounds. They picked up the scent of something or someone and took it back to whoever filled their water dish. They were smart, but this was not their plan. They did not talk to anyone besides him.

He knew their final destination: Naelan. The mention of "Twice-Cursed Traitors" was a name he knew. Across the sea and to the southeast, it was a nation of water mages lauded for their study of the elements and despised for siding with Shadow in the Great War. They were also hated by Shadow for quickly surrendering when the tide turned against them.

"Unblinking, fish-faced, sea creature," Faldir muttered.

Faldir's boots pounded into the creaky boards as she stormed down the dock. Her hood was down and her dark hair flowed freely to her shoulders. Her face was twisted into her usual scowl as she passed Tomis and motioned for him to follow.

"You didn't kill her, did you?"

Faldir rolled her eyes.

"No one named Johnathan Seers has left through these docks in the last few days. Legally anyway. Did he have any aliases while you worked together?"

They merged into the irregular currents of dock workers moving up and down the wide brick street. Shadows were cast by the masts of mighty ships. The din of the tides mixed with the stinking smell of brine, the shouts of workers, and the clip-clop of horse hooves.

"No, seeming legitimate was important. He was a fence. We did deals all over the continent. Some of our clients knew what they were getting into. Others were too vain to realize the only way to get goods like this was through unusual acquisition."

"Stolen. You are a thief, don't try to hide it," Faldir said.

"Stolen, pilfered, pinched, purloined, snatched," Tomis listed. He smiled, but Faldir's glower killed his grin quickly.

"And most of those were Pescan relics?" she asked.

"Mostly, but not by much. Lots of good Congressional and Margecein artifacts too."

Banners strung overhead proclaimed support to one political candidate or the other. Wealthy nobles skirted the dirty, work districts in polished carriages. Families ran errands. Teenagers found places to sate their boredom. Tomis could not escape the truth that Faldir hated every single one of them.

"What do you want with that Focus anyway? You've already got one, I've seen you use it," Tomis said.

"I'm not going to sell it, like you would."

"Be a better mage? Show it off to your magic buddies or your boss?"

Faldir almost rose to anger, but winced and stifled the curse that built on her lips. Tomis hit a nerve. They had a boss and she hated them.

"Where would Johnathan hide? What sort of place would he look for?" she asked.

Tomis thought it over, but a wriggling pang of guilt spoke loudest. You are selling out your friend for your own skin. He winced and pushed it away.

"Peter and I were movers. We would find relics, acquire them, and then move them to other markets for sale. John would get us clients and give us a cover. He was really good at not drawing attention to this sort of thing."

"You were grave robbers. I know this already."

"Freelance treasure hunter is the preferred term, thank you. That cover from John was important. If the Pescans ever got wind that its old relics were being bought and sold by congressional clients, it would cause a bit of trouble for everyone."

"So John might be here selling something at a market or auction?" she asked.

They left the docks, her footsteps guiding him to the north. They were on a long street that ran along the coastline. The irregular crowds of sailors were replaced with butchers, carpenters, and laborers who smelled of sweat. These buildings were made of simple slate walls and roofs. Their doors were propped open for any one passerby.

"He went clean a while ago," Tomis said.

"Anyone he could have been staying with?"

"He might be staying alone. I can never remember. I just turn my brain off when I hear words like family or retirement or hard work."

Faldir laughed, a short disbelieving noise, and reached into her pack. She retrieved a waterskin and offered him a drink. He did not realize how thirsty he was after all this walking and took it. She smiled as he handed it back to her. Those eyes reminded him too much of a hungry wolf.

"How might John respond to seeing you again? All these years and you just happen to be in Sallew at the same time?"

"Vague surprise? We left on good terms. He might be suspicious if he thinks he is being followed."

"Did you think you were being hunted before we found you?" Faldir asked.

Tomis shook his head.

"Shadowed steps are the quietest."

"So that is what you are? A Shadow cultist?"

"My family stood to lose the most when Pescavto surrendered. We were forced to flee our home and hide. We've done so for centuries. We're underdogs like yourself. You should be on our side of this," she said.

"I don't like sides myself, too messy. Loyalty, honor, too many circumstances where you are asked to do something unadvised."

"So you follow whatever creed benefits you the most?"

"It keeps me breathing," Tomis said with a genuine smile.

Faldir laughed again with that mean smile that would look more appropriate with fangs.

"You've made that much clear. Two people are dead because of you and you'll drink their killer's water as long as it quenches your thirst."

The comment cut deep like a knife, but he did his best to ignore it. That callus over his better half had some upsides. Tomis tilted his eyes upward. The long, coastal road bent inland ahead of them and then ran up a hill to the north of town. At the top was a shining light. He saw a round temple with a gleaming beacon at the top of it.

"And you can keep breathing if you do what I want. See that?"

Tomis nodded.

"Tomorrow, you will slip into that church and look around. It could be a safe place for him, they always welcome those who are versed in the way of Flame."

"You're going to need me to take a look?" Tomis asked. "I'd prefer company if you can tag along."

"Those zealots would recognize me at once. Consider this a chance to prove your loyalty."

"Oh goody, just what I was wanting."

Faldir gripped his collar and growled into his ear.

"You'll rest tonight. Once you arrive, do what you need to. Find Johnathan or better yet, find the Focus. Your life depends on it."

"My life, right. Bring back the Focus so you can kill me in a nice, quiet place," he said.

"You've been cooperative. Despite being a grave

145

robber, you are harmless. You have no spine, no spirit. Bring back the Focus or John Seers and you will walk free. I promise," Faldir said.

Tomis looked at the church on the hill. He got that tingling feeling that he used to get when he got something right. When the rumors of a relic paid off or a client fell for some overpriced product. They were on the right track and that terrified him.

"Don't think about running. My companion is an excellent tracker. Of course, you know that."

Tomis turned to Faldir. "You will spare me even if I don't come back with it."

"What?" Faldir asked.

"If the Focus is there, but I don't come back with it, you let me live. I don't have magic like you and we don't know how guarded they might be. You are walking me into an excuse to get rid of me."

Faldir stepped back from him. Her flustered glance sharpened into a predatory glare. "Are you bargaining?"

"And I'll need time. Won't be able to get there until later in the day. You know enough about skulking to know not to just waltz up to the door. I'll need to watch them, come up with a cover if I need to."

Her irritation boiled out of her eyes. Fingers hovering over the onyx rod at her hip, he could almost see her resisting the urge to kill him. Tomis finally had a wedge and, Flame bless, he was going to use it.

"Do we have a deal?"

She bit her lip and crossed her hands.

"If you come back with the location of the Focus, but not the item itself, we will talk. Don't overplay your hand, thief."

He doubted that she would kill him in public, but he

also assumed that he had eluded them previously. All the same, he had pulled a consolation from Faldir like blood from a stone. It would take some time getting back here tomorrow, especially if he didn't want to be noticed. Faldir jerked her head back where they came and motioned for him to follow. Tomis would survive one more day.

****

She chose a room within the darkened warehouse to commune. They made it back to the warehouse and settled in. Though she would be better suited to the night, this city knew Shadow too well. A lone shadow mage had no hope of resisting the combined vigilance of Sallew. If they were not ready to act, it was better to lay low.

Tomis and her brother were just beyond these thin walls. The thief was petrified of her hulking sibling. She did not worry about him causing trouble. Besides, he was too tired from roaming all over town. Faldir's legs ached as well, but it wouldn't do any good letting them know. A worm like Tomis would only wriggle if it thought it couldn't get away. She had to appear resolute.

There was one thing left to do. She tossed her cloak over the small window facing the rest of the warehouse. Darkness swallowed the room and the shadows swept around her like an old friend. Her eyes adjusted and the gift of her bloodline rendered the room into a dim nether light. Pescavto's oldest bloodlines bore this talent. Even without the light, they would never be lost. The rest of the office was scant. There was a desk with yellowed papers left unattended by the last taskmaster.

Faldir kneeled in the center of the room. She struck a match and a small flame bloomed in her hand. She closed her eyes as she did a hundred times before. Voices rose in the darkness. They were separate and one at once. They said different things, each voice belonged to someone else who dwelt in the darkness of shadows. They asked questions, told truths, and lied. As the squabble of voices grew, the match in her hand burned down toward her knuckles.

She listened for a particular voice in the chatter. An echo came to her, the dripping of water. It spoke into the shadows as she did. This voice spoke above the others in growling recognition. Her fingers snuffed the match.

"Father."

The shadows wrapped her in a cloak of shifting shade. She was no longer in an abandoned warehouse in Sallew. She could hear the drip-drop of tepid pools. The sound echoed off stone walls that were older than humanity. The muttering came to her next. Hushed voices spoke to each other at the foot of an altar. They shivered, cooed, and laughed as Faldir materialized before them. A dragging sound scraped through the cavern, the noise of reptilian scales on rock. The sound grew closer, a deep rumbling groan silenced the flock at the creature's feet.

"Daughter, what do you bring me?"

Faldir opened her eyes. She was in the deepest of caves, only able to arrive by Shadow's grace. Her mother told her that Father dwelt deep beneath the Elder Mountains, so far from the sun that Flame could never hope to reach it. He was not her father, but he was still the Father. He was the patriarch of her parents, her brother, and the rivals she killed for this prestige.

She looked up from where she knelt. Cloaked figures sat in groups along the edges of the narrow chamber, rooms above dug into the walls housed even more. The ceiling rose and rose until it went beyond her nether sight. A pool of cave water splashed and rippled as blind prawns crawled in the presence of something far greater. He towered before her. Even as the darkness could hold nothing from her, it was a spot of pure darkness in her eyes. Tendrils of shadow writhed like an amused cat's tail.

These playful shapes coalesced around the void that her eyes could not pierce. The shape changed as it breathed. Wider and then taller. Broader and then thinner. Something stirred inside the darkness and beckoned to Faldir with scaled hands. Each was tipped with claws like an eagle.

"I return to pass on knowledge, Father."

"You come bearing a note and nothing of substance," he said.

"I am close. It was stolen before we could arrive where the fire mage fell. We have captured the thief who gave us its location and he knows who possesses the Focus. Jonathan Seers, a retired thief of some sort."

Father stayed silent for a moment and tilted his head in the nest of shadows.

"Do you come seeking aid? To ask for help?"

Faldir looked at the ground and gritted her teeth.

"The quarry is in my grasp. They have no hope of escape."

"And yet you are empty handed. I thought you were one of my most promising children, Faldir."

"Do you care nothing for me? My brother and I march across the world and kill in your name. We are a pedigree, three-hundred years old, and I must fight to prove myself a member of this family."

"My brilliant child, heir of shadow mages, most promising of house Hramza." The darkness floated forward, talons clicking on stone and scraping as the foot lifted.

"You, more than your brother or your siblings or your parents, deserve a seat at my side. I wish to give it to you, but your weakness must be drawn out."

"I have no weakness."

"No weakness," Father simpered, "I can feel it in your cloying need. Were you ready, you would possess the relic and have begun your journey to Naelan. Perhaps you do need help."

"I need nothing. My brother and I will capture the Focus and kill those who took it."

"Good. There is the strength, the ice in your veins. You are so strong, Faldir, I could not bear to have you disappoint me."

Despite those promises, she was still an outsider to Father's coven of shadow mages. He still turned her brother into a scampering beast when he failed. She told herself this was it. This was the last challenge before she would be welcomed at his side.

"I will prove myself worthy to you. As a shadow mage and as a part of this family."

The shadows reverberated with a deep, booming chuckle.

"We will see."

The shadow pressed into Faldir again and she closed her eyes. The sounds of water and echoing voices washed away. Warmth returned to her face and the noise of a rolling wagon outside reached her. She was back in Sallew. Faldir grabbed her head, her shoulders tightened and her teeth ground together. She threw her head back and roared at the darkness with the hope that Father heard it.

Chapter Thirteen

Olivia, Josie, and John spent the next day on the church grounds. They eased into old habits without the stress of travel. Olivia's condition was the only reminder of the grim situation. Though Josie looked the other way on Olivia's continued lessons, she was distant at all other times. When she did address it, she was certain that they were manipulating Olivia.

There were only a few faces to suspect. Elza and Alkis lived in the church. Both of the devout mages hid very little from her. They were aided by a number of people who did not carry the gift. These few, maybe four at most, were dedicated to the Flame and not afraid to be seen in the company of mages. They watered the flowers, helped with the morning, noon, and sunset service, and delivered fresh linen to the guest house in the morning.

Their lodgings were meager, but it might as well have been a palace when compared to a horse's saddle. The wide windows captured the rising, eastern sun as it rose over the open ocean. The beds were simple, the mattresses filled with feathers and sheep wool. They were lumpy where you did not want it to be and flat everywhere else. There was one large, shared bedroom and an adjoining kitchenette. It reminded Olivia of a jail cell. There was nothing to become familiar with.

Despite this, she was relieved to sit still. Maybe the affliction was tinting everything in shades of anger, but this trip drained her in unexpected ways. She was not the only one either. John disappeared into town and returned with some food and more money than they set out with. When she asked about it, he told her to buzz off.

Around early evening, Elza collected her. The chief cleric's office was plain for someone of such wisdom. Olivia's eyes traced along a bookcase behind her amber-stained desk. A high stack of books overflowed from the shelf. Another shelf held some books, but also relics and icons. Each of them held some sigil of Flame, the sun, a scale, and more. The longer Olivia looked, the more she found to consider.

An oil lantern hung from the ceiling and several candles burned in ritualistic holders around the room. A window looked east, the forest only a dozen feet away from the glass pane. Elza sat on the floor and tented her fingers.

"Thank you for your warmth. The day is waning and now you make haste to others who need you. We make this affirmation as the Shadow nears."

Olivia matched the cleric's pose, unsure if she was supposed to join in the prayer or not.

"We light our torches as tribute to your journey above and as a promise of your return come the morning. *Parcha fo mea se lous as*, and we will return it to you when our time is at an end."

Elza turned over her hands and revealed her palms in a heart-shaped grip. Olivia recognized it as the symbol of the church, minus the sun that was usually affixed in it.

"Was that magic?" Olivia asked.

Elza smiled.

"It's a prayer we say before the end of the day. A

small thanks to the sun, avatar of the Flame. It leaves us to shine upon others. We should be grateful for its time and bid it goodbye as a friend."

It seemed more than a little silly. The sun certainly did not consider favors. A year or two of withered crops taught her that. The elements were vast entities. Olivia could not imagine that they could appreciate such a small thing as a prayer. However, it did remember her deep in the forest.

"But, it's going to rise again tomorrow whether you say thanks or not," she said.

"One would hope so," Elza said, "Do you have your Focus?"

Olivia grabbed the golden artifact at her side.

"Before we begin taming the affliction inside of you, we must give you dedication. You must learn to focus, on the Focus. Flame is emboldened by aggression. It feeds off it and grows stronger. The disciplined mage knows when to temper their emotions and close out thoughts."

Olivia leaned in closer. Her hatred of magic felt distant at the moment.

"Magic is not something you pick up after years of ignoring. That goes double for Flame. It is voracious as it is bold. Particularly for one so young. If you do not master your emotions, you will burn."

She thought of how the Flame begged to be released in the forest. How it had seeped out of her that night when her mother nearly died. The power felt like a drug, but it was a power that terrified her.

"I think I understand," Olivia said.

"Has it spoken to you?"

"Two days ago. It was so desperate to get out. It was

not like a voice in my head. More like a dog at the end of its leash. Thrashing and wailing, you don't need to understand it to know what it wants."

"It knows it can demand anything of you and so it does. We must give you discipline and control. In this way, we can stop it from freely burning. It is not a cure, but it can give us time as we look for one. No, keep your Focus raised. Always respect it. Discipline and respect for all magic. Even for the ones that oppose us."

"Even Shadow?" Olivia asked.

Elza fell quiet. It occurred to Olivia that no one might have been dumb enough to ask that question in front of her before. She agonized as the silence dragged for another awkward moment.

"We respect a wild cur because we know it can bite us. Now close your eyes and focus on clearing your mind."

Elza waited for her to follow the command. Her heart fluttered the way it did when she climbed a tall tree. Another day. Another leap. Another assumption that it would work out. Olivia closed her eyes. She tried to empty her mind, thoughts rising against her will as she looked for the Flame inside herself. The ruin fields south of home and the way the trees thrashed in the strong wind. Riding horses. Josie. Riding home to her family.

"Banish these thoughts," Elza said.

"How did you—"

"It's plain on your face. Concentrate."

As the memory left, a scream from the farm brought her back. She could see the horrid details of that night like they were playing before her. Blood on the ground. Green eyes glowing in the darkness. Her mother's teeth bared in pain. Sharp like the lumbira's. No, that was wrong. Her memories twisted and warped, hoping to make her suffer.

"Silence your mind. Find the Flame. Everything else is a distraction."

Blood spattered the walls of the Seers home. Tables were broken to pieces, and she stood alone in the house. The four-eyed beast held her fanged mother in its maw, fangs piercing her chest. She thrashed in its teeth and screamed for help.

Olivia was rooted in place, she wanted to run toward her mother. She was failing and she knew it. As soon as she took a step, the lumbira broke through the front doors of their home. A trail of blood and glass led into the darkness.

Come outside Olivia. I've found a way to teach you more, a voice said.

"Olivia, put these thoughts away. Wake up," another voice shouted.

The shining eyes in the darkness. The mentor. The monster. He stood just beyond the front door of the home. He held a blooming twig of applewood in his hand. His face was clean shaven. His skin was smooth and young. Shiny hair ran down to the nape of his neck and rose over his bushy eyebrows.

Yorker smiled, but his eyes glared at her in an unblinking stare. He beckoned with a wave of his hand as a pillar of fire burst to life behind him. The light glimmered off something squatting in the darkness. It was hungry for her spirit and the power that everyone else told her she had.

Hurry. It is waiting for us.

Olivia took a deep, gasping breath and immediately coughed as the air felt rough on her throat. She smelled smoke.

Elza rushed from candle to candle around the room. She smothered a fire that was spreading up one of her curtains with a wet towel. One of the tall candle holders was knocked over, but there was only a messy puddle where the candle should have been. Glancing around the room, Olivia saw every candle in the room was burnt up. The wax of the candles dried in long, oozing remains that cascaded down like frozen waterfalls. Only a few of them still held their wicks and burned. Elza smothered the last of the fire and composed herself. She handed a cup of water to Olivia before sitting across from her again.

"Your ability fits a wildfire. It is out of control. Powerful. Unwieldy. One other detail that is not helping, that Focus of yours is extraordinarily powerful. A skilled mage could do great things with it," Elza said.

Olivia swallowed the water with desperate gulps. It felt like she was dousing something within. She drank it down within seconds and steadied her breath before speaking.

"Is it the problem?" she asked.

"Perhaps. Bonding to a Focus is supposed to be a painful, lengthy process. When a Focus is made, it bonds to its maker. It is similar to ripping a part of yourself away when it changes owners."

"It has this habit of staying in my hand. I just pick it up and forget to put it down," Olivia said.

Elza's head bobbed low as she puzzled the relic in front of her. The unbending woman was replaced with a tenacious researcher. She seemed two decades younger by the speed and energy of her voice.

"It is incredibly odd. I've read some texts from the

Archive Primeval in Naelan, masters of elemental knowledge and experimentation. They suggest that a Focus may be easier to bond with if it passes to a blood relative."

"Do you know whose it is?"

Elza bounced where she sat. "I was going to ask you the same thing. Where did you find it?"

"In the ruin fields south of the Seventh. We never took anything before, we aren't thieves. This is the only thing I ever left with."

"A fire mage from the war perhaps? It is possible that this was some distant relative."

"I think my parents would have told me if my ancestors were mages," Olivia said.

"They might not have known. So much knowledge has been lost, entire families annihilated. We will try this again tomorrow. You should rest."

Elza took the empty cup from Olivia. She reached for a pitcher to refill it.

Olivia drank from the cup again and offered the Focus to Elza. "Don't you want this?"

"Why would I?"

Olivia blinked and her outstretched hand wavered. "Safety? Something about temptation or power or some other sagely proverb? I think it would be safer away from me."

Elza smiled and nodded.

"Though it would surely stop you from using more Flame magic, I am here to teach you discipline. It will better your relationship with it if you are around it at all times. It is a part of you now. Treat it accordingly."

Olivia pulled the Focus back to her and cradled it against her breast. "It remembers, doesn't it?"

"A Focus isn't really sentient as we understand it."

"I mean magic, the elements. Do they remember us?"

"They appear to. It is hard to speak to the personality of a literal force of nature or what it thinks about. We still know so little. But for my coin, they remember everyone who can speak to them."

Olivia pocketed the Focus and took another drink of water.

"I will retire to my quarters for a while. Take all the time you need. Just close the door on your way out," Elza said.

"Thanks."

Elza left the room. The kitchen was directly outside the door and the backyard was on the other side of the kitchen. Olivia took the cup of water with her as she left Elza's office. She closed the door and went to set down her cup when a shape rose from behind the table. It was tall and cast a large shadow across the room. Olivia nearly fell on her back before recognizing the ponytail and broad shoulders of her sister.

"Damn you, Josie. You scared me."

"Sorry, I didn't know it was you until you were too close." Her sister hunched down a little and leaned against the table.

"Well, you could have said something," Olivia said.

"Would a disembodied voice from somewhere in the room have helped that much?"

Olivia set the empty cup on the table. "What're you doing here anyway?"

"John's taking a nap. I haven't seen him this sluggish since he came home twenty ales deep and did not leave his room until he was dry."

"You weren't eavesdropping, were you?" Olivia asked with an accusatory eyebrow.

"Not at all. Just conveniently nearby to hear someone shouting about a fire."

Olivia pulled out a chair from the kitchen table and sat down, her hands shook as she did.

"It didn't go well. This thing, it's heightening my pain, my worries. I don't feel like my old self. I just about burnt down the church."

"You hardly meant it though, right? Eh, no reason to worry. These people love Flame. They would probably say thanks if you burnt the place down. Flame keep you indeed."

Olivia smiled politely, not ready to giggle.

"I'm just trying to make you laugh," Josie said.

"I know, thank you." Olivia drew a sharp breath, unable to shake the image of her dying mother. "I saw things. Bad memories on my mind, it was like I was living them all over again."

"You'll make progress, this Elza lady seems sharp for a mage. A little up tight, a little cold, but sharp. Let her muddle around, then we can figure out a way to get magic out of our lives for good."

"It's not *our* lives. It's my life," Olivia corrected.

"I'm looking out for you."

"I get that. This curse needs to be dealt with. I know that and we will. But I'm starting to think I can't walk away from all of it."

Josie looked at her for a long moment, another probing glare.

"It's only trouble. Ever since I found that thing and whatever business happened between you and Mage Yorker. This stuff isn't worth holding onto. You've been saying so for years," Josie said.

"Did you wonder if I was lying? Not just to you. Maybe I was lying to myself?"

Josie fell silent and leaned back from the table. Olivia rubbed her brow as a headache rose in her flushed forehead. This was not her, this was not how she wanted to treat her own sister, like some conniving opponent.

"Sorry, I'm tired and you don't get it. There is something that happened that I didn't tell you. In the ravine, when the lumbira found us again?"

"Yeah, you gave it the slip. You've always been fast."

"Not this time." She removed the Focus from her pocket and set it on the table. Josie's lip curled at the sight of it.

"I was cornered and lost. It was just a thicket of bushes and tree branches in that forest and I ran out of ideas. I was hiding, but not well enough. So I thought about my old lessons. I know that all happened before you joined our family, but before all the bad blood, I did learn a few things."

"That creep taught you to polish his shoes and run chores for him?"

"What else could I do? The Flame was bursting out of my chest. It wanted to get out and I asked the only other thing I thought of: Life. It remembered me, Josie. It was so happy that I came back to it. And using that magic, it saved me. I wouldn't be here if I didn't reach out to it."

Josie tilted her head to the side and cocked an eyebrow. Her lips bunched like she was going to spit on her.

"So we're a mage now?"

This was the fight Olivia dreaded. No, dread was not the right word. That would suggest that this could be avoided. She sensed that it was inevitable, especially after today. Josie's protectiveness would lead nose first into this argument. No avoiding it now.

"I don't know. Everything's still the same. Magic ruined the world, caused the war, split nations and families—"

"Oh shut up, none of that matters to you."

Olivia furrowed her eyebrows and the small, angry voice grew a little louder as her headache worsened. "What?"

"Whatever happened with that creep Yorker, that is why you hate magic. Sure, the history stuff is bad, but that doesn't involve you. Olivia, magic has not saved you. I've saved you, please see that."

"Josie—"

Her sister leaned over the table and pointed a finger in her face.

"Whose back did you sleep on the entire way here? Who gave you food and water when John went to sleep early at camp? Who held off the Shadow Wolf so you could hide in the woods? I've been there for you every step of the way."

"You have, I'm not saying you're not. I am grateful."

The angry voice told her to lash out. It felt like another voice in her throat. Like another brain in her skull. She dug her nails into the table and pursed her lips. Despite her best efforts, her thoughts began to blend together.

"It's messing with your head. Magic put us here, you can't go changing on me, I don't even understand you saying these things. Not after everything that has happened. It's not you."

"Life protected me in the forest. It saved me again when Alkis got me to use it yesterday," Olivia said.

"And we are here in the first place because of it. Life is different from Flame, yeah whatever. It is still nasty trickery that put my sister an inch from death's door and I caused it."

Olivia shook her head and stood. She tried to focus on that, but the Flame wanted her to go wide. Complain about her impulsiveness, it said. Assert your authority as an elder. This welp was out of her depth and needed correcting. She barely held onto the real thread: Josie felt guilty.

"This isn't your fault."

Josie sniffed back furious tears and her towering frame rose over Olivia. Her sister was trying to drown her grief with rage. Olivia thought that maybe they all had a little Flame in them.

"I grabbed it out of a skeleton's damned claw and gave it to you. I invited this chaos into our lives. Now you're joining it because some crone in a white dress told you you're special."

"Elza only wants to help. You're being paranoid," Olivia said.

"She seemed awfully keen to help when she found out you were afflicted. They both were."

"They're trying to help people."

"But I'm not allowed to listen because I'm not the one she is interested in," Josie growled.

Olivia rubbed her face. She knew Josie would not budge an inch. Why am I even fighting? She's useless, she's why I'm here. Her mind conjured words she dared not entertain.

"You should keep John company. You two can gaggle all you want about what's right for me," Olivia said.

"What does that mean?"

"You are not in charge of whether I use magic or not and you are damned well not in charge of my opinions."

"You would be dead if I wasn't here," Josie barked.

The heat surged and Olivia's world shook. Beads of sweat ran down her forehead and she staggered against the table. The Flame put words into her mouth, words she did not believe.

"If we hadn't adopted you, I wouldn't be dying right now."

Josie reeled back from the table as Olivia collapsed to the ground.

"Olivia? Olivia, help!" Josie shouted.

In the dimming, waking world, Olivia could see Josie's furious, tear-streaked face fade to black.

"Olivia, please stay awake."

Chapter Fourteen

A deep buzz thrummed in her ears. It changed pitch as it echoed through the dark. A man hummed a tune between rinsing flushes of water. Wooly bed sheets scratched between her fingers.

She was in a long annex. The crates of spare parchment and dried goods were stacked along the unpainted stone walls. The afternoon sun shined through the double-paned window. Alkis sat on a stool next to her, a bucket of water on the ground. He squeezed another flush of water from the towels before he noticed she was awake. His mouth turned up at the edges with a quiet smile.

"Welcome back. How do you feel?"

The smile faded into a focused frown as he felt her pulse with rough, callused fingers. She was too occupied with the aches in her joints to notice the flush in her cheeks.

"What happened?"

"You were doing what all good siblings do," Alkis said.

"Which is?" she asked.

He smirked and twisted the moist towel.

"The way she told it, you two were arguing and you passed out. She didn't say what you were talking about, but it must have been something tense if it agitated the Flame. Your Focus is safe. It's in Elza's office under lock and key."

"Did I lose control again? Did I start another fire?"

"Not a literal fire, though you might have stoked some embers with your sister that will need dousing."

The memory came back to her. The argument, shouting. Stars above, she remembered everything that she said. The whittling anxiety pulled her back against the bed. Nothing else mattered but making this right.

"Where is she now?"

"She's clearing her head in town. That or stew on it. I guess we'll find out. Your uncle followed after her," he said.

"I would never have said those things. I said we were better off without her. Stars, what was I thinking? I can't explain how it felt. I was out of control."

Olivia felt that it might be better to crawl into a hole. She could not imagine the pain it might have caused.

"The worst anger you've ever felt? It's not you, not the reasonable you anyway. Don't let it bother you too much," Alkis said.

She sat up on the cot.

"You're afflicted too?"

"No. I've been trained to use the barest amount of Flame, not enough to risk affliction. But when I wield it, I can feel it trying to creep in. The Flame is a part of us. It just excites our essence. It can spill over into," Alkis searched for the right words, "stronger emotions."

"You're a Fire Keeper?" Olivia said.

She heard stories about people with his talents. Fire Keepers wore a suit of smoldering, stone armor and only answered to the far-off nation of Katoia. Their touch could set you aflame and they did not know mercy. At least, as the stories said. He paused as he squeezed water out of the towel again and winced.

"Was. I left the order three years ago."

Looking him over, she expected to find a battle scar or a tattoo tallying his kills. His arms were not especially muscled, his eyes were deep and warm, and he did not fidget with an uncontrollable urge to murder and burn. This was not what she imagined a Fire Keeper to be.

"But you're just a monk."

"Monk-ish. It's not that specific around here."

"The stories I've heard say something else."

His calm demeanor cracked with a twist of his lip.

"Did you think of some big, armored soldier that puts entire villages to the pyre? Invulnerable, implacable, and coated in fire?" he asked.

Olivia nodded, frightened that he might confirm it.

"They're not invincible bloodhounds like they're made out to be," Alkis said.

They're human, just like anyone else, she thought. Maybe just as afraid as she would be, but with the tools to face down any challenge.

"Is it part of your training to give away weeks of your life to strangers?"

He shook his head and tapped his chest. "That part's all me. I'm sure you don't want to hear about it. You're not here by your own choice."

Elza was a bit of a schemer, but Alkis was something else. He cooked and cleaned. He did not quote scripture despite claiming he knew it. It was almost like he was just bumming a place to live, but chose a profession that was reviled.

"Actually, I would like to know. Consider it an official request," she said with a small grin.

He chuckled and ran his fingers through his deep red

hair.

"I guess since you're asking. I served the Fire Keepers for a few years fighting rebels and Shadow Beasts. The latter felt good, like I was helping people. But that wasn't the regular job. First and foremost, I kept people in line."

Alkis occupied his hands by playing with the moist towel.

"Years of service and I felt that I only helped the people in charge. If the poor were hungry to the point of revolt, we settled them. If someone expressed sympathy for another nation, they were questioned. If someone was afflicted with Flame, they were left to burn. I was taught it was a sign of weakness." He shook his head.

"So I left, walked away from my family, my friends… Elza gives to charities and the needy, but will help mages in need too, a rarity in these lands. So I joined her. I abandoned everything for a chance to help people."

Olivia was beginning to believe he was genuine, that he was not a mage with an ulterior motive.

"So what was I to you?" she asked.

"Someone who needed help worse than most other people. You felt like—" He stopped himself and waved away a thought. "It's stupid, never mind."

"What?"

"It's Church of Flame stuff. All that crap you don't believe in."

Of everyone here, Alkis kept to himself the most. He also happened to be the person who held her interest. She couldn't fight the instinct to let him be and nudged his shoulder.

"I'm stuck in this damn place. I'll just ask later if you don't tell me now."

He nervously adjusted in his seat. Despite a small pang of concern, she merely waited for him to finish.

"Fine. It felt like Flame put you here for a reason. You are my test, my proof that what I'm doing is right, that I made the right decision. I wanted to save the afflicted: here you are."

Her feelings were as clear as dishwater. She felt panic at the pressure and expectation. A small, needy part of her warmed at the sound of his voice telling her how much she meant to him. There was confusion about what would come next. Above all the smaller, confused emotions, she felt relief. It confirmed that her fears about magic might have been all made up. He was a mage who only grew more as he used his power. Not all mages were like her previous mentor.

Her face flushed. "That seems like a lot."

"Yeah, I didn't intend to tell you that. But you asked—"

"I did."

"—and it felt right to tell you."

The door to the room swung open and Elza entered. She wore her full ceremonial garb, the golden collared white robe. Her snow-colored hair was done into elaborate braids and a necklace emblazoned with a sigil of Flame dangled from her neck. Behind her, the voices of worshippers echoed off the walls.

"She wakes." Elza crossed over to them.

"I'm doing much better. I think I was agitated after our lesson," Olivia said.

"So you were. I shouldn't have left you alone. Alkis," Elza turned to him, "Could you supervise the end of the service?"

"Of course," Alkis said.

He stood and rubbed at his neck. An indecisive half-nod toward Olivia and a small smile was all he could muster. Focus in one hand, pail of water in the other, he closed the door behind him as he left. If there were mages like him out there, it meant she could escape Yorker's fate. Demonstrating control might calm Josie's suspicions to this entire place.

"I want to try again," Olivia said.

"So soon?" Elza shook her head and sat on the foot of the bed.

"I'm ready. Now I know what the risks are, we just have to keep trying."

"You have a natural talent for someone who is untrained. Most new mages have a hard time manifesting anything on their first attempt. Tell me about your previous teacher."

Olivia's vigor drained at the request. As much as what happened still haunted her thoughts, letting them out of her head seemed far more frightening. She wanted to exist in the now. The past was nothing but pain.

"He was your typical, about-the-neighborhood mage. He had the gift of Life magic. I just got bored. You know how kids are," she lied.

Elza said nothing. Her eyes did not move from Olivia and the silence slowly pulled out the truth. Olivia tapped her hands on her knee, unable to match Elza's stare.

"I'm not fooling you, am I?"

"No," Elza said, "Speak and walk with me."

Olivia grabbed a cup of water that Alkis left on the small bedside table. She took a long drink before following Elza out the door.

"I showed talent at a young age, maybe ten? My

mother tells me that I was making daisies bloom in her garden and cornstalks dance by the age of five. They decided to have me trained. We're well off, but they didn't exactly have plentiful choices for a mentor."

Elza kept pace with Olivia as they walked down the long hallway that led into the worship hall. All the parishioners had left. Only the distant sound of conversation outside of the church lingered.

"There was one mage in town: Clarence Yorker. He was more of a plant doctor than a teacher. He would purge a crop of blight or help you figure out why your pepper plants were slow to bloom, whatever you needed.

"My parents asked him to teach me and paid him as an incentive. He hesitated, but they were insistent to cultivate my gift. My mother said it was a part of me. She still thinks that. He agreed and I learned under him for three months. He lived on the north edge of town, a long ride from our farmhouse. There were a few times I stayed at his place so we could get to the next lesson bright and early. It was a lot for a child, but I was excited."

Elza listened with little emotion on her face. They passed through the wide hallways that ran along either side of the main chamber and into the central worship hall. The array of mirrors shifted so it no longer caught the light of the sun.

"The first few weeks were small lessons, very similar to what you've tried with me. I learned to listen to Life's voice."

"What was your Focus?" Elza asked.

"It was a rock, just a really smooth rock I found the first day I was at Yorker's farm. I painted it green."

Olivia smiled as the memory came to her. All this trouble with the amulet and she nearly forgot her first

Focus. They reached the steps before the dais and Elza gestured for her to sit.

"After two months, I was surpassing things that he thought would take a year or more to learn," Olivia said.

"You were a natural," Elza said with a smile.

"Yorker was like an uncle. I would stay at his house a few days of the week and he would be over at our farmstead for dinner on other days. Things were good, but he knew he was reaching the limits of what he could teach. Instead of just calling it there, he tried to push his own limits. He tried to make Water answer his voice. He spoke to the Earth, hoping to learn the secrets of making it move. He even explored Death. It wasn't so taboo for a frontier town that is accustomed to it. I don't think he had much success."

"What about the other one?" Elza asked.

Olivia nodded with a sad smile.

"He did. I don't know if it was an accident or if he sought it out, but he did speak to the Shadow. He did not seem too different at first. Of course, I didn't really understand what was happening. My parents had no capability to warn me against it in concept. All I knew was to stay home after dark. Yorker was certainly excited to be learning more things that he could teach me. I would stay up after my bedtime there and watch him."

Elza listened, but a knowing frown crept onto her face. Olivia imagined she knew this kind of story very well.

"He would walk to the edge of the fire at night, right on the line where the torches could not reach. I heard him talking, but I never understood. After a few weeks of this, I noticed he was frantic around sunset. I thought he was angry. Now I know he was steeling himself for what

Shadow asked him to do. He mentioned me to the Shadow from his earliest meditations. It wanted Yorker to prove his devotion for more power. It wanted a sacrifice."

Olivia squeezed her knees.

"One night, three months into his mentorship, he asked me to follow him outside after sunset. I was taught to listen to adults and I knew my family liked Yorker, but I was raised to avoid the dark. We all were. So I resisted."

****

Fourteen Years Ago

Olivia stood on the porch of Yorker's home and held the front door open. A bright torch burned in front of the house, stuck on a tall post. It reflected in the dingy, rustic windows. Beyond the fire light, at the edge of the yard, Yorker stood in the half-darkness. His long hair was tied back, a small beard clumsily bound into knots and spotted with beads. His teeth were barred in an unnerving smile that did not match his eyes.

"This is the next step, Olivia. It's safe, it only wants us to learn," Yorker said.

She shook her head. "Mom and dad say to stay inside the light. It's dangerous outside."

"A lesson taught to keep babies in their beds at night. Are you a baby?" Yorker asked.

Olivia shook her head again.

"Absolutely right, you're not. You will surpass me. But for you to do that, we need to take that first step."

Olivia was rooted to her spot on the porch. The confluence of worries put ice into her little arms and legs. Should she listen to her parents? Yorker was a friend though, and an adult. Olivia was taught to listen to adults that she knew. She set one small foot forward and then leaned back, unable to make a decision. Yorker groaned and stamped his foot. He kneeled down to her height.

"I want you to come with me. I need you to come with me, it won't tell me anything more until I do."

"What won't? I don't see anything."

"My teacher. It's in the woods right now. Come on, I'll show you."

Yorker yanked on her arm, nearly pulling her completely clear of the porch. She shouted and pulled at his fingers. They dug into her arm like a vice. Too weak to help, her feet dragged through the dirt.

"Clarence, stop!"

Tears grew in her eyes as the darkness neared.

"We don't have any more time." His smile snapped into a snarling frown. "She's coming," he shouted into the darkness.

"Let me go!"

A branch snapped in the darkness and the boughs of the trees shifted. A shape moved forward under the canopy, where the moonlight could not reach. Only the faintest glimmer of the torch light behind her reflected in its black eyes. It stank of mold and dirt. Tendrils of an even-deeper darkness swam around it like tentacles. It stood taller than a man, the details impossible to discern in the dark. Its eyes laid on her, flashing with the same shine as a wolf.

"Bring her closer," it said.

Olivia was too frightened to scream. She dug her fingernails into Yorker's skin and tore at his arm. He screamed and his fingers slipped enough to yank herself free. She ran back to the house, bounded over the porch, and closed the door behind her. Yorker's steps just behind her. She was not tall enough to get the top lock of the door, but she twisted the one she could reach.

"Olivia! Please, please come back!"

He pounded on the door. She ran beneath the table where they shared many meals and sobbed as she clung to a table leg. Yorker pressed his face against the window. He was half-lit by the torch outside. His teeth snapped and cursed, no longer the comforting man she once knew. She crossed her fingers and hoped the door would not give, the only thing she could think to do.

Yorker squinted into the window and saw her cowering beneath the table. His shoulders dropped, the rage disappearing at the sight of her. A gasping breath left him as he stopped shouting. He stepped back from the window and looked over his bleeding arm in the light. Tears gathered in his eyes.

"I'm sorry Olivia. I—"

His voice failed as he turned to the dark woods. Yorker leaned against the wall of his home and sat. In the distance, the trees thrashed.

"No! You don't get her. Never. Go away! I don't care anymore. You can keep it."

As Yorker spoke to the voice beyond the light, it almost scared her as much as his anger. He sounded looney to her. She wondered how she might get home if he completely snapped. After a moment, his voice faded and he spoke through the crack in the door. His voice was a weak, fragile thing.

"Go to bed Olivia, I won't bother you tonight. We'll get you home when the sun rises. I'm sorry."

****

Olivia rubbed her hands together and looked around

the temple built to venerate magic.

"If Yorker was tempted—I mean he was a seasoned mage. He had been practicing for years at that point. I never wanted to touch it again after that. My Focus, I don't remember what I did with it."

Elza watched Olivia as she struggled through her memories. The cleric did not move a muscle and watched her as though some further truth might surface. Olivia felt itchy under her eyes. Like she was being judged.

"What if I ended up like him? What if I didn't have the sense to turn away once I hurt someone?"

The high cleric perched her wrinkled hand on Olivia's shoulder. Her fingers pressed lightly on her, but it was enough to feel the comfort.

"Magic is a choice," Elza said. "You have a choice of how you use it. Your old mentor made his and they are not yours. For what it's worth, I never would have pushed you beyond what you were ready for."

"Would have?" Olivia asked.

"While you were asleep, I spent time reflecting on what I have gleaned from our lessons. I thought that you may have put the cure to affliction on my doorstep."

Elza sighed and looked up to the large, round window above them. Her sad eyes drifted from the sunlight overhead to the symbol of the church on the side of the dais. The woman made of fire, so strong in Olivia's eyes, finally showed the fading coals she was full of.

"All my years and I still am so small in the face of Flame's majesty. I cannot cure your affliction. If you remained here, it would only be a matter of time before you passed. You and your family must leave. And I intend to come with you," Elza said.

"Leave? We just got here."

The older woman shook her head.

"I have been trying to master Flame magic for decades. I know what it looks like when I am traveling down a road that will only become bumpier. Maybe if you showed up earlier we could have done something. Now the Flame is too strong, and it will not bow to you or to me. It certainly won't snuff itself."

Olivia tried to find the lie. She looked for the flash of deception in her eyes or the nervous frown hiding a plan in action. It never came. Olivia could hear John's voice in her head. He would certainly have an opinion of the best place to go. She could feel this new home slipping away, she wanted Josie and John nearby again. Before Elza told her any of the details, Olivia already knew it would mean more magic and more trouble. It would mean going deeper into this world she avoided for so long.

"What did you have in mind?" she asked.

"The Naelan Enclaves are home to the Archive Primeval. Generations of the world's most dedicated mages have made it their home. A fortress of research. A vault full of the collected knowledge of the elements."

"Naelan? That's on the other side of the world," Olivia said.

"Not as far as it might sound. As long as I am here to mentor you, I believe we can keep the affliction under control. Months if we are lucky."

"But what about the church? All this?"

"Cleric Alkis has long searched for purpose in his new life. He will be a fitting successor."

"You barely know me."

Elza nodded. "True. Our lot in life is to help the

177

needy, it is our call. This isn't all charity though. This is a chance for me to speak with the most wizened of sages in the world. I've been trying for years to find a cure for flame affliction, what if it's already been found?"

Olivia could think of one more question.

"When do we leave?"

One of the white-robed clerics walked into the worship hall and bowed deeply as they crossed the threshold of the worship hall. Olivia recognized him as one of the few people that assisted Elza.

"I'm sorry to interrupt, I just wanted to see if the new convert found you. He seemed so flustered. A life in need of guidance if I've ever seen one," the man said.

Elza looked to Olivia and then back to him. "New convert?"

"Yes, he was wearing white clothing. Very close to the clergy robes now that I think of it."

Elza stood and pointed at the door to the church. "Go find Alkis, tell him to come find me. Olivia, follow me."

Olivia walked close behind Elza. "What's wrong?"

"We don't have converts. Anyone can just show up."

They crossed through the kitchen to find her office door was still shut. Elza reached into her pocket and retrieved a small golden orb on a chain, small enough to be a necklace. She wrapped the chain around her fist and seated the golden orb in her palm. Now that they were close, Olivia could hear rustling and banging from inside. Elza flung open the door.

A man poured through every book, cabinet drawer, and container in the room. Papers were scattered. Tomes pulled from their shelves and carelessly tossed onto the floor. He wore a white robe as was described, but Olivia did not recognize him. His messy, dark hair clung to his forehead and large bags hung under his eyes. Thin and lanky, he jumped when they burst into the room.

In his right hand was Olivia's Focus. As his eyes went from Elza and to Olivia, his surprise melted for a moment. He seemed as though he might ask her a question. The odd expression passed as Elza charged the intruder.

"Thief!"

The intruder leaped across the desk as Elza swung her fist at him. She twisted her Focus down toward the open window. A gust of hot air blew against the window and the thief threw his hand up to cover his face. He did not see the window close against the gust and he ran face first into the glass pane. He cursed and dropped the Focus. His eyes cracked open, and he kicked Elza's chair toward her. The old woman tripped and fell to the ground.

Olivia grabbed a heavy book off the table and flung it at the thief. He turned in time for the spine of the book to catch him in his nose. Not waiting for his next move, she barreled into his chest. Even as he reeled from the blow, he quickly turned aside and she rolled off of him. He caught the windowsill and pushed the window open again. Within a moment, he slipped through the window, jumped back to his feet, and ran toward the tree line. Olivia heard other voices coming from the hall. She reached for the windowsill and prepared to jump over it.

"Stop! Don't go," Elza said.

"He is a criminal. We can't let him run," Olivia said.

Elza leaned over and grabbed Olivia's Focus from where it fell. She handed the relic to Olivia and looked out the window. The thief's white robes had disappeared into the forest.

"Our new friend is fast. A career criminal for certain. I doubt we would be able to catch him if we wanted to."

"I've crossed forests thicker than this on foot."

"And you likely were not afflicted at the time."

Olivia did not notice the heat building in her neck until Elza reminded her. The Flame was urging her to leap out the window as much as her own will. She worried that this was even an illusion and that the Flame might be guiding her thoughts.

Elza patted her shoulder. "Remember your temper. Control your breathing."

Alkis burst into the door, gasping for breath.

"What happened? Where is he?" Alkis asked.

"Out of our hair for now. I would not presume that we are done with him though. This place isn't a fortress, and he might return with friends. I was hoping not to get the town militia involved," Elza said.

She crossed the office and put a few books back on her desk.

"Like they will listen to us," Alkis muttered before he turned to Olivia. "Are you alright?"

"I'm fine. Elza was the one about to thrash the thief's hide."

"I knew you took after the old bird, always able to handle herself," he said.

"I hate when you call me that." Elza closed the window and locked it. "Alkis, you stay here and guard Olivia. There is a trapdoor under the kitchen table. Hide there if something happens before I get back."

Elza left the office, Alkis and Olivia following behind her.

"You're actually going to give them the satisfaction? If you tell the town guard about this, they'll just use it as a reason to throw us out of town. I can handle this," Alkis said.

"I believe in your capabilities, but we need eyes and light. We have to sleep at some point and I believe the thieves are going to rely on that. The sooner the better," Elza said.

"This seems a little extreme. He was scrawny. Let's just lock the doors and call it a night," Olivia said.

Elza slowed and turned to face the two of them again.

"You blow through my door with a relic from the great war. We have never had a break in over my thirty years here, but sure as the sun rises, we get our first the day after your arrival. *This* is no coincidence," Elza said.

Elza patted Olivia's hands and conjured the best smile she could manage. Anxiety built behind her eyes like a leaking dam.

"Stay safe child. Alkis, I expect you to be in one piece as well."

Alkis gave her a solemn nod and turned his Focus over in his palm. The high cleric walked out the front door and descended the long, steep road into the city.

Chapter Fifteen

Tomis tore off the white robe as soon as he broke through the tree line. He stuffed it into the hollow of a trunk and emerged onto the side of the long, coast-facing road. He got off it at the first opportunity and went down a narrow side street. His boots squelched across a congealed mat of political flyers papering the ground.

He almost had it. It was in his hand, his freedom guaranteed. Instead, he was lucky to have gotten away at all. How did that damned window close? He specifically left it open. Maybe he was getting soft after all. Tomis massaged his nose and winced at the touch. The other woman was spot on with that throw.

He knew that shade of dark blonde hair and the subtle wave of it, the strong chin, and her lack of hesitancy to jump into the fray. There was no mistaking it. Tomis knew in his bones that was John's niece. Tomis considered the chance that there were more, that the entire Seers family was in danger because of him.

His gambit failed. He hoped to steal the Focus and slip out unseen. John would not need to be involved, Faldir would get what she wants, and Tomis would walk away from all this, ready to run a nasty con on the next sap who hired him. Or find somewhere to hide. He hardly knew his captors. If Faldir had any sort of heart, sympathy even, maybe she would honor her word.

Now to stay alive, he would have to sell out John

Seers and his niece. The sun would set soon, not that the people cared. There were so many lanterns and candles, it was like night could never really fall here. He resumed his brisk pace and circled back around to the warehouses near the edge of town.

"I'm still breathing, doesn't matter how," he said to himself.

Tomis reached the front of the abandoned store and knocked on the door four times. A second passed before the door slid open and Tomis stepped through. A musky stink flooded his nostrils as he entered. Faldir sat on a chair in the middle of the room. She might have been trying to show an air of calm and control, but her hands fidgeted as Tomis entered.

"Where is it?" she asked.

He briefly considered lying to her.

"I don't have it. But! But, but, but it is there. I almost had it. Some of the clergy beat me up."

The Hooded Man growled behind Tomis. He pointed to the bleeding gash across his nose.

"And you left them alive?" Faldir asked.

"Yeah. Wait, do you think I am an assassin? I've never hurt anyone. Well, physically anyway. I don't want to go down what I've done to people financially, emotionally—"

Faldir rose, gripped the back of her chair, and flung it at Tomis. His reaction was a second too late and it collided with his right knee. He fell under it and grasped at his leg.

"Look! You know where it is. Just let me live."

Faldir walked over and gave his injured leg a small kick. Tomis winced in pain.

"I should be cutting your throat right now."

"What are they going to do? Smuggle it out of the city tonight? They worship the sun. They're too damn scared of the dark to go anywhere."

"Does it look like night? The sun has not died yet. They could be leaving right now. Tie him up," Faldir said to the Hooded Man.

The creature lifted Tomis from the ground and righted the nearby chair. He dropped Tomis into the seat with a solid shove and retrieved a bind of rope from a bag under his cloak. Faldir slipped on her travel cloak.

"You confirmed the Focus's position but did not bring it back to us. This falls into our maybe category if I recall. As much as you are a worm, you helped us and I am a woman of my word. I won't kill you here, as long as we retrieve the Focus."

"Wait," the Hooded Man said.

"Why would we wait?" Faldir asked.

"Wait for night. Sun still up."

She hissed with irritation. "We are leaving now. I don't have time for this."

The Hooded Man muttered something in his deep, feral tone. He finished tying Tomis to the chair and tipped it onto its back two legs.

Faldir leaned over Tomis and slipped a finger under his chin.

"If they are already gone or you were lying, we will come back and I will let my companion eat the beating heart out of your chest." Faldir's finger traced down his throat and jabbed him.

"It's there. I promise, it's there. Just let John live if you can. And anyone else he might be with."

Faldir's eyes narrowed and she grinned.

"So, he did bring family with him?"

"For me?" Tomis pleaded, "a favor for a pleading worm?"

"If anyone stands between me and the Focus, they will die. Too bad you betrayed your last, living friend for your own skin. If we find the Focus, there won't be any reason to come back, you've already helped us so much. Gag him and leave him in the warehouse. If the rats don't eat him, he will have plenty of time to commune with Shadow before he starves to death."

His heart fluttered in his chest. Death haunted him at every step; he could hear the scythe descending. He thrashed against his restraints, a nervous sweat building on his brow. There had to be another way. There was always a way out, things never went really bad.

"That wasn't the deal, let me go! I did everything that you—"

The Hooded Man clamped his hand over Tomis's mouth and dragged him through the narrow, cob-webbed hallway and into the pitch-black warehouse. As the light of the room faded into the darkness of the back room, Tomis considered that it wouldn't work out this time.

****

She planned to stomp around town for a few hours. Unfortunately, John decided to tag along. She told him what happened and left out the moment Alkis confirmed that Olivia was fine. Despite the danger of spending time in the city, he was determined to follow and brushed aside any concern of being recognized.

"I'm just stretching my legs. Might as well keep you company."

They walked down the streets of the city in one-sided silence. John insisted on chatting about everything. She was certain that he was trying to get her to think about something else. It was working. The more he made frivolous observations about the colors of doors and about the small birds that cluttered around spilled food, the more annoyed she was with him rather than with Olivia.

Their path took them along the coast and down to the southern edge of town. The chaotic web of docks was even more tangled up close. They were made of different kinds of wood and stood at different heights. Some signs were written in entirely different languages. Double-masted vessels were so tall that they needed pre-constructed ramps to unload their cargo. Bundles of barrels and crates were stored in mountainous piles to be wheeled into warehouses.

A horn called from the sea and blew three times. The first time registered no reaction from the idle dock hands. The second caused them to pause. The third sent several into a frenzy. People shouted and a few ran to a dock further down. A small crowd lingered at the end of the slip and looked out to sea. A man with a shaved head and a full beard stood at the front. He held an engraved, colorful seashell in his hand.

"She's listing to port," the bearded man said. "Open the doors. I can bring her up."

A merchant ship, sleek and capped with a lion's head on the prow, sailed into dock at frightening speed. The ship was tilted on its side and sunk lower toward the water line. The crew aboard were busy running down into the ship with buckets and cups, anything that could hold water. They would emerge seconds later and flung water over the side of the ship.

"It's jammed!" someone shouted from the warehouse door across from the slipway.

The salt-stained warehouse was tall enough to house one of these titanic vessels. A large beam sat across the double doors of a ship hangar. Several people were trying to force the crossbeam out to no avail.

"The beam's swollen. It's stuck!"

"Get it open. I won't be able to hold it forever," the bald man called back.

Josie ran over to join the people trying to lift the beam. Squatting to the right side of it, she flipped her hands backward and readied to lift it.

"Push when I say so," Josie said.

"Who the shade are—oh."

They fell silent at the sight of the towering woman.

"Let her help. You give us the word," the bald man said.

"Alright." She took a deep breath and flexed. "One, two, three!"

The beam squeaked as her muscled arms forced it out of the brace. It popped free and the three dock workers lifted it free of the left side. They pushed it aside and slid the double doors of the warehouse open. The slipway continued inside until it reached a set of wooden frames. Josie looked back at the ocean. The ship was coming dangerously close to the sea wall.

"How is one man getting that ship up here? They'll crash," she said.

One of the dock hands giggled. "Oh, you just let him do his thing, it's a treat."

The bald man stepped to the edge of the water. He closed his eyes and slowly lifted the seashell into the air and an azure glow gathered inside of the shell. As he did, the sea roiled. Waves manifested from placid water and pushed into the sides of the sinking ship. The waves built, one upon the other, and pushed until the ship began to rise. The sea rose with it. Water poured up the spillway as the entire ship rose out of the tide.

The mage carried the seashell in his hand like a toy boat, matching the ship's progress up the spillway. The roiling sea moved it onto land. Josie could not help but stare as the ship made its way up into the hangar. The crew watched over the railings of their ship. Some beamed in amazement and others were relieved to not be sinking.

The mage moved the seashell in front of him and took a few more steps to place it inside of the warehouse's repair rigging. The bow of the ship knocked into the far end of the frames and dock workers readied a set of ropes and a large brace across the stern. As the bald man let the seashell down, the bed of water splashed across the ground. A small tide washed over Josie's shoes as it returned to the ocean. John caught up with her and patted her on the back.

"By the Seventh and everything that walks, that was magic," she said.

"Water mages are a little limited to where they can do their stuff. Give them a little water and, oh boy, can they," John said.

The bearded man walked past the two of them and gave Josie a small nod.

"Thank you, miss. Would have been a sticky situation without you stepping in," he said.

"Well…" she stammered over her words, "I guess I had to help."

The crew threw down rope ladders or stepped out onto the repair platforms on either side of the ship. On the left side, the hull was scarred with large slices like someone had taken a titanic kitchen knife to it. On either side of the damage were O-shaped imprints dug into the hull. The dock workers got to work on repairs and the crew took a moment to appreciate dry land.

Josie told herself that she only helped because it was the right thing to do. If she knew there was a mage among them, maybe she would have felt differently. Of course, she knew it was a lie. She saw an opportunity to help and took it. Magic or not, it would have felt wrong to let the ship go down or crash into the docks. She kept her eye on the bald Water mage as she walked away. He stowed his Focus and helped the sailors down from the wounded vessel.

Warehouse crews wrapped up their day and followed these coastal streets to the many taverns and watering holes. An establishment named the Gray Whale boiled with voices and music, songs and cheers echoing from the open door. The evening sun had plenty of light to give, but a dingy light bulb buzzed next to the front door.

"That was nice of you to step in and help," John said.

"Back there? It's nothing. I'm sure that dirty mage could have handled it without me."

"They needed the help, y'know. But it bears remembering that sometimes stepping in is the wrong thing to do. An overstep, let's call it that." John spoke slowly, every word weighed and measured. John's roundabout way of talking was only funny when it wasn't directed at herself.

"What are you getting at? Out with it."

"Nothing. I'm just chit-chatting. I'm Uncle John, I don't scheme."

"Oh, what a lie. Do you listen to yourself or just drift

in and out?" she said.

"Anymore. I don't scheme anymore. That was another life and I promised your father I wouldn't talk about it," he said.

"A little late for that. We were almost killed because of that other life."

He ran fingers through his hair. "Yeah, don't remind me."

"You were a fence, right?" she asked.

He frowned. It tickled Josie to needle him like this.

"Where did you learn that word?"

"So that is a yes?"

"I didn't say that. Your wholesome country life shouldn't include things like fences and rackets and the like," he said.

"Well, I learned it from dad."

John shook his head. "Would you believe him? Don't tell them about what you do, don't show them how to pick locks, don't do this, don't do that. And he just turns around and tells you everything?"

"He didn't tell me everything."

For years, her dad did not even mention his brother. It was a shock to them all when he let them know that they had an uncle and he was coming to stay with them. She knew that John treated Josie like a niece and Olivia like a canker sore. To her sister's credit, she gave as well as she got. He taught Josie how to throw knives and told stories about the far edge of the world. Olivia was usually scorned for the slightest thing and forced to listen to his stories from a distance.

Of course, the thaw had begun. The two fought less and Josie would even describe it as co-existing. There was some sort of understanding building between the two of them. When they found out everything John lost, it was hard not to sympathize. She would never push her sister to make nice. Luckily, she didn't need to.

"You and Olivia seem to be getting along a bit better," she said.

"I always knew she was smart, how I usually give her trouble. Just figured that she wouldn't have the spine to cut it out in the world. The first daughter, the heiress, she's barely seen what's out there."

"John, we live in the world too. Just because Hasketter is remote, doesn't make it safe. It's just a different kind of danger."

"I know that now. Honestly, I regret writing her off as a silver-spooned, easy living, farm person. It was just so hard to get past it so soon after I lost it all. By the time I realized what an ass I was being, I couldn't stop."

"Because it was too much fun pissing everyone off?" Josie asked.

"It was easier to be angry."

Their conversation fell quiet again. They left the Gray Whale behind as they rounded a corner into a nearby market. Thinking about Olivia was a convenient distraction. Her mind was still on the dock, the ship, and John's chosen words.

"I knew what you meant earlier. I'm not dense," Josie said.

"What was I saying? I'm so absent minded and need to be reminded." John tapped his chin.

She scowled. "You don't have to gloat."

"Not gloating. Just observing."

"Two weeks ago, things were like they always were. We were at home, working, and doing chores. Harvest season will be coming around soon. I watched out for her. For my family. I understood all that, I had a use," she said.

"They look out for you too though."

"Them adopting me after the fire—" The words stopped in her throat. "After everything they've done for me, I'm the one who found that damn relic."

"Look Josie, you've been a sad sack since we left Hasketter."

"Ouch," Josie said.

John rolled his eyes upward and slapped his thigh.

"Sorry, I can do better. You've been struggling. I've seen it. Olivia has seen it. You need to let it go, because you don't owe us anything."

Only a few people traveled the roads as the sun crept closer to the horizon. A single group of vibrantly colored aristocrats played cards outside of a quiet tavern. The wind whipped over rooftops and fluttered a large flag. Where every other part of town was vibrant and occupied, this stretch of tile-roofed buildings had empty windows and rusty hinges.

"You've leaped to answer this problem. You helped her all the way out here. Even when the core problem, the thing that is really at issue here, is totally out of your control. You didn't make her use magic. You didn't know what it would do. I'm telling you this because things might get tough soon."

Josie's heart felt like it was on the verge of stopping for the last few days. This was not the hard part yet? The only thing she could imagine being worse was failure. If Olivia's illness progressed. The vaguest hint of her death almost sent Josie to her knees. It was her job to make sure that did not happen. She was the strongest and the fastest, but she still felt so lacking.

"Olivia is officially on a clock. The cure was a bust, so now we are hoping for a miracle. We're going to need you here. Can you do that?" John asked.

The answer was obvious to Josie: she would have to give even more. She nodded.

"I won't be nearby every time you need reminding. C'mon, let's get some food. That Alkis isn't a very good cook."

Every storefront around the small square was closed. Three carts were still open, but the owners were preparing to leave. Full of lettuce, carrots, and a picked over selection of grapes, they bought a small pouch full.

John paused as he handed over payment. He glanced at a row of abandoned storefronts nearby. They left the merchant behind to eat. She chewed on a mouthful of grapes when John stopped again. He turned to the closed store fronts and put a hand to his ear.

"Do you hear that?"

Josie craned her neck. The nearby nobility laughed loudly, the sound echoing across the plaza. She shook her head and swallowed a bite of food.

"That," John said.

As the laughter across the square died down, she heard a hollow banging sound. It echoed like a rock hitting the bottom of a dry well. Like a boot knocked against a wooden wall.

"No that's... oh it can't be though, right?"

It continued knocking randomly. As it continued, she picked up on a pattern: one knock, another knock, two knocks, one knock.

"We had a code back in the day... If one of us was in trouble, that was the code. One, one, two, one." John counted each knock on his fingers.

"Knocking?"

"A whistle, a horn, a knock. Anything. There's no way though, right? What are the odds of that?"

"What are the odds of a retired treasure hunter's friend being in town weeks after you get involved with a mysterious relic from the war?" Josie asked.

The knocking repetition continued. They followed the sound past store fronts until it led them to an abandoned store with a grimy window. A sign in the window said closed and a broken chain was coiled beneath it. John pressed his ear against the front door. The knocking came again.

"It's this one," he said.

John tried the door handle and pushed. When that failed, John threw his shoulder into the door. It did not budge. He stepped back and tried again, but only conjured a small cloud of dust. He stepped back from the door, but Josie's hand caught his shoulder.

"Would this be overstepping?" she asked.

"In fact, dear niece, it wouldn't be."

Josie stepped away from the store and charged. She lowered her head and then turned so that her shoulder collided with the door. It lifted from its hinges and smashed a chair that was propped against it from the inside. The storefront was long empty, only a few chairs scattered near a table. A doorway at the back of the room led deeper into the abandoned store. She rubbed her shoulder as John stepped past her.

"Tomis? Peter? Sweet sunlight, it's dark here. Do you have a light?" John asked.

Josie shook her head.

"Damn it."

He ran down the unlit hallway without a second

thought. The setting sun still offered enough light to see that the dusty floors were disturbed recently. There were three other sets of footprints beyond hers and John's. Josie could not track like Olivia could, but she knew the basics.

Two of them were recent, a set of drag marks where something was pulled. What puzzled her were a set of animal tracks alongside them. They were similar to a bear, but they walked on their hind legs. Two voices echoed from the darkened room beyond. Laughter rose up from the hallway as John stepped out of the cobwebs with a shorter man under his arm. His dark hair was flat. He limped on his right leg and nervously watched Josie.

"They grow them big out there, don't they?" the man said.

"That's my niece, Josie. Josie, this is an old friend of mine, Tomis."

"Oh, is he a crime friend?" she asked.

"She knows about that?" Tomis asked.

John waved a hand.

"It's not important, why are you here and tied up in a pitch-dark room?"

Tomis extended his fingers and turned his palms up. He chewed on his lip.

"I—I got into some trouble and I think they might be coming for you. We need to get out of here before they get back. Where's your other niece, is she around here too?" Tomis asked.

"Who? Who gets back?" John asked.

"Bad people. Shadow cultists, one's a void mage. Bad, bad people, John."

"How do you know Olivia?" Josie asked.

John fell quiet and his eyes narrowed.

"I might have run into her not too long ago. They made me check out the church. They want that Focus bad. What was I gonna do?"

Josie felt the urge to run back to Olivia as fast as she could. Whether she liked magic or not seemed to be such a small detail in the face of what Tomis said. The journey was not over. Olivia was not safe.

"Where are they now?" John asked.

Tomis licked his lips, a sure sign of an unwelcome answer to follow.

"The church, they're heading to the church."

John moved to the door and turned to Tomis. "You're coming too."

"What? I'm just an extra belly to feed, why do you need me?"

"Because you brought this madness onto my head. I can't make you come with us, but if you value the years we worked together, you owe me this much, at least."

John and Josie left the storefront and ran across the plaza. Tomis followed with faltering footsteps. She heard him let out a great sigh of resignation and begin running as well.

"Slow down, I'm coming."

Chapter Sixteen

Olivia walked from torch to torch around the church grounds. They burned with a dense, knotted wood. Doused in oil every night, weeks would pass before it needed to be replaced. The rest of the day was uneventful. No thieves returned, but neither had Elza. Without the high cleric nearby, she was on edge. The thief recognized her. Alkis waited by the front door as she finished up.

She turned over the Focus in her hand, oil pot in the other. The silence of the falling night gave her time to think. The cautious optimism about magic was becoming enthusiasm. There was no way to stop it. After a lifetime of refusing it, she felt that hesitancy was required. The unknown future made it worse. Her entire world was upended like dishware over a stone floor. Shattered beyond hope, there was the nagging thought that nothing would be the same again.

"Not much more to do. Elza should be back soon and then you can retire for the evening," he said.

"I was sleeping all day. That's the last thing I want right now."

They both stepped into the church foyer, the door to the main temple just ahead of them. The setting sun bathed it in an orange light that made the simple architecture seem regal. She could feel the history of their land seep into the walls of this place. Her time here was so fleeting. The hope in her heart could not douse the suspicion that she would not live to see this place again.

"Can I ask, did Elza share any details with you?" Olivia said.

"About you having to leave?"

She nodded. Alkis bit his lip and looked away.

"I shouldn't say anything. Cleric Elza is very particular. Meticulous as she is, I'd hate to upset anything she has in mind."

"Is there anything you can tell me? I don't even know if I can make it to Naelan."

"You can." He leaned against the doorway to the inner temple. "You're strong. Talented in magic and as determined as the old lady herself. Elza can teach you to control the Flame for at least a month. She is going to undersell you, but I've seen her do wonders," he said.

"How long before we leave? I would like to talk to my sister and I don't know if Elza is going to show up and whisk me away."

"There's still some time. I am sure your family will be welcome."

"What about you?" Olivia asked.

"Me?"

She was not sure why it crossed her mind. Alkis was certainly not a scholar like Elza, but his presence meant safety. She understood him. At least, she understood what she knew. He had no large plans at curing magical ailments or hurried city concerns. He just wanted to help her, even if he already saved her life once.

"Will you come with us?" she asked.

He grimaced at the question. Lips parted to answer, but he pulled whatever it was back inside of himself.

Alkis fidgeted with a portrait on the wall. His smirk was carved with a strained ease.

"I shouldn't. Someone has to watch after the church and the clergy. I already saved your life once, doing it again would be boring."

Elza was a juggernaut of knowledge and practice. Alkis made this all seem manageable. She considered asking if there was any way he could have come, some arrangement or deal. The silence between them held some sort of understanding. Maybe she had an ember of feeling for him. Would it be dangerous to tempt that line? She was hardly in the place to be thinking about her romantic future when her life seemed so fragile.

Her thoughts drained away as a growl reverberated along the walls of the temple. It burbled like the creatures that slunk in the dark places, but the slightest human tone made her shiver. Alkis reached for his Focus as Olivia grabbed her own. The creature bulged from under its black cloak, the flimsy fabric just large enough to mask its hulking form. Two hands, covered in coarse hair, were tipped with sharp talons. The deep hood shrouded the majority of its face, but it failed to hide a mouth of fangs framed by a set of clacking pincers. It stank like moist dirt.

"Stay behind me," Alkis said.

He raised his hand and a single spark lit inside of his Focus. It grew into a nest of embers before flashing into a sphere of light. Ash and cinder cracked to life and drifted to the ground as it spread down his arm. The Hooded Man dropped down onto all fours and lunged.

Alkis swung to catch the creature and the cinder armor flashed as the creature rebounded off it. It crashed backward into the prayer mats and its hood fell away.

Beneath it was a lupine face with chittering pincers. It charged once again and Alkis ran to meet it. He blocked the creature's next blow, but the other hand scratched his shoulder. Alkis shouted and shifted his footing. He jabbed the flaming fist into the creature's chest and it shrieked as hair and skin sizzled.

Olivia barely heard the crackle of rocks and dirt behind her. The hair on her neck stood on end as a warm voice rose within her.

Run.

She fell to the ground as a purple bolt of magic shrieked past her and crashed into the wall. A figure in a black cloak stood in the light of the dying sun. In her raised hand was a black, stone rod. Olivia did not wait for a challenge or explanation from the assassin. She dove out of the way as a second roiling shot blasted into the ground where she had been. Olivia ran into the center of the temple.

Alkis blocked another swipe of claws from the Hooded Man, cinder sparking from the shield over his arm. The creature's eyes followed Olivia as she ran to one of the four pillars that stood around the room. Alkis swung his embered fist into the creature's jaw. Teeth cracked, skin burned, and the Hooded Man backed away.

Olivia turned the wheel on the nearest pillar. The chains clinked and whirred above her as mirrors shifted up to face the reflective rod on the roof. The first mirror caught the setting sun's light and reflected it down the line. Brilliant light filled the temple and the Hooded Man screamed. The bright light sent him skittering back against a far wall with his hands in front of his eyes. Its sobbing wail was too close to a human sob.

The black robed woman entered the temple and

raised her Focus toward Alkis. Her killing magic leaped from the tip as he spun on his back foot to meet it. The inky blast burnt like fleece tossed into an open fire the moment it touched his magic. The magic hissed as it dissipated. The woman must have been used to killing with impunity. She flinched at the sight of her magic failing.

"A Fire Keeper. It's been too long since I killed a true disciple of Flame," the cloaked woman said.

"Just a shame I don't have my armor on me. Give me a minute and I can go get it," Alkis said.

The assassin's cold glare twisted into a gleeful grin. She thrust out her arm and a single beam of black magic connected with Alkis's shield. Faldir flowered her fingers outward and the beam branched into a dozen tendrils. They spread over the shield like choking vines and stabbed into the cinders. As quickly as one tendril evaporated, another one sprouted.

"Get to the kitchen, to the trap door," Alkis said through gritted teeth.

Cracks broke across his magical shield and flaked off as ash under the magical barrage. She ran from the shadow wolf and now this assassin. She lucked out twice. The cleric could only hold this for so long. Olivia would not put his life at risk. Olivia readied her Focus and stepped forward, but he pushed her back with his other hand.

"No. You can't risk it. Go, I'll be right behind you," he said.

A loose tendril of magic slipped around the shield and stabbed into Alkis's arm. He shouted as it left a blackened, bloodless wound. Olivia cursed under her breath. She grabbed the back of Alkis's collar and put her other hand on the small of his back.

"I'll guide you out. Just keep your eyes on her."

He adjusted his footing and stepped backward to follow Olivia. The grasping vines slowed as the woman stepped across the church's threshold. She pointed her Focus upward, giving Alkis a brief reprieve. A short blast cleaved through the network of mirrors above.

The top half teetered. Glass shattered and rained down in flashing shards. Each support failed after the other, light disappearing from the reflective panes. The glass slashed the prayer rugs to shreds and a severed chunk of the monolith crashed into the dais. The rain of shards was followed by a tide of shadows that swept into the hall.

Glass broke into steaming, blackened bits against Alkis's magic-coated right arm. Olivia winced against the small chips that dropped at her feet and she pulled Alkis backward. She turned and hauled the kitchen table out of the way as fast as she could. The square imprint of the trapdoor was barely visible, the handle hidden under a loose floorboard. She tossed the floorboard open and yanked on the handle as a howl echoed through the temple.

"We don't have enough time," she said.

Alkis let his shield of cinders dissipate and he grabbed the lip of the trap door. They lifted it open just as the Hooded Man strode into the kitchen. Olivia grabbed a plate from the nearby sink and threw it at the creature. It smashed to pieces and the creature ducked back into the temple. As it winced, Alkis dropped the trapdoor, and pulled Olivia out of the backdoor and into the yard.

The sun was nearly set, only a twilight glow burning

behind the tree line. The torches that Olivia lit only a few minutes ago were snuffed. Shadows shifted and crept toward them with wriggling, eager wisps of darkness. Alkis conjured another spark into his hand and let it grow until it bloomed into a new shield.

"Ignore what I said. Use your Focus," Alkis said.

"What about the affliction? 'You're not ready' and all that crap?" She looped her fingers through the grip on her golden Focus.

"That was earlier. You can either die slowly from flame affliction or let these creeps kill you."

"I still don't know how to use this damn thing," Olivia muttered.

The Hooded Man crashed through the back door and came to a stop. The woman was a few steps behind him. The creature circled around to hem them in. She loosened the tie of her cloak and let it fall to the ground. Her dark brown hair was tied back, her eyes locked on her prey. The Hooded Man was the beast, but she was the true predator.

"You're dying aren't you?" she asked Olivia.

Her voice made something inside of her shudder. The Flame wriggled and pumped her blood faster. It roared in the back of her head, a noise that sounded like a muffled scream. The woman's mere presence made the Flame shudder inside of Olivia.

"How do you know that?" she asked.

"I can smell it. You reek of burnt kindling. You should be resting, not fighting."

"Then stop trying to kill me."

"I did not expect you to move so fast. I will remember that next time." The assassin took a wide step to her left and the Hooded Man matched her move.

203

"I know someone who can snuff the pain inside of you. I can end this if you give me your Focus." the woman said.

Olivia's arm twitched as the Flame boiled in her chest. It pleaded with Olivia to kill this woman. She was certain that this woman did not want to help her, but the Flame was no friend either. Olivia knew what snake oil pitches sounded like. Even if it was for something she wanted worse than anything in the world.

"What do you want with it?" Olivia asked.

"Don't listen to the witch," Alkis snapped, "Her salvation would have you scampering around like this thing."

"Last chance. Give us the Focus and you will live, I swear on it," the assassin said.

Alkis chuckled. "A shadow mage bargaining? You must be desperate."

Reversing the tide of night, another light grew to the east. It was not the sun, but a bright orb of light glowing above someone standing on the other side of the temple. Her golden collar caught the light from her Focus as she neared. The golden ball at the end of the chain glowed like an ember.

"Your fight is with me, but you are welcome to run. The town guard is on their way." Elza sounded amused. "Surrender and I am sure you will receive a trial. I doubt it will be fair, but maybe they will spare you."

Faldir spit on the ground. "I would rather die than be the conqueror's dog."

The Hooded Man roared and lunged toward Olivia and Alkis. Alkis flashed his shield toward the creature and caught the first blow, the other claws swung at Olivia. She dodged the strike and kicked into the creature's ribs. It dodged Alkis's next swing and came back in with its snapping pincers and fangs.

Faldir's eyes rolled over black. Inky mist gathered around her hands and lengthened down each finger. She leaped across the entire yard with a trail of purple and black mist behind and crashed down toward Elza. Elza threw both of her hands toward each blow. The black, shadowy claws lashed against the light and the high cleric struggled to hold each strike. Her Focus grew brighter as it absorbed Faldir's attack.

Olivia and Alkis struck at the Hooded Man's flanks. When Alkis would block a hit, Olivia would kick. When it lunged for Olivia, Alkis brought his cindered fist down. The creature wheeled back as its flesh sizzled. Olivia felt a rhythm building, the two fighting together like it was a dance. Just as the tempo settled, the Hooded Man changed his pattern. The creature swung at Olivia, but then lunged at the Fire Keeper and struck him in the head. Alkis fell backward and his cinder shield broke.

The Hooded Man struck at Olivia with its claws. Olivia stepped backward. She punched the creature in the ribs, but the beast was ready for her. He grabbed her arm and with his other paw and pulled her toward his open maw. The Hooded Man's teeth sunk into her shoulder.

Elza's Focus grew bright enough to light the entire yard. Faldir brought both of her shadow-clad hands above her head and thrust down toward Elza. As the blow hit, the high cleric pulled the ball away with her free hand to create a taught chain. Light exploded from the Focus and a wall of fire rose in her hands. Faldir grimaced and fired a solid beam of shadow at the fiery shield. The high cleric marched toward Faldir, the flaming shield holding against the void magic.

Olivia tried to pull the beast off of her, but could not shift its bulk in the slightest. Her shoulder burned, blood dribbling down her arm. The lessons with Elza came to mind in the chaos. She focused on the flame within her, hiding in the dark of her mind. There was no time for peace or meditation. She imagined the darkness, the bonfire, and hoped it would listen. Olivia reeled her fist back, Focus in hand, and swung toward the Hooded Man's face.

A bright light flashed into existence as her fist collided with the monster. Its jaws opened and pincers pulled back from her shoulder. A bubble of cinder and ash glowed around her fist with a golden light. The Hooded Man scampered away and held its face.

"Father! Father please," he pleaded to the sky.

Across the yard, Elza's wall of flame bore down on Faldir. The void mage did not retreat a single step. Elza gritted her teeth and leaned over Faldir as though she might crush the void mage with her display. Elza's heels left the ground and she lifted onto her tiptoes. All her weight and will was bent down toward the shadow mage.

Faldir grinned and took one step back. She dashed to her left and dropped the beam of void magic. The wall of fire missed her by mere inches as it came crashing down. Elza tottered forward, not prepared for the void mage to retreat entirely. The cleric fell and Faldir stabbed into Elza's side with long talons of shadow. Faldir took a heaving, exhausted breath, twisted her fist, and withdrew the ethereal claws. Her eyes returned to their normal color as Elza collapsed face first onto the ground.

Olivia ran toward Faldir, but the void mage fired a salvo of void magic at Olivia. She raised the glowing orb of light in front of her and the shadowy bolts scattered against it. Olivia heard the sounds of people shouting and boots running up the main road. Torch light grew on the trees near the temple. The militia was almost there.

Faldir retreated back to the tree line where the Hooded Man whimpered. The darkness around them grew until it was a pool of pure darkness in the deepening night.

"I'll find you again, thief," Faldir said.

"Don't you run!"

Olivia saw the whites of Faldir's eyes last as the darkness swallowed them. Olivia neared the patch of midnight darkness and raised the bubble of light. The shadows drew back to reveal an empty patch of trampled grass where they once were.

Four militia guards ran into the back of the yard with lit torches. Armed to the teeth with longswords and short bows, golden armor and blood red helmets, they could not help a thing. Josie and John pushed past the guards, Tomis lingered behind. Across the yard, Alkis shifted and rubbed his head. Olivia turned from where the assassin disappeared and looked over to Elza's still body.

Chapter Seventeen

The torches were relit and guards paced the property. They shined torches into the darkened tree line and the windows of the unoccupied guest house. The group moved Elza's body inside of the church and laid her in the annex room. She was covered with a clean blanket, only marred by a few dapples of blood.

Alkis sat closest to the body. Tears silently ran down his bruised face. Olivia sat next to him with her hand on his shoulder. She closed her eyes and tried to find silence in the violence of the night. Beyond the fresh memories that wouldn't go away, she wondered what they would do next.

If the guards recognized John or Tomis, they did not care to act on it. No one was curious enough to ask. It barely crossed Olivia's mind, but she was too exhausted to worry. Maybe they were more concerned with the murder that just happened rather than one that happened half a year ago. Josie and John stood behind the two mourning pupils. Tomis stood near the entrance to the room and fiddled with a prayer book he found on the way in. One of the militia entered and stepped around Tomis.

"Cleric Alkis?"

He did not respond. His eyes lingered on the shape of Elza's corpse beneath the sheet.

"I wanted to let you know that militia will remain on property for the next couple of days. Additionally, we will be looking for the murderers, based on your descriptions."

Alkis looked at the guard with unfocused eyes and spoke in an unsteady tone. "Thank you."

The guard cast her eyes across the others and then left the room, stepping around Tomis again, who skittered out of the guard's way.

"*Parcha fo mea se lous as*." Alkis placed his hand on Elza's forehead. "Rest easy."

"A woman blessed by the triad, no doubt about it," John said.

Alkis nodded. "I let her down."

Olivia extended her fingers toward her sister. Josie stepped forward and set her hands on her sister's shoulders. Their anger seemed so small next to Alkis's grief. Olivia clutched her sister's hand tight. She prayed to whatever powers still listened that Josie would stay safe. John looked between his nieces with a small smile and then resumed chewing on his lip.

"She said we couldn't stay. She said my affliction was too strong, there wasn't anything she could do here. Nothing meaningful anyway," Olivia said.

"Is this true?" Josie asked Alkis.

The cleric rubbed one of his temples and turned in his chair toward them. "Elza might have been able to cure her if she arrived earlier."

"We rode as fast as we could," Josie said with an annoyed whine.

"It was hypothetical. Now that Elza's gone, I'm not sure how much time you have left."

Alkis stood up and walked past the bed they laid her on.

"You know this magic though. She taught you

everything," John said.

"It wasn't the learning part that is the issue. Truth be told, I learned more about Flame magic back home than from her. I was only allowed to be so strong without my armor. She pushed her boundaries. She did things I couldn't. Not safely anyway," Alkis said.

"We, uh. I mean, there's gotta be something, right."

John struggled for something to say. Tomis shifted uncomfortably on the other end of the room. He raised his hand to speak but stopped himself. Olivia glanced at the thief, a supposed friend of John's.

She recognized him for certain now. John explained to them that he was an old friend and was being held hostage. He broke in at their command, despite being a thief every day of his life before that. When Josie suggested beating the truth out of him, Olivia almost agreed.

"There's got to be some kind of cure or a treatment. Flame bless, there's a whole damn world full of people who could have tripped into this problem. You, Alkis. You're a Fire Keeper. Could your people help her?" Josie asked.

"Losing yourself to Flame is a sign of weakness in my homeland. They'd leave her to die at the city gates at best. At worst, they would make sure she burns out. I could try to tutor her, but it would buy us a few weeks at best."

Olivia thought Elza's plan would still work. What other choice did she have? Her body hurt from fighting and her head was numb from the night. Sleep sounded like the best thing at the moment, but time was a resource now. Every hour that passed was one less spent trying to reach the only possible cure.

"It would give me time to make the trip. The one that Elza wanted to do. It would get us to the Archive Primeval in Naelan," she said.

Tomis coughed and cleared his throat.

"What's that?" Josie asked.

"It's a den of water mages and traitors. They sided with Shadow during the Great War," Alkis said with a snarl on his lip.

"Yeah, centuries ago. Why is everyone so hung up on this stuff?" Tomis said.

Alkis gave Tomis an eviscerating scowl. His silence was as loud as nails on a chalkboard.

"We haven't talked about you yet either."

Similar to Olivia, when John revealed who their new companion was, he was as angry as Olivia. John's word meant far less to the cleric. By the look on his face, Olivia thought that he might kill the gaunt man in the corner.

"You tried to steal from us this afternoon, I'm certain of it," Olivia said.

"I was only there because they were going to kill you. My little visit—"

"Theft," she interrupted.

"—*visit*, was to try and spare you all. They just want the Focus. And I didn't steal anything, so it isn't theft. Just breaking and entering." Tomis crossed his arms.

"What do they want with the Focus?" Olivia asked.

"Because they like it? Shade, I don't know. It isn't like they gave an explanation for abducting me."

"Watch your tone," John said.

Tomis waved off John and kept talking.

"Faldir, that shadow mage, she wants it to hurt someone or do something. They didn't say much."

Alkis's burning glare did not taper off as Tomis spoke. "Are you certain we can trust him? Might be safer to hand him off to the militia."

"I trust him. I worked with him for more than a decade. I know when he's hiding something," John said, "But Elza had a point, who else knows magic better than Naelan?"

"You mean the same people who sided with Shadow?" Alkis asked.

"Elza thought it was a good idea. You said you don't know better than her. It's my life on the line. I don't need a few weeks. I need a cure. I understand that it is a long shot, but it's my last chance." Olivia sat back in her chair.

"It's also where Faldir and the other one is going," Tomis said.

The rest of the group turned toward him. He almost pulled into himself like a mollusk.

"The people who killed your, I mean, well. The scary pair, the killers."

Alkis looked back to Elza's body and rubbed his forehead. "Can we take this to the kitchen? She would have appreciated some quiet."

They all rose and left the room, Tomis quickly ducked out the door first. Alkis remained behind near Elza's body. Olivia followed the others toward the door, but looked back at the student and his teacher. He knelt down and removed something from his pocket, the golden chain of her Focus. Alkis cleaned a bloody smudge with the hem of his shirt and placed it on her chest. Alkis bowed deeply.

"I'll make this right. I promise."

He turned and paused, surprised that Olivia stayed behind. As much as Alkis blamed himself, Olivia could not escape the feeling of responsibility. There was so much madness in her life now. If she had never been afflicted, none of this would have happened. The thought haunted her, even as she recognized she could not have stopped Faldir.

"I'm so sorry," she said.

He began to speak, but coughed instead as the words caught in his throat.

"She died helping someone in need. There's nothing more she could have asked for. Come on, the others are waiting."

They walked in silence down the unusually quiet halls of the temple. Every candle and torch inside was lit. The white, slate walls felt lifeless. Glass and splintered wood littered the floor of the worship hall. Large parts of the mirrors hung like broken branches after a storm. The snapped monolith pierced the dais at the heart of the room. The chirp of crickets came through a broken window with the night breeze. In the kitchen, John poured mead into several cups. He kept the first one and drank it down in two gulps.

"Oh that is good," he muttered.

"I know for a fact it isn't. It's the cheapest stuff I could find," Alkis said.

John filled the other cups and passed them around to the others.

"Well, it tastes good to me."

"Haven't seen you with a drink since we got into town," Josie said.

"I figured I might lay off for a bit. Wasn't as hard as I thought it would be. Being chased by monsters is a good distraction." John finished pouring the drinks and raised his again. "To Elza."

They all raised their cups and drank in somber silence. Tomis broke the stillness.

"Why don't we just drop the Focus off with the city? They can throw it in a safe and you can sleep a little easier."

"I need it. Or rather, I might need it. It's the only thing keeping the Flame at bay," Olivia said.

"Also, their vaults aren't safe," Alkis said, "Lots of representatives with a lot of agendas."

"And a lot of palms that can be greased," John added.

Minute by minute, hour by hour. Tick tock. Their back and forth was literally killing her. Olivia took a large drink from her cup and set it down with a loud knock.

"We can kill two birds with one stone by going to Naelan. We get a chance to warn them that trouble is heading their way and it is the best chance for a cure."

She looked around the table and her eyes rested on Josie. Her sister leaned on her elbows and traced the grain of the table with her finger. She glanced up at Olivia with an anxious gaze. Their fight seemed so stupid now, but Olivia knew better than to dismiss it. Josie wasn't related by blood, but she carried her family's stubbornness.

"You'll come with me, right Josie?"

Her sister shook her head and blew a breath out through her lips.

"This was supposed to be the end. From Hasketter to Sallew and back, the cure was supposed to be here. Not only are you still sick, now we have assassins to worry about. A trip halfway across the world. More mages, more magic."

"It's the only way," Olivia said.

"I just wish we could go back home," Josie whispered.

"Magic can get her out of it. Take a look around, you're not in the backwoods of Hasketter anymore," Alkis said.

Josie glanced at John and then back to the table. She did not look happy or scared or even annoyed. She was angry. The frantic light in her eyes and quick breath made it seem like she might rip apart the kitchen at any given moment.

"I'll do this for you, Olivia. Only you."

Their troubles were buried, but not gone. It would have to do.

"We'll need a guide as well. Someone who has been overseas before and knows the region." John looked directly at Alkis. "Know anyone like that, Fire Keeper from Katoia? Next door neighbor of Naelan?"

"I was planning to come anyway. Olivia's still sick," Alkis said.

They caught each other's eyes and she could see the other thought behind them. Even beyond that nascent attraction, it was a primordial challenge for the Cleric. The other reason why he would follow her to the ends of the world. She was Flame's challenge, laid right at his feet.

"Well," Tomis blurted. He finished his drink and loudly placed it back on the table. "This feels like a family moment. I should get going."

"To where?" Josie asked.

"Anywhere but here. You people have a target on you. Faldir will be coming back."

"You're just going to leave in the middle of the

night? Who travels while the sun is down?" Josie said.

"You sure have a lot of questions and I don't have the time to answer them." He turned and walked toward the back door. John spoke as he was about to disappear from sight.

"You know, Tomis, you're probably safer with us."

Tomis stopped and turned on his heel.

"How do you figure that?"

John tilted his head one way then the other.

"True enough, we have a group of assassins after us and a treacherous journey ahead, but who do you think they're going to be looking for if they can't find Olivia?"

Tomis crossed his arms. "Well, they know who to look for. Why would they keep following me?"

"You know what, they seemed like such reasonable people when they were trying to kill us. You're probably right," Josie said.

John pointed at Alkis.

"And, we have a Fire Keeper on our side."

"Ex-fire keeper," Alkis added.

Tomis bobbed his head in thought. He looked out the window where a pair of militia patrolled the perimeter. She wished he would leave anyway. The crook would be a good distraction while they fled the city. Tomis was a coward and John had shown him the safest route. She knew better than to hope for her way.

"Do you still have your armor?" Tomis asked Alkis.

"It's not far."

"Can't imagine I'll be getting paid, will I now?" He winced and stretched. "You all make a compelling argument. I'm in."

Alkis walked to a nearby closet and removed some oils and wooden logs.

"Everyone get some sleep. It's been a long day and we leave as soon as we can tomorrow. I have one last thing to attend to."

He took the supplies and walked toward the side room where Elza's body rested. He was off to burn Elza's body and reunite her with the Flame she studied for so long.

****

The wind wailed against the walls of the guest house. Olivia couldn't sleep. She was too warm, the fire too hot in her chest. It was rising again. Though she was a long way from the desperate state she arrived in, the clock was still ticking. She passed out the day prior and woke up the next afternoon. To her, it was a long blur. The argument with Josie, the break in, the fight, Elza.

John snored on the other side of the room. He propped up his pillow and bag under his back so that he faced the door. His hand crossbow was clutched in his right hand, left hand laid over his chest. Olivia thought that any intruders might be terrified of the choking, roaring snore coming from him more than the weapon. Josie laid on her cot not far from him.

Olivia got out of bed and crept across the room to the front door. The hinges quietly squeaked as it opened. John grunted and his finger pulled on the unarmed trigger of the crossbow. She closed the door behind her and sat on the stone steps outside of the cabin. The cool, night air blew through her hair. A small relief. The flickering light of the torches kept the coiling shadows far from the sanctuary. A guard made his rounds, spear pole sunk into the ground like a walking stick on the route around the empty church. He gave a slight bow to her which she returned.

The door creaked open behind her and Josie stepped through. She settled on the steps next to Olivia, Josie's shoulders looming next to her shorter sister.

"Not quite the valiant sentry, is he?" Olivia smirked.

"He's trying. You can't sleep either?"

"No. I can't stop thinking about tonight."

"I can't stop thinking about tomorrow. That and the snoring," Josie said.

"It reminds me of the day before the big haul into town. Spend the entire day picking apples and you know there is a bigger day to come."

"Sleepless summer nights. At least those didn't have the fear of death lingering over them."

"Or shadowy assassins."

They listened to the trees and the distant crash of waves. Olivia did not want to bring up the fight yet. She knew she should apologize, but the idea of another hard conversation felt too awful to endure.

"It's been a week since we left home," Josie said.

"Is it?"

"I never imagined missing work."

Olivia laughed. She wished that the right words could flow as easily as the tide did. "Some normalcy would be nice."

"Do you think about home often?" Josie asked.

Olivia realized, with a pang of guilt, that she hardly thought about the life she was so prepared to take on, the mantle of responsibility she wanted. Considering it now, it seemed wrong. All that dedication to farming was just a diversion. It was difficult to admit that she did not want it anymore.

"I would be taking over the farm tomorrow if this hadn't happened."

She was ready to launch into her own anxieties that lingered in her head for days. A glance over reminded her that she was not the only one suffering. Josie needed firm ground to stand on.

"Mom is probably on the mend," Olivia said. "Corn will be almost full height by now. I hope that dad remembers to start picking the summer apples and not the amber ones."

"They both just have a lot on their plate. They're short both of us for harvest, assuming we don't get back until autumn."

"He's been doing this longer than either of us have been alive. They still have the farm hands. I'm sure people in town are being generous."

"You're right, they can handle themselves," Josie said, "so can you."

They did not meet each other's eyes. Both of them vented their pain to the stars overhead. Olivia looked first. Josie's arms were wrapped around her knees, her bent-over form looked like a boulder on the steps.

"I don't like this. It's out of my hands," Josie said.

"It wasn't in your hands, never was."

Josie looked away from the tree line and gave Olivia a small, sad smile. "What if all this was the easy part?"

This journey was hard for all of them already. Olivia was certain it was only going to get worse, but she could not let Josie suffer under that idea. With all the trauma of tonight, and what more might come, she wanted Josie to live on beyond these few awful weeks.

"I don't have time to wait. I've been so tired, burning up, scared. You were right earlier. I wouldn't have made it this far without you. That's why I need you if I'm going to go any further. We have to keep running."

"Don't give me that," Josie said and looked back at the forest.

"I wouldn't lie to you."

Josie fidgeted with a pebble by her feet.

"Don't forget that I'm looking out for you too. And so is John," Olivia said.

"I'm not that important, you don't need to be—"

"You don't get to carry this weight by yourself. We're in this together."

Josie's smile widened into her frivolous smirk, that wild and unworried grin that defied anything to cloud it. She wiped her eyes and stood up.

"I'm going to bed, just hoping that I can block out the snoring. Are you coming?"

"Not yet. I need a bit longer," Olivia said.

"Alright, see you in the morning."

Josie opened the squeaky door and walked back inside. Olivia watched the door close and then looked back to where the reflective tower once stood at the top of the temple. Her eyes traveled from the shattered roof, past the white walls, and to the patch of grass in the back yard where Elza died.

Chapter Eighteen

The shadows pressed against Faldir's face. The warmth of the surface was replaced with the clammy cold of her family's warrens. She clung to her brother. His sobbing came in heavy gasps. The darkness began to fade and the shadow dissipated.

A cave wall laid in front of her. An open stone door was carved into the rock surface, one foot thick and covered in Pescan runes. The written dialect had died out on the surface. Even Faldir did not fully understand them. Behind her, the blue lights of a shabby village lit only the merest piece of the enormous cavern.

Squat homes were made of driftwood from subterranean tributaries. Wooden doors were substituted with cloth. Shallow planter's boxes bloomed with luminous mushrooms and lichen. Pale creatures flapped thin wings as they wheeled above the scowling villagers who regarded the new arrival.

They wore drab clothing. Every single one had thinning, brittle hair and wide eyes. Their pupils shifted as they crossed from the unlit interior of their homes and into the shale rock streets. They chuckled and muttered. Some skittered away from her in fear, but most of them looked up at the stone doors in anticipation. She did not have time for their gallows entertainment. Her brother came first.

Faldir pulled the Hooded Man's hand away from his

blistered face. The girl conjured Flame, something Faldir did not anticipate. The young mage possessed strength of heart. It would be harder to break her than Faldir hoped. Those who clung to the light all broke in the darkness. She would be no different.

"You," Faldir said to a quivering, hooded villager who stood too close, "get medicine or I will hold you to account for his death."

He turned on his heel with a panicked nod and broke through the small crowd. She reached for her waterskin, but her fingers closed on nothing. She left her pack when she dropped her cloak. She held her brother as he hissed and whined.

"It's okay brother, we'll be okay."

"Fine. I'll be fine," he growled.

"We made them pay for this," Faldir said with an unbalanced cackle. "But they have so much more to lose. We'll show them."

The nearby torches fluttered in a non-existent breeze. Coils of shadow wrapped around the nearest torches and smothered the weak, blue flames. Clawed feet clacked over the stone steps before her. His darkness grew as he came closer, his vile form wrapped in curls of shadow. Behind Father, two others followed. The Hooded Man made an attempt to kneel, but fell onto all fours instead. Faldir focused on soothing her brother and crouched next to him. The only respect she could pay was to not match Father's gaze.

"The triumphant return, full of vim and vinegar. So eager," Father said.

They were in pain and all he could think to do was mock them. Her knuckles turned white as she clenched the hem of her brother's cloak. A wrong move would ensure death. That fear did not banish the hate inside of her.

"Where is the Focus?" he asked.

"It eluded us, but I know where it is going."

"You lie," Father said.

"We pursued as you desired. There were complications," she said.

His dragging footsteps crossed the ground between them and he grabbed her by the neck. He lifted her to his face and almost pulled her into the web of living shadow that surrounded him. A toothy grin and black eyes were seated in the armored, bumpy ridge of his brow and snout.

"You were so ready to prove yourself that you lost sight of what you were after. Your parents sat with me and awaited your return, ready to welcome you into the family. It's been so long for them."

Faldir looked at the two people who stood behind Father. She could see her father's wiry mustache poking from under his hood, his head bowed in Father's direction. Her mother looked up, her eyes were black as night, even the pupils lost to the changes that Shadow chose for her. Her mouth twisted into a frown.

"We did not retrieve it, but we learned much about the enemy," Faldir said.

He tossed her onto the cavern floor and moved to her brother, who struggled to compose himself. Faldir winced and rubbed her elbow as she stood.

"And you were not the one to suffer for your arrogance. Poor thing, look at him. He has been scarred by True Flame," Father cooed.

"A scar earned by battle with the enemy."

Faldir hoped that it might reframe this failure.

"It's a brand of the conquerors, a mark of shame. Do not sell me piss and call it gold," he said, "There now, we'll make you better."

The hooded villager approached with cloth, clean water, and a mashed pulp of medicinal fungus. He knelt next to the Hooded Man and washed the wound. Her brother groaned in pain, but restrained his movements. Father's claws stroked his throat, a silent command.

"She is hurt, Faldir is also—" the Hooded Man said in a small voice.

"I'm fine, brother."

She could feel small bits of glass in her arms and burnt spots on her face where the mage's fiery shield came too close. She ached, but any sign of weakness would invite his anger. If you could not serve Shadow effectively, it would change you to better serve it. Her brother's past failures twisted him into the clawed, hunched thing he was today. Father oversaw their defeat three-hundred years ago. For that, he was remade.

"The game is still on," she said.

"Your prey is wise to you. They know they are being hunted and will adjust tactics."

"It is a small group: three farmers from the Seventh, a thief, and a Fire Keeper. They had one other, a high cleric of the Church of the Sun. She is dead, killed in your name, Father." Faldir smiled at the memory of her last breath. He kept his back turned to her.

"Do not pander."

"One of them, the one who now possesses the Focus, is afflicted. She is being taught to control it, but she does not have long. A few weeks at most."

Father brushed his finger along the Hooded Man's face. Faldir was not sure she would yet survive. If he wanted to kill her, she would be helpless to stop it.

"They were outsiders looking for a cure. They will now seek the only place in the world that may have a cure."

Father's back went rigid. His claws pulled away from the Hooded Man and snapped together. A satisfied gasp escaped his lips. The past was his present. Things that happened during the Great War were stories to her. For Father, they betrayed him personally.

"Twice Cursed Traitors."

He would let her live for now. Her shoulders eased and she realized that she dug her nails into her hands.

"The target is the destination. If we can intercept them—"

"Do they know?"

Faldir's grin faded and repaired itself just as quickly. She forgot about Tomis. She thought over conversations they had, things she said. Had he listened carefully? Had she spoken of Naelan around him? No, certainly he would starve quietly in that warehouse.

"No, they do not."

Father floated toward her. She flinched at the outstretched talons, but they drew back and waited just before her face. He turned his palm and graced her cheek. The gray scales snagged on her skin with small, painful pinches. She swallowed this pain like the rest of it.

"You are the most promising of my descendants. Of those who do not yet dwell past this door, you belong here more than any other. But your ambition almost cost us everything. Your place as family will be granted once you have proven it. Do not let your need cloud your judgment."

Faldir glanced over at her parents. Her father lifted

his head, his pale white eyes saw beyond the walls of the cave, but left him blind to everything within. Her mother smiled.

"Do not disappoint us," Father said.

He dropped his hand from her face and gestured for her parents to leave. They turned at once and walked back through the stone door. The attending villager wrapped dingy, gray cloth around half of her brother's face and soaked it with medicine.

Father raised his clawed hand and whispers followed his gesture. A small tremor ran through the earth and dust fell from the distant cavern ceiling. The whispers grew louder, filling the air around them until they were answered by a chittering, feral screech.

"Your brother is a prodigious tracker, but we now must pursue by sea. You need my help once again. The unlit eyes of the ocean now search for the same quarry as you. Travel south along the coast at twilight until you see a black ship. They will grant you passage."

"We will not fail you." Faldir took a knee and lowered her head. The shadow pressed close to her again and the dim torches of the village faded from sight.

"I know you will not, daughter."

****

"Daughter."

Faldir spit the word onto the dry, shore grass. Faldir and the Hooded Man were on the quiet coast southeast of Sallew. She stewed all day long in the shelter of an abandoned shack. Her brother quietly scratched at his bandages. It was only once they left the ruined home that Faldir felt she could speak. In the dying light of the day, Father would not be able to hear her.

"He calls me family, but never treats me like it. Do

not disappoint, best of your bloodline," she growled.

"Do not mock Father."

"He wasn't there! I've earned my way into this family a dozen times. How many have we killed?"

"Twenty-six."

"How many relics have we claimed?"

"Thirteen," he recited.

"I cheat and kill and bury bodies and he leaves me with *this*."

Faldir sent a streak of energy crackling into the side of a tree. The blackened wood snapped and fell away from their path. She looked down at her arm and rolled her eyes.

"A tool that can be mastered by any idiot with a Focus."

"Better than nothing," the Hooded Man said, unimpressed by Faldir's outburst.

"I deserve mastery of Shadow, just like him. They all have it. The family, those allowed within the house. We've earned it."

Faldir kicked at the ground and looked at her brother as he hobbled alongside her. His snout barely peaked from below the tip of his hood. His pincers tittered as they walked.

"With everything you've given, they didn't even let you in."

The Hooded Man glanced from under his cowl at Faldir. They were still her brother's eyes, the ones that looked after her in the squat, desert huts of their childhood. Something flashed within them. It was a thought, something that he wanted to say. His pincers clattered again, but the sentiment passed and his eyes glazed over. He looked away from her with a grunt.

"You must try harder. Listen to Father."

The Hooded Man picked up the pace and walked ahead of Faldir. He barely fit under the cloak. His warped form was so twisted from the tall, lithe body her brother once had. She wondered what situation she might face if she failed now. Her brother glanced out to sea and pointed to the horizon.

"Black ship."

A boat emerged from the wash and spray of the waves. It was a small ship, large enough for a crew of twenty at most. The hull was slathered with black paint and pitch. No flag was flown from its mast and its prow bore a trio of sharp spikes, each of them a third the length of the ship. From over the railings, the haggard crew of warped sailors sighted their arrivals. They were not as changed as her brother, but no longer appeared completely human. A horn blew on the deck.

The sea boiled around its hull. Even as it cut through the waves, armored creatures covered in green shells chittered across the hull. She only caught glances of them: skittering legs, eel tails, and empty, glaring eyes on long stalks. The Hooded Man walked back to Faldir as they crossed the soft sands toward the sea.

"Focus on what you must do. For both of us."

Chapter Nineteen

Despite spending four days in Sallew, Olivia felt as though she had seen nothing. They would be boarding a ship soon, so she tried to drink in as many details of the city as she could. She minded their luggage at the foot of a dock.

The web of piers and ship masts seemed more like a forest when she was amongst the clutter. People came this way carrying barrels and then went that way haggling on dock taxes and import fees. The sun warmed Olivia more than she would have liked, but it was tolerable.

John bought passage on a merchant ship with most of the money that was left. Alkis signed the actual contract. John was eager to keep his name out of people's minds. The ship was a single masted vessel named the Sovarka. She recognized the lettering as Katoian, but did not know enough of the language to translate.

At the foot of the gangway, Alkis spoke to a somber man in a captain's coat. His collar was hiked up against the breeze. His beard and mustache were meager and uncombed, much like his short, brown hair. A pair of pale, green eyes concealed all emotion beneath them like a shallow sea. They stared straight through Alkis with a vague impression of boredom.

For his part, Alkis left the clothes of the church behind. He wore a simple vest, a brown shirt, and breeches. His dark red hair made it difficult to blend in, but the absence of a white robe gave him a chance to go unnoticed. His promise to tutor her would be fulfilled in transit. They would just need to work out a few details with the captain.

The Focus remained in her possession since last night. After what happened, she wanted it on her person at all times. Olivia found it calming to have her Focus nearby. The Flame did not fight her in the warmth of the day. It was happy. Clutched in her hands, it felt like a house cat watching her from its favorite spot.

"Hey, Liv," John called to her.

He emerged from the flowing crowd holding two bags. One was his own and the other was new and stuffed with goods. He sat down before he handed it to her.

"I figured I should be ready for the journey this time."

Olivia peaked inside the pack. It was full of camping supplies, alarm bells, oily deterrents against predators, and other gear that would have been useful last week. The bag was made from a tough cloth, heavy enough to stop a small blade.

"Not bad. I needed a new one."

"It's not leather, so don't get it wet."

"Where is Josie and your friend?" Olivia asked.

"I left them with some spending money. Tomis doesn't have anything except the clothes on his back. He needs a few things."

John straightened up where he sat and looked over at his niece. "I meant to ask you about all this. I backed your play at the church because I think you're right. We haven't had a moment to talk. Not since you and Josie fought."

"Since when do we talk?" Olivia asked.

"Just," he bobbed his head up and down, "I'm trying to be nicer, okay? And I need an opening for that."

Olivia hoped that they would be able to put grudges aside after everything they had gone through. Despite this, a small part of her only remembered the resentment. There was so much pain and doubt in her head. It was easier to close off another problem than confront it.

"I'm sorry for how I've been," he said. "It was just easy to be pissed at you. You had it out for me since day one."

"I didn't think you were my uncle at first. Maybe you scammed my dad with some sad-sap story about a lost brother or something like that."

He laughed harder at that than she expected.

"It would not be the first time I pulled that trick. I thought you were a silver-spoon-in-your-mouth, no fun type who was angry about me putting a wrinkle in your inheritance. And I'm sorry. You didn't deserve any of it."

Half a year of tension melted away inside of her and she could not help but smile. After the fear and exhaustion of the last few days, this felt like a cure to another affliction.

"I'm sorry too. I could have been kinder."

"I actually didn't come here to ask you about that though. You've had that Focus in hand since last night. What's more, I believe you were using real magic when we got there. I was worried that you slipped."

Olivia pulled the Focus toward her chest and glanced around. She felt like she did in the forest, like something was stalking just out of sight. Paranoia for sure. Perhaps some instinct from the Flame. These impulses were leaking into her emotions.

"It was like when the shadow wolf took my mom, but not the same. They hurt me, but it didn't just erupt from me. I called it and it answered. I asked for its help."

"Think you'll use it again?"

Olivia wanted to use it again. To feel the elements course through her was like taking a fresh breath of air. It would not really be living without it.

"Only if I need to."

"How do you feel now? You seem a bit flushed," John pressed his palm to her forehead, "and a little warm."

"That's normal these days," she grumbled.

"But you just manifested Flame and you seem fine. That's something to cheer about, eh?"

It kept her alive again. Her hesitancy was seeming thinner by the hour. She set out on this journey with so much anger. No matter any commitments she could make against it, no matter how much Josie did not approve, she knew it was impossible to say she would never use it again. If Faldir showed up, it was a near certainty.

"You don't think those two thugs will come back, do you? Between the four of us, we are not exactly helpless."

"Five of us," John corrected, "Tomis isn't too useful in a fight, but he has his talents. From what he said, those were not just thieves or common thugs. They are professionals. I've heard rumors about cults of shadow worshippers who went into hiding. I assumed they were all dead or gave up the fight."

"And their fight is with us, even if we didn't ask for it," Olivia said.

"We're fine for now. I just meant to observe that you are fonder of that golden doodad than you were even a few days ago."

He was good at reading people. Something she did not appreciate at the moment.

"I'm keeping it handy. Danger or not, this Focus has helped me three times. It might be time to start treating it with a little more respect," she said.

Would she be a different person if she had an actual teacher instead of Yorker? What if she did not smother that hope? She would not say it out loud and could only stand to think about it for a few moments at a time. She could not ignore that her staunch resistance to magic was breaking. Was it ever anger or was it always just fear? John nudged her out of her thoughts and nodded toward their ship. Alkis walked down the pier with a tiny smirk on his face.

"Greetings, Mister Monk," John said.

"The title is cleric. Or was cleric, not sure what I am now."

"You're our negotiator right now. All sorted out?" Olivia asked.

"Our fare is paid, we leave soon. They will sail directly toward Katoian Waters, stop in the Agrotik briefly, and then on to Naelan."

"Thought you said Katoia was a bad idea?" John asked.

"Knocking on the Fire Keeper's door is a bad idea. Agrotik is a farming town far from the capital. Help me with this."

Alkis leaned over to a large, stained wooden chest with brass binding. The initials A.B. were imprinted above the lock. It was hastily cleaned, but dirt still stuck to corners. John helped Alkis lift it.

"What is in here? So damn heavy, I took you for the kind that traveled light," John said. He set it on the ground and Alkis let it down as well. He pulled a key from his pocket and opened the lock.

"Don't tell anyone else that this is on board."

Alkis opened the lid part way. A suit of pale armor was set inside of it among red cloth padding. It was made of polished granite with dark metal joints. Runes were carved along the edges of the armor plates. Only the fringes bore any decoration. Small carvings of flames rose from the wrists and shoulders. The open-faced helmet was topped with a roaring lion crest. Alkis closed the trunk and locked it again.

"Each piece of that armor is priceless. Every set is unique to its keeper. With just my Focus, I am limited in what I can do. But when I put this on…" His face clouded with a thought.

"We wouldn't be hearing from the shadow thugs again?" Olivia said.

"Yeah. Things might have gone differently."

Olivia realized he was thinking of Elza. She looked around and picked up her bag and John's. "You help him with that. I can start carrying the others aboard."

Alkis broke from his thoughts and reached down to his end of the chest.

"Ready John?" he asked.

"You should've seen me on my best days. I could haul a wagon of product up a hill and still have the breath to sell them at the top," he said.

The two men carried the chest down the pier, Olivia in tow behind them. Salty water sprayed between the boards of the dock and the Sovarka buoyed up and down in the tide. Sailors shouted and grumbled as they prepared the canvas of the mast, tied up lines, and performed other indecipherable preparations. A large gangplank ran over the space between the pier and the edge of the ship. They crested the top and set the chest down on the deck.

"Better be worth it," John said and gingerly stretched his back.

"No choice in the matter. You want me as a guide, you bring the armor."

The captain loomed behind Olivia like a specter. His face was flushed and tanned from years at sea, but something about him felt drained and worn. The captain's green eyes seemed empty, preoccupied with something beyond the ship.

"Welcome aboard the Sovarka. I am Captain Yanna. Be kind to my crew, don't cause trouble, and this should be a pleasurable expedition for you all," he said.

"Captain, I'm Petra Cuza. This is my niece Olivia," John said.

Yanna made no effort to remove his hands from the depths of his pockets for a handshake.

"You must be the young woman Alkis spoke of. He said you have a condition. Some sort of disease," the captain said.

"It's a family curse of invalidity. I'm lucky to have missed it myself, right Olivia?" John said.

Olivia nodded stiffly. Lying so blatantly, with little preparation, was still new to her. If the captain suspected the lie, she could not tell it from his unblinking eyes.

"Alkis has paid an extra fare to allow the use of my quarters for treatment," Yanna said.

Olivia saw Alkis nod and followed his example.

"Good. That is a relief," she said.

"We just need daily time to administer medicine. I have a collection of leeches for bleeding. I would prefer it if your crew did not bother us at this time, it is somewhat unpleasant," Alkis said.

Yanna's features finally broke into something besides apathy. He wriggled where he stood and dug his hands deeper into his pockets.

"I cannot stand the things. You won't hear any grief from me. The berth is downstairs, there are several hammocks set aside for passengers. Claim some for yourselves. My quartermaster, Mr. Cretis, is below decks as well. Please speak to him when you can to register your arrival."

Yanna gave them a deep bow and went over a group of nearby sailors. John and Alkis grabbed the chest and trudged across the busy vessel to a set of stairs that ran below decks. John, Olivia and Alkis all gave polite nods or quiet murmurs of thanks as people stepped aside. The sailors waited with impatient smiles or shifted where they stood as if the extended stillness might kill them.

Small, covered candles lit the interior of the ship. The hallway ran from stem to stern and was wide enough for them to shoulder past others. They passed several doors, one leading to a galley with a large table and a bench, both bolted to the floor. Storerooms dotted this passage, each of them bursting with goods.

At the end of this hallway, the room opened into the berth. A tangle of hammocks, one suspended above the other, swung in the idle tilting of the ship. Sunlight beamed through several cracks in the ceiling, but it did nothing to lift the gloom. The few candles lit here were far too few for a space as large as this. Olivia could barely see the end of the room. Only a few sailors meandered here. Most were busy pinning letters next to their bed or fixing their personal effects to the posts nearby.

At the back of this wide room was a row of ten hammocks, each one nearly draped over the other. Olivia was not completely certain that Josie would fit in these. Above each of them was a wooden sign that read "Vateip-Passenger". Alkis and John grunted as they covered the final distance to the hammocks. They set down the chest next to one of the middle hammocks with a loud exhalation of relief.

"Why didn't I go shopping? Josie could have carried this thing herself. Think before you delegate, John," he said to himself.

Olivia dropped the bags in one of the other hammocks.

"Not to rub salt in it, but we have to go back up. We have a few more things," she said.

"And they will be taken care of," a quiet, slow voice rose from a handful of trunks that were being unloaded nearby.

A yellow-eyed man stood from behind an open box with a sly grin. He wore a sailor's outfit, but his cap was emblazoned with a stitched ship's wheel. His unkempt nails snagged on the cloth of his pants as he wiped one of his hands. He grabbed a ledger from beside the cargo and opened it to a particular page without looking.

"I didn't realize the Sovarka had servant service," Alkis said.

"It doesn't. I appreciate you bringing this heavy parcel down for us, but cargo must be stowed safely and carefully. There are rough seas ahead and I'd hate to see this lovely one's ankle get crushed by an errant travel trunk." He curled a finger toward Olivia. "Quartermaster Cretis you can call me. Cretter by my friends, and those who stay in line."

John sat on a hammock, still catching his breath.

"The captain said we would find you down here. I'm Petra, this is my niece Olivia and my friend Alkis. We have two more: Josie Cuza and Trevor Lanes."

"And they will be here presently? Not long until we cast off." Cretis carefully checked the parchment in his hands.

"Very soon. Flame willing," John said.

Olivia looked at her uncle, unsure of who Trevor was. He must have predicted her response as his eyes were already set on her. He raised his brows slightly and spoke before she could voice the beginning of the question.

"How long of a voyage are we expecting, Mr. Cretis? My niece has a condition and it is not well for her to be at sea for long."

Cretis scribbled a few more notes with a pencil before his wild eyes pulled away from the paper. They went to John and then to Olivia, where they stayed a moment longer than was polite.

"Illness?" he asked.

"Nothing that is catching, of course. We would not risk hard working people such as yourselves," Olivia said.

Cretis stared at her for another moment before looking at his papers.

"Yes, yes the captain mentioned a special arrangement. An afflicted passenger," he choked on a small, consternated noise in his throat.

"Terribly sorry to hear of your condition. Vague as the captain was, it sounded quite serious. And you are her caretaker then, Alkis?" Cretis drew a sharp line on the parchment, the tip pointing like it was a weapon, "You do not look like the apothecarial type."

Alkis waved a hand toward the quartermaster.

"An apprentice merely. My master is busy in town and I am to accompany them to Naelan where she can receive further treatment."

Cretis continued to smile, but the warmth was draining from his eyes.

"An expensive endeavor by the sound of it." He traced a line on the open page and frowned. "All paid for and ahead of schedule."

He closed the ledger with a deflated snap. Several rings, simple bands of metal seated with dull stones, clicked together on his fingers.

"I have your party marked as present, including those not here. Our cook likes to bless every voyage with his boiled, peppered potatoes. I recommend that you attend."

Cretis turned away and idly closed the crate he was previously sorting. He stalked out of the berth and to the stairs that lead to the main deck. Olivia sat on her hammock, unable to pull her eyes away from the quartermaster until he left her sight entirely.

"That's an odd one." John slid back into his hammock.

"An odder word choice: afflicted," Olivia said.

"It does just mean ill as well."

"We should be aware of other agents that might be looking for the Focus. Particularly one with yellow eyes," Alkis said.

"What about the eyes?" she asked.

"Could just be what his parent's eyes were, but it might also be the Wild Eye, an alteration favored by Shadow."

John sat up in the hammock with a finger raised.

"Let's not jump to paranoia before we've even set sail. Lots of people suffer small changes brought on by Shadow. Try getting caught in a mountain pass over winter and see if you don't come out of it with hairy arms and an extra set of incisors."

"But his interest in us specifically, the questions—" Olivia said.

"It all felt very intrusive," Alkis continued.

"Look, I'm as concerned as you all, but let's not rock the boat on day one. He's a quartermaster. It's his job to be nosy. Stars, we're the only passengers, I think. This is a trade ship, not a ferry. Of course he would make a note to meet us."

Alkis and Olivia shared a look. If she gave the lead, he would continue to needle. After facing down one pair of shadow cultists, she hardly wanted to let another go unnoticed. She decided to follow John's lead.

"You have a point, but please tell me that something about him was a little off to you," Olivia asked.

He rocked in his hammock and chewed on his lip.

"Doesn't hurt to be careful. We can't assume Faldir and her pet monster will be so brazen or that we might even see them again."

"We will see her again," Olivia said, "she won't let it go."

John nodded. "Well, don't get too jumpy. Here comes Josie and Tomis."

The two strode into the berth carrying their

purchases from town. Josie found a leather chest piece, her shining ax strapped over her shoulder. Tomis wore a set of clothes that were too pristine for how he skulked between the hammocks. He wore a pair of polished, leather boots, but seemed unsteady on soles that were not worn down.

"We got your friend some clothes and a new pair of boots. We only had enough shulten left over for a hunting knife for him. It'll have to do," Josie said.

Tomis set his bags down next to a hammock and riffled through his pockets. "Hopefully, I won't have to do any fighting. That's what you all are here for."

"We're here to get Olivia to Naelan. You are here to help," Alkis said.

Tomis waved him off. "You know what I mean. Here, a little snack for everyone. The bakery gave me a good price."

Tomis pulled a few biscuits from his jacket pockets. Olivia took one and rolled it in her hand. They were sprinkled with cinnamon, warm and spongy.

"These are fresh," she said.

"I don't know any baker who would give you a good price," John said and bit into it.

"Well, they didn't know they gave me a good price. Free is a good price, no?" Tomis smirked and bit into a second muffin. John rolled his eyes, but a small smile crept onto his face.

"I won't tolerate criminal behavior. What kind of friend is this?" Alkis asked John.

"An old friend. It's fine, Alkis."

"Yeah, don't go crying to the city guards over it. Just some yeast, flour, and a pinch of cinnamon," Tomis said. Alkis frowned and sat on a hammock in between John and Olivia. Despite his protest, he still swallowed down the last of the biscuit.

Olivia thought Tomis was shiftier than John could ever hope to be. In addition, he was not bound here by anything other than John's soothing assurances of safety. She did not plan to make an issue of it, but she would keep as close an eye on him as she could. The biscuits were delicious though and he could have kept them to himself.

"Oh, by the way," John said to Tomis, "Your name is Trevor now."

Tomis shook his head. "I hoped I wouldn't have to be Trevor again."

"It's a perfectly fine name. What's wrong with it?" Josie asked.

"It's not the name, it's what I've done with it. There is a standing charge of theft on Trevor Lanes in Shavuhnsten. A few other places too."

"I wonder why," Alkis muttered.

Josie reached over and took another biscuit from Tomis's pocket. "I don't know, he might be useful to have in a pinch. I'm coming around to the idea of having a thief nearby."

"Don't get any ideas from him," John said.

"Because you are the model of good parenting?"

John went to speak but was cut short by a horrendous ringing on the deck above. A bell clanged and the pace of the sailors up and down the hallway quickened from their already exhausting pace. A voice hollered above deck.

"Stow the gangway and prepare to cast off!"

Chapter Twenty

Olivia found her favorite spot in the shade of the afterdeck. The westerly wind blew across the cold, ocean water and whipped a chilly breeze to her seat beneath the helm. As long as the ship sailed south, south-east, she could rely on it for a few hours of the day. With little else to do, she resorted to watching the crew go about their business.

The Sovarka ran like a well-timed watch. The crew rose at the same time every day, driven by the chipper urgings of Mr. Cretis, and the night shift retired in short order. Breakfast was provided to everyone. More happened over the course of the day, but it was a garble of sailing jargon to her. It gave her the impression of control though. There were no accidents or strange happenings. Her only source on sailing the high seas were novels: pirates and sea monsters. Thankfully, she found the real thing to be tame.

The captain was as inscrutable at sea as he was on land. Only when the seas grew choppy did he raise his voice. He told Olivia that they were underway and left Congressional waters yesterday. They were now in the Trade Sea, the long and narrow ocean that spanned the relatively short gap between the continents. To the west, the Congress of Six and Shavuhnsten. To the east, the Kingdom of Margecei and Katoia. Far to the south-east was Naelan, their destination.

Olivia took a rag and dipped it into a bucket of water next to her. She pressed it against her forehead. The shade and the frigid ocean water made for an effective treatment. It was not permanent though. The vitality she felt at the Church of the Sun was fading and it had been days since her last meditation. Alkis was not allowed to use the captain's space as they were promised. Despite his rising frustration, the captain did not seem bothered by the complaints. Yanna was too busy to allow it, but said that they would be allowed in today.

Josie, pale as a sheet, staggered up from below deck and shuffled to the railing of the ship. Her eyes opened only long enough to see where she was walking. She wavered on her feet even more than the bobbing of the ship would have done by itself.

"I won't be right after this, you watch," Josie said.

"Still not used to it?"

She hobbled over to Olivia and sat down.

"It's unnatural. This floating on the water business. I don't care for magic. I hate boats."

"You should go below deck. Less horizon to focus on down there," Olivia said.

"It's not the water, it's the bobbing. I can't shake it. Above deck, below deck, it's all the same."

"Almost lunch time. That might help?"

Josie gagged. "Don't speak of food to me."

Olivia rubbed Josie's back. There was no helping her, but at least this was the sort of distress that would not kill her. Olivia could live with that.

"I'm out of advice. You'll just have to suffer."

Alkis emerged from below deck followed by Captain Yanna. The dour, high-collared captain fumbled with a set of keys in his hands, pale green eyes set on the two women by the afterdeck.

"Still growing your sea legs, Ms. Josie?" Yanna asked.

"If one more person makes a nautical jab, they are going overboard," she said, not looking at who was nearby.

"An action that would land you in irons for the remainder of the journey," the captain said.

If it was a joke, his tone did not capture the mood. Josie finally realized who addressed her, but could not conjure the fortitude to improve her temper. She merely restrained it.

"Apologies, Mr. Yanna. I don't feel so good."

"Captain, not mister." He dropped the keys into his pocket. Dropping to eye level, he gestured for her to look at him. He took her chin in his hand and set his fingers against her neck, carefully checking veins and glands beneath her skin.

"First time at sea?"

Josie nodded.

"Her heart beats at a healthy pace, no sign of jaundice. If your condition does not improve, I have some wine and wormwood in my quarters. It has eased my own sea sickness at times."

"A captain who gets seasick?" Olivia asked.

"An acquired condition, much like yours. Mine only comes and goes though instead of your perpetual fever." He turned to the doors leading to his quarters.

The captain fished his keys out of his pocket again and flipped to a shiny, brass key. He turned the lock and held the door open for his guests. His cabin was lit with oil lanterns and was the brightest room on board by a wide margin. The porthole windows on either side of the ship were doubly reinforced with metal slats across them. The sunlight was barely able to filter through. Harpoons were set into a rack on the far wall. A small trophy mount meant for a skull sat empty. An extra-large hammock hung from in the far corner and his desk sat across from it.

"You have the next two hours to work whatever malady it is you must excise from her. If there is one at all." He walked over to his deck and locked some of his desk drawers.

"I am sick, I guarantee that," Olivia said.

He shook the last drawer forcefully and stared at the two of them from across the room.

"But it certainly is not the curse of the invalid as you claim. I do not appreciate being lied to when I believed that I was giving charity to the weak and vulnerable."

Alkis leveled a finger at the captain.

"How dare you accuse us. Our details are our own business."

The captain slammed his palm on his desk and a vein bulged in his forehead. His unshakable calm threatened to shatter. He did not shout or snarl, but his growly voice somehow made it worse.

"Lodgings on a quiet merchant ship at a favorable rate for a girl on the edge of death. That is what you bartered, but here she stands flushed and lively. I demand answers."

"We are not thieves or rogues if that is your concern," Alkis said.

"So when my quartermaster tells me of a suit of granite armor in our stores, I am to assume you are missionaries of the church?" Yanna said.

"No, Alkis." Olivia pressed her hand into his chest.

"We should tell him."

Alkis looked at the captain and back to her.

"You know how people react to mages. How do we know he won't toss us overboard?" Alkis whispered.

The worry crossed her mind. Despite the many who worshiped Flame as a giver of light and life, none of them showed any love of magic. It was an odd dichotomy she was not familiar with before coming on board. They merely wanted to venerate Flame for protecting them from Shadow, but had no desire to wield it.

Of course, these were the best cases. Some onboard reminisced about mugging mages for their belongings or just for satisfaction. They were taught magic ruined the world the same as herself. She understood there was no way to deviate from this path now. The same prejudice she used to carry was now turned back on herself.

"We have to trust someone. If we don't cooperate, we are going to run out of options," she said.

Alkis nodded after a moment and stepped back.

"Captain Yanna, you were deceived because of the nature of our departure. We are being pursued. Two brigands who serve Shadow attacked us at the Church of the Sun. They were after something in our possession," Olivia said.

Yanna arched an eyebrow.

"That was you? Were they after that armor?"

"No, it is something of mine. It is a Focus."

Yanna looked between the two of them for a moment. His fingers reached for a picture frame on his desk.

"You're afflicted. He's helping you control it," the captain said.

"How'd you guess?" Alkis asked.

"I have some experience with the chaos that the primevals can bring into our lives." Yanna looked up and turned the picture frame face down. He stretched his neck and wiped his palms on his coat.

"Thank you for your honesty. I suspected the worst and for that I'm sorry."

"There is nothing to apologize for, Captain. There are some of your crew that we suspected of ill motives as well," Olivia said.

He tilted his head and slid his hands back into his pockets.

"Who?"

"The quartermaster was keenly interested in Olivia's condition and the circumstances of our trip."

"Mr. Cretis is a trusted sailor of mine, but his position is not of my choosing. quartermaster is an elected title on my vessel, as it is on most," Yanna explained.

"And it naturally follows that he would inquire about us on your behalf."

"That is a fair assumption, but I gave him no order to interrogate you for details. His duties are to ensure that our supplies are accounted for and the crew are heard. I would put the fear out of your minds. You are quite safe."

The captain walked past them and opened the door.

"Are you going to tell Cretis about me?" Olivia asked.

"Not if you wish to keep it a secret. As I said, I know the mania that follows the lives of mages. I knew one that dealt with too much of it. If I can spare you the pain, I would," he said.

They were not able to shake the quartermaster's attention. However, knowing that the captain could be trusted eased her.

"Thank you."

He bowed his head to both of them, his face placid and emotionless once again.

"Close the doors behind you when you are done. I will be along to ensure my belongings are still present and accounted for." Yanna closed the doors behind him as he left.

Alone together, she wanted to strategize their next move. With Cretis still watching closely, her secret was not entirely safe. Alkis held up a hand as the captain's boot steps crossed the deck and out of ear shot.

"Cretis absolutely knows about your affliction. I'm sure of it," he said.

"It doesn't bode well, but he also might just be a peevish busy body. Cretis is still bound by his duties and to the captain's will, which is thankfully with us. I am not sure how much more he can do."

Olivia pulled her Focus from inside of her jacket. Alkis paced across the room and looked over the captain's desk.

"For now, we do what the captain said. We will put that worry beyond our minds and focus on the lesson at hand."

Alkis pointed at the large rug that covered most of the floor.

"Let's roll this up, put it back when we are done."

"Would that qualify as touching his belongings?" Olivia asked.

"I don't think he would appreciate burns on his rug."

They left the roll of cloth to the side. Olivia sat in

the center of the room. Alkis reached into the bag and removed a stone gauntlet. It was a piece of his much-vaunted suit of armor. The stone plates were a warm, tan color and the edges were chipped and worn. Alkis wiggled his fingers as he slipped the glove on. Olivia could see his Focus, the chipped slate of stone with the gem set into it, was seated in the palm.

"You ripped your Focus out of the suit?"

"More like chiseled." He stared at the gauntlet on his right arm as if it were talking to him. He smirked and flexed his fingers with an appreciative slowness. She thought of the way that her Focus spoke to her, or maybe it was the elements reaching out to her. Her own Focus felt like a part of her now, like a child quietly humming. Her mind bent toward it at all times.

"When was the last time you wore it?"

Alkis sucked in a breath of air and balled his hand into a fist.

"I buried it three years ago and swore to never use it again."

"Does it remember?" she asked.

Alkis paused and then nodded. "It remembers that I broke my oath. The only reason it might still listen to me is because it doesn't want to go back in the box."

"When you have it on, how does it work? Do you start flying around or something?"

Alkis giggled and glanced at Olivia with his warm eyes.

"When Flame first came to our aid, it gave us True Flame. It was a piece of itself that we could use to drive back the Shadow. The first Fire Keepers had no idea that they were signing their death warrants by using this gift. So we learned to channel the Flame into our armor. This limits what we can do: no fireballs, can't burn down a forest with a thought, can't drive back the night with a small sun."

Alkis brought a fist toward his chest and bent out his elbow away from his body. A light appeared inside of his palm. He opened his fingers and the spark in his palm faded.

"But we can augment our own strength or durability and purge almost any disease from our bodies."

"Almost any?"

"Well." Alkis gestured to her. "One we can't fix. But that is why we're here. Take the Focus in your hand. Elza wanted you to focus on mediation. You found the Flame and now you are talking to it. You showed that at the church."

"That is the end of it though, right? We don't want to push it any further."

"At this juncture, my job is to teach you the basics of Flame magic. It started eating you up because you didn't have a relationship with the Flame. You stuck your hand into the furnace without understanding how hot it was. Give me your hand."

Olivia put her other hand forward. He held it with his armored hand and closed his eyes. She was surrounded by people who did not know a thing about magic. He was an expert, someone who had answers instead of rumors. He opened his eyes and let go of her hand.

"It's content, at least as much as it can be. Its progress has slowed." He asked, "What did Elza teach you about the Focus's position?"

"The elements take a clue from it, sort of guess what you want."

"Good. It's especially useful when you don't have time to think."

He cocked his arm back and an ember sparked in his hand which grew to a small flame. Ash and cinder burst from the gauntlet and the stone surface came to life. Veins and cracks inside of the material grew red hot and glowed against the pale granite. It shimmered with heat. Small flakes of cinder dropped from it.

"Held like this, it knows I want to break something," Alkis said.

"Not me I hope." Olivia smiled.

Alkis squinted, not understanding her until he noticed that the fiery fist was raised in her direction. He relaxed his fist and the flame faded.

"Are they alive?"

"Yes and no. They don't have thoughts or moods like you and me. Best as I can tell, they are imbued with a fraction of the person who made it. When you use a Focus, you are putting a part of your life force in contact with the primeval elements. It's the only thing that can get their attention."

Olivia looked over her Focus again, tracing the curve of the red gem seated in it.

"So this might remember who used it last, who made it?"

"Very likely. It is strange to me how it bonded with you. I would assume that you were lying for some reason, but you're not like that. Here, you try what I did." He raised his fist again, but did not conjure magic to it. "We will go slow though, ease you into it."

Olivia brought her hand in front of her and closed her eyes.

"Find the quiet moment that you found with Elza,

push out the noise."

His voice rumbled in her ears. She thought of his warm eyes looking at her across the floor and wondered what he saw in her. She flushed at these thoughts and pushed them away. Left alone in the quiet, the bad memories poured back in. She heard her mother's distant scream. Green eyes loomed in the shadows and the pillar of flame crackled in the distance. Yorker sat in the flickering darkness at the edge of the fire.

"Focus."

The eyes faded and she walked closer to the fire. Yorker slipped into the darkness and the fire loomed large in front of her. It was larger than last time and now resembled a bonfire that stood twice her height. The flames spilled over its bounds with flickering, seeking tongues of red and yellow. It sought kindling.

"I found it," she said.

"Now, raise a fist like me."

She balled her hand and raised it before the tower of fire.

"Now imagine the flame in your hand. Invite an ember to your palm. Not to you, invite it to your palm."

She looked at the fire.

Come to my hand, she thought.

The flame rose and whispered toward her arm, but did not cross the gap.

"Try speaking," Alkis said.

"I want to think it. No one else says anything."

"And most everyone else you've seen is an experienced mage. You'll get there, but not right now."

"Flame, come to my hand," she said.

The fire in front of her burst forward and wrapped around her arm. She gasped as the heat bloomed against her skin. It danced around her arm like a curious snake.

"Now pull it back," Alkis said.

Olivia gripped the tendril of flame in her fingers and pulled it from the bonfire. It bloomed in her hand and boiled down to a small cinder, a spark in her palm.

"Open your eyes," he said, a laugh held in his chest.

She realized the heat on her face was not completely imagined. A sphere of shimmering heat shimmered around her fist. Embers sparked off it as they had from Alkis's hand. She could feel the heat coursing from her heart to her arm, the Flame cooperating with her. Alkis grinned and looked between her and the sphere of magical fire.

"You're a natural."

She smiled back but was quick to look at her fist again.

"Damned luck, look at it."

It would be a lie to say she was not exhilarated. The elements were like a nagging voice in her head, a dull vibration that would not go away. Yet, when she channeled them as she did now, the nagging feeling turned into music. Her heart beat with the flow of the primeval and suddenly it felt as though the whole world danced to her tune.

It's beautiful.

"Don't get distracted. You are going to send it back, ready?" he asked.

She nodded and closed her eyes.

"No, open them."

"What?" she asked.

"Consider it a challenge." His grin refused to leave his face. She nodded and focused her attention on her fist.

"Good, now address it. Send it home."

Olivia found the pulsing center. The white-hot ember bloomed in the middle of her Focus.

"I do not need this ember, take it back," she said.

The heat guttered. The cinders ceased flaking from the sphere and it dimmed lower and lower until it was snuffed. She flexed her fingers and drew her hand down into her other one. She laughed and felt her palm. It was still warm.

"I did it."

"Very good, ready for more?" Alkis asked.

Olivia nodded. "What's next?"

Chapter Twenty-One

Josie spent a great deal of time with John and Tomis over the next few days. Alkis and Olivia would disappear to the captain's quarters for training. Even after they were done, Olivia was distracted. So fascinated by the powers that she swore off for years, Josie recognized her sister less and less.

For the first two days, Josie was occupied with groggy, stumbling sea sickness. No part of her life prepared her for the dominion this illness held over her. People from the Seventh boasted about their constitution and adaptability. Josie failed that first tenant entirely. So she aspired to live up to that second principle.

The third day marked a definite shift for Josie Faros. She rolled out of her hammock and did not feel the urge to grasp it for balance. She skipped breakfast that morning, but walked the halls with a familiar clarity she feared was gone for good. The revolting nausea was gone. By that evening, she appreciated a setting sun at sea for the very first time.

Captain Yanna's tight-lipped nature only grew more tense as they went further out to sea. He could pass for a walking corpse, glassy eyes watching the waves around them. When he was not tied up with his inner thoughts, he gave jargon filled orders that were as hard to decipher as his own thoughts. Olivia said that he was a friend or at least had no intention of harming them. Josie was not as assured about the quartermaster.

She was aware of the nosy, yellow-eyed man. As the only passengers on the ship, he had plenty of excuses to talk to every single one of them. However, his attention was unquestionably on Olivia. He screwed up his face and buried that hooked nose in his ledger whenever he was rebuffed. Something about Olivia got under his skin. For now, Cretis made a habit of taking his lunches on the bow so that he could watch Olivia and Alkis come and go from the captain's quarters. Olivia was not the only one to suffer his presence. The first day at sea, he made a point to speak to Josie.

"A woman of your size, gib-faced appearance, and prodigious strength, surely you've worked as a menial before. Now, now, you're not attending any masquerades, don't give me that look. So if I need you as another pair of hands to swab the decks, what is your going rate?"

Only John's hand around her wrist and an agile dodge from Cretis stopped her from laying the quartermaster on his back. John cursed at Cretis for the insult, but the yellow-eyed creep got away without consequence. She understood the danger of attacking someone who was in charge of the vessel, but she still dreamed of ways she could pay him back.

John made his best attempt to appear relaxed. He slept in, or at least appeared to with his hand laid over the small dagger on his belt. He joined the crew for card games in the evening, but never bet more than ten coins across the match. Whenever there was an argument over gambling payouts among the crew, he was generous enough to spot a needy debtor from his own pocket. Josie wondered how much longer he could keep this up. Uncle

John, described as a rogue by his own brother, was the most risk-averse person onboard.

This left Tomis and Josie with time to burn. The crew worked in shifts and there were always a few idle hands throughout the day that whiled their time away with cards, stories, and other ways to thrill the dull hours. Josie insisted that Tomis teach her a card game called Stoking. Her uncle protested, likely not wanting to add another gambler to the pool. However, when challenged to come up with a better pastime, he relented.

"It is all about keeping your own campfire going," Tomis tapped at the Ace of Easts placed in front of her, "Each player has their own fire, mine being the Ace of Norths here. The fire will need kindling every turn or it will go out and you lose. The rest of the cards in your hand can either be fuel or hazards. Fuel keeps your fire going, hazards increase the cost to keep your opponent's fire going."

"So the betting comes in on whose fire is higher at the end of the round?" Josie asked.

"Correct."

"And there is an advantage to going last, you see everything that's been set out before you."

"Or you go first and are really good at reading people," Tomis said.

Tomis recited the rules with a lively energy. She was happy to have a distraction. The wiry, nervous, and haggard thief that she met slowly turned into a wiry, nervous, and well-rested teacher. Over their sessions, he taught her how to spot a tell or spin a lie. She learned the best ways to cheat at cards and a few useful ways to get out of paying your debt at the end of the night. He also taught her how to take a hit.

Tomis reminded her of John, but a John that was out-of-sorts with himself. He was certainly the black sheep. Alkis openly distrusted him and Olivia did not speak with him beyond polite conversation. Over the course of their days, Josie noticed that his nice clothing was disappearing. When he showed up one day wearing the ugliest, worn shoes, she was compelled to ask.

"They think I've only played cards a few times," Tomis said with a grin, "I've proved as much over these few days. When we sit down for our last game before we make port, I'll break them so badly that they will have to give me the shirts off their backs."

He giggled and pounded the table.

"But it's a game and the results are not decided. There is a degree of luck to it," she said.

"Well, yes."

"You don't see the danger in wagering everything on a single game after slowly losing everything beforehand? If you lose, you've just made a bad bet with extra steps."

Tomis shrugged.

"I lost the boots, but won some coin in the end. I put up one of those nice, soft cotton shirts we bought. I knew the sailors would have an eye for something clean and warm."

"You've thought that far ahead?" she asked.

"Supply and demand, young lady. Eventually, I made enough actual money to put up real bets. Feed the pig plenty of carrots and meat. Come time for slaughtering, it will be a ripe bounty."

"Seems risky," Josie said.

"Oh, horrifically so. What else am I going to do though? I pulled you all into this incredible trouble. I already owe John for the clothes. Who knows when I'll get another gig. Or when I can stop worrying about some shadow cultist sticking a knife in me."

"And if you lose, if your gambit does not work, then you stay in John's debt and we have to keep helping you."

Tomis shrugged again. He swiped up a bit of cold mashed potatoes from his lunch plate onto his finger and popped it into his mouth.

"That is the risk we take."

Josie laughed.

"What?" he asked.

"You're crazy."

"There is a certain thrill to it. Lose everything, win big. I've done both a lot. Okay, the first one more often than the second. I've yet to make a bet that didn't pay off in some way though. There's always an upside."

Josie narrowed her eyes, her smile still on her face.

"So why do you do it?"

Tomis stretched his arm down the table and hooked a basket of oranges with a finger and dragged it closer to them. He snagged one, peeled a patch of skin, and took a bite.

"What does it matter to you? You heard your cleric buddy, I'm bad news."

"He's been in a church for the last three years, of course he is gonna have a certain reaction to ne'er do wells."

"Careful with that word. I do well quite often."

"You're out there on your own. No one to hurt, no one to help. Being part of a community is comforting, but it's all relationships and politics," she said.

He took another bite from the orange and listened.

"Who is growing the same thing as who, who can sell it better, is there enough food to cover the weaker yields for winter. There's just a lot of structure. People talk about passing on the farm to this son or that son-in-law. Olivia will inherit the farm; we're going to have to suffer some gossip for that."

"I got the sense that folks from the Seventh didn't particularly care if a man or a woman did the tilling," Tomis said.

"Most of the time it is. We all get taught how to field dress a deer, but once you get into family politics and who-owns-whose land, suddenly people love to cite the way things are elsewhere," Josie said.

"You're both capable. Who's to say you don't shake things up?"

"Slowly going that way anyhow. She wouldn't be the first female heir to a farm as large as ours. Just hope Olivia doesn't let tradition get in her way. She is so hesitant at times, it kills me. Wouldn't say that to her though, that stays between us."

"So you think you could run it better?" Tomis asked.

Josie never gave the idea too much thought. Her attention was on paying back her adoptive family. Earning her keep as it were. She never told them this and they never asked for it. The idea of claiming the farm as her own almost sounded funny. That was Olivia's fate. At least, that was what she assumed her fate would be.

"No, no. It's not like that. She's earned it and I was more than happy to help her run the place. I could handle the day to day: make sure the livestock are fed, tend to the horses, work with the field laborers, that stuff. She could handle the big stuff like finances and property law, blah, blah blah."

Tomis idly peeled the orange and yanked another ripe piece from it.

"That was until all this mess happened. I've spent my whole life in the Seventh. The Seers family took me in when I was young, my family farm burnt up with my folks in it. I had nothing and they've treated me like one of their own. If you asked me three weeks ago where I would be in thirty years, my only answer would be in Hasketter."

Josie gestured to the galley that they sat in.

"And now look at all this. I've barely seen anything of the ocean and there is a whole other continent."

"The yearning desire to see more. I get you," he said.

She scoffed and thought about cursing. He completely misunderstood.

"It's not me who wants to see more. I can't wait to get off this floating casket. I never cared for magic and neither did Olivia. Now she is upstairs messing with that stuff and the redhead, which has only gotten us into more trouble," Josie said.

"So you are left here wondering if there will even be an Olivia in Hasketter?" Tomis asked.

Even though she was getting to that, it still made her squirm to hear it out loud. Her first instinct was to double down. She was used to being strong and sometimes that meant letting everyone know you were. Doubt could pick someone apart as easily as a knife. If Tomis knew she would not tolerate magic, or change, maybe that could shift things. She was starting to think it would just make things worse. That left Josie with only one other option: adapt.

"You travel a fair bit. You've met mages and all kinds of people. Right?"

A weasel smile flashed on his face. Maybe he thought the sudden change of topic was a joke. He settled and rolled the half-eaten orange in his hand.

"You could say I have, sure."

"And your whole situation is mostly your own doing. You cheated people and hung around those with poor intentions."

"That stung a bit to hear out loud."

"What I mean is, you're still here. Just knowing different kinds of people didn't sink you. Knowing mages didn't leave you insane or maimed or dead."

"No, no, it didn't. You know people are pretty much the same. Doesn't matter if they can speak to birds or whatever. And, well." Tomis pulled his fingers tight in his hand and waved away a thought.

"What?"

"It's family stuff, I don't know any better and I shouldn't read into things."

"You do open your mouth often, but I'd like to hear it this time."

Another wry grin and he ran his fingers through his thin, dark hair.

"Just because you're so far apart, doesn't mean you can't coexist. That's the only way the world works, getting along with each other. If we all just stamped our feet and turned away, we'd never get anything done."

Josie did not miss what he was actually talking about. Even though he was not a parent, not a father, not even a role model, he still carried a wisp of wisdom. Maybe it was something she would carry someday. And if she did not have it at this point, maybe something would mold it inside of her.

"But, what about looking weak? If you swear up and

down that you hate cabbage, then one day you say you love it, what's everyone supposed to think of your judgment?"

"Hopefully, they realize that people can be wrong. But, again, that's just me. Food for thought."

The cook snorted as he walked into the galley with armfuls of carrots, tomatoes, and onions. He hummed a slow melody. The cook stumbled into Tomis's chair and lost a few vegetables to the floor.

"Sorry, sorry. Didn't see you, you all have your appetite? Tonight marks the end of summer and I've got a vegetable soup in mind. Good bits of broth and some Shauven Flatbread for dipping," the cook said as he picked up the dropped food.

"Busy night for you then?" Josie asked.

"Indeed, the whole crew will be in attendance save for enough people to keep the ship sailing."

"We won't go far then," Tomis said and put up his feet.

Chapter Twenty-Two

The galley was never this full. Dinner time was always a busy time, but there was at least a third of the crew out to hold the night shift. They jammed into the doorway, crammed hip-to-hip on each of the few tables. More leaned against walls with the bowls in hand.

Olivia and Alkis found Josie and Tomis already waiting. John joined later and squeezed in so close to another sailor that it would have been roomier for them to throw their arms around each other. Across the room, Cretis reclined against a wall with a bowl held in the crook of his wrist. He smiled and listened to a red-face sailor next to him, but Olivia did not miss that he could watch all five of them from his vantage point.

They all slurped on shabby spoons that had never seen a quality soap. Carrot ends, onion peel, and chewy bits of herbs floated in the broth like icebergs. It made for cautious slurping, but the savory zest made Olivia forgive the faults. She soaked some bread in the broth when a shrill clanging disturbed the low mutter of voices. At the front of the room, Captain Yanna leaned against a counter with his own bowl. His spoon knocked it four more times.

"Thank you, sailors of the Sovarka. A hand for our cook, the patient Hazim Fens who makes the haul on this boat a bit more joyful with every morsel." The crew clapped and slapped their bare palms onto tables for the portly man.

"And a thanks to our passengers for a quiet ride. Their presence is unusual, but they have played gracious guests. No matter the forces they contend with, they have been most considerate."

The crew gave a smaller round of applause and table thumping. Cretis looked bored. She could almost see him fight the urge to roll his eyes. All the same, she caught his yellow eyes from across the room. He twitched his lip and gave a small nod. You might have everyone fooled, she imagined him saying.

The applause trailed off and Olivia took another slurp from her bowl. She was used to disaster at this point. When they sat down, she half-expected Cretis to interrogate her in front of the whole crew. From how he sulked against his seat, he looked defeated.

"This meal marks the end of summer. It also coincides with our transit back into territorial waters. We are nearing the coasts of Katoia and Naelan. Our passengers will be glad to hear they will depart in a matter of days. The rest of you will be glad to hear that we will be remaining in harbor at Naelan for a week after we arrive. So ready yourself for leisure, you all have earned it." The crew banged tables, whooped, and clapped again. This one was louder than any before it.

"We have enjoyed a calm voyage. No creatures of Shadow nor tempests of Water. I raise a glass now to the Triad: Earth, Water, and Flame. May the Water move us swiftly, the Earth come to us without delay, and Flame protect us," Yanna said.

The crew answered with a mixture of ayes and nods. Some repeated the captain's last line and bowed their heads in reverence before drinking. Olivia clinked her cup against Alkis's and then Josie's. The other two were out of reach and she merely lifted it toward them. Something still nagged at her. It was the same kind of buzzing that she felt in the presence of Flame or Life. She could barely perceive it.

"I think we might get out of this yet," Alkis said.

"I wouldn't be so fast to assume that." Olivia poked at her soup.

"Only two days left in the journey. What harm could he do?"

She thought about all the hardy, quick-to-action people around them. Their difficulties were knitted for the most part, but she did not miss the way that Josie avoided her around lunch time. It was as though she did not want to be reminded of what Olivia was practicing. Clearly, she found the thief to be better company than herself. The same sentiment was strong among the rest of the crew and they did not have the familial connection to restrain them.

Olivia found it difficult to put the magic away once the lesson was over. As she sharpened her craft, the more she felt it around her. Floating on the ocean, she could still feel the scurrying of small rodents below deck and the algae blooming on the underside of the ship. The Flame purred in her chest, fed and happy. It was growing, certainly, but it felt like a slowly rising tide rather than a crashing flood.

Olivia had another set of eyes and ears. It was like when she was young and unafraid of this power. She ran her fingers around the cheap, wooden bowl and imagined heating it to a scalding boil. How would they react? Could Cretis incite the crew so quickly?

"As long as we're on this ship, we aren't safe."

Olivia lowered her voice. "We have no idea how these people might react to a mage. Two of them to boot."

"Unfortunately, she's right. We have to keep our guard up a while longer. Has he kept his distance or has been hounding you still?" John said.

"He's stopped pestering us immediately after lessons, he doesn't come by to quiz us. All he does is watch," Alkis said.

All the obvious interdictions had stopped. Still, she could not shake the feeling that he was like a wolf stalking a larger pack. It was thrown back a few times after being too bold. Now he waited for some other opening.

"But he isn't done," she said.

"We could be done with this if you let me at him," Josie whispered.

"Don't even think about it. He might be ready to kill to defend himself. Can you say the same?" John asked.

Josie glimpsed the thought and hunched over her near empty bowl. "Just don't think we should let him bully my sister and everyone else."

"That's the way things are sometimes." John glanced across the room at the yellow-eyed man. "Then we don't give him anything. If he is being quiet, we go quiet as well. Think you could get away without meditations for a day?"

Olivia did not like the idea of bottling it all up, but knew the stakes. One slip, one piece of provocative suggestion and they could find this to be an unwelcome ship. She also had no clue how the Flame inside of her might respond to a sudden deprivation. It was peaceful prior, but she learned it was anything but predictable.

"I guess it wouldn't hurt," she said. "What do you

think, Alkis?"

The cleric balanced on the back legs of his chair.

"It should be fine. One day won't set her too far back. But we are dealing in matters of weeks now. An hour, a day might be acceptable now, but we might wish we had it down the road."

John toyed with a ring on his finger. His face pulled tight as he considered the gamble, but then chuckled.

"What?" Olivia asked.

"Never easy with you is it?" he asked.

There was a time she would have considered it a barb. Too much happened to miss the real intention of what he said.

"I wouldn't want you to get bored like you were back home. This is far more exciting, isn't it?" Olivia asked.

"All the same, we're getting you back there." John raised his cup. "Swear on it."

Alkis and Josie were quick to toast, but Tomis continued slurping up more warm stew. Josie jabbed him in the ribs and he spit a bit of soup back up.

"Don't act like you don't care," she said to him.

Even with the prompting, Olivia saw the flash of hesitancy in his face. He hid it and raised his cup with a plastered, warm smile.

"You're right, a friend of John is a friend of mine. I'll do my best," Tomis said.

They clinked the wooden cups and went about the remainder of their meal. Conversation strayed from Cretis, magic, and her affliction, but Olivia's mind never wandered far. That dull hum still lingered. Looking away from her table, she caught Cretis giving them a glance before stepping out of the room.

He hiked his coat up over his neck, but his eyes glittered with manic anger. It reminded her too much of the bandits on the side of the road. She considered telling everyone else, but wondered what good it would do. Cretis was restrained by Captain Yanna's warnings and his methods were rendered pointless. With so little time left, it was probably frustration she had seen. Nothing more.

****

The sea lashed against the hull with a dull crash. It almost drowned out the snoring of sleeping sailors. Olivia laid in her hammock, hoping that sleep was moments away. She gripped the hilt of her hunting knife and adjusted in her hammock.

The Flame was growing again. It still sought kindling. Like a dog allowed to run across wide fields without a leash, the occasional exercise stopped it from acting out. However, she was running out of room to let it play. Her improved condition did nothing to ease her mind. She would burn out in time, but she had a real chance now. Once they disembarked in Naelan, it was a short distance to the Archive Primeval.

The ship rolled and creaked with unnerving moans. A storm rose as the sun set. Just a temperamental squall, the boatswain told them. The night crew could certainly handle it. She drifted closer to sleep knowing her family were near.

The boat shifted again and a creak followed. She hardly noticed the first time, but the second and third creak pulled her from the promise of sleep. She looked around the sleepy berth with a bleary eye. The candles were extinguished save for the small lanterns in the main hallway that ran from bow to stern. The forest of hammocks waved back and forth. Sailors turned in their sleep while others were so quiet that they might have been dead.

The candles just outside of the berth flickered, but the light did not return. They remained as a low spot of red fire, almost snuffed in the candle holders. Even the light from the portholes, dismal as it was, shrank to nothing. Her heartbeat pounded louder in her ears as whispers rose in the darkness. She went to rise against the hammock, but cold ropes pulled her against the netting.

Bundles of shadow wreathed around her hammock, under her arms, and across her chest and thighs. She flexed against them and tried to scream, but found the same cold feeling across her face. She bit against her misty binds, but they would not break. She looked up from the black ties as a shape loomed closer.

He wore a simple undershirt and trousers. His hair was a tangled mop of curls that only made his yellow eyes more distinct. Cretis held his hand in front of him, fingers flexed like a cage around a small bird. One of his rings glowed with a dull, purple light.

He said nothing as he came closer to Olivia, his eyes were drawn to the bags that sat beneath her bed. His incisors peeked from behind his lips, sharper than they ever should have been. He gripped his fingers tighter and the shadowy ropes tightened around her. She pressed with all her strength, but found Shadow unbending. Cretis leaned down and sorted through her bags, his other hand inches from her throat.

The Flame surged inside of her. He was close to her Focus, his fingers scraping around inside of the bag. It was afraid; she was afraid. She looked over to her sleeping friends, but the room was too dark to see beyond her assailant. She was alone while this ghoul sorted through her things.

The shadow pulled tight around her neck. She gasped for air and kicked her legs. She felt his fingers slip around her Focus as if he grabbed her leg. Her heart pounded in her chest and she felt tears well into her eyes.

"A bit of a gamble by me, just taking it off you. But I'm short on time. It will be so sad when they find your corpse in the morning. Guess the affliction moved faster than they thought it would," Cretis whispered.

He leaned in and kissed her forehead. The Focus, held in his free hand, came as close as it would get. With the light fading, she pressed forward with one arm and drew the other one back. She won only a few inches of movement, but it was all she needed. Her fingers caressed the golden artifact and she screamed one thought to the pillar of Flame in her mind.

Burn.

Her hand erupted into a ball of light. Shadow hissed and scattered from it as the bindings came undone. She pressed it into his chest and full, leaping flames erupted from her fingers. Smoke filled the air and a roar of fire sent every sailor falling from their hammock or screaming awake. Cretis stumbled across the room and her Focus clattered to the ground next to her bed. She grabbed it and drew her hunting knife from her waist. Blood pumped through her veins. The Flame would not wait and it pushed her further into a witless rage.

Olivia crossed the distance to the still-smoking Cretis in two bounds. It was hard to tell that he was alive between blistered skin and smoking hairs. She did not worry for family, fair judgment, or law. Ending his life was the only thing Olivia could consider.

She leaped on him with a feral yell and swung the knife. His hand flew up to block the blow and her blade lopped off the fingers of his hand. Olivia drew the knife back and readied to drive it down when a hand grabbed her from behind. Another hand yanked her off Cretis.

"He has to die. He has to die!" she shouted.

Several sailors pushed her against one of the wooden supports in the room and yanked the knife out of her hand. Josie bullied past the many waking sailors and struck one of them. The chaos of the room turned against them in that instant. Olivia saw only a swarm of bodies and fists as John, Alkis, and Tomis tried to separate the crowd from Josie. Her sister fought hard for someone unused to brawling. Olivia breathed a sigh of relief when the furious voice of Captain Yanna bellowed through the berth.

"Enough of this! All of you."

The tide of violence settled. Josie pinned a man to the floor with her boot and another one throttled her from behind. John and Alkis stumbled out from a crowd of people that collapsed into a heap of bruised faces. They only looked marginally better.

"The girl stabbed Cretis. She tried to murder the quartermaster," a sailor said.

"But he was up to something odd. What was he doing here after hours?" the cook asked.

Captain Yanna helped up a sailor from the ground. Bright, furious eyes swept from person to person across the room and settled on Cretis, who laid on the ground where Olivia left him. His eyes trailed to Olivia and went to the golden Focus in her hand. Cretis giggled and spat blood onto the floor as the entire room followed the captain's gaze.

"What did he do?" Yanna asked.

"He's a shadow mage. He tried to kill me," Olivia said, her voice hoarser than she expected it to be.

Cretis offered no defense. He chuckled like a fool and clutched at the stumps of his fingers. The captain leaned down to him.

"Are they lying?"

Cretis giggled, his body shaking with laughter.

"It doesn't matter, nothing you do matters," Cretis said between his fits.

"He's looney," the cook said, "he's had it out for the passengers since they boarded. Trying to sully the girl's honor, I bet."

A group of sailors moved toward the cook with curses and balled fists, ready to defend their quartermaster's reputation. The captain stopped them with a raised hand.

"Enough of this. Put him in irons and pull him top side. We'll get the truth out of him there."

"You're going to trust their word over his?" one of the crew asked.

"I said do it. We'll sort this out now. You five," Yanna gestured to Olivia and her companions, "be along quickly. Don't make me shackle you as well."

Those who maligned Cretis were quick to drag him from the floor and bind his hands. Shackles appeared a minute later and locked around his feet. The remainder of the crew, just over half, stood by with uneasy faces. They gave Olivia dirty looks before following their captive quartermaster to the main deck. Olivia walked over to her family.

"You're bleeding. Water and fire, what did he do?"

Josie asked.

Olivia's clothing was stained with droplets of blood. She winced as she felt her midsection. It felt like a papercut wound around her body wherever the binds of Shadow clutched at her.

Alkis kept an eye on the last few sailors who made their way out from the berth. He stood in front of Olivia and the rest of them, his armored gauntlet already slipping over his hand. John was busy loading his hand crossbow.

"I'm so sorry Olivia. I had no idea he would—"

"Neither did I, it's fine. We're alive," she said.

"No way that lunatic doesn't end up in the brig for the remainder of the voyage," Josie added.

Tomis wandered over to Cretis's severed fingers and the rings that rolled around on the floor. He picked up a silver ring that was seated with a dull, gray gem.

"What did he mean, 'It doesn't matter'? They could hang him for this, of course it matters what they do," Tomis said.

"Like I said, he's a lunatic. Less thought spent on him the better," Josie said.

"No, he's got a point. How did he know what to look for?" Olivia pulled away from Josie's grasp.

"I haven't seen a messenger hawk or pigeon anywhere on this ship. He couldn't have let them know unless he was dropping bottles into the sea. And with this storm, I doubt that would make for a useful trail," John said.

Alkis shook his head and looked between Tomis's rings and Olivia. She was coming to understand a little bit more of what was possible when magic was an option. With Alkis's tutoring, she was learning just how much was possible with magic at play.

"Shadow is everywhere and nowhere. He could easily have been talking to Faldir this entire time. He has his own room. Flame bless, no one could catch him unawares if he was careful."

"We have to get up there and warn the captain," Olivia said.

Josie readied her polished ax. John finished tying his gauntlets over his arms. Tomis held his hunting knife with a shaky grip. He looked over the knife like it might bite him.

"Go ahead, I will need a minute to get the suit ready," Alkis said.

Olivia's eyes caught his. "Be quick."

He winked and nodded for her to go. Under the amber candlelight, she wished they had more time to know each other. Those feelings did not go away, not since the church. If anything, they intensified as he brought her into his world. The fear she felt for the Fire Keeper was long gone. There was some other restlessness in her heart, but this wasn't the time for it. Now she was afraid there would never be such a time.

With Josie, John, and Tomis at her back, she marched up the stairs and slipped the Focus over her fingers. The deck was lit with as many lanterns and torches as the crew could gather. Cretis was roped to the ship's mast, hands behind him and neck dangling forward. His body shook with the occasional giggle, but his fit of laughter was over. Captain Yanna stood in front of him with a saber in hand. The circle of onlookers made it feel like an execution. The wind whipped across the deck and sent the torches flickering to small pits of flame. They reached the main deck as the gust died and

Yanna's voice rose with it.

"Confess what you've done. I'd rather you cool your head in the brig than throw you overboard."

"I would be quite comfortable in the deep. My friends will find me," Cretis said.

Sailors muttered with worried looks.

"Pure madness, how much did he have to drink?" one of them asked.

"Confess," Yanna pleaded.

"You're not the one I need." Cretis stopped himself. Olivia pressed through the crowd and into the firelight. His mouth went slack.

"She's the one I want to confess to."

The captain turned and pointed to the afterdeck behind them.

"I don't need you riling him up. Wait over there, I'll deal with you all in a minute."

"I told you some days ago that we are being pursued. We believe he might be in league with them. We're all in danger," Olivia said.

"She brought it up for all of us to see. How nice not to hide it." Cretis eyed the golden Focus on her hand.

"She's a mage?" someone shouted from the crowd.

"This whole voyage is cursed, it's a wonder we haven't caught fire," another one said.

The murmuring grew into a dull thunder. Olivia lowered the Focus to her side, images of an angry mob crossing her mind. It was one thing to face it in theory, but the reality was much worse.

John waved his hands at the crowd and shouted over the building hysteria. "Quiet! Captain, you need to put as much speed in these sails as you can."

Yanna shook his head. "The cover of night is buying

us time, there is no way for them to know where we are unless we've been tailed."

"It's possible," John said.

"No, it's not," Yanna spat. His temper pushed to the surface. "My daughter tempted the powers of Water with her gift. I learned that it was a power you must respect and keep at arm's length. I've done my best to do that and I've tolerated your use of it because you have been compliant and kind. Do not lecture me on what is and is not possible at sea."

"She's not telling you what's possible at sea. She's telling you what's possible at night." John's tone of voice would have sounded appropriate intermingled with swears.

"Captain," a man in the crow's nest squinted into the distance, "Vessel off of our stern and closing fast, northwest."

"What flag does it fly?" Yanna shouted back.

"No flag and no lights."

Olivia's stomach fell as the ship crested a wave. It was Faldir. The obsession in that woman was clear the moment they met. She truly would chase Olivia to the ends of the world. The crowd of sailors broke from the circle and looked over the railing. The deranged man laughed again and nodded toward her.

"You've damned us," Yanna said to Cretis.

"Not all of us. You could always hand her over. I'm sure they would be pleased."

John held Josie back. Her ax was raised at her side, ready to strike.

"Let me end the miserable worm," she growled.

"Flame fades. It will abandon you or it will consume you. Shadow was there at the beginning, and it will be at the end," Cretis babbled.

He looked away from Olivia as his captain stepped toward him. Yanna raised the point of his saber and ran the quartermaster through. Olivia watched the sword draw out of Cretis and her Flame squirmed with satisfaction. She hated the feeling, but the fire still throbbed in her veins. It wanted her to watch. Cretis whined in pain, but his voice choked as Yanna twisted the blade in his guts. No one gasped in surprise or moved to stop him. Tomis stepped back from them and nervously looked at the horizon.

The yellow-eyed madman kept his eyes on Olivia as the light faded from him and his breath grew shallow. He slumped in his binds and fell still. Only his head rolled with the sway of the deck.

Josie stuttered out a few words as she watched the man die. Olivia felt the urge to shield her sister, but the Flame basked in the violence. It ached against her skin, the promise of release not far ahead. Enraptured by Cretis's death, she could only worry about her sister from afar. The Flame had her now.

"Captain, we need a heading. Ship is closing," the boatswain called from the helm.

"Crew to arms," Yanna bellowed, "full sail to port and run her along the wind. We'll see if we can lose them."

A bell rang on the ship and the crew scattered to find anything suitable for a weapon. Deck axes, harpoons, knives, and paddles were readied with equal trepidation. The Sovarka turned and a shape loomed out of the shadow. Gray sails buffeted in the breeze as the black hull rose into view. A trio of spikes were leveled at the side of their ship.

"Brace!" the lookout shouted.

Chapter Twenty-Three

"Brace! Brace and prepare for boarding," Yanna shouted.

Whatever crew members remained above deck rallied to their captain. They grabbed on to ropes and railings. Josie grabbed Olivia with one hand and the railing of the ship with the other. John dashed to the center of the foredeck and held onto a rope that ran up the front end of the sail.

The dark ship crashed through a rising wave and the trio of spikes pierced the hull of the Sovarka. It shuddered with a cracking groan that made Olivia think the ship would surely fall apart. Sailors lost their grips and hurtled across the deck. Torches were snuffed by a wave of sea water. Lanterns broke and littered the ground with shining shards of glass and small trickles of oil. Josie gasped as she fought to keep her grip on the railing, but held firm. The dark ship lurched forward as it came to a halt.

A woman in a dark cloak stood on the prow of the other ship, an onyx rod in her hand. Faldir had found her again. Behind her, a number of physically warped, sullen crew members waited. Captain Yanna flourished his saber in the light of the dying torches.

"I am captain of this vessel and request your surrender. Prepare to be boarded. Our ship is ailing and we will need to requisition yours to complete our journey."

"Is that a threat?" Faldir asked.

"Let me make myself clear: surrender or die."

"If that is your choice," she said.

Faldir gestured forward and the sea erupted with thrashing bodies and snapping claws. A dozen creatures climbed up the sides of the wounded vessel. Their dark green shells were covered in barnacles and stank of fish. Spider legs, tipped with sharp hooks, carried them toward their prey. A long eel's tail stuck out from the back and a chomping pair of jaws opened to let a seeking tongue lash forward.

John aimed into the wet maw of the nearest one and fired. His aim put the short bolt right into its mouth and a gout of slime exploded from it. He drew his short sword and swiped at another creature's legs as it scampered in his direction.

Josie roared and swung her ax down onto another one of the crustaceans. The blade cracked its shell in a single stroke, black ichor spurting from the wound. Not quite dead, the creature stabbed into her leg with its hooks. It pulled itself toward her, the toothy maw opening for her knee. Josie kicked with her other leg, broken fangs rolling away. Its hooks ripped from her leg.

Olivia readied her Focus as a third creature circled her. She opened her fingers.

"Give me an ember."

The Flame answered and a cinder grew into a shining orb of light. The monster gurgled and lashed its tail against the deck before it lunged toward her. She stepped back from a pair of raking hooks and kicked the crustacean in its maw. Olivia brought a hammer blow down onto its shell. Heat radiated from her strike and the creature sizzled. It squealed. The shell steamed and cracked. It came in for another bite, but Olivia grabbed one of its jaws. It tried to close its teeth around her hand and only found burning magic.

"We have to get off this ship," John said.

He sliced another leg from a creature and then plunged his sword into the fleshy side of its shell.

"Where did Tomis go?" Josie asked as another monster broke from the water and climbed up the railing behind her.

"No time. Where are the lifeboats?" John turned and knocked a crab-monster back into the water.

Olivia looked back at the stairs that led below. Alkis was still below deck. Her mind imagined him swarmed by these things all alone. He was far more capable than she could be. She only hoped that his armor was as terrifying as the stories suggested.

"There is one at the back of the ship, but we have to wait for Alkis," Olivia said.

"We have to get to that lifeboat. Now," John snapped.

"Without him, I die. I'm not cured yet."

John cursed and kicked at a dead creature.

"Fine, we find the lifeboat and double back. Maybe he will be up by then."

The ship began to list, and large waves washed onto the far edge of the sinking vessel. Large oars extended from the sides of the dark ship and paddled backward. It withdrew its prow from the hull of the Sovarka. The hull groaned as twisted metal and splintered wood fell away from the wound.

Of the crew, only the captain was left alive. Dead monsters littered the deck with spears stuck into their maws and shells cracked open. Fallen sailors were shredded by hooked talons or throats ripped out by snapping jaws. Captain Yanna sliced and leaped among the creatures, reaping a tally from the horrid things. He backed up into the group of three, Josie swinging her ax into the face of a beast next to him. Yanna turned, saber raised, and stopped.

"Lifeboats?" Yanna asked.

They nodded.

"We're going for the one at the back of the ship," John said, taking the moment to reload his hand crossbow.

A howl echoed over the ship and the group turned to see a hooded beast leap onto the deck. Faldir followed, rolling after she landed. The Hooded Man bounded across the deck toward Captain Yanna, the hood falling back to reveal his twisted form. Josie lowered her shoulder and charged into the monster's side.

She saved Captain Yanna from his claws, but the momentum carried her backward. He crashed through them and the group scattered where they could. John rolled to his feet and fired at the Hooded Man. The bolt lodged into his back, but barely slowed the monster down. Josie's ax swing was knocked aside by the creature's swift paw. His talons cut into Josie's arm.

Yanna extended a hand to Olivia and helped her up. She felt like she might combust at any second as the Flame pulsed inside of her. The fear of death was strong enough to shake the blood thirst that overtook her before. He leaned on her shoulder and tried to catch his breath.

"Breathe, I saw your friend Trevor run toward—"

A streak of dark magic screamed through the air and pierced his back. It cut straight through and tore away a piece of railing inches away from Olivia. Captain Yanna dropped to the ground without another sound. Faldir pointed her Focus at Olivia and smirked. She fired a second bolt.

Olivia raised her fist in front of her and imagined a shield. Heat blazed through her and a disc of light and cinder burst into existence. The void magic evaporated into mist against it, but Faldir did not wait. Her eyes clouded over black and dark magic weaving itself into claws around her hands. Faldir lunged across the deck and night swallowed up any light in her path. Her shadowy claws broke against Olivia's shield. A second strike came forward and Olivia stepped back.

She was exhausted. Olivia could channel the Flame, but it was no match for this experienced assassin. The heat rose inside of her. It wanted to break free and set the entire world ablaze. It wanted to burn this void mage and consume the ship for kindling. Olivia wanted to let it free.

No, she thought, hold the line. Just hold.

Across the deck, Josie's ax was knocked from her hand as the Hooded Man threw his weight into her. She fell back against the doors of the captain's quarters, the cloudy-glass windows shattering and cutting her skin. John lunged forward and stabbed at the Hooded Man's side. The beast's claws rang as they deflected the killing edge of John's sword. The beast swung back and ripped chunks of wood from the wall as John retreated up the stairs of the afterdeck. The Hooded Man's blood looked black in the faltering torch lights. Josie roused herself and grabbed her ax from the ground. She looked across the deck to Olivia.

Josie took a step toward her, but stopped when she

heard her uncle scream. The Hooded Man ripped the helm clean from the ground and tossed it toward John. It caught his side and sent him sprawling toward the back of the ship.

"Go!" Olivia shouted from across the deck as she blocked another one of Faldir's hits.

Josie grimaced and ran up the stairs toward her uncle.

Faldir swung upward and sent Olivia tumbling backward. The void mage's eyes cleared and strands of void magic sprung from her Focus. They grew in number and overwhelmed the shining heat of Olivia's shield. The Flame built under her skin. It felt like her blood was boiling. Her mind was overwhelmed with screams, green eyes, a man sitting at the edge of a fire, and now of this horrible woman bearing down on her.

Ashes burst from her Focus and she collapsed backward, her magic snuffed. Olivia was only left with the inferno in her heart and the freezing chill of sea water on her face. Faldir pointed her onyx Focus at Olivia and smiled.

"I'll spare you a slow death."

A wave of heat blew Faldir off her feet as the words left her mouth. Across the deck, wooden planks cracked and smoked beneath granite, armored boots. Runes and cracks inside of the armor plates glowed like coals. In one hand were the shredded fragments of a crab monster, dripping with black ooze. The other hand gathered a bright ember in the palm. Alkis glowered at Faldir from under his suit of armor. The air shimmered around him like an oven.

"You're better off running," he said.

Faldir sneered as she rose to her feet. She directed

her Focus at Alkis and a streak of black energy lashed toward him. The Fire Keeper lifted his hand and the shot dissipated as it struck him. Faldir launched another beam, seeking tendrils of shadow branching from it. Alkis slowly walked toward her, unbothered by the shadow mage's efforts.

A light grew in Alkis's hand and he dropped the pulped remains of the monster from the other. Alkis closed his fist and a burst of light lit the deck like another sun. Faldir's magic disappeared.

"Brother!" Faldir shouted.

On the afterdeck overhead, the bleeding Hooded Man turned from his two opponents and lunged down. The weight knocked Alkis forward to his knees, but the beast leaped off Alkis as the incredible heat singed him. He scratched at the burning stone armor and recoiled. Faldir brought her Focus upward and fired a hail of inky, purple death at the Fire Keeper.

Olivia ran for the afterdeck. Up the stairs, John helped Josie up from the crumbled remains of a barrel. A red stain spread across the side of her shirt and blood dripped from cuts on her legs. Pieces of cracked glass speckled her left shoulder. John pointed to the back of the afterdeck. A lifeboat hung from a rope pulley just below the railing.

"Get it ready for us," he said.

Olivia loosened the knots that kept the lifeboat tied tight to the ship, but it swung and wobbled on its own. She hoisted herself up and looked inside. There, a figure huddled under one of the seats. The hiding sailor looked up and sighed in relief. He pulled off his hat.

"Thank the Flame, is John safe?" Tomis asked.

"Tomis? You've been hiding this entire time?"

Olivia asked.

John brought Josie to the edge of the railing and pulled the lifeboat even with them. Tomis smiled desperately and mouthed the start of a dozen excuses before settling on one.

"I kept it here. The crabs didn't even notice me," Tomis said.

"By the triad, at least you're alive," John said.

"A lot of help you were," Josie grunted.

She winced as John helped her swing over the railing and into the lifeboat.

"Alkis is on the deck. He helped me escape, but we can't leave him," Olivia said.

"Are you crazy? We have a way out right here and we're all in one piece!" Tomis said.

John took one step onto the lifeboat and stopped. He looked between the deck and Olivia, the noises of the fight carrying over to them.

"If we move fast, we can make it without him," John said.

"No! If we leave him, then you've condemned the both of us."

It was her burning heart that put the thought in her mind. Not just the desire for survival, not just the chance of seeing home again. It ached to keep her newfound friend alive. Regardless of what he could be in the future, right now he was a friend in need. John wiggled his head side to side with a small, frustrated gasp.

"She's right! Water and fire, she's right," John cursed.

He loaded his hand crossbow and Josie began to rise from the lifeboat, ax in one hand and the other pressed into her side. She gasped in pain and fell back onto the seat.

"Tomis, keep her safe and be ready to cast off when we get back," John said.

Olivia and John crossed the afterdeck and headed to the fight beyond. Josie made an exasperated noise as Tomis barely kept her inside of the lifeboat.

"You better come back!" she shouted as they reached the top of the stairs.

Alkis held his own, but was pinned. One arm was restrained by the Hooded Man, his snapping jaws dangerously close to Alkis's face. The other was raised against a solid beam of void magic. It slowly chipped away at the burning shield. Licks of darkness broke from it and blistered the wood of the ship, leaving crackled scars along its path.

John aimed at Faldir with his crossbow and fired. The bolt caught her in the chest and she drew back from the hit. Her aim tilted the tip of her Focus down. The beam of killing magic sliced through the hull of the ship like an ax through a sapling.

Alkis seized the Hooded Man's throat with both hands. The twisted remainder of a man writhed in the air as Alkis lifted him free of the deck. The Hooded Man screamed and choked against the burning gauntlets. Alkis grabbed the shoulder of the Hooded Man and twisted. Faldir's brother died with a hollow cough and a wrenching snap.

The ship lost its battle against the currents and splinters shot into the air. Timbers snapped, beams broke, and sea water rushed into the lower decks. The two halves of the ship pulled from one another and Alkis tumbled through the frail doors of the captain's quarters like a boulder down a hill.

John fell backward toward the railing. Olivia jumped for him, but crashed against the railing and knocked the wind out of her lungs. She gasped for air and John gripped her hand before tumbling over the side of the ship. The only thought in her mind was not letting go. The world spun, but she could feel him squeezing her hand.

His crossbow tumbled into the seething water below. John swung his feet toward the ship, but his boots slipped on the hull. She could hardly focus. Her lungs burned as she gasped for air, only aware of John. Everything was dulled by the loud ringing sound in her ears. John nodded at her, a desperate, encouraging smile on his face.

They were family. Despite their differences, she knew that much. They both had long roads that led them here, each filled with their own troubles. There was never any hope for them to understand each other from the beginning. All that mattered was they were finally here. Olivia pulled him up toward the deck when a blinding pain flashed in her head.

Faldir drove Olivia's face into the railing. Her nose cracked and blood filled her mouth. The world spun and Olivia could barely see John. Faldir's fingers twisted at her hair and she cursed under her breath. John reached for a knife in his belt and slipped his fingers around to the blade.

"Fight it, Olivia!"

She just needed to hold on. If she could reach her Focus, they might have a chance. John whipped the knife up in his hand as Faldir raised her onyx Focus at his chest. A bolt of void magic shrieked past Olivia and struck John in his heart. He went limp as it carved through him and blasted into the roiling sea below. His fingers slipped from Olivia's and he dropped into the black water below.

Faldir smashed Olivia's face into the railing again. The world around her faded to black. She felt something being pulled from her hand. Faldir struggled to take it, golden and shiny. Olivia's mind sharpened in time to see Faldir pry the Focus away from her. She rose to hit Faldir, but the void mage easily dodged. She cracked Olivia across the jaw and spots bloomed in her vision.

Pounding steps shook the boat as they crossed the splintering wood of the deck. Faldir ran down the Sovarka as the dark ship sailed near to the prow. A smoldering giant pursued her, but slowed as he passed Olivia. Faldir leaped from the railing and landed onto the deck of her ship.

John is dead. Her mind could not escape the thought as her consciousness dimmed. Everything was a tumult in the world beyond, but only this one fact mattered to her now. It was his charge to keep them safe, but she knew she had failed her vow in return. Bring everyone back to the farm. Instead, John Seers's grave would be the crushing depths of the sea.

Stone hands lifted Olivia. They were warm like rocks left out in the sun. Alkis dashed up the stairs toward the afterdeck. The lifeboat began to descend. Alkis leaped over the railing and into the small boat as it plunged into the cold, empty sea.

"Where is John?" Tomis asked.

"Maybe he fell overboard, circle around and look for him," Josie said.

"Olivia, can you hear me?"

Alkis removed his helmet and gave her a small

shake. The vault of the night sky choked the light from the burning ship. Small raindrops plinked off Alkis's armor.

"He's gone," she rasped.

"What?" Josie leaned over Olivia.

"I couldn't save him."

Josie shook her head. The darkness closed in around Olivia again. She felt sleepy.

"No, you're confused. Olivia, please stay awake."

"John, are you out there?" Tomis shouted toward the few pieces of the Sovarka that were still above the waves. Faldir's ship disappeared behind the rolling waves.

"I tried."

Olivia closed her eyes, nothing left to fight. The fire in her chest burned too brightly and it hurt to breathe. She thought it might be easier if she slept for a bit.

Chapter Twenty-Four

The taste of salt on her lips. Grit rolled between her toes.

Waves crashed nearby.

Birds sang to the tune of the breeze.

Someone dragged her through broiling sand.

The ship sank. Faldir took her Focus, the splash of water, the taste of copper, and then John fell. It rose up like a waking nightmare and sent her skin crawling.

Olivia jerked to life. The patchwork of clouds above occasionally broke to let the sun peak through. Their lifeboat was beached next to the weathered hull of an ancient warship. A coast the color of ash and dirt spread around them, barren of trees. A mountain range, capped with snowy peaks that gleamed like sugar, ran across the land like a distant wall. They were in the midst of an ancient battlefield reclaimed by nature.

Siege weapons were buried under snarls of ivy and brush. Dry, bone-colored grass grew in between discarded shields, blades, and arrowheads. Glimpses of ivory stuck out from the ground. A pile of armor laid next to where a single bone thrust from the earth. A wind-ravaged flag waved in the wind. Any indication of its loyalties were bleached away by the ages.

Sweat ran down her face. The heat of the sun was overshadowed by a rising tension within her chest. The Flame was restless. The bonfire in her mind grew into a wildfire. Josie swung in with a hug, nearly knocking Olivia flat onto her back.

"Thank goodness you're awake."

Her red eyes shined with emotion held for too long. Tomis stood a few paces away from them. He crossed his arms and ran his fingers through his hair, attention elsewhere. Alkis bent to a knee next to them. His smile was happy, but grief haunted his features. It was not grief for him, but for her.

"Olivia, when we first got into the lifeboat you were saying some things. Do you remember?"

Josie rocked on her knees. "Is he gone?"

Tears built in Olivia's eyes. She could smell the briny seawater he fell into. She could hear the shrieking bolt of magic that ended his life. She closed her eyes, afraid that if she kept them open that she would see it happen again.

"He's gone."

Tomis came closer to them, but kept his distance. "If he fell into the water, he might still be alive. It's long odds, but I've heard stories—"

"Shut up," Josie snapped.

"Faldir did it, she killed him," Olivia said.

Josie collapsed into Olivia and a sob heaved from her chest. "No, please."

Alkis set his hand on Olivia's shoulder. "He passed saving all of us."

Tomis stared at the ground. His hands hung loosely by his sides, caught between thoughts. Josie rose from Olivia's shoulder and snarled at Tomis through her tears.

"You coward, if you helped, he might still be here."

Her knee gave out and she stumbled forward. She held her side as Tomis retreated further away from her.

Alkis tried to hold her back, but she pulled her hand from his. Josie pointed at him and advanced closer to the shamed thief.

"You didn't see it, he was hiding."

"In the lifeboat?" Alkis asked.

"People died. We were in danger. You were right behind us. What happened? Figured our decisions were out of your hands? Decided that my family wasn't worth your time?"

Tomis shook his head.

"I couldn't help you. Look at me, I'm skin and bones. I'm just a thief."

She charged at Tomis and struck him in the stomach. He flinched against the hit, but didn't see her other fist coming. Her knuckles collided with his jaw and sent the thin man onto the ground. Josie went to pounce on him, but Alkis barely held her at bay.

Olivia rose to help, but stopped as a needle of pain stabbed into the back of her head. It felt like a dagger twisted in the base of her skull. She closed her eyes and screamed as the pain shot down her spine, buckled her knees, and forced all other thoughts out from her mind.

She was accustomed to misery. The affliction tested her in ways she never expected. This was worse. It felt like it might kill her. The world was too bright, sounds echoed in her ears. For the briefest moment, she was ready to give up entirely.

"What's wrong?" Josie limped over to Olivia's side, her fight with Tomis set aside.

"You have to meditate," Alkis said. "The Flame will be growing quickly now."

"Not... Flame."

Olivia writhed on the ground as white-hot pain shot

down her spine and coursed into her arms and legs. She could almost hear the pain, a shrill ringing in her ears as her brain tried to peel itself in two. Gasping for air, she reached for the quiet of her mind, the silent space where she had some control over herself. In that haunted darkness, she could barely see into the dark past the blinding pain shaking her skull.

"In my head, it's in my head. My neck," she whimpered.

"Where's your Focus?" Alkis asked.

"Faldir took it."

Just as she felt she would have to scream, it stopped. She wriggled her fingers into the sand and rose to her knees. She left one hand against the back of her neck, afraid it might return if she was not careful. A small headache lingered in the center of her skull.

"What is happening to me?"

Alkis bit his lip, a nervous light in his eyes. Olivia waited for him to speak, praying that there was some small explanation for this. Only the lingering pain of the Flame in her chest willed into movement. If that pain returned, she thought she might die right there on the beach.

"Faldir is trying to change its loyalties," he said, "It will take some time and it will be excruciating for the both of you. She won't be able to use it until it answers to her."

"Will it kill her?" Josie asked.

Alkis did not answer. He shaded his eyes and looked at the barren land around them.

"How long?" Olivia asked.

"A few days, maybe a week. The process will only make your affliction worse."

Her spirit sank lower. It nearly dragged the rest of her down with it. Facing a death sentence was not a novel thing anymore. Before now, she had hopeful friends and a road ahead. It did not seem impossible. As she sat on the ash-colored sand, that last chance seemed to be collapsing.

"Where are we anyway?" Josie asked.

"I think we're south of Katoia. Those are the Border Mountains. South of them lies Naelan. We're close Olivia, we're so close," he said.

The pain bloomed again. Olivia winced, but a vision filled her mind.

A woman sat in front of a flickering candle. Olivia's Focus laid on a table in front of her. It was Faldir, a pained expression painted on her remorseless face. She screamed, but did not pull her hand from the relic. The pain blossomed like a ball of pins that grew larger. Faldir grabbed her head as Olivia's hands grabbed her own. Faldir's fingers left the relic and the pain dimmed.

Josie pulled Olivia upright, helpless to ease the pain.

"Where do we go?" Josie asked.

Alkis pointed toward the mountains.

"This is a neutral land: no towns and no forts. However, there are small, supply keeps built for people who get lost. If we can get to the foot of those mountains, we should be able to find one. They will give us food and hopefully help us get to Naelan."

Tomis brushed himself off as he walked toward the trio. His eyes made no effort to look at them, like a dog that knew it was in trouble.

"I know one is half a day's walk from here. I used to hide out in those mountains on the crossover from the Shallow Sea. Plenty of hiding spots for people like me."

"Bastards and liars?" Josie said.

"I know I've done nothing to earn your trust. John is—" Tomis cleared his throat. "I did nothing to help. If you let me, I can try to make it right to you all. I know these roads."

Olivia massaged her forehead. Laying down and dying wasn't an option, even though surrender sounded like a relief to this pain. She wanted to throw a rock at Tomis, but Olivia was out of options. Any help was welcome. Even if it was from a spineless bastard like him.

"We still don't know if you sold us out on the Sovarka."

"Or that you won't leave us for dead when trouble inevitably shows up?" Josie added.

Tomis held out his palms. "You can't, but I am telling you that I won't."

Alkis scooped Olivia up in his arms. She pushed against his grip, but his hands kept her there. She couldn't ignore the flutter in her heart at the gesture. The urge to help herself was louder and more familiar.

"Put me down, I can walk."

"I'm certain you could. Without your Focus, you are on a clock. All that you have is your own strength, so you need to keep every bit of energy you have. We will have to carry you."

"I can take her too," Josie said.

"I may need you to, it is going to be a long walk. Unfortunately, the criminal is our best chance at finding a supply point."

Josie scoffed and looked between Alkis and Olivia. She would not find the consensus she was looking for. Olivia gave her a small shrug. Josie found who to blame for John's death, but Olivia wasn't sure it was the right person.

"We're keeping him around? We should throw him in the ocean."

"The time for punishment will come later, but right now we need to remember why we are here. We can still make it to Naelan in time if we hurry," Alkis said.

Olivia glanced at the sky and tried to measure the hours left. "The day is halfway done. We have four, maybe five hours before sunset."

"We'll settle in after a few hours. We're probably safer here than farther inland," Tomis said.

Alkis shook his head.

"We can't wait. We will have to travel through the night."

"What?" Olivia asked.

Alkis was brave, but the suggestion was suicidal. It went against everything they were taught about staying safe. The darkened wild around the Seventh was bad enough. The stories about these far lands, cluttered with the remnants of old Shadow cults and unmarked graves, kept Olivia up at night.

"Are you nuts?" Tomis's voice broke, wincing at the mere suggestion.

Josie grimaced, but said nothing. Olivia looked for assurance from her sister, but Josie's somber mood told Olivia that there was nothing better to do. Alkis was right.

"If we wait for daybreak, that will be another six hours Olivia does not have. Every minute is precious," Alkis said, "We don't have much time."

****

There was one waterskin between the four of them

and no food. They were tired and bruised, but they continued despite the aching pain in their feet. Tomis could not think of anything to say that would be welcomed by the others. So occupied with their own thoughts, six hours passed in what felt like half that time. Finally, a moment to mourn John, but they would never have a body to bury. Alkis soldiered on with Olivia in his arms.

The sun slid behind the mountains. Its dim light would remain for only another hour. Driftwood was collected, everyone's sleeves were ripped, dried as much as they could be, and wrapped around the sticks for makeshift torches.

Despite how much terror they had been through, the coming night brought a new panic to his heart. Not everywhere was as pacified as Hasketter and Sallew; there were only Shade Rats to contend with, Needletooth Foxes, and the occasional Swooping Howler. He heard about what night brought in other lands, but reassured himself that they were just stories. No matter what they faced, they had a Fire Keeper with them. He hoped that it counted for something.

Tomis walked on Alkis's left side, nearer to the desolate inland. Not that it mattered, everything was dark now. The open sea glittered under the moon, the only measure of their progress. He was grateful to walk through the tall grass rather than the shifting sands of the beach. It only came up to his knee, but he could imagine enormous bugs hiding in the blades of grass or a cluster of those crab-monsters in the foliage ahead of them.

He looked back to the group and his fears of monsters were replaced by a pang of remorse. They were all tired. Empty eyes traced the ground in front of their path. He was certain each of them were grieving everything behind them or dreading what lay ahead. All this pain was his fault. He was blameless for the affliction, but they might have made it to Naelan without him. Wandala would still be alive. John would still be here to look after his nieces.

Josie noticed Tomis, but ignored him again after a moment. Though they all despised him, Josie's silence bit like frostbite. He had seen the pain in her eyes many times before: parents, former lovers, conned tradesmen. It never bothered him. This time it cut him to the bone and he knew why. These women were the only legacy of John Seers, and they hated him.

Despite being jostled by Alkis as he adjusted, Olivia slept without a worry. Tomis was glad that her sleep was peaceful, even if it was just exhaustion catching up with her. There was no delaying the affliction now. There was no hope but to march forward against the night.

"Tomis, how close are we?" Alkis asked.

"Not totally sure, but we should be getting close. Maybe another few miles at most."

"Shouldn't we be able to see them? A tower out here in this barren plain, it should have a signal bonfire or something," Josie said.

"You would think so," Alkis muttered.

A twig snapped in the darkness. As Tomis swung around, a pale shape moved beyond the edge of his light. He stammered and blinked. A tremor rose in his hand as he tried to make sense of what he saw. It looked like a person, but it was too lithe, too pale. There were big ears, too large to be human.

"Did any of you see that?"

Alkis slowed and turned toward the fields of high

grass. Josie's wide eyes watched the same spot as Tomis.

"I did."

The surf crashed behind them with a dull roar and the dreadful silence of night came after. Josie held her torch up higher and Tomis gasped. In the shifting light, two dozen pinpoints of light stared back at them. Tomis knew a predator's eyes when he saw them.

"Shit."

Alkis shook Olivia awake and set her onto her feet. She stumbled and leaned against Josie, her face flushed and sweating. Roused from her dreams, her face contorted as she took in the terrifying sight.

"What the hell are those?"

"Korsch." Alkis gathered an ember and his suit pulsed with heat. "They used to be people who lived in deep valleys and caves. At some point, they stopped being human. They're not supposed to come this far out of the mountains."

His ember grew brighter than either of their torches. Pale shapes scattered like bugs, hunched figures standing on two legs and staring with round, black eyes. One of them screamed in a harsh, too-human tone that sent the four of them stepping back toward the sea. Others answered the cry with whooping shrieks. Alkis raised his glowing arm, the light keeping the hungry horde at bay.

"Stay in the light. They can't stand anything other than darkness. Just move slowly, we have to keep moving."

The Korsch made clicking noises and called to each other in cooing tones. Tomis yelped as something ran into the surf just behind them. Its hairless body squatted over a pair of strong legs with overdeveloped, grimy toes. Their knife shaped ears swiveled after their quarry as they moved further down the coast. Its eyes gawked at him like a corpse's gaze. The thing ran back through the rising tide and out of the moonlit water.

"Do we just keep walking?" Alkis asked.

Olivia shook her head and cleared her throat. "I don't have any better ideas."

One of the creatures crashed through the tide with a whoop and ran straight for Josie. Tomis leaped in its way and brandished a torch. It gnashed at Tomis with small, needle-like teeth. It retreated back from the light, but Josie raised her torch to swing. For a moment, Tomis thought that she might break his head open instead.

"Down you idiot!"

She swung over his head and something shrieked behind him. He fell to his knees without thinking, face first into the chilly, ocean water. His torch hissed as a wave washed forward and doused him. Tomis shook the water from his head and inspected the hissing stump of his torch. It was soaked through. A shoddy light to begin with, he doubted it would have lasted much longer anyway.

"Will it light?" Alkis asked.

"I don't think so."

They were pinned against the coast, the circle of pale things barking at them from all sides.

Chapter Twenty-Five

Gnashing teeth and glaring eyes gathered around them. The Flame pushed against her chest, her pulse racing in her veins. Olivia clung to Josie's arm against the sick, shaky feeling in her knees. She wanted a weapon. She wanted a shade-damned break. Alkis held the line against these things for the moment, but she did not miss how they came closer.

Josie kicked at the scampering thing that nearly took Tomis's head off. The growing chorus of hooting swelled as more Korsch joined their brethren. There had to be something she could do, some sort of respite from this nightmare. Olivia closed her eyes and reached her fingers toward the sand underfoot. The quiet of her mind pulsed with the thrum of a bonfire. The heat on her face could have been the hot breath of a snarling predator in the waking world or the Flame within her mind. Either one would kill her soon.

"Please, help us."

She reached out to Life, the quiet voice that found her in the forest. Echoing in her mind, only the roar of the fire inside answered her. Perhaps it could hear her screaming for salvation, but it would only be a whisper without her Focus.

Olivia opened her eyes as Alkis shouted at a pair of the creatures. They inched closer into the light, but skittered back at the flaming juggernaut in front of them.

The mob shifted and a flicker of light glittered in the distance. It was far and faint. Olivia blinked as she tried to make sense of it. It was not a hallucination or trick of the light. A handful of low-burning torches were hardly visible behind the wilderness and the growing mob around them.

"Look!" Olivia pointed past the creatures. She could barely see the base of a distant tower beyond the low fire. "We need to break through them. Got anything for that, Fire Keeper?"

"I can light up, but I can't keep you safe," he said.

Josie pulled Olivia tighter to her shoulder. Her younger sister took gulping breaths against the pain in her side. "You run in front of us. We will keep up."

"You're going to need help carrying her," Tomis said.

Josie snorted and spit near his feet. Olivia was furious with Tomis, but the need to survive surpassed it. She gripped her sister's wrist and jerked her head toward the tower.

"Can you be pissed later? We're going to die if we don't work together. You're too hurt to carry me alone. Don't try to hide it."

"We don't have time for this!" Alkis took a swipe at the horde. The Korsch screamed and pulled back.

"Damn it, fine! Take her right arm, I've got her left," Josie said.

The ember in Alkis's hand dimmed, the light closing around them. It pulsed to the rest of his suit. Veins and sigils in the armor brightened against the gloom. Tomis and Josie lifted Olivia by her shoulders.

"Ready?"

Olivia nodded her head.

"Go!"

Alkis closed his fist around the ember and his armor pulsed with fire. It thrummed with white flame as he bulldozed into the line of creatures ahead of them. Josie and Tomis took off after him, Olivia's feet barely scraping at the ground. The heat from his armor was like a campfire blowing into their faces. They gasped for breath through the hot air and ran ahead blindly.

The creatures shrieked as their prey stormed into them. The rest of the pack followed them with furious howls. A clawed hand swiped at the back of her hair. She knew they were only a few steps behind. Their ragged breathing mingled with the cacophony of hungry throats.

The front gate of the tower was open. Josie's footsteps outpaced Tomis. Just enough to make Olivia nervous, but not enough to leave them behind. If Tomis wasn't helping Olivia, she was sure that Josie would leave him behind. Alkis was a molten boulder. Any creature that darted into their way was trampled by smoldering stone. They were only a dozen feet away. Just a bit further. All memories of their rivalries and differences seemed so small with the howling hunger right behind them.

Alkis tore dirt and grass out of the ground as he turned to face the swarm. The fire drained from his armor and gathered in his hand once more. The ember turned into a glowing flare that burned like daylight. The Korsch reeled back. The teeming swarm of dozens crashed into each other. Tomis, Josie, and Olivia ran past Alkis and into the light of the tower. Alkis smirked as he stepped inside the ring of torches and left the pale monsters to gnash their teeth.

Olivia collapsed to the ground, shortly followed by

the other three. She gulped in the cold, night air. She would have laughed if her lungs did not hurt so bad. Josie leaned on her knees and cackled.

"That actually worked? Oh, don't make me do that again."

"You doubted us?" Tomis asked between breaths.

"Mostly you," she said with a smile.

Alkis pulled his helmet off. Spread on the ground, he looked over to Olivia and raised his eyebrows and cocked a smile. It was an infectious grin she couldn't refuse. Bound behind all that armor, it reminded her that there was a friend in there.

"How the hell did you do that? What does that weigh, a hundred pounds?" Olivia asked him.

"The magic helps the load, but it doesn't stop you from breathing in a bunch of hot air."

Her breath at least somewhat evened as she pushed herself up on shaky legs. The Flame was itching for more. Without food or a decent amount of sleep, she felt frail. Not even when she collapsed at the Church did she feel so close to dissolving entirely. Alkis rose and helped her steady on her feet, a thankful smile shared between them. They both turned to the quiet stronghold ahead.

The fort was surrounded by a circular stone wall. It was slightly taller than Josie and small lanterns were set into it every ten feet. The main gates, a pair of wooden double doors, hung open. The grounds within were populated by a few small tents and storage hovels along the walls. Food, lumber, and other goods were stowed away. There was a squat, wooden structure the size of a small house on the other side of the fort.

The tower was made of stone slabs. A banner hung from one of its four windows. It flew the sigil of the

Katoian Empire: a styled fist wreathed in flame, and the shades of crimson that accompanied that mark. Alkis entered first.

Something was wrong. There was no clattering of armored boots or alarm bells. All she heard was the thud of Alkis dropping to his knees in front of a crumpled shape on the ground. A corpse laid on the ground in front of the Fire Keeper. It was not the only one. The dimly lit common ground of the fort was a slaughterhouse. Guards fell where they stood, weapons dropped before they could land a blow on their attacker.

The door to the tower was ripped off its hinges. Iron rods, fired from coilguns, were stuck into the inside walls. This was not a raid from marauding monsters or a battle with a warring faction. Olivia could almost track where the carnage had gone. Someone came inside the fort to find supplies. Once they opened the gates, the slaughter began. She glanced over another corpse and confirmed her fears. This guard was struck by a single bolt of magic. The wound was surrounded by a ring of black, brittle flesh.

"Void magic. Think it might have been her?" Tomis said.

Olivia had almost forgotten about that specter. The Reaper, a symbol of death, came with the autumn across their fields when the leaves fell and the old creatures died. This being was not a real being, but that did not stop the superstition. It was portrayed as a cloaked figure, wickedly twisted by Shadow magic. She knew better now. The Reaper was very real and it was a woman carrying an onyx Focus.

"Who else?"

Faldir had no problem killing, but it always served a

purpose. She only struck where she needed to be. Senseless slaughter for its own sake was new. It was awfully visible for someone who clung to the literal shadows. What other presumption would people make after they saw these wounds?

"Faldir is hardly subtle, but this isn't right. She has what she wants, why do something so risky?"

"She needed disguises," Tomis said.

Josie busied herself with lighting every unlit lantern she could find. She wandered away from them and went toward the small shed on the other side of the grounds. Olivia crouched next to one of the guards. She could not suppress the gasp she made as her knees bent. Her breathing was shallow. Every time she tried to take another one, it felt that her lungs might burst if they held it for too long. She balanced herself with one hand on the ground, her elbow shaking ever so slightly.

This guard's neck was broken. She had been stripped of her armor, but it was nowhere to be seen. Olivia looked across the killing ground and saw several more bodies that were discarded in the same way. They all had their armor taken from them and were dumped unceremoniously next to one another. Tomis silently counted the bodies over her shoulder.

"You said something was going to happen in Naelan," Olivia said.

"Yeah, something about revenge. You can't just waltz into the Archive Primeval. It's a fortress."

"Unless you have a way in."

He nodded. She had assumed Faldir was too fierce, too personally involved in this, to think of anything other than to hide who she was.

"Dress yourself up like a Katoian diplomatic envoy,

fly the empire's flag, and dock. Stars, they might arrange a meeting with her target for them."

"Just kill their target and get out?" Tomis asked. "Or start a war, sow doubt on who fired first. Katoia and Naelan don't have a great history. They ripped each other to pieces during the war. When I was Faldir's prisoner, they called Naelan 'Twice Cursed Traitors'. Revenge for old grudges. Seems like a lot to go through for some payback."

"Or it's something more. If you're right about sowing doubt, maybe this is just to set the stage for something else," said Olivia.

A plot to pit their enemies against one another: the bearers of Flame on one side and the Twice-Cursed Traitors on the other. If Naelan and Katoia suspected the other, they would barely need a reason to start fighting. From there, who knows the destruction they could wreak. What chaos could the shadow mage sow with the eyes of the world drawn to this new war? Now *that* sounded like Faldir.

Olivia walked back toward Alkis. Tomis lingered near the dead in quiet reverence. The Fire Keeper sat by the first dead body they found. His eyes shifted over the other bodies across the grounds and then returned to this first one. The body was tall, but bent onto itself as it had fallen. His sword was only a few inches from him, just out of reach. Alkis's voice was broken when it left his throat.

"I knew these people. I was embedded with them as a Fire Keeper. They called me the Banner Hammer. I put back drinks with a few of them."

It was just like Elza. Something inside of him cracked when his mentor died and now it was broken into a dozen pieces. His shoulders heaved with a sob. His lips twisted with anger. She could not let him bear this.

"It's not your fault, Alkis."

"What am I doing here? I abandoned my oath. Raised as a child to be a Fire Keeper, my father, his father. I made that oath, and then gave it up and walked away from my friends. I left to help people, not just enforce rules."

He turned to face Olivia. "Sure, I fed the needy and gave to the poor. But here I could save a life. Flame put you in my path, Olivia. And this is where it led me?"

"All this? It isn't your fault. You left to help people and *you did*. If you were here for them, you would have given up on yourself. That pledge you made to the needy wouldn't even exist. Flame did not ask you to help me, I called it. You joined us and have helped me get further than I had any real hope for."

"And it has been nothing but death and failure since. I return home, clad in my armor, and find my friends are dead. And that charge, that greater purpose, it's over. I wanted to help people and I shattered everything I knew to do it. All I have for it is a stranger that stumbled into a death sentence."

Her heart twisted at his words. This was just a shade in his eyes, that had to be it. Josie and Tomis might be able to get her to Naelan, but Olivia would not leave him broken. Too many people had suffered for her already.

"I'm still here."

His warmth had evaporated with the last bits of his magic. The man in front of her was nearly broken. Alkis stepped back from her, tears trickling from his face as he clasped his head. Olivia held her lip as stiff as she could manage. She let him try to find his way out of this darkness, confident that he would not lose himself. She had to have that hope. There was so little for her to rely on. Alkis was one thing she could not cast aside so easily.

Alkis looked back with a trembling lip. The storm had passed.

"I didn't mean—"

"I know."

She walked closer to him. Every step was an effort now. Alkis needed something to lean on. Knowing that she could help him now was the only thing that kept her standing. Alkis gestured around the fort.

"I couldn't save Elza. I couldn't save my friends. I forsook my oath for a new one. I wouldn't let the afflicted burn. I wouldn't turn a cold shoulder to the needy. I would save people, not conquer."

Olivia placed a hand on his armor. She wanted to throw her arms around him and weep into his shoulder. She thought of her own shattered life. Everything that she left behind would never be hers, even if she survived. Her faith that she would survive this journey dimmed.

"It's not forsaken. As long as you try, you've not failed. You've helped us get this far. Just a bit further now, right?"

He rested his forehead against hers. Olivia's eyes traced across his lips, his freckled skin. She breathed in the warm, smoky scent that drifted off him. He felt warm. He felt like a place to rest.

"So much pain and blood has been shed because of me. And you're scared that you might be next," Olivia said.

Alkis wiped his face before answering. "This is something darker, this shadow cast over the two of us."

"We're so close."

His hand traced down her arm. He pressed his nose to hers. Alkis was so close, she could reach out and claim him there. It was hard to doubt the feelings that bubbled in her chest. That small root that flickered next to the Flame within her. Olivia was so distracted by the chaos and dread that she didn't notice it flower.

"It's not that," he finally said. "Being around you, listening to you. I haven't felt this in a long time, maybe ever. I know you've felt it too. Right?"

She could not resist it, but the trembling in her arms grew worse. Her resistance had hidden it this far, but she was at the end of her rope. It wasn't the time or the place. Her death would only hurt more if there was something to mourn. All the same, she was running out of the will to hide.

"I have."

Olivia tried to cup his chin, but seized as a burning pain shot through her. She gasped and collapsed forward. Alkis caught her. The world swam together in shades of brown, red, and black. She pressed her fingers against the warmth of his armor and took a deep breath. Olivia winced as her muscles cramped. Despite the ache, she bit her lip against it. She would not be weak. Not now.

"Finish that oath. Get me to Naelan and they won't have died in vain. Give me a chance to make this right to John and Elza and everyone else."

Before Alkis could speak, a voice broke the silence.

"Hey! I found something."

Josie appeared from around the tower with a horse. She had fitted it to ride and lead it by the reins. It munched on some hay as they approached. She palmed an apple for it to eat next.

"They have a stable back there. It looks like Faldir,

313

well—This is the only one who made it." She brushed the horse's mane before taking stock of her compatriots.

Olivia straightened herself as best she could, still leaning against Alkis for support. Alkis lowered himself so that she could rest easier. They shared a glance before they turned their focus to the horse.

"I can't ride the horse. Never mind that I'm lousy at riding, I can't leave this armor," he said.

Tomis returned to the group, hands knitted together.

"It's just armor. Fancy armor, but still."

"We might need it if we run into Faldir again," Alkis said.

"I can take Olivia. I'm good to ride." Josie tried to step into the saddle, but fell backward and barely caught her footing. She gasped and held her side.

"Water and darkness you are," Tomis said.

"Well, who else is going to take her?"

Tomis shrugged and held his hand up. Olivia grimaced. She did not think John's death was all his fault. It was her curse that dragged him from their home. However, Tomis was a snake and a liar as far as she was concerned. His recent contrition wasn't enough to forgive him, but Olivia could recognize the unfortunate truth; Tomis was the only person who could deliver her to Naelan in time.

Josie snorted. "We're really doing this?"

Tomis crossed his arms and crossed into the middle of the group.

"Firstly, I am a gifted rider. Secondly, you don't have a choice. Alkis can't ride."

"I can't ride *well*," Alkis said.

"And Josie, you're still healing. I'm sorry for what I did. Take this as my first step toward redemption, eh?

Trust me, I can get us to Naelan hours before anyone else. Guess who had to run from various authorities and pissed off customers for the last ten years?" He jerked his thumb at himself.

Josie and Alkis looked for another alternative. Their faces were tortured at the idea of putting their faith in him, but Olivia's eyes never swerved from Tomis. These last two weeks had taught her to give things another chance: the Elements, John, the world. Olivia decided to give one more second chance.

"Help me up, will you?"

"Just want to grab some water for us really quick. Just a moment," Tomis said before running off toward the tower.

"Olivia," Josie groaned.

"I don't have much time. I can feel it. I'm parched, tired. I'm not going to argue with you."

Alkis went to the main gates and conjured Flame into his armor again.

"I'll make sure the way is clear for you."

Tomis ran off to grab some supplies from the tower's stockpiles. Josie listed off a dozen reasons not to trust him when he stepped into the tower. Josie walked in between the horse and Olivia. She raised her shoulders and screwed up her face. Olivia recognized when Josie was trying to be tough.

"He's a thief."

"Josie."

"He's a spineless cheat who is bad at cards."

"Please."

"He left John behind before and he let him die on that ship."

"Josie, this isn't your decision. I am leaving with

Tomis and that is the end of it."

Olivia conjured strength into her voice. It was the tone that she used to use to send errant farm hands scattering for their tools. It only lasted for a second, but it was enough to break her sister's protests. The towering girl seemed to shrink as her lips pinched together. Josie sniffed back tears.

"I can't lose you. If you're out of my sight, what can I even do? I'll go mad if I have to go home alone. I can't do it, I won't."

Olivia took her sister's hands and squeezed as hard as she could. The thought that she would never see home again crossed her mind before. She banished it whenever it tried to surface. It was naive to think Josie would not recognize it, but she still hoped. Olivia wanted to tell her that would never happen and that all this would end perfectly. It would be a lie and Josie would know it.

"You're still my kid sister, but you deserve the truth. We are past the time that we can take our chances on luck and comfort. The truth is scary, just like the world. It's up to us to be brave in spite of it. We can hide in our delusions and hope things will just work out or we can fight with everything we have. Spitting and cursing and biting, don't leave anything behind. Fight dirty if you need to.

"That's what I need you to do, Josie. I'm going to leave and I need you to fight to get back to me because I am going to be fighting just as hard to get back to you. I can't promise this is going to work out, but if you fight as hard as I'm going to, I know we'll both see the other side of this."

Josie wiped the tears from her face and straightened her back. She thought over Olivia's words for a moment before wrapping her arms around her. Olivia collapsed, burying her face in her sister's shoulder. The tears stung as they drained from her.

It was not a lie. Olivia would fight with everything she had left to get back to Josie. Even if the sisters did everything they could, she knew the odds were stacked against them. So she enjoyed this embrace, knowing that it might be the last time they spoke to each other.

"I love you, Liv," Josie said.

"I love you."

Tomis left the tower with a bundle of supplies under his arm. The sisters let go of each other and Tomis guided Olivia to the horse's saddle. She climbed up with barely any breath left in her. Josie balled her hands into fists as Olivia climbed onto the mount. Josie grabbed the back of Tomis's shirt as he walked by. He dropped the bag on the ground and she pulled his ear within biting distance.

"Whatever happened with my uncle aside, you're in charge of keeping my sister safe now. You see her to Naelan or I will not rest until I find you. Get me?"

Tomis nodded as fast as he could. Josie let him go and he scooped up the bag of supplies and threw it over his shoulder. Olivia did not raise her voice. The thief could use a little extra motivation. The journey ahead of him would not be easy either. To his credit, he sounded more confident in this than anything before it.

"That's a promise." Tomis stroked the horse's mane and whispered to it in low tones.

"You've got an opening," Alkis called from the front gate. "Only a few of them out here. Best take off before they get too curious."

Tomis climbed onto the saddle in front of Olivia and

took the reins.

"I will be expecting you and Alkis in a few days, understand?" he said.

"That goes double for me," Olivia said.

Josie smiled through the tears running down her face. "I'll be there."

Tomis whipped the reins and the horse galloped back into the wilderness. As they whipped past Alkis, Olivia reached her hand out to him. He broke from his watch to touch her hand. It was a fleeting embrace, but the only goodbye they would manage. She barely saw his smile beneath the armor before they rode out of the gate and took a sharp left onto the road. Chittering creatures scampered after them with no hope of catching up.

For the second time, Olivia watched the only comforts in her life vanish behind her. Josie and Alkis disappeared around the bend of the fort's walls. They plunged into the midnight wilderness around them. There was nothing but uncertainty ahead of her, but Olivia was determined to use up the last drops of her life conquering it.

Chapter Twenty-Six

Her white knuckles gripped the table as the ship pitched to starboard. The dull ache at the base of her spine wouldn't go away. Faldir almost put the Focus away after tasting the agony she would have to endure for days. This storage room was emptied for her purposes and the crew were warned not to disturb her while she was inside. It was readily obeyed. They did not know what she was doing or why, but they respected their captain and feared her.

The crew were a motley assortment of warped, shadow worshippers like her brother. Desperate for salvation to their pains or greedy for the power that the night held, they signed away their normal lives for that distant promise. Peasants, barons, academics, it did not matter what they used to be. They were all twisted to a new purpose. They were only a little better than the murderers in Sallew or the thieves who escaped the Sovarka. The ones who killed her brother.

Focus, focus for the both of us. Her brother's voice came back to her.

"I'm sorry. I'll do better."

A single candle hung from the ceiling on a shabby fixture. The shadows circled around it like sharks in the sea. She was certain that Father was listening to her screams through them. She suspected that he wanted her to suffer for this power. Her cloak hung from a nail next to the door. Her prize sat on the table in front of her. Adar's Focus gleamed with unnatural polish for something so old. She bled to claim it. People died to bring it here. Now she was afraid to even touch it.

She imagined Father's probing taunts. Your brother is dead, you have the means for revenge, are you still too weak to honor us? He would make sure to trot out her parents again and let them sob in front of her. Would they sob? They damned her brother to a life of servitude with no chance to be family. She acquired the Focus at the cost of his life. If she failed this next step, would she suffer worse than he did?

She gritted her teeth and prepared for the next round. When the Focus called her master, she would have the power to prove them wrong. She would show them just how worthy she was. She would make her brother's death mean something. They would suffer.

Faldir closed her eyes. Father and her brother faded from her thoughts and she was left alone in the darkness. She found the quiet in her mind, the place where she put her hate. Sparks of violet void magic filled the shadow around her and she directed her mind to the Focus in her hand.

"Fill this vessel. Take residence in it."

The Focus shook. A pin prick of pain stuck into the side of her head.

"Open. Open to me. You have a new purpose. Don't be scared."

Void magic clouded around her fingertips. It probed the shining metal and the Focus trembled at every assault. A sharp pain exploded across her skull. She dropped her head low and clung to her chair.

Her old Focus writhed in her pocket. It did not want

to leave. Her brother had given her the hunk of onyx and she chiseled it by hand. It carried her through hard years. It made her strong. This new relic held such power. The remaining essence of the dead mage would be bent to serve Shadow. It pained her to give up her old Focus, but there was no alternative. Only it would grant her the power she needed. She kicked the chair away from the table and leaned over it. Stabbing pain flickered up and down her arm, each time stronger than the last.

The Focus put an image in her mind: a flash of the afflicted mage on the back of a horse.

"Forget her."

She couldn't break now. Probing spikes like dagger tips worked up and down her neck. Another vision came to her: a voice, a horse, mountains.

"Olivia," someone said. "Hold on, we're getting close."

Olivia and Faldir opened their eyes. She could barely think through the fatigue. A mountain range towered nearby, the peaks breaking through the clouds. A wall of stone, tall as the heavens, narrow like a throat. Those were the Border Mountains. They were close to Naelan. They were awash in the sun's intolerable warmth. Faldir felt the Flame burning Olivia from the inside out. It was easier to break a Focus if the owner was dead. There was less for it to hold on to.

The vision cut to black as Olivia's eyes closed. Faldir could feel Olivia in her head, their thoughts and memories bleeding together. Olivia stood next to her in that quiet moment, a hand pressed to her mouth. She gasped against a sob and shook her head. Faldir felt her pity. She despised it.

"You've done nothing for them to hate you so

much," Olivia said.

"Leave me."

"They aren't worth it. Flame bless, he is using you."

"You're lying. Envious. Jealous that I am so close."

"Family isn't a bargaining chip. That isn't how it should be."

Faldir repressed the impulse to agree.

"No. You're wrong, you have to be wrong."

"I felt that. You know this is wrong, don't fight it. You're miserable. And all the murder and bloodshed they ask of you will never make it right. This is what family is. This is what you should feel around those you love."

Olivia's memories poured through Faldir's mind: the smell of hay and grass, soft beds, the crunch of a ripe apple, belly laughing at family dinners. Hard work. Disappointment. Yorker, the end of those times, a craving for perfection. Olivia strove to be strong and came up short as Faldir did. Despite her faults, she was accepted. It felt wrong.

"Please, you are killing for something they will never give you," Olivia said.

"You don't know how it felt. You weren't there."

"And they never should have asked that of you. I'm so sorry that you endured that, but you don't have to follow them just because they raised you. Do you really want to be like them? Like a monster?"

"Just die!"

Faldir winced and let go of the Focus. Olivia faded from view as the connection faded. The memories of plentiful fields and laughter dimmed. The relic sat on the table, unphased by her suffering. Faldir tasted blood. She couldn't be right. Olivia was a liar, a charlatan of Flame.

Faldir was taught that the minions of Flame would lie. All the same, it hurt more than she liked.

She drowned this pain, like all the other pain she felt. This power would set things right. It would get her all the recognition she ever craved. They would love her when she was strong.

She pocketed the golden Focus. As she slipped into the sleeves of the cloak, she watched the pithy candle above the door. It was so weak, but still burned as brightly as it could against the shadows that circled it. It was how Olivia felt moments ago. Faldir opened the door and blew the light out.

The galley was not far. The stink of brine mixed with the odor of gristle. Bare seasonings mingled with the smell of meat. It smelled like a joyless meal. She found the cook in the cramped kitchen. His bat-like ears moved before the rest of his head followed. His pupils dilated, the golden irises thinning.

"Where is the captain?" Faldir asked.

The cook's eyes lingered for a moment longer before he went back to his job, one of his ears still pointed at her.

"At the helm. We're almost out of the storm."

"How do you know?" she asked.

"I can smell it."

Faldir left the cook to his duties. The rest of the ship was as dimly lit as her chamber was. Small candles were left as an afterthought. Their tiny flames flickered against living shadows that salivated at the light's imminent death, like a cat toying with a wounded mouse.

Faldir pulled her hood up and climbed up to the deck. Rain pattered onto her shoulders and a boom of distant thunder rolled overhead. The sun was hidden by a veil of storm clouds. The crew members cleaned the deck and dried it where they could manage. Each one was changed by Shadow: a woman with knees that were reversed like a dog's, a man who seemed more bear than human, a sailor who tied down loose ropes with chitin-covered tendrils for hands.

The captain was by the helm as the cook predicted. He spoke with one of his crew. They both looked ahead and would occasionally gesture toward the barely visible coastline. The captain loomed over the sailor. His shoulders bunched higher than they should. A reptilian tail extended behind him and twirled around his own boots. Pointed ears poked out from his messy hair. His left eye was marred with a blood-red pupil that drifted free of the other one. He dismissed the helmsman before he bowed to Faldir.

"Mage Faldir, how goes your meditations below deck?"

"Making progress. I won't need much more time."

"Perhaps we could bring you an iron maiden or have you drawn and quartered. Screaming does seem to be your chief exploit."

"Cute." She crossed the afterdeck and looked out across the sea. All she saw was mist, waves, and the barest hint of a distant shoreline.

"We have to move faster. The schedule has moved up."

"On whose word?" the captain asked.

"On mine, as heir of the first blood line. I carry his authority with my voice."

The captain snarled, but lowered his eyes.

"I apologize. My crew are hard pressed getting us through the squall. We are about to break from it, but they will want rest and food. We've sailed across most of the Trade Sea in remarkable time. You must recognize that."

"I recognize that my brother perished on this trip when you and your crew could have helped us."

The captain had refused combat aboard the Sovarka, citing concern for his crew. She left with a brother and returned alone. They held a small ceremony to mark his passing two days prior. It tempered her anger, but it did not fill the void. She still needed their ship to sail and his crew to escort her to the archive. Despite Faldir's calm demeanor, the captain took a back step from her.

"Most regrettable, he was like us. Branded by the creator and made to serve a grander purpose. We mourned him."

Faldir choked out a mean cackle. "With candles. What an honor for someone who dedicated his life to snuffing the Flame."

He spoke through gritted teeth, hands clenched at his sides. "It's a tradition, ma'am."

"I am not here to honor your traditions. You have a job to do and we very nearly failed. Shadow has given you its boons and you are still too weak."

The captain did not answer. He knew to speak further would invite death. Faldir tested his silence with a long gaze, her lips pulled back into a sneer. After a moment, she looked away. Killing him would be an inconvenience.

"You did get us through the storm quickly, I will commend you for that. Allow them to rest in small shifts, minimum reduction. The thieves we pursued? They survived the Sovarka and will arrive at the archive soon."

"Do they know that we are going there as well?"

If Father learned this, she would lose everything without an attempt. The clouded sunlight was enough to banish the deeper shadows on the deck. Father would not hear them. She grimaced as the truth crawled from her lips.

"It is likely one in their company may know."

"Then speed is required for us to succeed."

"And such is my command. Understand me now, captain? Are the disguises ready?"

"My men have cleaned them. I've picked a party to join you once we land. You won't be able to stay long. There are only so many questions that we can fake. So many tests that we can pass before they figure us out."

"The Focus we acquired turned a farmgirl into a talented Flame mage overnight. Through me, I could put fear into Father's veins. It will be quick."

The captain frowned. "How much does Father know?"

"He will have to approve. He is not the one risking his neck for our cause. His meddling might doom us. Any delay, any change in the plan, could spell disaster. My brother will have died for nothing, and your crew will be captured."

The captain grasped the helm and adjusted the course slightly. His roaming red eye followed the coastline along the far horizon.

"You should go back downstairs. That Focus isn't yours yet."

Faldir stared into the back of his head, her fingers gracing her onyx Focus. She was uncertain if it would answer her. Loyalties were shifting between the two Focuses. The consequences of using either would be unpredictable. If the captain figured that out, she worried about what he might do.

Faldir descended the steps to the deck and headed back below deck. The captain called for sails to be opened and other preparations to be made. It was clear to the crew that Faldir would work them to the bone as long as it met her goals.

"Worms," she said to herself.

She held her head high and did not match the glare of the sailors. She wanted them to be angry. Their rage would motivate them. Their fear would keep them in line. All of them knew they were expendable if they crossed her. She felt their eyes on her as she crossed the deck. Not much longer now. Vindication was just one day away.

Chapter Twenty-Seven

Wiping sleep from his eyes with the back of his hand, he tweaked the reins and commanded the horse to keep its pace.

"C'mon, just a little further."

It ran like it knew a life was at stake, but the horse was nearly spent. Tomis was at his limit. He barely ate in the last two days or slept since the Sovarka sank. They stopped long enough for the horse to rest and for Olivia to cool off. That was the only reprieve available. Tomis swore that steam rose from her limbs the last time she dumped a handful of ocean water down her neck. That was the last time she was awake.

Olivia was like a sack of coal in his arms. She wouldn't wake up no matter how hard he tried. She still breathed, but her heartbeat was frantic. Tomis supported her in the saddle. His legs spasmed with cramps and his arms shook. He tried flexing different muscles to relieve the ones he used up. Even those efforts, completely illusory at best, were tapped out.

Still, he urged himself to keep riding. He was determined to make this count. He rode against the night with screaming monsters on his heels. He crossed the foothills of the Border Mountains through rain and wind. He wore his body thin and did it all for someone else. The only thing that could keep him going was the vague sense that it was the right thing to do.

The storm clouds parted to reveal a shining bright day. The sun already was past its midpoint in the sky. The slopes of the mountains were well behind him and his journey was nearly over.

He grinned through the pain as he looked down the road ahead. Azure spires rose in the distance. The enormity of the city clouded most of the horizon in front of him. He was not there yet though. Small farms clustered next to the road. Figures in sturdy, blue shawls called water from wells and sent it sprinkling over fields of crops. He thought about stopping and talking to these people on the outskirts, but he was almost certain they would barely know how to help her or where to take her.

He needed whoever lived in the not-so-distant blue spires. They would know how to save her. They would give him a chance at redemption. His mind wandered to fictional scenarios where they would drain the fire from Olivia and all would be forgiven. They would see that he was not a plague on the Seers family. He would have helped them at the end.

Before he went too far down these waking dreams, the horse whinnied. The road ahead was bisected by a coursing river. He pulled on the reins and the horse slowed to a stop. It gladly broke its pace and trotted toward the river for a drink.

The current flowed out to sea at a torrential pace. He would certainly be swept away if he stumbled into it. It was dark with depth, the bottom too murky to see. There was not a bridge within sight. Up and down the river from where he looked, it was uncrossable. On the other side were brick homes, each with a small farming plot, rows of grapes, or livestock milling about in their yard.

He climbed off the horse and Olivia slumped off the

saddle. Tomis set her down as gently as he could. He brushed her soaked hair from her face and felt her forehead. Olivia was burning up. She put off heat similar to a low hearth. Her lips were chapped and parched. Tomis opened his waterskin and tipped it toward her mouth. Before the water could touch her lips, she pulled back and grabbed her head.

"She's—she's in a tunnel. She's in the city," Olivia muttered. Her voice was a hoarse growl.

"What?"

Her teeth pulled back and she looked beyond him, her eyes full of terror. Olivia screamed and twisted into a shaking ball of pain. This was not the first teeth-chattering nightmare she suffered. Some lasted for minutes and others for hours. Olivia muttered about things that were not there or people she never met.

"In my head!"

He braced her neck and arms as she shook harder.

"Olivia, it will pass. Come on, fight through it."

"No!" For a moment, Tomis thought it was Faldir's voice coming from her mouth. "It hurts, it isn't like they said. It isn't like they said! Help me. Olivia, help me!"

Her voice cut out as she slumped into a coughing fit. Her eyes drifted open. Tomis prepared for the next seizure, but it never came. She looked around the road for a brief moment before leaning into his arm.

"It's gone," she whispered.

"A short one? Who said we couldn't catch a break."

She shook her head and took a shallow breath. It sounded like a wilting breeze blowing through a graveyard.

"No, my Focus. It belongs to Faldir. I can't feel it anymore."

He thought that maybe it was for the best that the Focus was gone. Looking at Olivia now, drained and dying, he second-guessed himself.

"There's nothing we can do about it right now," he said.

She closed her eyes. He was glad to see a measure of pain fade from her face as sleep took her again. He laid his pack beneath her head and helped her settle onto it. Nearby, the horse had drunk its fill and laid down. Tomis walked to the edge of the river and made sure he had not merely overlooked a bridge. No one was in sight, maybe eating a meal or resting. He had no compunction against being rude.

"Hey! You all, over here. We need help!"

The door of the nearest house swung open and a woman poked her head out. Her blonde hair was cut short and barely went lower than her ears. Her small chin pouted as she knitted her eyebrows.

"*Carsa an eig he lar?*"

"I don't speak Dasoi," Tomis worked through the bits of it that he knew, "*Chain ei*—umm, *caord agam.*"

"Stop, you're embarrassing yourself."

She approached the river's edge. Another farmer walked out of their field of turnips and yelled something in Dasoi. She answered and waved him off.

"You said someone is hurt?" Her accent lifted the ends of the spoken word.

"Dying, she's afflicted with Flame. We've been riding all day to get to the archive. I only stopped because… well, where are the damn bridges?"

"You're from afar, yeah?"

The woman pulled a smooth stone from her pocket. Blue letters were engraved above a line that ran around its circumference. She held the rock low to the ground and spoke a few words. The line on her Focus glowed white and the river bubbled. The currents broke in different directions as dark shapes rose from the depths. The woman brought her Focus up from the ground and the shapes rose with it. Small pillars of water pressed slabs of stone upward. The algae-covered rocks slotted together as they bobbed just a few inches above the water line.

"You can call me Caira. I watch this section of the river. Bring your friend and your horse across."

Tomis lifted Olivia from the ground and called the horse over, which obeyed.

"My name is Tomis. This is Olivia."

"And your horse?"

"That's not my horse. Just borrowing it."

When they reached the other bank of the river, Caira lowered her Focus. The great stones sank to the bottom and the current resumed its ferocious pace.

"We heard there might be a cure for affliction here," Tomis said.

"Cure? What kind of stories do you outlanders tell?"

Caira put her hand to Olivia's forehead. Other people heard the commotion and came out of their homes. They looked like any other people save the favor for blue fabrics and the pendants or rings everyone wore. Many stood on their steps and watched while a few others came closer.

"She's sick?" one of them asked.

"Afflicted. She's a mage. How long has she been afflicted?" Caira asked.

"Just under a month, a little longer? I'm not sure."

"That long?"

"She's had some help. We left our companions behind, but they should be catching up soon," Tomis said.

"I'm no expert with the plague of fire. You will need to get her to the archive. East of here, across the lake." Caira pointed inland.

"Further? My horse is worn down, I don't think it can go any longer at speed."

"No need. Maelin," Caira called.

A child stepped out of Caria's home. The young boy scampered down the steps and to his mother's side. She spoke a few hurried words in Dasoi and pointed to the horse.

"My son will take it to our barn and look after it," she said.

"And what about us?"

She walked to the edge of the water and waved her Focus back and forth. She spoke and several slabs of rock floated upward again. Caira stepped onto one of them. The other slab, made up of three large rocks pressed together.

"We will ride the river."

Tomis lifted Olivia from the ground with a wince. His body was almost spent, but he was preoccupied with the unnatural display in front of him. There was plenty of magic throughout his life, but he kept it at arm's length. He knew plenty well that it was as destructive as it was helpful. After this brush with Flame and Shadow, he was even more reluctant to trust it. However, it was not just his life on the line. He pursed his lips and walked to the edge of the river.

"I just… step on it?" he asked.

Caira nodded. "Trust me. Water is not tricky like

Flame or Shadow."

"That isn't what I'm worried about."

He stepped onto the stone with one foot and made a small leap with the other. The water built up under the platforms and they moved forward.

"You must sit. We will be moving fast," Caira said over the babbling current.

Tomis kneeled down and supported Olivia's head. The current grew faster and small rapids built around them. The stone slabs tilted slightly backward so the waves broke against the front like the bow of a ship.

They zipped along the surface of the river. Forests of water reeds swallowed entire sections of the nearby shore. Horrendously fat toads leaped for safety as they passed by. A light mist formed over the land, the small homes and farms obscured in fog.

After a few minutes, the river opened up into Lake Locrih. It was not quite an inland sea, but stretched further to the south than Tomis could see. The city of Uncanan stood on the shore behind them. Its tall, blue towers rose up from a dense collection of wooden buildings. Canals pierced into the land like streets of water. A number of small docks dotted along the shore's edge. There were only a few boats, each of them rigged as a fishing vessel without nets or reels. A mage on one ship raised an enormous globule of water from the sea, a school of fish trapped inside. The mage gestured and various fish were propelled from the globe of water and into one of three tall baskets.

Dozens of people zipped across the lake and every one of them possessed a Focus. Some rode slabs of rock or metal as Tomis and Caira were. Others stood on long, narrow boards. A few piloted wide boats that glided through the water. Young children zipped across the water on pot lids and planks of wood. One of them zoomed through the gap between Tomis and Caira, which brought a bout of curses from Caria. Tomis did not know Dasoi, but he understood the timber of profanity.

Tomis was so enamored with the people nearby that he almost missed the glittering palace to the east. The Archive Primeval hung over the far edge of the lake on wide supports before spreading inland. The structure's turrets were like peaks of a crown, each one lit up with libraries and halls. Algae-covered, stone supports ran deep into the water and held up the densely packed hallways and paths that looped around the central towers in flowing patterns.

The portions built on the far shore were older and blocky. They lacked the architectural grace of the lake side, but were regal in place of the ethereal beauty of the former. Greenhouses overflowed with fruits and vegetables. Blooming flowers the size of cabins covered walking paths. A network of bird houses housed every shade and shape of bird Tomis could imagine.

"Wish you could see this, Liv," Tomis whispered.

Caira's magic moved them across the lake in less than an hour. The full size of the Archive Primeval dawned on Tomis as they drew closer. It was larger than most towns. Its supports were thicker than the oldest oak trees. Every brick and stone looked older than humanity, as if the Elements had woven this place into existence. Caira guided them to a wide, sloping ramp that dipped into the water.

Tomis's platform skidded off the water and ground to a stop on a stone path. He forced his sore limbs into action and lifted Olivia again. She weakly pointed at the spires that rose above them like mountain peaks. Her eyes drifted open for a few moments before closing again.

"Naelan?" she asked.

"Just a bit further."

He looped around the exterior paths before joining with another walkway, Caira bullying her way through groups of sages and learned mages twice her age. In the chattering tongues nearby, there were accents and languages from around the world. Some were old enough to be grandparents, others as old as him. Very few were any younger. Some wore a sort of uniform: navy-blue robes with official pins and badges. Others were common clothes, admittedly of a high quality. There was no air of leisure. This was a place of debate and evaluation. Every scholar was too buried in their work to care about the new arrivals or were quick to size them up. None interfered, even when they saw the ill woman in his arms.

The outer hallways were open to the evening air. Small pillars ran up to arched ceilings where lamps burned above their heads. Stone benches lined the interior halls. Caira and Tomis stepped into the first large door they found. It opened into a lofty interior hall. Water-propelled platforms rose and fell on the inside, letting someone at a third-floor entrance descend to the first within a minute.

They were approached by a pair of mages that carried an air of authority that Tomis avoided as a child. Unlike the other scholars, these two were plainly not buried in their own research. They reminded him of guards.

One was a woman in light leather armor. A military badge was pinned to her shoulder, a shield with water flowing around it. Her dark, braided hair ran down her back and faded to a pale white hue near the ends. A pale and bleached scar cut across her eye. The mace in her right hand was studded with sharp ridges, blackened by frequent heat. The pommel of the mace extended further than normal. A yellow gem, similar to Alkis's, was embedded at the end of it.

The other was a man in a black, leather coat that ran to his ankles. His gloved hands were notched on his hips, elbows stuck out behind him. He wore a pair of ovular glasses that looked more like goggles with their brass rims. A trimmed mustache and goatee the color of loose gravel spread around his mouth and jaw.

"Mages, we require your assistance," Caira said.

Tomis knelt down to rest Olivia on the floor and the two mages knelt with him.

"What's she sick with?" the man asked.

"Flame affliction. We've traveled so far to get here," Tomis said.

"You're safe. We will do what we can," the woman said. "Mulvey, take a look and tell me what you see."

Mulvey, the man with the brass-rimmed glasses, pulled off the glove on his right hand and laid it on her forehead.

"You seem very tired. You both rode here?" the woman asked.

"Oh it's nothing. Just haven't slept in a day or so. I'm fine, help her, not me."

"You can call me Juno. My friend is taking care of her, let yourself rest. I'd rather not have you collapse." She turned to a few gawking scholars who stood nearby.

"Go to the apothecary and bring me some blankets and let them know we will be along shortly."

"She doesn't have long," Mulvey muttered. He opened his eyes, his pupils fading from blood red to a warm brown.

"That bad?" Juno asked.

"It's a wonder she is still alive," he said. "You've done well, what are your names?"

"Tomis."

"Caira. I'm a river watcher. Poor things caused a scene calling for help."

The scholars returned with a few blankets. Juno took one from them and draped it over Tomis.

"Caira, I need you to take Tomis to a quiet place and let him recover for a while."

Mulvey lifted Olivia from the ground. "Alright little kindling, let's see if we can't cool you off."

Through the suffocating fog of exhaustion, he thought of ripping Olivia out of Mulvey's arms. The imperative was drilled into his brain: protect her. It was what John wanted. There was nothing else in the world that mattered more than that. Tomis's body finally reached its limit. His head swam and his throat ached for water. The slightest suggestion of success allowed his own needs to surface.

"I need to go with her."

"No, you are staying here for now." Juno held a hand in front of him.

Mulvey carried Olivia off into the grand hall and headed for a set of doors to the left.

"I promised someone. I have to make sure she is alright."

Juno steadied him and placed her hand on his chest,

her Focus gathering a small glow. Warmth returned to his limbs. A sense of peace overcame him as the lights around him grew fuzzy. It felt as though he only just woke up and could easily fall back into a deep slumber.

"You have delivered her. You've done everything you can. Leave the rest to us. Scholar Iona will want to speak with you once you've rested. It isn't every day an afflicted Flame mage walks through our doors. Caira, make sure he rests alright?"

Caira guided Tomis back toward where they came from.

"Come on now, let's have a sit and look at the lake. Naelan sunsets are a beauty."

Tomis looked at the far door where Mulvey and Olivia passed through. He waited for the guilt to speak, for the pang in his chest to well up and tear at his heart. It never came.

He followed Caira to a lakeside corridor. She eased him onto a bench and his eyes were drawn to the glittering lake. Beyond the dark blue water and the small flashes of people flitting it, the spires of Uncanan stood against the dying light of the day. Lights flickered in the shadows of the great towers. Every alcove and balcony shone in the amber light on one side, the other cast in inky shade. As the sun tilted lower, the city almost glittered as much as the lake and the sea beyond.

There had to be a cure here. If it did not exist in this dazzling center of civilization, what other hope could they have?

"I need to get back home. Will you be okay here?" Caira asked.

"Is there a cure?"

"What?"

"Earlier, you mentioned something about stories we tell outside of Naelan. We came here because if anyone knows how to cure flame affliction, it would be the people who trust magic more than anyone. Right?"

Caira closed her hands together and looked out over the city.

"I've never heard of a cure for the plague of fire, but maybe the scholar will know something I don't. Take care Tomis."

She left him sitting on the bench, staring out at the glittering blue city that he had fixated upon for the last few days. The charge was delivered. His journey was done. Despite this, he was not convinced she would live.

"I tried John, I really did."

He rested his eyes and fell asleep seconds later.

Chapter Twenty-Eight

"Help me," John said.

He tottered at the edge of her bed and black water rose behind him like grasping hands. Yellow eyed monsters lurked inside the waves. Some were people, some were snakes, some were wolves.

"Don't let go."

The waves swallowed John as he tumbled backward. Olivia brought her legs underneath her and reached forward, ready to leap into the abyss after him.

She woke up. The distant wash of waves that came through her window was the only lingering memory of her dream. John was not here, there was no predatory black water lurking at the foot of the bed frame. The Flame burned in her chest like a hot pepper lodged in her chest. It scalded the back of her tongue. She had not felt such heat since the middle days of summer.

She sat in a pool of pale, moon light that left the edges of the room darkened. The cream-colored sheets were smooth enough to be silk. A pail of water sat on the table next to her and vapors of frost drifted from the still water. Crystals of ice clustered around a small charm that dangled into the bucket. Several candles burnt in a silver candelabra perched on a bedside table.

Something shifted in the shadow. A match struck to light and a man wearing brass-rimmed glasses rubbed his eyes with his free hand. He groaned and lit a candle on a table next to himself. The candle revealed Tomis sleeping in a chair next to him. He nudged Tomis, who jumped awake and blinked a few times. The man with round-glasses crossed over to her. He nodded to Olivia as he blew the match out.

"Evening miss." The man flipped his pocket watch open. "Patient has woken at quarter till one."

Out the window, a jet-black lake reflected the moon in its rippling waves. Beyond it, she saw the towers of Uncanan. The city was so much darker than what Olivia grew up with. There were no grand beacons, no braziers, and no walls of light around the city.

"Symptoms have advanced, but she seems to have recovered consciousness. Well, we will need to check that to confirm," he said to himself.

"Who are you talking to?" she asked.

He tapped his temple.

"I do my best work when I speak aloud. Oh, names, right. Professor Mulvey, at your service."

He extended his hand and she reached out to it without a thought. As she did, he spun her wrist face up and pressed his fingers to her wrist. Panic flooded her mind and her heart pounded against his ribs. Olivia was restrained against her hammock again, a strange man grabbing at her. She was a young girl, Yorker dragging her into the darkened forest.

Olivia jerked her arm away and swung her balled fist into Mulvey's jaw. She reacted without thinking, the swing not quite her idea. The Flame had sprung to life and put motion into her limbs.

"Damn! I was just looking for your pulse." He rubbed his jaw.

"I'm so sorry. You surprised me."

"No surprise parties for you."

Tomis wore a foolish grin as he crossed the room. "Oh thank the triad you're awake."

"I don't remember much past the day we left. I'm glad to wake up again," she said.

"I'm just happy you're alright. It was close."

"I'm grateful. Thank you."

His smile thinned and he gave an awkward nod, somewhere between an accepted compliment and dismissal. "As for this one. I've never seen an apothecary with such poor bedside manner."

"I prefer the title doctor. Guess I shouldn't be surprised you don't know the difference. I apologize miss, I'm used to working with," he tilted his head as he chewed on a thought, "bodies."

"Dead bodies?" Olivia wrinkled her nose.

"My field of expertise. May I take your wrist? I promise it won't hurt."

Olivia offered her upturned wrist. He stared into space as he pressed his fingers against her veins. She didn't need the pressure of Mulvey's fingers to feel her heartbeat. It hammered in her chest like it had so many times since that night back in Hasketter.

"Interesting." He let go of her wrist. "Iona should be down shortly."

"Who is this Iona you people keep talking about?" Tomis asked.

"Scholar Iona, she basically runs this place. She's been around longer than anyone else and knows more than anyone else. Anyone inside these walls anyway."

Mulvey sat back in his chair.

"And she might have the cure?" Olivia asked.

The professor pursed his lips and looked at Tomis.

"You should tell her."

It was plain on his face. She might as well be dead. Trembling fear crept up her arms and she laid back in the bed. She thought about the journey from home to here. She thought about summers in the Seventh and ripe apples in autumn. She remembered the family graveyard that the Seers family tended at the edge of their property.

"There is no cure. Not one that they know. However, they said the scholar has been researching flame affliction for years. They were insistent that Iona will give the final word on treatment," Tomis said.

It was a polite death sentence. What other choice did she have other than to accept it? She was too tired to fight. If the end was coming, she thought that setting things right was a noble pursuit. Oliva placed her hand over his.

"You didn't have to come. You could have stayed in Sallew. I'm sorry that I didn't trust you at first."

"I mean, it was safer, right? Like what John said, we had that Fire Keeper and you folks around me. It just turns out it wasn't as safe as I hoped. And besides, I didn't exactly help on that ship. We both know what happened."

"Josie might have you pegged as John's murderer, but he wouldn't have been on that boat if I wasn't around. You got me here. No matter what comes next, you tried. From what I've heard about you from my uncle, that is more than what you've done through most of your life."

Tomis moved away from the bed. He jammed his hands into his pockets and took in a deep breath, as if preparing to plunge into an ice bath.

"I was never in it to save you or your sister or that

stick in the mud, Alkis. I've burned a lot of people, but no one died on my account. Once I got mixed up in this business with the Focus, one of my oldest friends died for it. Then a stranger who did nothing but help me."

Tomis ran his fingers through his hair. His eyes did not leave the floor.

"There's something I need to tell you. I'm the reason John's dead."

"You couldn't have helped. I've thought about it, trust me."

"No Liv, I mean we're in this mess because of me. I told them where to find the Focus. When they couldn't find it, they tracked me down and were going to hold me to account for that. I played the only card left. I sold John out."

He vomited his confession forward like it would kill him if it remained inside any longer.

"I heard about your accident on the farm, where John was staying. I heard that three members of that family took off for Sallew. It was a guess and I used it to stay alive. I was so convinced that I could keep him out of it, that I could pull some trick and warn him. I thought I could steal the Focus and they wouldn't have to deal with you at all. But I knew damn well this only ended in one of two ways. John pulled the short straw."

Tomis rubbed his knees, but kept his eyes glued to the floorboards. She adjusted in her bed. It all seemed too coincidental at times. That feeling nagged at her the entire way here. The awful irony that Josie and Olivia started this, but trouble found them after all. He *was* a snake.

"Then I lost him. We all lost him and the danger wasn't gone. I need this, Olivia. I need you to get better."

She fumed in dreadful silence. Every word and outrage she could conjure didn't seem to be right. Even as the impulse to empty her bucket of water on his head crossed her mind, a small voice pleaded his case. He's a snake who saved her. He didn't have to ride through day and night to get here. She remembered all the second chances that she gave over the last few weeks.

"If you don't forgive me, then what am I supposed to do with myself? I've not just cost Peter, Wandala, all those sailors, and John."

Someone knocked at the door. Mulvey stood to open it and Tomis took the chance to leave the room. He murmured an excuse as he sidled past the new arrival. Olivia made no motion to stop him and laid back on the bed. She hesitated on the precipice of anger, too tired for rage. She settled for a cold shoulder and thought over what she would tell him when she could.

Faldir. She remembered the other reason why they came here.

An old woman with thick-lensed glasses entered the room. Her blue eyes scanned the small chamber and settled on Olivia. She was shorter than Professor Mulvey by almost a foot. Deep wrinkles were carved into her face like cracks in a boulder. She wore a maroon robe with tattered sleeves. Her gray hair ran to her shoulders and a pair of glittering, teardrop earrings hung from her ears. She closed a book in her hands, a finger stuck in the pages.

"I am told your name is Olivia." Her voice was quiet, but her delivery was succinct and sharp.

"There are people coming to hurt you. Her name's Faldir, they're shadow mages and they're already in the city. You have to get ready," Olivia said.

"No need for any more alarm. Your friend already told us, we will discuss it in a moment. I apologize for my peer, Mr. Mulvey," Scholar Iona said.

"Peer? I thought you were his boss or something?"

"He aged better than I." Iona pulled a chair close to Olivia's side and sat down. She flipped the book open again and searched for her spot. It had a warm, brown leather binding with yellowed, dog-eared pages peeking out from it.

"How are you feeling, dear?" Iona did not look away from the book as she spoke.

Olivia fell back in her bed again and hoped she would not have to rise before this was resolved. "Not wonderful. I'm thirsty. Everything is so warm."

Iona gestured to the chilled bucket on Olivia's bed table. Mulvey grumbled something before pouring Olivia a glass.

"So focused on the task before him, he forgets all else," Iona said and looked up from the book, as she finished the page. "Well, Olivia, I welcome you to the Archive Primeval of Naelan. We accept any mage from any land, provided they forsake claims and loyalty to Shadow. Before we could consider your residency, there is the considerable matter of your affliction."

Olivia laughed.

"Residency? I came here to find a cure. You're mistaken, I don't know what Tomis told you."

"A talented mage from the Seventh Republic, who fought her way across the ocean from assassins and monsters all the while maintaining her own bulwark against the most insidious illness known to humanity. Yours is just the kind of mettle we want."

"Tomis told you all that?"

"Some, but the elements had more to say. The lake and I are old friends," Iona gestured out the window, "The lake is a friend of the river, who is a friend of the sea, who is a friend of the river that divides the Seventh, which was once rain that fell onto your family's apple orchards. It took a while, but I found answers."

"It doesn't matter. I will be gone soon. I can feel it," Olivia said.

"Is that so?"

"Oh shut up. Stop playing games with me. I know you don't have a cure."

Olivia couldn't tolerate any more uncertainty. It was rude, but she figured that there wasn't anything more to keep back. The Flame wanted her to rage. She considered giving it what it wanted. However, the scholar waited with a mother's patience that no tantrum could disrupt.

"They should have told you that only I can rule on whether there is treatment. Are you ready to listen? Or should I keep the good news to myself?"

Olivia's stomach jumped at the words, but she did not dare to get her hopes up.

"Good news?"

"Very few people have survived the affliction. Only two in fact. One was a member of the archive. The other was from a far land. You will be the third, I hope. This affliction wears on the body until your vitality is spent and you die. Life mages have a particular gift against the Flame. They can manipulate nature around them. Consequently, they might also manipulate the sibling of Life: Death."

She let this linger in the air between them. Olivia flinched in her bed at the mere mention. Death was almost as unthinkable as Shadow as the two dwelled in each other's presence often. To wield Death as a magic was to foul the fruit of the world. What was worse, to use it without careful consideration could easily make you a victim of your own power.

"It's unthinkable," Olivia said.

Mulvey shifted uncomfortably in his chair and stared off into the corner of the room.

"It's inescapable. Life becomes death becomes life becomes death becomes life. It's a cycle, the great wheel. Most Life mages spend their entire lives without venturing onto the other side of the road. You are an exception to that trend."

"I'm not a Life mage though. I'm not even a real mage."

Iona shook her head.

"I would ask you to reflect on your use of magic. When has it gone well for you?"

Olivia thought about the forest with the lumbira, healing off of Alkis's life force, making flowers bloom as a child. Even though it answered her with increasing frequency, Flame felt more like a companion.

"Handling Flame has helped me," Olivia said.

"In times of great emotional turmoil?"

Olivia nodded.

"The elements, save for Shadow, are loath to let a mage suffer. They will respond to the gifted. You are exceptional. Please recognize who and what you are," Iona said.

"Do you even have a plan?"

Iona shut her book and leaned forward with a hardened scowl. She reminded Olivia of Elza for the briefest moment.

"It's a gambit. There have only been two survivors for a reason. There is no stopping the Flame inside of you. The only result is to let it burn until it has nothing left to consume. You have to die, Olivia. You must die and then Life has to bring you back to us."

If she heard that anywhere else, Olivia would have thought it was a joke. She looked between Iona and Mulvey, hoping to find clarity in a plan that sounded like insanity.

"I don't understand."

"The elements know that we will need you. You are not the only person upon whose shoulders we will place our hope, but you are one of them. When I spoke to Water, it told me about Faldir. Her kind have circled us for centuries. A random death here, a suspicious fire, or a dead body with void wounds. Only we see the wider connection. Everyone else chalks it up to circumstance or an accident. They never went away. They will never forget their wounds."

Iona slid her glasses back up the bridge of her nose.

"There's a war coming, Olivia. Flame showed us that you are up to this task. It is up to Life to ensure that Flame's attention does not take your gift for good."

"You're insane," Olivia said.

"But I am asking it all the same. Our peace is hollow. It's a dying tree in a field and a storm is gathering. We might need you more than you need us, Olivia," Iona said.

"She's right for it."

Tomis stood in the doorway. His hands shook, his nerves surely telling him to run away as fast as possible. All the same, he was here fighting his own nature. What else did she have to lose? She decided to give him one more chance.

"I can help, if you have any need of a no-account rogue," Tomis said.

"Apprehending Faldir will be dangerous. Sure you're up for it?" Mulvey asked.

"He is," Olivia said.

Tomis swallowed and raised a finger. "We're going to need more people."

"We've already requested soldiers from the city. We will have all the hands we need," Mulvey said.

"Not them. My sister, Josie, and a Fire Keeper named Alkis. I need Josie to get through this. You'll need Alkis to stop Faldir. They landed with us north of here and have been walking south since."

Iona turned to Mulvey.

"Think we have the time to give them a lift?"

"I'll speak to Juno."

Mulvey set his chair back against the wall and left.

"In the meantime, we have to get ready," Iona said to Olivia.

"What if you're wrong?"

The scholar opened the book in her hands and resumed reading.

"I'm usually not."

Chapter Twenty-Nine

Tomis checked the clock tower for the sixth time. It was almost noon. Hours had passed since Juno departed to find Alkis and Josie, but they had not returned. Olivia was off with Iona, preparing for death. Worse than any of these things, the woman he feared more than anyone else lurked somewhere nearby.

"They aren't going to make it back in time, are they?"

"It does not appear so," Mulvey said.

They stood in a small tower above the grand Hall of Currents, the eastern entrance to the archive. Through a spyglass, Mulvey watched the long road that wrapped around the lake and led to the front door. It was busy, but even Tomis could see the squad of five Katoian soldiers heading their way. Tomis worried about what might be in the wagon that they pulled behind them. He fiddled with the buttons on his left sleeve.

"Why don't we just jump them right now? We don't have to let them into the archive at all."

"They could make it to the forest and go to ground. We would have no capacity to find them until they decided on the best time to strike us. These aren't thugs like you and me."

"I take offense at that word. I've sold artifacts worth more than any amount of coin you'll ever see."

Mulvey scoffed.

"And I'm sure all of that was legally acquired and consented to be sold. I may not have made much mucking about, but I know your mark."

Tomis had not figured this mage out yet, but there was something familiar in his eyes. He looked at Tomis like a target: the quality of his clothes, his possessions, and his demeanor. The other man looked for weaknesses and hidden weapons. It was the same kind of glance that John, Tomis, and Peter had mastered years ago.

"Enough of that. Why are you so relaxed?"

Mulvey shrugged and kept his eye on the road. "I've seen a lot. Also, I don't like their odds."

"No Fire Keeper. No mace-wielding Juno. Your boss won't be there and neither will Olivia."

Mulvey turned from the window and shouted down the hall. "They're approaching, take your positions!"

He gestured for Tomis to follow him. "Downstairs are ten soldiers on loan from the Naelan High Court, ten senior mages who pull security duty around here, and then there's me."

The guardians, referred to as the Shield of the Archive, were academics who had some experience with violence. They slipped into casual robes and stashed their Focuses in their pockets. Each was ready for a fight, but posed as stuffy bookworms.

A fountain dominated the middle of the grand hall. Water spouted from the mouths of enormous fish. The center was fashioned like a great crashing wave. It spouted the mage's weapons: an unlimited source of water. Elite soldiers of Naelan waited within side passages. Covered head to toe in plate armor, each trained in the art of war for a decade. The trap was set. Mulvey walked to a point in front of the fountain, a distance from the front doors. He traded his normal leather jacket for the traditional blue robes of the archive.

"Tell me, do I look accomplished?"

"You look, uh. Well, hmm."

He did not. Tomis would not believe that this hardly shaven man was any sort of commanding sage of the primeval.

"Yes or no?" Mulvey said.

"No. Not in the slightest."

"What? I've got the robes and all, the whole thing."

"It's the hair, the glasses."

"What's wrong with my hair?" Mulvey asked.

"You said you know my mark? Well, everyone else gets yours, friend. You've been out of the game too long."

Mulvey cursed under his breath and pointed to the other side of the room. "Go hide. If they see you, they will know something is up."

"What's the signal?"

"I think you'll know. Just don't do anything until the others do."

Tomis went to a spot under a pair of winding staircases as the main gate swung open on its venerable hinges. The lanterns flickered as the wagon crept inside the hall. Tomis found an angle underneath the grand staircase from which he could observe.

The mock soldiers let the wagon rest on the ground. Mulvey stepped into their path and waved them over. They were a grisly collection of mercenaries. Rough skin and patchy spots of fur peeked from under their ill-fitting clothes. Some were too large for their shirts, their shoulder seams ripping. Aside from the seal of the Katoian Empire on their breast, they were cheap stand ins for the real thing.

"Where are you?" Tomis muttered to himself, "Where are you, witch?"

"Welcome, soldiers of Katoia. I recently heard of your arrival and did not expect to entertain guests. I apologize that we do not have a proper welcome for you," Mulvey said.

One of the imposters pushed forward. She was muscled and tall, her hair twisted into an amber mane. The fur puffed from under her hat and hem of her shirt, red and gold tones shining against blotchy skin.

"Your welcome is fitting. We seek Scholar Iona, the one in charge. We were sent to parlay with her directly."

"And your name is?"

"Does it matter?" she grunted.

"It does, actually. I want to ensure you are properly introduced as the envoy to your nation. Such difficulties between our people, details do matter."

She growled like a feral dog.

"Hartwin. Will that do?"

"It will. However, hmm." Mulvey cupped his chin in his hand.

"What?"

The others bristled at the delay. Each was more monstrous than the next. Tomis wondered if they were always this way, caught between human and beast. Did the harbormaster deem this dreadful collection acceptable or had they become worse? Maybe they changed to better suit the bloody task. They might have been as repulsed by their new forms as Tomis was.

"That isn't a very Katoian name. Do you have a seal of order?" Mulvey asked.

Hartwin snarled and flexed her right arm. Veins

pulsed and fingernails popped from her hands with a bloody splatter. The lanterns fluttered again as the shadows deepened. She brought her arm backward as talons burst from her fingertips then thrust them into Mulvey's stomach. He gasped and gritted his teeth.

"Your cooperation is not necessary," she said.

The other cultists drew their weapons against what they thought were librarians. Instead of fearful cries and panic, these bystanders stood their ground. Each drew a Focus and gestured toward the invaders. Water broke from the fountain and flowed through the air. The streams of water cracked into the shins of two and sent them falling onto their faces. They tried to rise only to find the water gathered around them. They were bound by it like a straitjacket and pulled high off the ground. Soldiers burst from the side doors with spears raised. The other two shadow cultists turned to fight, but wailed and dropped their weapons.

Hartwin buried her claws deep into Mulvey's gut, blood running in streams onto the ground. He gasped for air and reached for his pocket as Hartwin dragged him toward the stairs.

"Back! He still breathes, but I will end it.".

Tomis crept behind her and kicked into the back of her leg. It did nothing to her other than reveal his position. The rage of a cornered animal burned behind her eyes. As she moved to lunge at Tomis, Mulvey held her where she stood. The bleached skull of a small dog was clutched in his other hand. Runes carved into the top of its skull blazed with a blood red light. This was not the dull orange glow of Flame magic. Tomis heard of magic that glowed red. He knew it was the color of carnage. It was the color of death. Mulvey's eyes faded to a matching hue.

"Stay, darling. I need you."

Hartwin's skin paled and drew against her flesh. She screamed and swung a clawed hand toward Mulvey, but he twisted her arm out of place and she toppled to her knees. Mulvey's gory wound knit together. It scabbed and healed within moments as magic coursed through him.

The hair on Tomis's neck stood on end. He realized that Hartwin would die in front of him. She looked dry. Her eyes bulged in their sockets and skin cracked. She twisted against Mulvey's iron grip to no avail. The husk of what was once Hartwin dropped face first on the ground and her arm ripped from its shoulder without a drop of blood left to bleed.

Mulvey let go of the withered arm and slipped off the blue robes of the archive. Those around him avoided his gaze and focused on the four prisoners. After Mulvey's display, none lifted a finger of defiance.

"You weren't just a thug," Tomis said.

Mulvey tried to fix his ripped, bloody shirt before giving up, and pocketed his Focus.

"I used to be a lot meaner."

A horn blew outside of the archive. Mulvey turned toward it and smiled. "Your friends are here. Just in time to avoid the unpleasantness."

Tomis walked by the four prisoners and looked them over. None had the piercings that studded Faldir's chin. Their eyes were wild shades of green, orange, and yellow. None of them possessed anything that looked like a Focus or matched the unflinching defiance he grew to fear.

Panic rose in his chest. He dared to adjust one of

their chins to make sure. She wasn't here. She wouldn't delegate this to anyone, she should be right in this line up. He jumped inside the wagon and rooted through the few boxes within. Carrots, sprouts, a spade. Tomis tossed them aside, but did not find a secret latch or hiding place.

"What's wrong? Battle's over, we won," Mulvey said.

"She's not here."

"Who?"

"Faldir. The one running this whole thing. None of these people are her."

Mulvey furrowed his brow. "No one else entered. Maybe she sat it out?"

"Impossible. There's no way she does that. She was obsessed with this. She lost her brother over this."

"Maybe they betrayed her? These shadow types aren't too loyal, you know."

"No, she's too scary for them to do that. With the Focus, Flame knows what she could do."

That's right, she had the Focus now. Faldir spoke about it as if it were a weapon, something that would make her more indomitable than before. Now it was hers. Shadow surprised Tomis time and again. His blood ran cold as an idea popped into his head.

"This was all a show."

Alkis burst through the front doors with Josie right behind him, followed by Juno and the others. Josie looked around the room and set her eyes on Tomis.

"Where is Olivia?"

****

She slipped through the darkened places in this bastion of traitors. No, Faldir traveled from one part of herself to the next. She was the darkened corners of the world now. The moment she joined with the Focus, something reached from the other side and leaped down her throat. The pain was indescribable. It grabbed her tendons and yanked as it crawled inside of her, but she felt her mind fade. She lost who she was as this new entity put her on puppet strings.

Once it was stuffed into her, all that fear dulled. Her worries seemed so small compared to the crushing will that lived within her. The world dissolved into shades of gray and black. Everything beyond it made her head throb and her body burn.

Find them.

The thought was not hers, but a suggestion pressed against her ear. The voice swaddled her like a filthy blanket. This was not Father. It was something stronger. Her arms moved on their own and led her to the next motion, the next movement. Faldir the marionette was pushed along the thin veils of shadow. A trio of guards crossed a set of stairs, from the light of a torch and into a shaded portion of a hallway. She reached out and wrapped herself around them.

Grasp, squeeze, crush.

She left them motionless in the hallway. Someone screamed. A scholar opened a nearby door and bathed the hallway in light. She hissed and retreated.

Keep moving. Find Iona.

Through the darkness, she felt dozens of people tread across her. They all raced to find the scholar, a useless effort to protect her. Faldir watched each one and found that they went toward a chamber on the western side. Their path divined, she pushed herself into every shadow they crossed.

Her hands rose up around their ankles. Her fingers

poked at their eyes. Some knew enough magic to conjure small embers against her. It only bought them time. They could never hope to cross the cordon she raised.

She left a part of herself in these many shadows and traced the path to a small room along the western hallways. There was nowhere else she could be, but she was not alone. Faldir hated the light burning in the afflicted woman.

Olivia.

The strings pulled her from the world of gray and black and threw her toward the world of color and light. It was a hard shove that jerked her neck around, no thought toward the pain it inflicted.

Kill them. Bring them into the dark. I will be with you.

The feeling in her limbs returned. She chose a shadowed corner across from the room. A part of her wanted to run from the dark places if it meant staying away from whatever haunted her thoughts. Even with this small degree of freedom, it lingered at the edge of her mind.

Worry about it later, focus on the goal.

It sounded like her brother's voice, only deep and distant. He was right. She could not spare a moment. She would not throw away her brother's life. She would not abandon her quest. Family, acceptance, revenge: it was all so close at hand.

Chapter Thirty

Olivia's breath was weak. She lost the ability to
sweat two hours ago. Her stomach stilted at the idea of
food, but growled in need. Olivia swallowed with a dry
throat and hoped that Josie and Alkis were close. She
hoped Tomis would be able to help them. She hoped that
this all would work.

"Eyes up, dear. No time for daydreaming now," Iona
said.

Over the hours, more books were brought full of
arcane diagrams. They cluttered tables at first. Then Iona
set them on the ground. She assured Olivia that she
would pick it up in just a moment while she read from
another book. Those other books also went on the
ground. Now there were stacked towers of books rising
around them.

Candles lit every dark corner of the room. Iona
explained that Shadow often stalked in Death's
footsteps. It was best not to crowd the room. A small
fountain babbled beyond the door. It was carved into the
wall and ran to a small pool at its feet. The airy hallways
breathed with the warm breeze of early autumn. The
open hall looked over the lake and the city beyond it.
Olivia wished she could rise to see it.

"You have no Focus and we hardly have time to
make one. Even bonding to an already existent one
would be too difficult for you in this state," Iona

muttered.

"I bonded with the first one I touched. Maybe it's just as easy as that?"

Olivia was too weak to get the sarcasm across, but Iona thought it over. Her finger traced across a paragraph in a book.

"The previous owner of that Focus died a long time ago. We also do not have a Focus from a dead person on hand. Maybe if I went into the storage I could find one. It's worth the effort at this point, even if I cannot be present to examine it. Assuming of course there are any down there." Iona set aside the book in her hands. "Can you remember the last time you spoke with Life?"

"It was in a forest. I was in danger, scared." It hurt to speak.

"Keep that frame of mind handy. Preferably not the scared part, wouldn't want that."

Olivia did not laugh or smile. There was no one here to see her and now she suspected they would not make it in time. She never gave much thought to how she wanted to die. A warm bed surrounded by family crossed her mind at one point. It was unoriginal, but seemed nice compared to other possibilities.

"I won't be able to see my family again," Olivia said.

Clouds rolled across the sky outside. The sun dimmed and a shade of gray swallowed the archive. Iona reached for a book and thumbed open the first page.

"It's okay to be scared. I ask for your faith in me, but you hardly know me or this place. I didn't lie to you, Olivia. I know my stuff."

"You said you are usually right."

"That's true."

"Usually isn't always."

"Well, we don't have any better—"

"I'm tired of hearing that. I don't have any better options, but I am still going to lose everything. So don't just sit there and shrug when I'm the one who will be dead within the hour." She tried to sound angry, but even a raised voice exhausted her. Iona rubbed her hands together and conjured a warm smile. Even as Olivia's mood worsened, the old woman never cracked.

"Every person who has come to me with flame affliction, whether they survived or not, were determined people. They faced fear, they failed, they doubted. When the time came for them to do what they needed to do, they didn't waver. Even when there was no chance of winning. Olivia Seers, I can gladly say that you will join those ranks. Regardless of what happens, I know your family will never doubt that you tried with all your heart to get back to them."

The lanterns in the room flickered and dimmed as a dark spot grew across from the doorway. Iona rose from her chair and drew her Focus, a silver rod tipped with a blue gem. The whispering shadow swelled as tendrils licked out of the darkened corner. The inky spot spilled into the hallway and a cloaked figure emerged from it. A smile and a piercing-studded chin poked from under the hem of the hood. Her teeth were now adorned with sharp fangs that almost slipped past her closed mouth. The golden Focus was threaded through Faldir's fingers.

Olivia spent plenty of time thinking about how she did not want to die. If Faldir was her executioner, she hoped it would have been a fight. She sat up in bed, fear pushing a desperate spurt of energy into her limbs. The Flame wanted the Focus back, even as Olivia knew it would not answer her.

"Leave us be. She is already dying," Iona said.

"About time."

Faldir's voice was trailed by its own shadow. As she spoke, another voice mimicked her words. It was like thunder following a strike of lightning. "I'm not here for the thief. I'm here for you."

Iona gestured toward the nearby fountain and water burst from it. Spiraling streams arched over Faldir's head and wrapped around her. The streams tightened and merged into a restraining sheath of water. Iona pointed her Focus toward Faldir as she threw the bed sheets off Olivia.

"We're cornered. You have to get up."

Olivia rose from the bed with a gasping breath and fell against the side of it. Black dots appeared in her vision. She was nearly too weak to think.

In the hall, Faldir was swallowed by shadow again. Her misty form slid from the watery binds and settled to her left. It rose back to her full height as she stepped out of it. Beams of void magic ripped through the air like a crackling swarm of black needles. Iona brought her hand upward and a fiery shield grew from her palm. The void magic vaporized against it.

Iona stepped through the doorway and into the hall. The water followed the Focus clutched in her hand. They zipped through the thin shield of simmering heat and hissed as they reached a boiling temperature. The thin streams of steaming water knocked Faldir backward. They wrapped around her throat and twisted around her skin. Faldir lifted a hand and slashed downward, shadow rose and fell in a similar motion. A thin disk of void magic cut the stream of water and the shadow lingered between the two mages.

Iona reached toward Olivia, still slumped over the bed and gasping for breath.

"Olivia, you need to come to me!"

Billowing clouds of shadow rushed toward Iona. She conjured more water from the fountain and brought it toward her flaming hand. The water drove into it and more hot air billowed out. It pushed the dark clouds backward and the light of the ember held back the shade.

"I'm trying," Olivia said, "Just another moment."

She took a few steps toward Iona. Without any way to save herself, Olivia fumed at her helplessness. She conjured the last of her strength into the next few steps. Her lungs throbbed with every breath. The lights grew fuzzy.

"Remember your last breath. Remember how you spoke to it in the forest," Iona said.

The shadow billowed over Iona's head like a thunder cloud. She saw the gathering attack a moment too late. The clouds pushed down and swallowed the older woman. Bright purple needles of void magic emerged around the cloud and drew back. Olivia staggered to the door frame and reached into the cloud of shadow. She felt an arm and pushed. They both fell onto the floor and the needles missed their target as they drew together.

Olivia could barely open her eyes. Planning how she would organize the harvests on the family farm, chasing down an escaped foal, the non-stop ride to Sallew, none of these compared to the peace that took her now. Iona drew more water from the fountain, so much that the spout ran dry for seconds afterward. The water slid across the floor and then rose across the hall. It split the hallway, shadow building on the other side.

"Just hold on a little longer. We need to—"

A swirling mass of void magic bloomed on the other side of the watery wall. It thrust forward and Iona shifted her shield to take the hit. Water splattered to the ground as pulsating purple energy crashed into the last of Iona's flame magic. Iona slid backward, but her defense still held.

The darkness surged around Iona, who brought both hands to her Focus and a bright flare emerged from it. The light blossomed and pushed back the swirling gloom. Faldir raised the Focus above her head and the shadow pressed closer, threatening to crush Iona.

The flare was originally so bright that it nearly lit the hall. Now it was reduced to a candlelight. It was all that kept Iona from being swallowed entirely. She chanted and asked the elements for more aid, all to hold the line.

Faldir stepped next to Olivia and the storm of shadow followed with her. She kept one hand raised toward Iona, but turned her attention to the dying woman at her feet. Faldir's pupils were black circles within bloodshot eyes. Even as she directed her power to suffocating Iona's light, the darkness still licked from her back and under her arms.

"Hello again," Faldir said, the other voice mimicking her.

Olivia could not conjure any words. She opened her mouth to swear, but only a tired moan came out. Faldir flourished the golden Focus before her. The gem seemed clouded with the horrid magic that coursed through it.

"I had the hardest time pulling this from you. It liked you. It still does. I'm sure if you tried, you could rip it from my hands. You could save Iona and everyone who will die after her."

Faldir lowered the Focus toward Olivia.

"Come on. Try."

Quartermaster Cretis had been cocky enough to taunt her and Olivia made him pay. She reached deep and tried to bring her hands up. She would snatch it from Faldir and turn its power back on her. Olivia fidgeted as her shoulder rose, her arms darted up, but her hand flopped just short of the relic.

Faldir snatched her hand and crushed her fingers in a vice grip. The pain sharpened Olivia's mind. She reached her thoughts out to the elements. None of this mattered if she did not listen to Iona's plan. Faldir's magic probed her heart. She was searching inside Olivia the same way that Mulvey did. This time, Faldir grimaced and drew away.

"It's so bright. The Flame has consumed you. So much for happy memories. So much for that family you taunted me with. They're useless to stop this."

Life, I need you. Listen, Olivia thought.

"Because you are weak. Love is weakness, mercy is a crutch, and you would never survive in my shoes. You have to see it. How could you deny it?"

Faldir grabbed her by the throat and lifted. Shadow pulled away from Iona to lift Olivia into the air. Sleep pulled on Olivia's mind. Darkness crept into the edges of her sight and her thoughts grew murky. The elements, it was the only thing she could remember.

She knew this would be the last sleep. If she gave in, that would be the end of it. There was no resisting it. Instead of conjuring a final insult for Faldir or looking at the kind woman who would surely die after her, she closed her eyes. She spread her fingers and imagined them moving through the soft earth and prickly grass.

"You're too far gone. I will let your Flame burn you out. So close now, so much for family. In the end, you are alone. You were wrong. I've proved it to you. Damn it, say something!"

Faldir's voice raised in pitch with a desperate wail. Olivia tried to put this witch's rambling out of her mind. She thought of the tall trees, the orchards, and the forests.

Hear me please. Olivia drew a ragged, gagging breath and opened her eyes long enough to see someone walk up the stairs at the end of the hall. There was a simmering suit of armor and Josie's tall figure.

"Olivia!"

The voice echoed down the hall as everything faded. Olivia closed her eyes. Her final breath left her lips.

"I'm ready to listen.

Chapter Thirty-One

Faldir loosened her grip on Olivia's throat. Her body tumbled to the ground and buckled like a ragdoll. Glassy eyes stared down the hallway at her sister. Only a vague suggestion of pain was the left in her features. Despite how close they came, they failed her.

"Not like this," Alkis muttered.

Josie's scream ripped from her throat. She took a step forward and charged at Faldir. Daggers of shadow and void magic arched down the hall toward Josie. Alkis stomped after her and ignited his armor. Blisters of cinder dripped from the joints as he threw himself in front of Josie. The dark magic rebounded off his armor and threw him backward. The Fire Keeper fell to his knee and spat blood onto the ground.

Iona's light finally grew and broke from the trap of shadow that held her. She opened her palm toward the fountain's water and gripped at the air. A small wave of water burst from it and flowed across the floor at great speed. It caught Iona's feet and washed her the rest of the way down the hall until she arrived next to Alkis. She brought her shield up once again.

"This isn't your fight," Alkis said to Josie.

"She killed Olivia," Josie said.

Faldir fought back a giggle that rumbled like thunder. "Let her try, Fire Keeper. Better to die with bravery in your heart than simpering in a corner like the rest of you will."

Faldir idly swatted toward the fountain against the wall and a boulder of void magic smashed it to pieces. The flow of water weakened, but still gurgled from the damaged spout. Alkis pulled his fist tight and snarled.

"Don't tempt me, witch. I can show you real fire."

"Neither of you have the strength to kill me. Surrender the old woman to me and I will let the others live."

Behind Iona's shield, Josie fumed.

"What am I supposed to do then? I won't just sit here."

"She's right," Iona said. "We can't beat her. Neither you nor I have practiced True Flame. We need the sun."

"There's a lot of floors above us, lady. We don't exactly have a window to open," Tomis said.

Faldir brought a storm of shadow raining down on them. Arms of darkness, fingers tipped with daggers of purple, void magic, rushed forward. Iona swept her hand forward and Alkis slammed his palm into the ground. A wave of fire left his suit and lit a small distance in front of them, their magic combining into a sizzling wall of light and heat. The sea of clawing shadows burnt apart as it neared the barrier, but her magic was perceptibly weakened. Alkis turned to the others once Faldir's magic scattered.

"Josie, take Mulvey and Tomis. Search this place for mirrors. The sun is on the east side of the building. We are on the west. Get as many as you can and try to bounce the light into the doorway at the bottom of these stairs."

"Give me some time, that's gonna take a minute," Josie said.

"What do you think I plan to do?"

Mulvey palmed his Focus. Magic seeped into his hands as his eyes tinted red.

"She wants you, Iona. Let me fight."

"No," Iona barked at her colleague. He flinched and the pulsing, red magic faded moments later. "You have nothing to fight with. Go."

Josie, Tomis, and Mulvey ran down the stairs. At the bottom was the eastern great hall. The arched room was two stories tall and ran across the entire structure before merging with the western hall, a narrow gate separating the two. Works of art depicting mages of the old world, landscapes, and majestic animals decorated the walls. A handful of other scholars and visitors from town took shelter behind a nearby table and watched the staircase.

"What's happening?" one asked.

"Never mind that. All of you, get as many mirrors and glass as you can and bring it here."

"What? Why?"

Josie rolled her eyes and pointed at a nearby door. "Just do it!"

They jumped at her command and ran off toward separate wings of the archives.

"Josie, you go into the western hall through that gate. There should be a privy chamber or two there. I am going downstairs to check the privy on the next floor. Tomis, you need to stay here and organize anyone who shows up. Get their mirrors and start setting them up to bounce the light at those stairs."

"Me?" Tomis said. "Why me? I'm good at gathering stuff."

Josie and Mulvey went their separate directions without another word. Tomis bounced on his feet and looked at the stairs. The battle above shook a trail of dust from the rafters. At the end of the hall, a gate led out to sunlight and safety beyond it. This wasn't his fight. He was dragged into it. He did all he could for John, he was sure of that. Tomis was convinced that there was no good to be done if he lingered right where the thunder would come down. He took one step toward the door and stopped.

That annoying wriggle in his chest had grown stronger over the last few weeks. He imagined that Josie might really need him. Would Olivia rescind her forgiveness if this half-baked plan actually worked? What if he ran after they washed up on the shores of Naelan? The bones in his back seemed to root him in place as he realized he had no choice but to remain.

"I guess I'll just wait. Waiting for the fight to come down those stairs with a perfectly good way out of here right behind me. Very unadvised."

Even as he complained, he felt more right about this than anything he had done before.

****

Iona gathered a shield of light in her hand and lifted it as a bolt of void magic zig-zagged toward them. It crashed against her magic and scattered, but her shield broke into a flash of fire and ashes.

Faldir's assault pushed them down the hall to the top of the stairs. Alkis's back foot was almost to the lip of the first step. He struck at a monstrous face of void magic that emerged from the shadow. Purple fangs reared back as his fiery fist broke it into a vapor of dark smoke.

"There has to be a better spot," Alkis said.

"No choice, we need time for Olivia to wake up," Iona said.

"What?"

The suggestion took Alkis's mind from the battle at hand. That momentary slip allowed a spear of shadow to slip past their defenses. The black tendril grabbed Iona's arm and lifted her into the air. Alkis jumped from the ground and cut through the shadow with a burst of cinder. Iona fell and winced before conjuring more magic. The wound was mottled with blackened tissue, but the Scholar pushed through the pain.

Alkis turned to answer the next blow, but found that the storm of shadows had slowed. On the other side of the hall, behind Faldir, a burst of light burned a path through the shadow.

"For the Flame!"

Juno charged through the darkness and swung into Faldir's shoulder. Shadow coiled around Faldir's arm just before the mace hit and sent the shadow mage tumbling to the ground.

"For the Flame!" Alkis answered.

Juno swung down to deliver a killing blow, but the darkness coiled upward and swallowed her. It spread up her arms and wrapped around her mouth. Her arms were pulled outward and shadow lifted her into the air. Juno's furious voice was muffled behind the dark binds. The light of her mace flickered and then went out as Faldir rose from the ground.

Faldir raised an open palm and snapped her fingers together into a fist. As she did, Juno screamed through the whirling darkness and the sound of rending flesh and snapping bone followed. The shadow twisted and wrung around her, elbows and knees moving in unnatural directions.

Alkis grabbed Iona and threw one of her arms over his shoulder. As Faldir turned the shadows toward the stairway, the pair disappeared over the first few steps and into the stairway below. They descended the steps as wisps of shadow crept along the walls like the arms of a horrid octopus. Each one spun forward and put out lanterns along the walls.

Iona raised a shield of light as they retreated. The shadow was bottlenecked behind them, forced to smash down the narrow stairway. Alkis heard Faldir's steps close behind them. The shadow pushed on Iona's magical shield and it wilted. The heat weakened and the light dimmed. Alkis leaped over the final few steps and dropped Iona behind him.

At the bottom of the steps, the twisting curls of shadow spread beyond the stairs. He conjured another ember into his hand, but let it grow in strength. It spread from his arm and across his chest.

"I spurn you no longer. Show me True Flame."

A shimmering layer of embers covered him from head to toe. He groaned as the stone armor singed his body and it grew hotter than ever before. He became a beacon of light, the entire great hall lit by the Fire Keeper. The embers burst and True Flame leaped from the runes cut into his armor. His scream echoed down the hall as Flame licked down his arms and legs.

He raised his hands toward the stairs and a burst of fire rushed up the stairs. The Shadow reeled back into the hallway as the Flame chased after it. It flew up the stairs and stormed toward Faldir. Shadow and void magic peeled back, burned and scattered, and the shadow mage quivered as the fireball came to meet her. For a moment, Faldir believed that she failed.

The pain was too much, the fire too hot for his flesh to bear. Alkis fell to his knees and the fireball collapsed into a wave of hot air. Alkis coughed and pulled the helmet from his head. His hair was burnt off. Streaks of raw, torched skin ran across his body. He hesitated to conjure more flame, but he knew what the stakes were. He had to make this count. He did not save Elza, he did not save his friends, and he did not save Olivia. He would sell his life to make sure the witch died. As he struggled to his feet, Faldir emerged from the stairwell with a billowing cape of shadows.

"Alkis, get down!" Tomis shouted.

Alkis looked behind himself and was nearly blinded. Dozens of people all lined up glass and mirrors from countless rooms. The sunlight from the west entrance bounced across the hall and hit a series of mirrors almost a half a mile from where he stood. It reflected down these two rows, each mirror facing each other at a slight angle until the light was catapulted toward the stairway.

"Now!" Josie shouted.

The nearest dozen mirrors turned to catch the light. Alkis fell out of the way and golden rays poured over Faldir. Shadows sizzled and evaporated with a shriek. The deep, thundering voice that mimicked Faldir bellowed by itself and the walls shook. As the shadows shrank, Faldir pulled her remaining void magic to the golden Focus.

She directed it toward the ground with a thunderous blast. The stone floor cracked and fissures shot through beneath their feet. Forgotten roots and dirt showered down walls. Sprigs of weeds and clandestine beetles were exposed as the floor pulled itself apart.

Fissures arced to the walls and shook portraits from their hooks. Lanterns broke and sent burning oil onto the people below. They leaped out of the way of falling debris, dropping their mirrors in a rush. The ground shifted and sent others falling to the side. Several soldiers fell back, off balance in their heavy armor. Glass shattered and metal clattered onto the ground as the chain of sunlight was severed.

At the foot of the stairs, Faldir picked herself up from the ground. The shadows began to grow around her once again. Iona went to stand, but her own shadow sprang to life. It wrapped around her arms and legs and pulled her tight against the ground.

Alkis failed to stand. Blood gathered at the joints of his armor. It hurt to breathe and his skin bristled against the armor as he tried to move. All he could do was watch as Faldir lifted her Focus in the air like an executioner's ax.

"This is for my brother."

Chapter Thirty-Two

She felt wet dirt between her fingers. Roots and mold clung to her. One force pulled her upward and the other drew her down. She pushed her fingers through the moist earth and pulled. A voice rattled the dirt from below. It sounded like the skitter of beetles burrowing toward a fresh corpse.

THIS ONE IS PART OF THE CYCLE NOW, Death said.

Her part is not yet played, Life answered.

Soil tightened around her legs, the worms pulling downward.

SIBLING, GIVE IT TO ME.

The dirt loosened and she slipped further down. Bones and ashes intermingled with the earth around her. She held onto the roots and the roots held onto her, fingers of bark gripped her hands. The soil drew downward as worms and maggots wriggled at her ankles.

THE WHEEL MUST TURN.

It will continue to turn without this one. Her survival will lead to more entering the cycle.

The worms and maggots let go. She climbed up through the dirt.

IT IS BURNT. IT HAS NO MORE LIFE.

She was never meant to be kindling.

Her fingers broke through the surface. She clawed at the grass above and wriggled against the hungry dirt.

THE WHEEL MUST TURN.

It will turn, sibling. Just let this one go for now. She will not escape you forever.

Her arms broke free of the grave. The roots wrapped around her shoulders and knotted. The warm voice pulled so hard that it almost broke her bones. The last tugs of the dirt yanked at her heels, but still threatened to pull her down once again.

FINE. THIS ONE IS YOURS FOR AS LONG AS YOU CAN KEEP HER.

And the next time she goes, there will be no arguing.

Olivia gasped for air as her head broke the surface. In the dark of her mind, only the glow of torch bugs and luminescent fungus lit a tall tree where a flame once burned. She pulled herself free and rested against the bark. The ground was singed, but small sprigs and saplings broke from the dirt.

The Flame was nowhere to be found.

****

A tremor shook the floor and Faldir staggered away from her waiting victim. The shake strengthened and mortar fell from the ceiling. The wall above the stairway cracked and roots pushed through. Seeds accidently left in the mixture awakened to a mage's call. They grew in moments, becoming winding roots worthy of a centuries old tree.

Faldir leaped aside as a chunk of masonry fell away from the ceiling. The shadows drew in around her like a protective mother. The roots pushed aside portraits and molding. Plants ripped from the ground across the entire hall. A woman emerged from the chasm where the stairwell once was. She was carried forward by a bed of roots and plants that twisted around her.

Olivia held a flowering knot of wood in her right hand. Her hair hung free around her shoulders and dirt stained her formerly sweat-soaked clothing. Roots steadied her feet as the enormous bulk of plant life pushed through the stone walls.

"No," Faldir said, her voice low and ragged. "You're dead. Flame burns kindling!"

"Don't do it, Faldir. You won't win their love even if you succeed."

Faldir gnashed her teeth and screamed. She lifted her Focus toward Olivia, but the vines near her feet moved to action. Grasping plants grew around her feet and spread up her body. Faldir lashed at the roots with her void magic, cutting the plants to bits as they tried to bind her. The shadows rose and spread in the darkened hall. Claws of inky midnight flew at Olivia, the swirling clouds ready for blood.

Olivia closed her eyes and raised both hands. The voice was with her again, but not the distant tone that she barely found before. It spoke in her ears like it stood beside her. Its calm voice was not afraid of the Shadow. Neither was Olivia. The magic pulsed through her like her own blood. It whispered in her ear and directed her eyes to the ceiling above.

Roots burst from the ground and traveled upward. They burrowed through the stonework. It found moss that grew in the shady spots of the roof. It found dandelions that grew inside of stuffed gutters. Roots wrapped around supports and rafters and then pulled them aside. Wood splintered as the roof came apart. Beams of sunlight poured down through the crumbling roof and spilled over Olivia. The cloud of shadow evaporated as it streaked toward her.

The sun shined through the hall as the plants and roots ripped the ceiling open wider. Josie grabbed two people by the collar and pulled them out of the way of a collapsing pile of stone. Tomis pulled Iona to safety, only a few steps away from Faldir. Within moments, the ceiling widened until the entire hall was lit by the early afternoon sun.

The shadows shrieked and scattered to the dark places of the archive. Faldir shielded her eyes from the light as they faded from midnight black to dark brown. She gestured forward with her hand and shouted, but nothing followed her command. Her cape of darkness was wicked away like dirt washed away by soapy water. Shadow would not even grant her the gift of murderous void magic.

"Don't you leave me!"

She screamed as she did many times before, her wrath directed to the final hollow of shade beneath a collapsed stone pillar. A grand root broke from the ground and lifted her from the ground, tightening around her arms. A strong vine snaked around her wrist and slapped the golden Focus from Faldir's hand. It clattered to the ground far from her reach. In the warm sunlight, Faldir grew quiet and looked at the broken ground below her.

Alkis could not take his eyes from Olivia.

"By the Flame," he said.

Josie laughed and clapped her hands. Tears ran free down her face as she jumped and cheered. Others joined her with applause and whooping. Tomis nodded to himself and pounded his fist on the earth. Olivia's platform of vines and roots lowered her to the floor. She leaped from it and ran to Josie. The sisters threw their arms around each other, Josie practically pulling Olivia off the ground.

Alkis limped over to them with an uncontrollable smile. Olivia looked at him and walked over to meet him. The thrill of living again almost darkened to see him on the edge of death. At least, he looked as though he was hauled out of an oven. His injuries did nothing to dim his mood.

"What happened to you?" she asked.

"I tried doing what you did. It didn't quite work out."

"I can heal you. That looks like it really hurts."

"In a minute, just another minute." Alkis tried to smile through the pain and winced. "I'm just, I'm so happy you made it."

"His little display bought us time. Just enough too," Tomis said.

Olivia gave Tomis a deep nod.

"Thank you. I was hoping you would stick around."

"Well, I figured I needed to do something good before I pulled another jerk move in the future. I'd rather be an unpredictable scoundrel than an unreliable one."

Alkis stepped closer to Olivia and took her hand. He smiled, but tears welled up in the corners of his eyes. He leaned forward and Olivia caught his weight on her shoulder.

"We need to heal you, you're injured."

He nodded, his eyes not straying from hers. "I thought, we thought we lost you for good. I'm just happy to see you."

Mulvey and Iona lurked behind the group. The scholar cleared her throat and nodded to Olivia. The group returned the gesture. Alkis tried to bow for a moment, before leaning on Olivia again.

"Our duty is to help the weak and we recognize those who help us in turn. You all went above the call of duty to protect me and save this archive, even if with some significant property damage," said Iona.

Olivia looked up to the broken ceiling. Stonework, hundreds of years old, was reduced to a pile of pebbles. She could feel the wriggle of bugs and roots. Life babbled in her ear, already mending ripped roots. Olivia loved every syllable it spoke to her. Her eyes settled on Faldir, still held captive in the twisted root in the center of the hall. The void mage watched them as they spoke. As their attention turned to her, she looked away.

"What do we do with her?" Mulvey asked.

Alkis stumbled forward, his Focus conjuring a minor glimmer of light. He gritted his teeth as the first suggestions of fire returned to his armor.

"I can think of a few things."

Olivia grabbed the pauldron of his armor and held him back. Once, she wanted Faldir dead. She murdered John, tore Olivia's life to pieces, and hunted her through the worst days of her life. Still, Olivia could not forget that moment in the ship's belly. She felt the pain that wracked Faldir. The shadow mage did not choose this life.

"Enough people have died today. Leave her to Iona."

Alkis spluttered a few half words and pointed his finger at the captive witch, but then stopped. He nodded his head and closed his eyes. Faldir said nothing. She turned her head to hide from the sun beating down on her.

"Put her in the armory," Iona said to a nearby

soldier, "there is a cell there that will do for the time being. Get as many candles as you can find."

Iona came closer to Olivia and clasped her hands together. The scholar's composure had not shifted a little. Perhaps the only change was a slight grin that refused to go away.

"I told you I tend to be right about these things."

"Here I stand." Olivia showed the knotted root in her hand, a new Focus.

"And we need to talk about your future. The archive is interested in all mages who have something to add to the magical record, especially those who have saved it from shadow cultists."

The specter of her future returned. Olivia felt Josie's eyes on her. She only confided these things to John, maybe to Alkis during their lessons. She could not imagine returning to that life, but something still held her back.

"Oh no, I've got a farm to take care of, fields to rotate. There's a whole life waiting for me."

"Sis, that's a pack of lies."

Olivia looked over to Josie, expecting her face to be overjoyed at the idea that this was all over. Instead, Josie shook her head and took a deep breath. Josie nodded to the enormous root that held Faldir.

"Look at everything you did. Everything that's happened, it's miraculous. Incredible. I was so sure that this was just a passing thing, but the magic won't go away. And it's like, it works for you. I can't ignore that anymore. I love you Liv, but you can't run from this."

Olivia did not understand the emotion that bloomed in her. There was fear of loss, the fear of losing her sister. If she stayed, she would be leaving everything she knew.

However, heaped upon this sadness was a mountain of happiness and confirmation. She knew this was what she wanted.

"What about the farm, our family?"

"I've got that handled, or at least they'll understand. It's what mom said before we left. You found who you are. Don't throw that away for tradition. Don't throw that away for me."

Olivia smiled and turned back to face Iona.

"Residency?"

Iona nodded. "We can find you a room, likely something small for the time being. Your connection with Life magic and adeptness at bonding with Focuses, we will have quite a few studies to prepare. They won't be boring days. We're going to put you to work."

Iona turned to Alkis and raised her eyebrows.

"As for you, we always have plenty of room for all mages. You served honorably."

He shook his head. "Ask me later. The burns are really starting to hurt."

Iona led them down the hall, Alkis leaning on Olivia's shoulder. The scholar snagged the golden Focus from where it fell. Olivia was glad to be rid of it, but still felt a twinge in her heart. It was gone from her forever.

Chapter Thirty-Three

Faldir steadied her breath, the remnants of a nightmare on her mind. She dreamed of a titanic child playing with a doll. It cackled and flung the plaything around in its gnarled fist. When it pulled on one of its arms, pain spiked through her wrist.

All that darkness, he would have seen it all. She didn't know if his eyes were here in Naelan or if Shadow whispered it to him. He had to know by now. Faldir failed her family and her brother. Tears did not come. Instead, she shook at the idea of returning to him. A part of her imagined ways that she might stay away from them forever.

She was held in a cramped cell, her bed pushed into a corner with two buckets at the foot of it. One filled with water, one empty. The rest of the room was arrayed with stowed weapons and armor. She was surrounded by six oil lanterns, four more covering the corners of the room. Through a narrow, barred window, she could see the golden day beyond.

This cell was somewhere below the main levels of the archive. Above her head, those scheming bastards pilfered through books. All Naelan was convinced that the world would move past what they were.

Faldir knew better. You could never escape what you truly were. She could swear off the powers of Shadow, but she would never shake off its mark. In the eyes of the world, she was a dangerous prisoner. She was a failure. Faldir chafed against these labels as they piled on in her head, but could not figure out how she could have avoided this fate.

Three guards lingered outside of her cell.

"Well, look who's awake," one of the guards said.

Her memories from the possession were scattered. Some did not feel like her own recollections, but like a story she was told. For now, she felt like herself again. The thunderous voice did not echo in her ears. Each flex and twist of her fingers was her own choosing. The relief was short lived as she remembered what Shadow did with those who failed it. She flicked her tongue over her teeth and stopped at the razor prick of her canines.

"No."

She rose from the simple cot and looked into the pail of water. Her familiar face stared back up from the water. Bruised, but still herself. She opened her mouth and choked a scream in her throat. It wasn't all a nightmare. The consequence now poked from behind her lips, ivory and sharp. Her canines were grown into earnest fangs and the other teeth sharpened into points. She was not a beast, but was much closer to one now.

"I served it to the letter. I did as they told me to."

They lied to her, just like Olivia said they would. Shadow only twisted those who failed it. Even in the throes of its power, as she killed in its name and gave her own body for it to inhabit, it changed her. There was no appeasing the darkness. She was never really family to any of them.

"Not so strong without your dirty magic, are you?" the first guard asked.

She sat back on her bed and ran her fingers over her

teeth. If Father ever found her, if Shadow took her again, it would treat her like clay. Her brother's failures were less than hers. What sort of beast would she be molded into?

"I hear they are considering the death penalty," said the second.

"You don't say?" said the third. "We haven't executed anyone in almost a century."

"Serves her right. Even the Pescan throne doesn't want anything to do with them," said the first.

Faldir's eyes were drawn to a shadow on the other side of the room. In the faintest spot, barely perceptible between the many lanterns, the timid darkness shifted on its own.

"No, didn't you hear? The House of Tides wants to ask her some questions," said the third. He leaned against the bars and whispered to Faldir. "Play nice and you might just rot in a cell until your dying day."

She leaped off the bed and stepped toward the bars. The guards flinched. It still felt good to be feared.

"So bold now that I'm in a cage."

Faldir drowned the fear in her chest. There would be no return to Shadow, never again. She swore on her brother. Whatever fate waited for her behind these bars, it would not be in darkness.

A man in a black leather coat entered through the armory door. His steps clicked on the stone floor of the chamber as he crossed over to the cell, face twisted into an irritated scowl. She recognized him from the hall. They called him Mulvey. A stupid name, as most Naelanean often had.

The noisome guards fell silent, their humor dried up by his mere presence. Mulvey glanced around the room, looking between the light set around her. He settled on the same, small shadow she saw and pushed one of the candles toward the darkened corner. If there had been the slightest chance of Father listening into their conversation, it was gone now. He stepped up to the bars and crossed his arms.

"Faldir, was it?"

She sneered at him and sat back down. The guards were harmless in the grand scheme of things. This one was notable. He stank of Death. It was difficult to discern, but impossible to lose once you found it. This man gorged himself on the living to fuel himself.

"I'm surprised you're not locked up with me. Death mages are almost as feared as us. I think if there were more of you, we'd be second fiddle."

Mulvey turned to the guards and gestured for them to leave. They marched out of the armory, eager to escape the presence of the two dreaded mages. He dragged a stool a few feet away from the bars and settled onto it. Mulvey toyed with the tips of his gloves, his stare unphased behind the brass-rimmed glasses. If he was as old as she suspected, then there was little she could say that he had not heard before. Faldir took that as a challenge.

"I'm not the one in a cell, so let's talk about you. I've been permitted to offer you some leniency on your sentence."

"What did they offer to put your powers on a leash?"

"If you cooperate, the death sentence is off the table. Duration of imprisonment will be reduced depending on the quality and amount of information provided."

She leaned forward on the cot.

"You could kill everyone here if you really tried.

I've seen your kind do it before."

"You will be moved to Deep Holding in the foundations of this place. Location of your confinement is non-negotiable."

"Or are you too weak?"

Mulvey's eyes flashed with a hint of red. He stood from his stool with a low growl, but Faldir didn't quiver. She heard that Death magic was excruciating, but her knowledge was too important to lose. He wouldn't lay a finger on her. The red in his eyes faded and he smirked. Adjusting his glasses, he sat back down.

"You don't scare easily."

"I've seen worse," she said.

"I'm sure you have. And I've seen worse Shadow cultists than you. You still look human, except for those little additions." He gestured to her teeth.

Faldir looked at the ground and rolled her tongue over the extended canines in her mouth. The pain was still fresh. It would be sometime before she could bury the shame. It was a mark of her defeat that would never go away. Alterations from Shadow were impossible to fix, an indelible brand.

"That isn't your business."

"I don't blame you for being rude. You deserve to be sore. You've been used. I've met my share of your kind and know they won't be happy that you lived. They would prefer you dead so you can't talk."

"Shut your mouth. They were my family."

He raised his eyebrows above the brass eyeglass rims.

"Were?"

Faldir couldn't bring herself to let the entire truth out. It was pointless to pretend that they would rescue her at the first moment or dedicate themselves to revenge in her name. She was a loose end now. If they did anything, they would silence her.

"You can't trick me into thinking you're any better."

"It's no trick. You're not the only one to be burned. My kind are a nasty bunch, you're right on that. We don't have the monolithic organization that you do. We're separate clans, feeding off the world to extend our lives so that we can dance and drink and screw to our liking. If we do run into each other, it's like two packs of wolves. One has to prove themselves the dominant pack. I've burned my bridges, Faldir. It hurts as much as you think, but you don't have to turn your back on everyone."

She wrapped her arms around herself. Faldir took in the cracks and grout of the stone floor. Like a spider web of broken relationships. Her family was beyond her forever, for now. She wondered if there were any bridges left to burn.

"I'm not telling you anything."

"Of course. You're too close to things. We're going to give you a few weeks to stew on our offer. In fact, I'm allowed to remove the penalty of death that is hanging over you. All I need for now is something small. Just tell me you'll think it over."

She looked up from the floor. It seemed too easy.

"You'll forestall my execution if I tell you I'll think it over?"

Mulvey nodded.

"It's obviously a lie if I say that."

"Perhaps. Probably. Very likely. Time has ways of clearing the air. I'm your enemy right now, but you will figure out that I don't hate you like everyone else. I understand where you've been. I know the guilt you carry around. I know you're scared of them. There are ways past this. You can get that new life that sounds so nice. However, the price is cooperation. You could do worse than working with someone who's walked a mile in your shoes."

Faldir wasn't sure if a clean start ever crossed her mind until today. It did not sound untrue to her though. A Death mage would certainly know something about escape. She doubted that he was lying. Maybe there was a way out, some way to leave all of them behind and find something new. At the very least, she would not miss the chance to take advantage of Mulvey's idiotic offer.

"Fine. If it keeps me alive, I'll think about it."

"Which is?"

She swallowed. Faldir often mocked Father, but it felt different to say it to someone who wasn't her brother.

"I'll consider being your informant."

Mulvey smiled wide and rose from his stool.

"I'll look into getting you some real food. Get some sleep. We'll talk soon."

Mulvey pushed the door open again and the three guards scurried in as he left. They were quick to resume their jeering, but she didn't listen. She leaned against the wall and ran her tongue along the sharp fangs in her mouth.

It was likely she would not tell them a thing. Of course that was the only choice. Faldir was not a slave. She would not wear their collar like that simpering Mulvey. Her power was a product of her own unswerving determination and unrelenting drive. She was not a spineless tell-all like Tomis. She would meet Death at the hands of these traitors and that would be the end of it.

Despite this insistence, she listed all the things she knew in her head and wondered how much damage it would do to Father and the family that betrayed her.

****

The streets of Uncanan were as full as Sallew, but lacked the worrying tumult. Everyone felt the world around them thrum and vibe with the tides that broke on the shoreline. Nearly everyone was like Olivia: gifted. Almost everyone could command the elements around them. Of course, not everyone was at Iona's level or even Olivia's. She learned the majority of people knew just enough to get by. Very few could feel the magic flow through the air like Olivia did.

It was a new home, but it still felt like the far away land she knew it as. She could go about as a mage without recrimination. These people seemed put off if you didn't reach for magic as a way of solving problems. That was not a concern for herself. Olivia wielded power greater than some would gather in their entire lives, but barely knew enough to keep a handle on it. Luckily, Life seemed less inclined to chaos. When she reached out for it, the answer was always mild. It demanded nothing of her, though she could feel the presence of Death somewhere nearby. She was uncertain if this was something all Life mages felt or if her defiance of fate had pissed it off.

Towers dominated the heights around her, every one of them a singular style of subtle carvings and smooth walls. She learned that the entire city was built with magic, the stone melded by Earth mages. Near the edge of the docks, these towers grew infrequent and were replaced with store fronts.

The archive gave her several changes of scratchy

clothing and fresh bed sheets. Her new Focus, the twist of knotted wood, never left her side. Iona found her a small room on the third floor of the archive. An old storage room before her arrival, it smelled of old books and candle wax. It was barely large enough to fit in the small bed she was provided, but it was hers. Not the inheritance she thought she'd have by now, but somehow more promising than a family farm.

When she set out from Sallew, she worried about what sort of mage she was. Olivia was not a madman like Yorker or a warrior like Alkis. She did not think of herself as sagely, much like Elza or Iona. Olivia thought of Faldir. They could not have more different lives, but the two women shared something. They were both haunted by ambition, driven by the pressure of family. She was a murderer, but Olivia felt that she understood the mad mage locked away somewhere in the archive.

It frightened her to no small degree. Olivia did not know how to feel about the past, still full of regret. Yorker would never truly leave her, but she could replace that memory with something new. Maybe with Naelan or her cramped room. As she rounded through one of the grand avenues, she saw someone who might be able to fill the pain that still lingered.

Alkis leaned on a crutch near the end of the dock. Josie and Tomis stood next to him. The worst of his burns were mended, but his left arm was held in a light sling. Thankfully, Flame did not afflict him. His experience as a Fire Keeper barely kept it out of his heart. Magic healed the worst of his injuries, but he still bore the scars from the fight. There was only a trace of his auburn hair left. For the time being, he left his Focus in his room. Iona suggested that it was dangerous to reach out to Flame until he healed.

Josie wore a clean, leather jacket and held a bag in her hands. This endeavor did not darken her petulant vibe in the slightest. Tomis swung his bag over his shoulder and cast an eye to the passenger ship nearby. The thief cut his hair down to an orderly, clean cut. He claimed it would meld into his new life easier. Olivia reached them as a voice bellowed out from the nearby passenger ship, calling for all passengers to board. Josie smiled wide as she joined them. Alkis leaned a little heavier onto his crutch.

"I thought you were going to miss us. Cutting it a little close, huh?" Josie said.

"I wouldn't miss this. I am here, aren't I?"

"It's almost that time. Ready Tomis?" Josie asked.

The thief rummaged through his bag to ease some last-second anxiety.

"I've got a few things to take home with me. They don't sell pipe-herbs like this back home."

"Just for personal use, right?" Alkis asked.

"Of course." Tomis nodded. "All ten pounds of it. I wouldn't dream of selling it for a profit. I wouldn't dream of doing it in your presence."

"Give him a break. He's earned some roguish behavior," Olivia said.

Alkis bit his lip and shrugged. "I bid you a good trip and wish you luck when they check your bags."

"I wouldn't be a professional if I didn't have a plan, would I?" He went to laugh, but the noise died in his throat. Tomis rubbed at his neck. "I'm gonna miss the both of you. I know I wasn't always the most dependable."

This was the end for now. Tomis's words brought it

rushing forward for her. It was easy to know something was coming. In the moment, her sister ready to leave her in a strange land full of unknowns, she pursed her lips and fought the tears.

"You did your best Tomis," she said. "I can't say we forgive you for everything, but you were there when we needed you. You better be the best farmhand that my parents have ever seen."

"Don't worry. He will have a damn good taskmaster." Josie slapped his back and he jumped in shock. He recovered himself and gave a nervous smile.

"I assume you'll be visiting eventually, right?" Tomis asked Olivia.

She nodded.

"Damn right she will be," Josie said.

She wrapped her arms around her sister and Olivia held her back. Olivia did not think of the danger they faced. All she could think was the harvest ahead, the explaining Josie would have to do, and the farm that would move on without her. It was sad, but she knew it was necessary. Her mother was right in the end. This was a part of her that would never go away. She enjoyed the last embrace they would share for some time. Josie wiped her eyes clean, sniffed, and nodded to Alkis.

"You best keep her safe, Shield of the Archive."

Alkis rolled his eyes and hobbled toward the towering woman with an open arm.

"I already hate how that sounds."

Josie hugged him, eliciting a few pained groans from him. She let go and patted his shoulder. Her sister looked back to Olivia. She felt the sentiment from her sister: this was it.

"I love you," Olivia said.

"Love you too, sis."

"Casting off in two minutes. Two minutes, sharp."
The captain stared directly at the group from the bow of
the vessel.

"Come on. Time to go, Josie," Tomis said.

They turned and headed toward the ship. Olivia
watched the gangway until it was pulled away and the
sails were raised. Josie found a spot on the port side of
the ship and waved to them as it weighed anchor and
pulled out from the dock. Olivia followed it until it left
the harbor and wheeled north.

"It'll be alright. If Josie can do anything, she can
certainly handle herself."

Her breath caught in her throat as Alkis set his hand
on her shoulder. It wasn't new, he carried her for quite
some time after they washed up on these shores. She
gave him a small smile and squeezed his hand.

"I know. At least you have some direction."

"Only because Juno died for us. It would be wrong
to refuse it."

He hobbled onto his crutch and nodded toward the
city. Olivia walked slow enough to keep pace with Alkis.

"It's not that. I feel like I'm not out of place. I feel
more at home than I have in years. Back in Hasketter, I
bled for every ounce of respect I had. It never came easy.
People don't second guess me here. I'm just another face
in the crowd."

"Belonging, how awful. What will you ever do in a
place that doesn't gossip about you because of what you
are."

Olivia swatted at his arm, aiming for a spot that
wasn't covered in bandages.

"I was getting to it. You didn't hear what Iona told

me after I arrived. She made it sound like I'm a part of something much bigger than just Faldir."

His smile dimmed. She appreciated his good humor, but was glad that he understood the gravity of this arrangement.

"Mulvey filled me in a little bit. Something about a war with Shadow. Your abilities were fostered by the Elements. Sort of out of the frying pan and into the fire."

"What am I supposed to do with that? I'm grateful for her help and getting over my issues with magic, but it feels expected of me. What if I'm not the person they thought I was? I can't promise them what they're asking for."

Alkis was not so quick to banish these worries. His smile furled under a thought, a sign of something he held back. She remembered how he described his mission with her. Flame put her in his path. It was as consequential of a feeling as what Iona confided in her. Olivia faced a daunting future, but Alkis was directionless aside from a vague duty to help the archive. He had the opportunity to leave, but still involved himself in her affairs. She wondered if he still thought himself tied to her fate.

"Are you so eager for danger that you're looking forward to the next thing?" He did his best to bury the uncertainty behind a joke. It did not help her, but his smile was too earnest to hate.

"Not eager, but it's not easy to ignore. What do you think, seriously?"

"I think you died and then came back. I think you've demonstrated more skill than some Fire Keepers I used to know. I think you fought your way halfway across the world when a lot of other people would have rolled over and died. You're strong, Olivia. Don't overlook that.

"They're asking a lot of you and who knows what the future might entail. I know you can rise to the occasion, but I also know you're not alone. No one will send you off alone to face down all of Shadow. You were so busy telling Josie to not carry everything on her back, you forgot to remind yourself of the same thing. I won't abandon you."

Alkis slowed and cleared his throat. He pivoted on his rigid leg and leaned on his crutch.

"At the tower, I never really got the chance to thank you. I lost hope. Elza was gone, all the lights were going out, and you told me just what I needed to hear. I can say I saved at least one person. It means the world to me that you're here."

Olivia's face flushed. She often thought about what she wanted to say. He showed her that it really was a gift and not a curse. As much as she helped him march forward, he did just as much and more for her.

She wanted to nuzzle into his neck and feel his arms around her. To talk into the late hours, ask him a thousand questions, and answer as many in return. It throbbed in her heart like it might kill her if held for too long. Every time she felt this, it was the wrong time. It had been nothing but wrong times since they met. Standing in the shade of this grand city, just the two of them, it did not feel like the wrong time. For once.

"At the tower, when everything seemed so bleak, I felt something between us. I had felt it for a while. Ever since we met. And I was sick with the affliction or being chased by Faldir. I had so much to lose and I didn't want to find even more that would hurt me."

Her fingers inched toward his and he slipped his

hand around hers. Alkis was possessed with that same sparkling energy, his eyes focused on every word she said. Olivia could not fight the grin that crept over her lips as she answered.

"I thought that maybe you were just grateful for my help. All the same, I thought as much too."

The touch of their fingers pulled them toward each other. Olivia was scarcely aware how she drifted closer to him. Her eyes slipped from his face to his lips. For that moment, she didn't carry the hopes of the archive. She wasn't a stranger in a city dripping with magic. Olivia was a woman who wanted to feel Alkis against her.

"And now that we're here," she continued, "just you and me, I was hoping we could explore that. A new world, a new chance—"

He leaned toward her and she brought her lips to his, her hand caressing the side of his face. Alkis smelled like she imagined, warm with a hint of citrus from whatever soap he used. Her heart pounded like it did in the days before, but each pulse was bursting with life. Each one made her feel as if it might send them both cascading over the rooftops in each other's arms. Their lips parted and they came back for another. She pulled herself against his chest.

They stood there for only a matter of seconds. However, it felt like they stood there for minutes when they pulled apart. Her fingers toyed with the light fabric of his shirt, the manic grin refusing to go away. Alkis chuckled and leaned back onto his crutch.

"I've wanted to do that for so long."

"Worth the wait?"

"Every minute of it."

They moved down the street under the buzzing

lights of the city, hand in hand. It was a city for her, full of people who understood the whisper of trees in her ears and the tickle of grass underfoot. She would miss her family dearly, but could feel in her bones that this was where she belonged. Olivia would finally blossom after years of fighting the roots under her feet.